Praise for *New York Times* bestselling author

MAGGIE SHAYNE

"A tasty, tension-packed read."
—*Publishers Weekly* on *Thicker Than Water*

"Maggie Shayne demonstrates an absolutely superb touch, blending fantasy and romance into an outstanding reading experience."
—*Romantic Times BOOKreviews* on *Embrace the Twilight*

"Maggie Shayne is better than chocolate. She satisfies every wicked craving."
—Bestselling author Suzanne Forster

"Maggie Shayne delivers sheer delight, and fans new and old of her vampire series can rejoice."
—*Romantic Times BOOKreviews* on *Twilight Hunger*

"Shayne's haunting tale is intricately woven.... A moving mix of high suspense and romance, this haunting Halloween thriller will propel readers to bolt their doors at night!"
—*Publishers Weekly* on *The Gingerbread Man*

"Shayne's talent knows no bounds!"
—*Rendezvous*

"Maggie Shayne delivers romance with sweeping intensity and bewitching passion."
—Bestselling author Jayne Ann Krentz

"Shayne's gift has made her one of the preeminent voices in paranormal romance today!"
—*Romantic Times BOOKreviews*

MAGGIE SHAYNE

DEMON'S KISS

MIRA®

ISBN-13: 978-0-7783-2497-3
ISBN-10:   0-7783-2497-4

DEMON'S KISS

www.MIRABooks.com

Printed in U.S.A.

You know

Prologue

— ◄— ►—

"**I** need you to kill someone."

Rhiannon stood on the leaf-strewn path where Reaper had agreed to meet her, long hair and longer dress dancing on the night wind, and she wasted no time on preliminaries.

As greetings went, it wasn't the warmest one he had ever received. But it *was* the most common.

"Of course you do," he replied. "Why else would you have asked me to come?"

Her smile was slow. Her eyes held a dangerous glitter. "Normally, of course, I would prefer to do this sort of thing myself," she told him, moving closer. Her sleek black panther moved beside her, each step slow, sinuous, silent, its head level with her hand, bumping against it every now and then. "But the circumstances forbid it, I'm afraid."

"And what circumstances are those?" Reaper asked, curious. He began walking, remaining close to her, but not touching. He didn't like touching.

The hem of her velvet dress stirred the gold and russet leaves that lined the footpath. It was a trail that

wound through a secluded park, high in the hills of
Virginia, a wilderness tucked between cities, and a
popular route among runners, cyclists, walkers and nature lovers. Right now, though, in the deepest part of
the night, the park was deserted. The only sound to be
heard was that of the wind, crackling across the few
brittle leaves that still clung to the surrounding trees.

She didn't answer him, just kept walking at his side,
her fingers scratching the top of Pandora's huge head
every few steps, eliciting a purr from the panther that
sounded disturbingly like a growl.

Reaper probed more deeply, using a tactic certain
to work with the arrogant Rhiannon. He knew her
well enough to know how to bait her. She was, after
all, his maker. "This rogue you want killed must be
the most heinous in history, if he has you too afraid
to face him yourself."

She stopped walking and swung her head around,
a sharp, swift movement that brought her long raven
hair snapping over one side of her face. "I fear *no one,*
my friend. And you know it. I'd like nothing better
than to break his bones one by one, while bleeding
him in between."

He nodded, knowing she was fully capable of carrying out the threat, and furthermore, would likely
enjoy it. "So why call me?"

"Because he's not just a lone wolf, Reaper. He's the
leader of an entire pack of them, a pack who will turn
on anyone who threatens their precious alpha male.
And as much as I hate to admit it, I'm not a lone wolf,
either. Not anymore. I have a mate, Roland. I have

friends, family, now. Precious children—important children—are a part of that family."

He lifted his brows. "You speak of the mongrel twins born to the half-breed vampiress they call the Child of Promise."

Her eyes narrowed. "Be very careful when you speak about those children, Reaper. I love them as if they were my own."

He held up a hand, understanding. "I get it. You can't risk bringing the wrath of a pack of killers down on those...*special* children. Well, you were right to contact me. I'm the perfect man for the job."

"You sound awfully sure of that," she said, calmer now. She pushed her hair behind her shoulder and resumed walking, staring upward as she did. He followed her gaze. It was a moonless night, crisp and clear, with stars glittering like ice chips from a cold, black sky. The chill air tasted of apples and smelled of rotting leaves. "You haven't even heard the details yet, so how can you know?"

"Because I *am* a lone wolf. I have no family or friends to worry about. Nothing is precious to me, and there is no one that I love."

"Liar."

He shot her a look. "It's the absolute truth."

"Rubbish. There's the boy."

He averted his eyes, looking anywhere but at her. "What boy?"

"Reaper, honestly. The mortal, with the baggy jeans and bad video-game addiction. Seth, isn't it?"

"He's hardly a boy anymore. And as you're aware,

he's one of the Chosen. You know perfectly well that we vampires have no choice where those rare humans who possess the Belladonna antigen are concerned. They can be transformed, can become like us. It's not affection, Rhiannon. We're *compelled* to protect them."

"Yes, I *do* know that. And I also know that for each of us, there is one of them with whom the bond is far stronger. Seth is that one for you." She stared at him until she made him look back. "You care for him," she accused.

"I care for no one. He's a nuisance. If I weren't forced by nature to look after him, I'd stay a thousand miles from him at all times, I promise you that."

She thinned her lips, shook her head. "If that's true, then I pity you."

"Don't waste your energy, Rhiannon. I'm an assassin. I was a killer in life, and I remain one in death. It's what I do."

"And you do it well."

"Better than anyone."

She studied him for a moment longer, then sighed and nodded. "The details, then. He calls himself Gregor, and he hunts throughout the Southeastern states— here in Virginia, the Carolinas and Georgia, that we know of—taking the innocent, the young, any victims he desires, and encouraging his gang to do the same."

"How old is he?"

"No one knows. The trail of corpses—the victims he doesn't bother trying to hide—started appearing about a decade ago, as near as I can trace."

"And who made him?"

"No one seems to know that, either."

He frowned at her. "That's unusual."

"He's an unusual criminal, Reaper."

Reaper rubbed his chin. "I like to know all I can about a mark before I go after him, Rhiannon. Without knowing his age or the identity of his sire, there's no way for me to begin to calculate how strong he might be."

She looked away momentarily. "Well, if it's too much of a challenge for you…"

"I didn't say that." He barked the words without thinking, then went silent, seeing the mischief in her eyes and the slight smile tugging at her full lips. She knew how to get a reaction out of him, too, he reminded himself. "Tell me what you *do* know, then."

She nodded. "I have no idea how many are in his gang. Rumors run the gamut from ten to fifty. His apparent right-hand man is known as the Jack of Hearts, and slightly more is known about him. Probably because of the trail of broken hearts and empty bank accounts he tends to leave behind him wherever he goes."

"A con man," Reaper said.

"And an excellent lover, or so I've been told."

"Anything else?"

"Yes, and this is…disturbing. Part of his gang—the bulk of it, in fact—is rumored to be made up of… creatures unlike any I've heard mention of before."

He stopped walking, frowned at her. "Creatures?"

"Vampires—only…not."

"Then…what?" he asked.

She blinked rapidly, scratching her cat's head more

slowly as she considered her answer. "Bear in mind, this is second- and third-hand information. I only have rumors and reports to go by. But it's said these creatures are large, powerful blood drinkers, who seem to have no thought or will of their own. They obey Gregor mindlessly—even to the point of self-destruction."

He lifted his brows. "Does such a creature exist?"

"I've heard of vampires who've learned to make slaves of ordinary mortals. They do this by drinking their blood and giving them a drop or two of their own in exchange. This leaves them weak and increasingly dependent upon the vampire, much as a drug addict becomes dependent upon his chemical of choice. But they're still mortals. Weak, eventually mindless, yes, but only mortals. These creatures are strong, large and, apparently, immortal. An entirely different breed. No one, not even the oldest among us, can guess how Gregor made them."

Reaper nodded. "Clearly, we're dealing with a brilliant mind. I hate clever villains. What else do you know, Rhiannon?"

"Not much, I'm afraid. Only that Gregor and his gang are dangerous, a pack of rabid animals. They murder innocent mortals. They bring the danger of discovery—and the wrath and hatred of those who already know about us—down on the heads of every vampire in existence. They must be destroyed. But you'll need to be very careful."

"Not to mention very well compensated."

She pursed her lips and tugged a drawstring bag from her sash. He hadn't noticed it there, and no wonder. It was black velvet, like the gown itself. Holding it up so it dangled by its strings from her long, dagger-tipped fingers, she said, "*Very* well compensated."

He took the bag, which weighed at least two pounds and jangled musically when he shook it. He didn't bother opening it. He trusted her. If she said it was fair, it was fair.

"One hundred thousand in gold. These krugerands are only the down payment. You'll get the rest when the job is finished."

"A hundred grand, huh? You must really want this Gregor dead."

"Not just me," she told him. "The oldest, the most powerful and the wealthiest among us have contributed to this cause, Reaper. You have their blessing."

"The blessing of the damned. That's rich."

She tipped her head to one side, frowning. "You're exceedingly bitter, aren't you?"

"Am I?"

"I'm only trying to tell you that if you need assistance, there are many of us waiting to offer it."

"I won't need help."

"But if you do—"

"I work alone." He turned and walked away from her.

"Contact me when it's done," she called after him, that air of command in her voice a note that was familiar to him and natural to her.

"I won't need to," he said. "You'll know. I will be in touch all the same, though, to collect the rest of my payment." He tossed the pouch of gold coins and caught it again as he moved out of sight.

1

─ ── ─

Seth Connor was cornered and low on energy, crouching on the top of a crumbling crypt in the middle of a cemetery. Toxic sludge had seeped in, covering the ground on all sides, so getting down and running for it was not an option. He wouldn't last long if he stepped into that muck. Besides, he was surrounded by zombies—half-witted, yeah, but still dangerous. The sludge didn't seem to bother them, or maybe they were just too zoned out to notice. Still, between them and the bubbling green chemical cocktail down there, he wouldn't stand a chance. He was going to have to try to jump the gaping distance between where he was, and where he needed to be—the roof of the caretaker's cottage. And it was a long jump. He wasn't sure he had enough juice left in him to make it.

But standing still wasn't an option, either. He shouldered the shotgun, emptied it into the mob of zombies, who were already trying to climb onto the roof themselves, just to clear himself a path, then pushed off hard. His body somersaulted through the air, once, twice, three times, poisonous muck flashing beneath him with every flip, and then it seemed to be getting closer. Hell! He stretched, straightened, reached—and just barely caught the edge of the cottage roof with his fingertips.

His legs dangled. Zombies were reaching for him, grabbing on, trying to tug him down. He kicked at them, then managed to draw his handgun. Hanging by the fingers of one hand, he peppered the bastards with lead.

They fell away. He dropped the handgun—a hell of a loss, but he might be able to find another at the next level. Tugging himself up onto the roof of the caretaker's cottage, he took a look around and saw the path to safety: a power line suspended from the roof's far side. He headed for it, hopped on and tightrope-walked his way to Level Nine.

Blowing a relieved sigh, Seth dropped the game controller onto the coffee table, stood up and stretched the kinks out of his back. It had taken a while to get through that last level, but the feeling of triumph, though bright, was only fleeting. It was a game. A fun distraction from the constant waiting that had become his life. He didn't even know what he was waiting *for*. But the sense of nervous anticipation, that electrical charge just before a lightning strike, that feeling that something *big* was about to happen, had come on stronger today than it ever had before.

He was destined for something important. He'd always known it. But he was getting awfully bored waiting to find out what it was.

His phone rang. He jumped, that was how tightly wound he was. Then he grabbed it with the half-formed notion that this might be the call that would start him on his way toward whatever it was he was supposed to be doing. A glance at the caller ID box wiped that notion away. It was only J.J. calling from The Hole, the local sports bar where Seth had been promoted to manager.

Sighing, he picked up the phone. "Yeah, pal, what is it?" It was always something.

"Seth, I don't know what to do, man. Tommy's supposed to be on grill, but he went home sick. We're out of grenadine and the dishwasher's acting up again. And we're packed tonight and short on staff."

"Dude, you call me every time I have a night off."

"It's a crisis, Seth."

"No. It's normal. A crisis is when things are unusually bad. This is stuff that happens all the time. Normal, J.J. You gotta learn how to handle it."

"I'm trying, but there's only one of me."

Seth lowered his head, then sighed and figured what the hell. It wasn't as if he had anything else to do. Maybe go to bed early. Maybe dream about *her* again. The beautiful little redhead with the eyes that looked right through to his soul. The one who had something to do with his destiny. The one he'd never met, but had dreamed of for as long as he could remember.

He sighed. She would be there waiting in his subconscious, no matter what time he went to sleep. "I'll be right over, okay? Meanwhile, call Bobbie to come in and handle the grill. She's closest, and she always loves picking up extra hours. Call Tanya in to wait tables. She goes right by the liquor store on her way in, so have her pick up a couple of bottles of grenadine on the way, and that'll tide us over until the truck arrives tomorrow. I'll be there in five minutes."

J.J. sighed audibly. "Thanks, Seth. You're a freaking hero, you know that?"

Yeah. Some hero. Master of broken-down dishwashers and missing waitstaff, he could leap stumbling drunks in a single bound. He closed his eyes and shook his head, before grabbing his hoodie off the hook by the apartment door and yanking it over his head on the way out.

Four hours later, the bar was closed, stools upside down on the mahogany counter, chairs upside down on the tables, floor freshly mopped and filling the place with the scent of pine cleaner. Seth was heading out for what was left of the night, which wasn't a hell of a lot.

J.J. was beside him, carrying the money pouch, which they would dump in the bank's night-deposit box on their way to the parking lot on the corner. His out-of-control brown frizz was being held hostage underneath a worn-out, stained-up Yankees cap. He shuffled his feet when he walked, and he slouched too much. Seth thought the kid needed a lot more than just on-the-job training if he ever wanted to get ahead in life.

Then again, Seth thought, who was he to talk? Okay, maybe he didn't have J.J.'s lack of self-esteem. But he was still in a job that was going nowhere, in a life that was nothing but filler, waiting for the big fat hairy deal he'd always believed was his destiny. He was meant for something big. He knew it. And tonight it felt closer than ever.

One block to the bank. J.J. was whistling the theme

song from the newest *Rocky* film. Traffic was nonexistent, and the pavement gleamed.

"Can you believe it rained and stopped again while we were in the bar, and we never even knew it?" J.J. asked.

"Yep. The Hole is like its own self-contained world."

"World?" J.J. echoed. "Nah. Small town, maybe. Better yet, it's a self-contained soap opera. It's got all the characters down. There's the dirty old man, Henry, who can't think about anything but his dick and gets away with sexually harassing every female in the place because he's a hundred and two."

"Henry isn't thinking about his dick, J.J. He's trying to remind himself he's still a man. Patting a waitress on the ass when she passes close enough for him to reach is about the only way he can still manage to do that. Although, I think he'd feel more like a man if one of them would smack him, instead of smiling and patting him on the head as if he's cute and no real threat. They could at least pretend to be insulted."

J.J. lifted his brows. "I never thought of it that way. What about Mrs. Brown?"

"Shauna?"

"Yeah. Everyone knows she's married, but she comes in every night, drinks until she's messed up, then hits on every stranger who walks into the place."

"They never hit on her back, though."

"So?"

"Think about it. She's a good-looking woman, J.J. If she really wanted to get laid by some stranger, she wouldn't have any trouble. She's not really trying. If anyone shows any interest, she backs off like mad, until they take the hint and leave. Then she keeps drinking until she starts crying, and then she has me call her a taxi." Seth shrugged. "She's miserable and just wants to be loved. If her husband doesn't wake up, I imagine she'll eventually work up the strength to walk. Until then, she'll just keep being miserable, I guess."

"You really see things about people," J.J. told him. "What do you see in me, Seth?"

Seth shrugged and didn't look J.J. in the eye, because it was such a sappy and un-guy-like conversation to be having. "A kid with a lot of potential. You can do anything you want to, J.J. You just have to grow a pair, you know? Like tonight, you could have made some decisions, solved some of those problems on your own, and taken the consequences, good or bad, yourself. But instead, you called me, to save yourself from having to take any chances."

"Why take chances if you don't have to?" J.J. asked.

"You know how I got promoted to manager, J.J.?" Seth didn't wait for an answer, just went on. "There was a major crisis at the bar one night. Manager had a heart attack and got rushed to the E.R. Bartender was his wife and went with him. Head waitress had to drive her there. And there I was. But I jumped in and handled it. Made some calls, got some people to fill in for the bartender and waitress, managed the place myself all night, and kept things going like clockwork. Next thing I know, I'm getting a promotion and a raise. *That's* why you take chances when you don't have to. No risk, no gain, pal."

J.J. nodded. "I think I get it."

The streetlight was flickering. Later Seth would think that flickering streetlight had almost seemed like a warning. But right then, he paid it no more attention than he did the little shiver that tiptoed up his spine for no obvious reason.

Then, in the next second, someone crashed into his back, slamming him to the sidewalk so hard his chin split. Then fists pounded on his head. Pain exploded behind his eyes. Shock and surprise made his heart hammer, but he reacted anyway, rolling and flinging the bastard off him, then scrambling to his feet to take a quick look around.

J.J. was lying on the ground, face-up, with some big SOB kicking him in the ribs. Seth hurled himself at J.J.'s attacker with everything he had, and the two of them sailed bodily into the alley.

He landed on top of the guy. The other one jumped on him before he could even draw a breath. But he managed to shout, "Run, J.J.! Get the hell out of here! *Run!*"

And that was it. One of the bad asses picked him up, spun him around, then knocked him flat again with a fist to his jaw. As he lay on his back in the alley, he caught just a glimpse of J.J. running for dear life, already a block away. Then the thugs—there were four of them now, and he was damned if he knew where the other two had come from—were all around him, blocking his vision. He couldn't see anything except legs in faded, torn jeans that hung loosely, and the front ends of unlaced Columbia suede work boots, with the tongues sticking out.

"Gimme the money bag, asshole," one of the thugs said.

Seth smiled slowly, but it hurt, so he stopped. He figured his lip was split, and maybe his jaw was busted, too. He wasn't going to tell these bastards that J.J. was the one carrying the bag. Not just yet. Give the kid time to get clear. He figured his own ass was grass, either way. "Why don't you take it from me?" he asked.

"My pleasure."

The beating *really* began then. And there wasn't a hell of a lot Seth could do about it. He tried to get a few blows in, tried to block the punches and kicks with his arms, but eventually he was hurting too bad and bleeding too much to do more than curl up like a boiled shrimp and wait for them to get tired.

He wondered, after a while, if this was it, the big shining moment he'd always known he was meant for. Maybe his entire purpose in life had been to be here tonight, to take the heat off J.J. So maybe it was J.J. who was truly meant for something big. Maybe he would end up being president or something. And Seth was just a pawn, a sacrifice for the greater good.

Damn. He had always thought it would be something more. And his biggest regret was her—the girl he'd been dreaming about for so long. Could he really die without ever once meeting her face-to-face? It didn't seem possible, but it looked pretty damned likely.

After thoroughly tapping the vampiric grapevine, Reaper's only lead to Gregor was a spoiled rich vampiress who called herself Topaz. She lived in a mansion on Emerald Isle, in North Carolina, and rumor had it that she'd recently lost a substantial portion of her wealth to a vampire con man who'd broken her heart. No one had heard the man's name, but his description matched that of Gregor's sidekick. The M.O. was right, the location was right, and Reaper was pretty sure his gut instincts were right, too. The con artist must have been the vampire known as Jack of Hearts. And if he could find Jack, he could find Gregor and the rest of the rogue band.

So he was on his way to Emerald Isle when the sensation hit him. First it was a sense of nervous energy, a clenching of his stomach, a twitching of various muscles, a surge of epinephrine. Fight or flight. But it came for no reason. He wasn't in danger.

No, but someone is.

He felt pain, then. Excruciating pain. Not his own.

And then he sensed the essence behind it, the aura that came whenever one of his kind came into proximity with one of theirs, or whenever one of his kind was in dire need. The feelings were coming from one of the Chosen.

And not just any one of the Chosen. But *his.* Seth Connor. The young man was in trouble. And the bottom fell out of Reaper's stomach in spite of himself. The kid was always in trouble of one kind or another, but the pain he was feeling now… This was no minor scrape.

"God, now of all times?" Reaper rolled his eyes and told himself that Seth was proving to be exactly the kind of nuisance Reaper had told Rhiannon he was. He told himself that, even as he stopped everything he was doing to race to Seth's aid. He reminded himself that there was no choice. He hadn't been lying when he'd told Rhiannon that he was compelled, as were all vampires, to protect and watch over Seth's kind. If he could have ignored the call, he thought deliberately, determinedly, he might very well have kept on driving.

Yeah. Right. And just who do you think you're kidding, Reaper?

So he obeyed his instinctive need to go to the younger man, and go fast. He took an exit, following his senses, his intuition, and as he got nearer, he realized it was a damn good thing he had.

Reaper felt the cold breath of his grim namesake nearby and knew that Seth, his own charge, was near death. He skidded the car to a halt, leapt out, turned and ran, moving so quickly that he was invisible to human eyes. Moments later, he was at the mouth of an alley, where four upright men were kicking and beating one who lay on the ground, curled loosely in on himself.

Reaper didn't speak, he just moved. His first blow sent one man smashing into a wall, where his head took a chunk out of the cinder block it hit. He grabbed the second one by his nape and hurled him through the air, not bothering to watch where he came down, though he heard glass breaking. He grabbed the third by his hair and slammed his face into the ground. And then he delivered a kick to the solar plexus of the fourth that probably split his intestine apart. And all of it in the space of two seconds, possibly less.

Finally he knelt beside the young man, his cast-iron

stomach churning as he bent closer. Seth's face had been badly beaten. His eyes were swollen and purple, his nose broken, lips split, jaw unhinged or broken. His own mother wouldn't have known him. Reaper knew him, though. He knew his scent, his essence. His restless, frustrated energy.

As much as he disliked physical contact, there was nothing else for it right then. Reaper slid an arm beneath Seth's shoulders and lifted his head up from the concrete floor of the alley where he lay. His body was as broken as his face, but it didn't show as much to the naked eye.

"Did J.J. get away?" Seth asked. His voice was coarse and soft.

Reaper narrowed his eyes, then probed the younger man's mind and saw the scene unfolding through Seth's memory. The attack. The other, even younger, man, J.J., being beaten. He saw what Seth had done, taking the attackers on himself to give J.J. the chance to escape. He could easily have gotten away himself, but he hadn't. Reaper sensed that J.J. had. "Yes, he's safe," he said.

Seth sighed and closed his eyes. "I'm glad."

Seth was dying. Or else he wasn't. The decision was his.

"Open your eyes, Seth," Reaper said. "I need to talk to you."

Seth wasn't sure if he was alive or dead. The pain was fading, and so was everything else. He felt as if he were falling farther and farther away from everything real. And then an insistent voice, a man's voice, one that was oddly familiar to him, made its way through a long and winding pathway from his ear to his brain.

"Open your eyes, Seth. I need to talk to you."

He tried to obey—something about that voice made him want to—but he couldn't. And really, he *didn't* want to, not all that much. He was dreaming about her again. She was so real, so freaking real, this time. He could feel her when he touched her. Soft skin, masses of coppery hair he couldn't stop stroking. Her petite frame, her soft voice, the uncertainty that always seemed to linger behind her eyes.

"I really don't have time for this, you know. If you don't wake up and give me an answer, I'm just going to have to do it without your consent."

Consent? Do *what* without his consent?

"Seth, honestly, I'm nearly out of patience." The man sighed, and when he spoke again, his voice was different. It held some kind of power that hadn't been there before. "Hear my voice and obey, Seth Connor. My will is yours. Do as I say. Open. Your. Eyes."

Seth realized he was alive after all. He had to be, to hurt this bad. He supposed he had to wake up and pay attention if he wanted to keep it that way. He hated leaving his dream girl behind, but maybe this way he would get that chance to meet her for real after all. Yeah. It could still happen.

That hope was what drove him to gather his strength, what little remained of it, and open his eyes. Barely. They were swollen and sore, and his vision wasn't any too clear. But the form that took shape, very slowly, before him, was that of a man, probably no more than a few years older than he was himself, and yet way, *way* older in some unnamable way.

"I…know you," he managed to mutter. "I've…seen you before."

"Yes, you have. I pulled you out of the river when you fell in, back when you were ten or eleven. And I dragged you out of the car wreck that killed your parents when you were sixteen, just before it went up in flames. There were countless other times when I helped you out of one scrape or another. None quite this serious, though."

Seth's mind was spinning, because all of a sudden he *did* remember. "How come I didn't remember—I mean, until now?"

"Because I didn't want you to."

The guy hadn't aged, Seth realized. Of course, he'd been beaten senseless, and his vision was blurry and it was dark, but somehow he didn't think it was a mistake. The guy looked exactly the same as he had those other times. Dark hair, brooding features, deep-set eyes that almost looked haunted. "Who are you?" he managed to ask.

"Your protector, for lack of a better term."

"Why?"

"Not by choice, I'll tell you that much. The rest will have to wait, Seth. You don't have a lot of time."

Seth nodded, and it hurt when he moved. "I'm dying, huh?"

"Yes, I'm afraid so. Your mortal life is ending. There are internal injuries. A ruptured spleen, I think, though I can't be sure. You're bleeding inside. It won't be long."

"I didn't think it would be over this fast." Seth tried to look around, but there were only out-of-focus shapes in the darkness now. His vision was narrowing, shrinking inward, so he squinted at the man again. "What is it you want me to do, before I…go?"

"I'm a vampire, Seth. I wish I had time to tell you all that entails. But I can only give you the barest of basics. I'm one of the undead. I live by night, and blood, not food, is my sustenance, though I do not need to kill in order to live. That's a myth. I never age. I'm powerful, strong, fast. My senses are heightened beyond anything you can imagine, and there are extra ones, as well. All of this can be yours, too, if you choose to become what I am. You need only tell me."

Seth stared at him and wondered if he was hallucinating.

"The alternative is death, and whatever waits beyond that," the man went on. "The choice is yours. But you need to make it soon, Seth. You won't be able to remain conscious much longer."

And in that moment, everything became crystal-clear to Seth. Everything in his life fell into place, all the pieces interlocking, to form the outline of a jigsaw puzzle. There were still pieces missing, almost the entire inside of the thing. He couldn't see the design, the picture, only that outline, that form. For the first time he could see its shape, see that it was real. *This* was the destiny he'd been sensing all his life. This was the first step on the path of the life he was meant to live—the path that was going to lead him to *her,* at some point along the way. He was sure of it. This was the beginning of something big. And as it turned out, it was something far bigger than even he had ever imagined.

"I want to live," he said. "I'm supposed to. There's something I have to do."

"Is there? And what would that be, Seth?"

The man sounded almost amused. Didn't matter. Seth knew it was real. "I don't know all of it yet. There's a girl—a woman— God, she's something special."

"Really?" Amusement was shaded by something far darker now. "She have a name?"

"I don't know it…yet. But I know I have to find her. And I know there's more—something major I have to do. So I'd better take you up on this…this vampire thing. 'Cause the alternative is to die, and I'll never get it done that way."

"You'll never get *anything* done that way. So be it, then," the vampire replied. And then he leaned over, and even as Seth told himself there would probably be some far less dramatic way to accomplish the thing than the one so common in pop fiction, the man bent closer, tipped Seth's head back and sank his fangs into Seth's throat.

He felt them pierce the skin, pop into the vein. There was pain, sharp and somehow good, and then there was the most incredible sense of release—not orgasmic, but more like a pressure cooker suddenly letting off steam. It rushed out of him, this pressure and tension and frailty, and pain, too. It rushed out of him with the blood that was rushing out of him, into the vampire's hungry mouth.

He tipped his head back farther, willing the stranger

to take it all, and he felt his life ebbing away, flowing out of him with every swallow the vampire took. And then the creature lifted his head away, wiped his mouth with the back of his hand and lowered Seth to the ground.

Seth's vision cleared, and he lay there on his back, in that alley full of trash, staring up at the glittering stars far, far away.

"You're dying now. Just as you begin to do so, Seth, I'll bring you back. Don't be afraid. Just relax and let it happen."

Seth tried to nod, but he sensed that nothing moved. Then, just before it all went black, he glimpsed her. Just for an instant. Her long, thick, copper-red hair hung over one shoulder, and her huge brown eyes pleaded with his in a way they never had before. He saw her more clearly, *felt* her more clearly, than he ever had. Her eyes were darkly lined, exotic and slanted. Her body was small, lithe but incredibly powerful. She was *wild,* he sensed, and then he sensed something else. She was caged.

She was begging for someone to help her. For *him* to help her.

It wasn't a dream. Not this time. It was real. He was really seeing her, somehow, in his mind. It *wasn't* a dream. Everything inside him reached for her, yearned for her, and then everything in him simply stopped. There was darkness, silence, no sense, no feeling, and then…

Bam!

Sensation slammed into him like an electric jolt. He went as rigid as a flat-lining patient when the paddles were applied.

But there *were* no paddles. There was only a wrist, which he was holding to his mouth with both hands, and from which he was drinking just as greedily as if he were dying of thirst.

He *felt* beyond feeling.

He *sensed* beyond belief.

He tasted and saw and heard and smelled a million, million things all at once, and knew them all. Jerking the wrist away from his mouth, pulling his head back, he sat there, blinking, *reeling*.

"It'll be all right," the vampire said. "It takes some time, but you're going to get used to it."

Somehow, Seth doubted that. "God, she's real. I mean, I always knew it, but I doubted—I wondered. But she's real. She's so real, and she needs me."

The man frowned at him. "*Who* needs you?"

"The girl," Seth told him. "We have to find her. We have to go to her. But I don't know how. I don't know where she is, or—"

"Okay, okay, you take it easy now. We'll get to the bottom of this, all right? Don't worry. Right now, you just need to…rest. Just rest and let your body adjust to the change. Okay?"

Seth nodded, lowered his head, closed his eyes and muttered, "Okay."

2

—◆—

Vixen paced from one end of her cell to the other without breaking stride. Her steps were small and light and smooth, and she tended to walk on her toes. She didn't like it here. She didn't like the people who were holding her. She didn't like the bars that held her captive or the fact that she couldn't simply squeeze out between them. She could have, once. Before they made her into whatever sort of demon she had become. But she hadn't been able to change since.

"Vixen, is it?"

The one called Briar leaned against the cage from the outside. Her hair was wild, wavy, thick and mink-brown, like her eyes. She was very young, must have been made into one of *them* at an unreasonably early age.

Then again, so had Vixen herself.

"What do you want?" Vixen asked. She gathered her hair, pulling it around to the front of her, so it hung over one shoulder, and stroked it. Whenever she was nervous, she tended to stroke or play with it—her way of touching her own nature, reminding herself of who and what she truly was. Not one of *them*. *Never* one of them.

"It's not what I want," Briar said. "It's what Gregor wants."

Vixen shrugged. "What does *he* want, then?"

"He wants you to help him. After all, he's helped you."

"He caged me. In this body. In this cell."

Briar shrugged. "In the cell, maybe. Not in the body, though. You can still change."

Vixen lowered her eyes, shaking her head slowly. Her throat felt tight, and odd, warm fluid filled her eyes. "I was in human form when he…bit me and drank my blood as if I were a chicken. *He* made me… whatever I am now. I tried to shift back, but—"

"You were newly made, and you were weak and frightened. That was six months ago, Vixen. You're stronger now. You have to try again."

Vixen looked Briar in the eye and shivered. She always shivered when she caught the scent of the darkness that lived in that one's soul. It was cold and frightening.

"Try, Vixen."

Vixen sighed and shook her head side to side.

"Try, Vixen," Briar said again, but she said it differently this time. There was anger in her voice. "Try, or go to sleep hungry again."

"I don't mind going to sleep hungry."

Briar sighed and reached up to the wall, where the long metal prod rested on a hook. Vixen flinched, and backed up as far as her cell would allow.

"Fine," Briar said, "I'll play with you for a while,

and *then* you can go to bed hungry. How's that sound?"
She stuck the rod between the bars, and no matter how
Vixen twisted away, she couldn't get beyond its reach.
It touched her belly, and jolted her so hard her head
snapped back and her knees buckled.

She curled on the floor, trembling. "Please, don't."

"But I enjoy it so." Briar poked her again, in the
neck this time.

Vixen jerked away, and her head hit the floor.

"Now, you're going to try for me. Aren't you,
Vixen?"

Vixen opened her mouth to answer, but she
couldn't get words out. Briar stabbed the rod in the
small of her back, and she arched and cried out, form-
ing the word *yes* on her agonized scream. When it died,
she lay there on the cold stone floor, shaking uncon-
trollably. "Yes," she whispered. "I'll try."

"Good. I'll give you an hour to recover. And if you
make me torture you again, Vixen, it's going to be
something a hell of a lot worse than the prod. Understand?"

Vixen nodded, the motions jerky and tight.

"One hour." Briar turned and walked away down
the echoing stone hallway, taking the light with her.
Vixen heard her feet ascending stairs, and then the
slamming of a heavy door. She was alone. Her senses
wouldn't deceive her about something so simple. She
was alone, here. The only prisoner of these cruel sapi-
ens.

And yet, she wasn't alone.

There was a mouse family living on the other side of

the room. They'd made a nest in one of the deep chasms in the stone, and they huddled there out of sight whenever one of *them* came into the dungeon. But they would come out for her. Oh, they wouldn't get too close. After all, she'd spent a good many hours of her life as one of their natural predators. But despite that, they sensed her animal nature, and her pain and distress. They were curious.

They came out now, though she'd felt them coming even before she saw them. She heard their little squeaks as they conversed and began hunting the floor for any crumbs, shooting looks her way as they went.

You won't find any crumbs around here. Those ones don't eat food. She thought the words at them, as images and ideas, not as a language. And she knew they understood. They hurried across the floor, to the loose board in the bottom of the door that led outside, and squeezed their tiny bodies through it.

She hoped they would gnaw it some more as she had tried to convey they should. If she could shift, she would need the board to give a bit more to allow her to squeeze through easily—though she might be able to fit even now, if only she could change.

Even when the mice were gone, she still didn't feel entirely alone.

There had been someone else. She'd sensed him all at once tonight, when one of the drones had taken her outside for a well-guarded and far too short walk. Gregor wanted her healthy—weak, and half-starved, but basically sound—until he figured out whether he could use her or not. So she was granted a nightly walk. And tonight, she'd felt him. A male. A kind one. He had seemed so very real, and so near that she had even lifted her head, sniffing the air and feeling with her senses to try to locate him, even identify him. Human or animal or vampire—she couldn't be sure. And then she had realized that he wasn't close to her, not physically. But in some other way, he was. Incredibly close. And he was coming—coming to help her. She had felt it, known it.

He had told her so, somehow.

She had closed her eyes and focused on that feeling with everything in her. "If you're coming to me," she'd whispered, "please hurry. If I have to stay here much longer I'll die. Please hurry. I need you."

And just as suddenly as it had arrived, her sense of that other person, the male, faded entirely the moment she was ushered back inside, through the cellars she thought of as dungeons and into her cold cell.

She hadn't sensed him again since then. She wondered now if she had only imagined him, and she sank to the cold floor, lowering her head as despair crushed her.

But she didn't allow it to hold her in its grip. She lifted her chin, and she vowed that she would escape these creatures who held her. She was smarter than they were, more cunning, and more in tune with her senses and her instincts. If they were right, and she *could* shift back, then it would not take her long to make her way out of here. She would slip away at the first opportunity.

And then she would be free. Free to run and play and *live* again.

But even then, it would never be the same. She could

never go back to what she was before. She knew it, sensed it. In a very real way, her life was already over.

Seth opened his eyes and lay very, very still, because *damn*. Everything was *different*.

"Ah, you're awake," the vampire said.

Seth blinked, amazed, because, yeah, the guy was a vampire, and it was real and now he was...he was...

"What's wrong, Seth?"

"Your voice. Dude, it's like I can hear every vocal cord vibrating when you talk."

"I know."

"I can feel the air touching my skin."

"You can probably hear the grass growing, if you listen for it," the vampire said.

"So I'm either tripping on acid, or I'm..."

"You're a vampire. Your senses are heightened. Magnified. Everything is impacted. You'll feel both pleasure and, unfortunately, pain, at levels almost beyond endurance."

Seth closed his eyes. "What a trip."

"An endless one," the man said.

Seth lifted his head, realizing he was in a car, and that the other man was driving. The road was dark before them, the lines flashing by at an alarming speed. "Where are we going?" A little voice deep inside told him he knew damn well where he was going. He was going to *her*. He didn't know how, or exactly why, but he felt it. He was getting closer to her with every mile.

"North Carolina. I was on a mission when you interrupted me, Seth. I don't have any more time to waste."

"I *interrupted* you? By what, almost dying?"

"Exactly."

Seth searched the vampire's dark face, awaiting an explanation he seemed reluctant to give. Finally, the man nodded as if he'd decided on something. "There are a lot of things you're going to need to learn in a very short time, Seth, and this isn't the most important among them. But I'll try to sate your curiosity all the same."

"Gee, thanks."

"You don't need to thank me. I'm your maker, your sire. Your father, in a way. It's my duty to educate you."

"I was being sarcastic, pal. You don't have much of a sense of humor, do you?"

"I've never seen the need for one."

"You ever…make any others?"

The vampire frowned at Seth briefly, before returning his gaze to the road. "You have a rare blood type, Seth. It contains an antigen called Belladonna. Humans with this blood type tend to grow weak and die young. They also tend to bleed excessively."

"I've always had the bleeding thing. I knew about the antigen—makes transfusions tough to come by. I didn't know I was gonna get weak and die young, though."

"You would have, eventually. Now you won't. But you know that. What you don't know is that only humans with the Belladonna antigen can become undead, Seth. Such mortals are known among us as the Chosen. All vampires had the antigen as mortals. And all vampires sense mortals with the antigen, and are compelled to aid and even protect them."

"You're kidding me. Hell, that's why you've shown up before. Helped me out when I got into trouble."

"That's why."

"But…why you, why not any others? I mean, there *are* others, right?" He sat up straighter in the seat, surprised that the movement didn't hurt him. Last he remembered, he'd been beaten within an inch of his life. "How many of them—of us—are there? And where are they? Are we going to meet them? Is there some kind of a—"

The driver actually smiled, and it was such a stunning thing to see that Seth went silent. That dark, morose expression faded for just a moment. But then it returned so swiftly that Seth almost wondered if he'd imagined the change. "May I continue now?" the vampire asked.

"Yeah. I just… There's so much I want to know."

"And you'll learn all of it, in time. For now, I'll continue with the part I've begun. For each vampire, there is one mortal with whom the psychic bond is particularly strong. For me, that mortal is you. That's why you've seen me before. That's why I've helped you when you've been in trouble in the past. And it's why I could not do anything but come to you again when you were near death."

Seth nodded slowly. "I appreciate it."

"If I'd had a choice in the matter, I'd likely have continued on my mission and left you to live or die on your own."

Hell, this guy was one cold son of a bitch, Seth thought.

"Careful. I can hear your thoughts, you know."

Seth's brows rose high. "You…?"

"But you aren't wrong. I *am* a cold son of a bitch."

"Damn."

Again the vampire smiled, just slightly this time. "I'll teach you to block your thoughts. It's just further evidence I made the right decision in bringing you along with me. Initially I intended to transform you and leave you behind. I only realized after the deed was done that a fledgling vampire as clueless as you wouldn't last a week on his own."

"Hey, ease up there, pal. I think I could have managed just fine on my own."

The vampire looked at him briefly, brows raised, a look of skepticism in his dark eyes.

"I'm not kidding," Seth told him; then he turned to gaze out the window, amazed that he could see for miles, and that everything was as clear as day to him, despite the fact that it was dark outside. "I've been waiting my whole life for this. I mean, I didn't *know* it was this, but it has to be. I always knew I was meant for something big, something important."

"The girl," the vampire said. And Seth shot him a look. The man shrugged. "You mentioned her, earlier."

He nodded. "She's part of it. But there's more. Maybe this mission of yours. What is it, exactly?"

"I've got to kill someone."

Seth shivered and looked down at his hands in his lap. "Hell."

"Don't worry. He's in dire need of killing. And I have no intention of letting you become involved. I work alone."

"Well, you *did.* But, uh, I'm kind of here now, so—"

"I work alone."

Seth nodded. The vamp was a cranky bastard. He realized, as the man shot him a look, that he'd heard that thought, too. Seth attempted a sheepish grin. "Sorry. This is gonna take some getting used to."

"Mmm."

"You know, I don't even know your name."

"Reaper," the vampire said. And that was it, nothing more.

"Reaper. Huh. Well, hell, I guess it fits." Seth was quiet for a moment; then he sent the guy a smirk. "So can I call you Grim?"

"No."

Not even a smile. Seth sat back in the seat, realizing that joking wasn't going to go over real big with this guy. He flipped on the radio and began looking for a decent station. "Reaper, you saved my butt back there. I owe you, you know. So if you decide you *do* need some help with this mission of yours, you just say the word, okay?"

Reaper looked at him with one brow higher than the other.

"Don't look like that. You don't know me, pal. There's not a lot I can't do."

"I don't doubt it. And I'd lay odds your friend J.J. will never forget what you did for him last night."

Seth looked at him, because that statement had almost sounded…approving. But there was no sign of it in Reaper's face. So Seth looked away, saying nothing.

"If there wasn't much you couldn't do before, Seth," Reaper told him, "then believe me, there is considerably less you can't do now. There are a few things you should know immediately, however."

"Shoot," Seth told him.

"You're extremely flammable. Stay away from fire. Sunlight will kill you, slowly and painfully. That part of the mythology is true."

"How about a stake through the heart?" Seth asked.

"A stake through any part of you could kill you, but not because of the stake. We tend to bleed excessively, and bleeding out is one of the ways we can die. However, if you get cut and can stanch the bleeding until the day sleep, you'll heal with the sunrise. Always remember that. If you can stay alive until daylight, you'll survive."

"Okay. How about a crucifix? Will that hurt me?"

"Don't be ridiculous. We're not devils."

"Sorry." He'd offended the guy. Hell, who knew vampires had pet peeves?

"You need blood to survive," Reaper went on. "You can get it from blood banks. You don't need to take victims. You're going to feel pain a hell of a lot more than you did before. It's one of the things that can lay you out. It can be *that* debilitating. But the balance to that is you'll feel pleasure more intensely, as well. The older you get, the more intense your senses become, and your other powers, as well."

"What other powers?"

"Running with great speed, leaping incredibly high, telepathy, mind control, sheer strength."

Seth smiled. He thought of his latest and most impressive feat to date. Besides saving J.J.'s life and becoming a vampire, that was. "I wonder if I could leap off the top of a crypt, somersault three times and land on my feet on a roof a dozen yards away."

"I wouldn't be surprised," Reaper said.

"Could *you* do it?"

"Of course."

Seth smiled a little. "Yeah, but could you do it over a toxic swamp full of zombies?"

Reaper frowned at him briefly, then shook his head as if puzzled and returned his attention to the road. Seth found a radio station he liked and cranked the volume. He was surprised that Reaper didn't reach out and snap it off again, and even more surprised to see the cranky bastard's foot tapping in time every now and then.

They rode that way for three excellent songs in a row; then the station launched into a block of commercials, so Seth turned it down. "So where in North Carolina are we going?" he asked.

"Emerald Isle. Rather near Wilmington."

"Uh-huh. Is that where the guy you have to kill is?"

"I don't know."

Seth waited. Reaper didn't say more, though. "Hey, come on, fill me in. You seem like a decent guy. You wouldn't be after this dude if there wasn't a reason."

"I'm a killer, Seth. An assassin. It's what I did as a mortal, and it's what I still do. I'm very good at it, but there are…there are things about me that make me as dangerous as hell. You're not safe with me. No one is. Keep that in mind, and keep your guard up. Don't trust me. Don't trust anyone."

Seth frowned, studying Reaper's profile. "Is that my first lesson on being a vampire?"

"That's your first lesson on being alive. It should be everyone's."

"You're intense, you know that? Are you always this serious? This freaking...dark?"

"Yes." Reaper glanced sideways at Seth, and then sighed. "There is a gang of rogue vampires, led by a man called Gregor, who've been murdering humans at will. Young, old, innocent, it doesn't matter. They leave bloodless bodies, with fang marks in their throats, lying around where they can be easily discovered. They have to be stopped."

"Damn straight. You can't just go around murdering innocent people."

"I'm more concerned at their lack of discretion. It exposes our existence to people who might otherwise never know of it. And that puts us all at risk."

"Oh." Seth nodded. "So what's in Wilmington?"

"A vampiress who might know something of the gang's whereabouts."

"What makes you think she knows?"

"She's beautiful, incredibly wealthy, and it's rumored she recently had her heart and her bank accounts broken by the same man. That sort of game is one Gregor's right-hand man is extremely fond of playing."

Seth nodded, and wondered if this vampiress with the broken heart was the woman he was looking for. He was still full of questions. But he decided to give Reaper a break. Then he reached up for the rearview mirror and tilted it down to check out his face. Sure, the pain was gone, but he had to be bruised pretty badly.

However, when he looked in the mirror, there was

no reflection. A wave of nausea rose up in him, and he pushed it down.

"That's another one of the myths about us that are true," Reaper told him. "And your bruises are gone. They healed with the day sleep. Everything did, just as it always will."

Seth licked his lips, leaned back against the seat and closed his eyes. "One more question, okay?"

"Only one?" Reaper sounded skeptical.

"For now." Seth opened his eyes, wanting to see the guy's expression for this one. "That stuff you told me about the Chosen, and about every vampire having one special one, one that he's more connected to than any other?"

"Yes."

"Well, I'm a vampire now, too, right?"

Reaper nodded.

"So do I have a bond with one of the Chosen, too?"

"Yes. One of the Chosen—or, possibly even one who's already become a vampire. The bond remains even after the transformation. You may not know who it is right away, but yes. There will be a powerful connection, a pull. You'll know when that one needs you. You'll feel compelled to help."

"Could I have felt that bond even before I was changed over?"

Frowning, Reaper glanced at him. "I don't see why not."

Seth was pretty sure he already felt it. Had felt it all his life, and then, more potently than ever, just as his mortal life had ebbed away. The beautiful thing with the coppery red hair and the huge brown eyes. She was a part of his destiny. He'd never been more sure of anything.

For just a moment he started to panic. What if he was supposed to be helping her right now? What if he couldn't find her in time? What if...?

And then he felt it. Just as surely as day followed night, he knew it. They were going the right way. He was doing exactly what he was supposed to be doing. The fate he'd been waiting for was at hand. He'd never felt this way before. He knew it was dead-on-balls accurate.

He sighed and tried to relax. He was on his path, on his journey, doing what he'd been meant to do his entire life. And he was going to do it right.

3

━━━◆━━━

"I hate him. I hate him, I hate him, *I hate him!*" Topaz hurled a 1945 Waterford cut crystal vase into the wall with so much force that it dented the surface before it exploded into a thousand glittering bits.

It wasn't as satisfying as smashing his face would be, though. God, when she thought about how she'd been with him, the things she'd done. She'd been utterly uninhibited, willing to do anything, try anything, experience anything, because she was sure she was safe in his hands. That he was just as enamored of her as she was of him. That he loved her.

He'd convinced her of that.

She'd allowed it.

"Liar!" She kicked an oak rocking chair out of her path as she paced the mansion's great room. It hit the fireplace mantel and broke into three pieces on the way to the floor.

Topaz was enraged. She needed to feed the fury inside her, and stored blood wasn't going to do. Not tonight, not with the memory of *him* so alive in her mind.

She'd been making progress getting over him. Or

she'd thought so. And then that freaking gossip of a vampiress, Dorinda, had to bring it all crashing back on her. With her, *Oh, honey, I just had to come by and see how you were doing,* and her, *I know exactly how you must feel.* All of it bullshit, all of it just a way of leading up to the real reason for her visit. which was to impart the news that Jack had been seen several times in Savannah, in the company of a very young, very beautiful vampiress no one seemed to know anything about.

Dorinda hadn't come out of concern. She'd wanted to gossip and gloat, and twist the blade Jack had driven into Topaz's heart. Dorinda was jealous. She'd wanted Jack for herself. The lucky bitch should be grateful she hadn't gotten him.

It galled Topaz that she'd been so transparent, so idiotically in love that she'd revealed it to everyone she knew. So that when her money vanished, and her lover with it, everyone knew that, too. She'd been publicly humiliated. She'd been used. And she'd been robbed.

And hurt. Though she would never admit that to anyone, ever, not even under torture. But she'd been hurt more than she had ever hurt in death or in life. And she didn't think the pain was going to end any time soon.

She had really loved the bastard.

She grabbed a jacket, slung it on over her glittery tank top and designer jeans, not because she would feel the night's chill, but because it was a cute jacket, leather with fur trim at the collar and cuffs in a shade of pale mink that exactly matched her hair.

Topaz enjoyed nice things. And while she wasn't

destitute, by any means, Jack's thievery had set her back substantially. He'd taken her for a half million, convinced her to let him invest it in something she should have known sounded too good to be true. As it turned out, it was something that didn't even exist.

"Bastard."

She flung the door open and dove into her bloodred Mercedes SL-500, and then she drove at high speeds, searching for trouble.

A couple of hours later, she found it.

She didn't know what city she was in. She'd been following her senses, not road signs. There was a killer here. Yes. She would have settled for a wife beater or a child abuser, or quite possibly someone parked in a handicapped spot without a permit, but a killer was better. Less chance of morning-after doubts.

She parked the car and tried to quiet her mind long enough to focus. She needed him, needed to vent the rage that was boiling over by now, needed the solace that came with the blood. Like morphine, it eased her pain. Like mother's milk to a newborn, it comforted and calmed. Living blood, more than any other kind. And that was what she needed.

It wasn't often that the pain got this bad, but when it did, a human had to die. She wasn't a rogue. She wouldn't take an innocent. Not only because of the regrets that would leave imprinted on her heart, but because it would bring the wrath of the entire undead community down upon her head, and she didn't need that.

Over the years, Topaz had learned how to control the

filters in her mind, to raise and lower them at will. She lowered them now, briefly, like opening floodgates to the thoughts and senses of thousands, perhaps millions, of mortals within her range.

Noise came in from all directions, deafening, maddening, perhaps, given time. But worse than the noise—far worse—were the sensations. Pleasure, pain, heat, cold. And still worse, the emotions. Nearly crippling in their intensity. Hurt, grief, joy, fear, love.

She wasn't new at this. For ten years she'd been honing her skills, and now she put them to use. She filtered through the myriad signals her mind received, taking her time. She had all night, after all. She filtered out the joy, the love, the anger, until she'd eliminated everything but the fear. And then she explored still further, until eventually she felt something promising.

Cold, stark fear. And pain with it. There, yes, she felt it, and homed in on it, focusing, shutting out everything else now.

Not far from here. Not far at all. Topaz opened the car door, got out, clicked the lock button and turned, scenting the air now, in addition to following her sense of the woman. And then of the man causing the fear and the pain. Yes. This way.

She moved, enjoying the click, click, click of her three-hundred-dollar Italian stilettos on the sidewalk. As she got closer and the signals came clearer, she moved faster, faster still, until she was only a blur of motion to mortal eyes. And then she stopped, standing beneath a fire escape, staring up at an open window. He was there. And he was busy.

Topaz bent her knees and pushed off, soaring upward, landing on the fire escape right outside the window with barely a sound or an effort.

She stared into the apartment. A woman was lying facedown on a pretty white carpet, while a man humped her from behind. He had a knife in his hand, and it was near her throat.

Topaz climbed through the window and stood there, four feet from the couple on the floor. "Are you about done, there, pal? We have some business, you and I."

He stopped humping, swung his head up, met her eyes. His own registered shock. "How the hell—" And then anger. "Get the hell outta here, bitch, or you'll be next."

"Oh, do you promise?" she asked in a higher than usual voice. "Come on, baby. Do me right now. I want you *bad*."

His eyes narrowed. The apartment was neat, and scented with vanilla. Probably a pleasant place, until this asshole had come to fill it with terror and strife. Topaz wasn't enjoying her visit here. She didn't intend to hang around any longer than necessary. "Put the knife down and let her go."

"I'll cut her. I'll cut her fucking throat if you don't get out of here." As he said it, he gripped a handful of the woman's hair and lifted her head. The blade was pressed to her neck. She had a little too much makeup on, and some of the mascara was running under her pretty blue eyes. Big earrings, big hair, tiny skirt, and a top that was about the size of a Band-Aid. Probably a prostitute, a classy one, judging by her good looks and her apartment. But to jerks like this guy, a whore was a whore, and this one deserved whatever she got.

"I'm out of patience." Topaz lunged forward so fast that he could not possibly have seen her move. To him, it must have seemed that she just disappeared, then re-appeared an instant later right beside him as his knife went sailing across the room and right out the window. It cleared the fire escape, and by the time it clattered to the ground below, Topaz was picking him up off the woman, one hand clasping him by a large handful of his thick head of hair.

The woman tugged her tiny, tight skirt down as she scrambled to her feet. She ran to the door and was out of there without bothering to say thanks. But that was okay. Topaz had her prize.

She turned the man to face her. He wasn't struggling. He was scared. Clearly, he'd picked up on the fact that she wasn't exactly human. Finally. It had taken him long enough. But at long last he knew something was off.

"What the hell do you want?" he asked.

"I want you to look me in the eyes and say you'll never hurt me."

He frowned. "I won't."

"*Say* it."

"I'll n-never hurt you."

"Tell me I can trust you."

"You can. You can trust me, I swear."

"Tell me you love me. Call me baby."

"I love you, baby."

"You fucking liar." She jerked him to her, and sank

her teeth into his throat so deeply she scraped bone. She didn't drink, she gorged. She feasted. She tore his flesh, and she enjoyed every minute of it.

As she drank she saw them, the women he'd raped in the past few years. There were dozens. Most of them alive. But he'd killed the last three—no, two. Only two. The one tonight was supposed to have been number three.

Well, no more.

When she'd drained him, and his warm blood was flowing through her, soothing her, easing her rage, she felt every tense muscle in her body uncoil. She felt release. Relief. And it was good.

She flung his considerably lighter corpse over her shoulder, anchored him there with one arm and swiped her lips with the back of her other hand. Then she climbed out the window with him, jumped easily to the ground and headed back toward where she'd left her car. If anyone saw, they didn't speak. It wasn't the kind of neighborhood where people were likely to butt in, and she was moving so fast it was unlikely mortal eyes would be able to tell what she was carrying.

She flicked the button on her key ring, and her trunk popped open. Then she tossed the body inside and slammed it closed. She knew a nice swamp where he would sink out of sight and probably not emerge for a good century or two—if ever.

Topaz got behind the wheel, started the engine and said, "That could only have been better if it had really been you, Jack." She tried really hard to visualize herself ripping into his jugular and sucking him dry.

But instead she imagined sinking her teeth into him in passion, not anger, and sipping from him while he slid his cock into her and drove her wild. God, it had been so good with him. It had never been that good before. She didn't imagine it ever would be again.

And instead of feeling better, she just felt more pain. Oh, the rage was gone. She'd sated that. Temporarily. But not the hurt. Nothing could ease the hurt. How could she still want him, even while wanting to kill him?

"Maybe I'll just have to kill him, then. Thanks to that gossipy bitch, I have a pretty good idea where he is." Unfortunately, there wasn't time for traveling tonight. It would be daylight by the time she dumped the body in the swamp and made her way to the safety of her home.

She put the car into gear, spun the tires a little as she pulled away from the curb and cranked the volume on the MP3, choosing the playlist she'd named Madder than Hell. The first song to come on was Alanis Morissette's "You Oughtta Know." Fitting.

…you told me you'd hold me until you died—till you died—but you're still alive!

She was going to do it, she thought. She was going to find him, hunt him down and make him pay. Make him suffer the way he'd made her suffer. Sure, she'd been too devastated at first to think of vengeance. But that part was over. Now she was just fucking angry.

She was going to kill the bastard, and while she was at it, she was going to get her money back. Tonight, just as soon as the sun set and darkness fell, she was going on the hunt for Jack Heart, to make him pay for what he'd done to her. *No one* treated her that way and lived to tell the tale.

No one.

4

━ ◆ ━

Roxanne O'Mally was twisted into what a nonpractitioner would have called a human pretzel when the broomstick standing beside the front door tipped over. Well, tipped over wasn't really what it did. It hurled itself to the floor as if bent on suicide.

She frowned, then slowly untwisted, rose from her yoga mat and padded barefoot, not to mention stark naked, to the broomstick, bent and picked it up. "Company coming," she muttered. But the emphatic nature of the message seemed to suggest there was more to it than just the traditional signal of a toppling broomstick.

Roxy would have told herself she was being overly nervous, except that she'd been having odd feelings for days, and bad dreams three nights in a row. An evil spider weaving a web in the middle of a busy sidewalk. A bear trap set and baited in the heart of a wildlife preserve. A sense of someone waiting around a corner, just out of sight, someone dangerous, about to spring, but not on her.

Roxy reclaimed her unfinished drink—a tall glass

still half full of her own special blend of vegetable juices and empowering herbs. "Let's just see about this," she said as she pulled on a satin robe, slid her feet into matching slippers and scuffed to the table in the middle of her rain forestlike living room. She had filled the place with man-sized waterfall-fountains, tub-sized misters and more plants than furniture. She kept the humidity level at eighty percent in here. God, she loved her home.

Taking a seat, she sipped her drink, then set it down, picked up the tarot cards and began to shuffle as she thought about opening herself to messages from spirits. Then she laid the cards out in a careful pattern.

The Hermit. That card usually indicated an inner journey. But the thought that came to mind when she saw it was of her dearest friend.

The other cards that fell around it, though, didn't make sense. He was surrounding himself with... family? But he didn't *have* family. He was a loner. Someone was conspiring against him. He was in danger in the near future, but also...

"Right now." Roxy jumped to her feet, raced to her bedroom and pulled on clothes just as fast as she could. A flowing skirt, a clingy Lycra top, a pair of bamboo sandals. She hoped it was a warm night, and pulled on a black felt shawl as she raced outside, deciding the car was a far better option than the van.

She didn't know exactly where he was. But they had a bond, and she was counting on it to guide her to him.

God, just let it be in time.

Vampires, she thought, rolling her eyes. Sometimes they were more trouble than they were worth.

"It's going to be daylight soon," Reaper said. "Can you feel it?"

Seth frowned, and searched his senses. "I feel... *something*."

"Describe it."

"It's kind of...dense. Heavy."

"Yes, that's the lethargy. Be aware of it, always. You must never be caught by the sun's rays. They'll burn you alive, Seth."

"Okay," Seth said as the vampire steered the car onto an exit ramp. "So we're gonna find someplace to hole up for the day, then?"

"Yes. Tonight will be soon enough to visit this vampiress."

"Cool." Seth supplanted his impatience by conjuring images in his mind of where they would spend the day. Some crumbling ruin, an abandoned warehouse, maybe a crypt in a cemetery. "So tell me something, will you?" he asked.

"I might."

"How long have you been a vampire? I mean, are you, like, centuries old?"

"Do I seem old to you?"

"Well, you seem pretty wise and pretty powerful, so yeah. I guess that makes you fairly old. That's not an insult, is it? I mean, to a vampire?"

"Age is power. To call a vampire old is to call him powerful. It's not an insult."

"So?"

Reaper looked at him, narrowed his eyes, then nodded once. "I've been a vampire for a little more than a decade."

"Who made you?"

Tipping his head to one side, Reaper seemed to study him, then said, "I suppose I had all the same questions when I was newly made. I wanted to know if the way I'd been brought over was unique or fairly common, what others had experienced, how many of us there were and how far back we went."

"So? You gonna tell me?"

"I don't know how many of us there are. I don't know how far back we go, though I've heard at least as far as there has been recorded history, and beyond that, who can say? I can tell you about my transformation, though."

"Yeah?"

He nodded. "I worked for…the government. In a covert capacity."

"You said you were an assassin," Seth reminded him. "Military? CIA?"

"I could tell you, but then—"

"You'd have to kill me." Seth grinned. "You actually made a joke."

"Just because I don't use it often, doesn't mean I lack the capacity for humor," Reaper pointed out. "At any rate, I was on assignment in the Middle East, and I was ambushed by a small, disorganized band of extremists. They got lucky. I took a dozen bullets, maybe more. They left me for dead, lying on a dusty street in Syria. The shooting spree had frightened any potential onlookers into hiding. I was alone and dancing with death right then. And that's when she came."

"She?"

Reaper smiled a wistful smile when he said the name. "Rhiannon. Most incredible creature you've ever seen. You want old, that one's old. Her father was a freaking pharaoh."

"No way."

"I swear. Her real name was Rianikki, the way I hear it. She changes it every few centuries when she gets bored. And she gets bored easily. She's got a hair-trigger temper and paper-thin patience and a black panther for a pet."

Seth smiled slowly, fascinated, dying to hear more.

"So she leans over me, and she says to me, 'I was honestly having a wonderful evening—it's open mike night at the Kazbah, you know. But you had to go and get yourself shot, didn't you? You couldn't have waited? Even another hour?'

"Hell, I couldn't talk. I just lay there with my mouth open, wondering if I was hallucinating her, or if she were an angel, or maybe a demon, come to take me to the other side. But she keeps talking. She says, 'You're gonna be dead in about a minute, my friend, so you need to think fast. You can become a vampire, like me, and live. Or you can die. And I'd take time to explain to you all that being a vampire entails, but there's no time. Some of the mythology is true, some isn't. All in all, I think it's a wonderful existence. Eternal youth, strength and ever-increasing power. No more sunlight, but that's a small price.'

"I really thought I was losing it. But she just leans

closer and says, 'Time's up. Yes or no?' I didn't say anything. I didn't know what to say. And then she said, 'Fuck it, then. I guess I get to decide.' And she sank her teeth into me, and— Well, you can figure out the rest. I woke up a vampire."

"Wow. That's…that's incredible. Is she—is she around here? Will I ever get to meet her?"

"I have no doubt you'll cross paths with Rhiannon one day. But no, she's not in the area at the moment. I took on this mission partly so she wouldn't have to. She has…other things going on that need her attention right now."

Seth frowned as Reaper stopped the car at a traffic light and put on his left-turn signal, which would take them into the parking lot of a Motel 6. He blinked, and said, "You're kidding, right?"

"About what? Rhiannon being too busy for this right now?"

"This," Seth said. "You're serious? We're staying here?"

"Why not?"

"Well…I don't know. What about the windows? Won't the sun get in and toast us?"

Reaper reached into the backseat for what looked like a gym bag. "Duct tape and heavy black fabric. I never travel without it."

"Note to self. Get a gym bag and watch reruns of *MacGyver.*"

Reaper frowned at him, clearly not getting the joke.

Seth just shrugged. "Never mind."

The signal changed, giving them a green arrow to

make their left-hand turn. Dropping the bag, Reaper turned the wheel and pressed on the gas.

Neither of them saw the semi coming until it hit them, and then there was nothing but noise, shattering glass, groaning metal, squealing tires, the stench of hot rubber and a whole lot of hurt.

A crowd was gathering by the time Seth opened his eyes, picked up his head and tried to get his bearings. A woman was making her way through the bystanders, coming closer, shouting at them to get the hell out of her way. Seth couldn't see her. There was smoke and it was kind of—

Smoke.

Hell, that couldn't be good.

Seth turned in his seat to mention it to his companion, but Reaper was out cold, and Seth smelled blood, thick on the air. "Oh, shit. Reap, come on, man. Wake up." He shook the limp shoulders, but nothing worked. Then he saw where the blood was coming from. A jagged piece of metal was sticking out of Reaper's thigh, blood oozing from around it.

The woman who'd been doing all the shouting was closer now, rapping on his window. "Get out of there! It's gonna go up."

"Give me a sec." He released his seat belt, then Reaper's, then took his belt out of his belt loops, wrapped it around Reaper's thigh, just above the wound, and pulled it tight. Any tighter and he would have risked busting the femur. Gritting his teeth, he yanked the metal out.

Blood oozed all the same. He had to stop it.

Hands pounded the glass again. "You need to get out *now*."

He ignored the woman, grabbed the duffel bag, and wrestled with it until he got the duct tape out. Then he tore off a piece with his teeth and used it to tape the gaping skin together. A second piece, and a third for good measure.

The smoke was thicker now. His lungs were burning. The woman was tugging on the passenger door, but it wasn't giving. The driver's door was no good, either, mashed up against a telephone pole.

He leaned back, braced his feet against the door, and yelled at the woman to stand back. She did, and he kicked with both feet. The door popped open, almost easily. Hell, he'd forgotten about how much stronger he was now.

He put his back to Reaper, pulled the man's arms around his shoulders from behind, and, with people reaching in, pulling to help, he managed to get them both out of the car.

They'd moved about thirty feet away, into the darkness lit only by the glowing lights of other vehicles, when Reaper's car blew to hell and gone, the explosion knocking Seth to his knees, with Reaper still on his back.

And then that woman was there. "Come on, boy. Come with me. Daylight's on the way, and so are the police and paramedics."

Seth stared at her, shocked. How could she know daylight was their enemy? She had long carrot-orange hair—not coppery, like his dream girl—that curled from top to bottom, and it was impossible to guess her age. There was something about her, some familiar *feeling,* almost like a scent.

"You're just a fledgling, aren't you?" she asked Seth. "I'm Roxy. I'm one of the Chosen—that's what you're sensing. Raphael is my friend."

"His name is—"

"Raphael Rivera, aka Reaper. And only his best friend would know that. Now, come with me, while they're all distracted by the explosion. Hurry."

She helped him to his feet, Reaper still on his back, and led him toward her waiting car, shouting, "I'm a doctor, clear the way! I'm a doctor!" as she went. She opened the back door, and Seth eased Reaper in, onto the rear seat.

The bleeding hadn't started up again, so Seth got into the front, and then Roxy was behind the wheel, driving so fast that Seth felt himself gripping the dash until his knuckles turned white.

Reaper moaned from the backseat when she took a corner too fast; then he spoke. "Roxy?"

"Yeah, it's me."

"No one else drives like that."

She laughed softly.

"Are we being followed, Roxy?"

She glanced up into the rearview mirror. "What do you think I am, an amateur? Why?"

"Because that was no accident. It was a vampire— not quite a normal vampire, but a vampire all the

same—driving that rig that hit us. And it was delib-
erate."

Roxy frowned and swore, using a streak of profanity
Seth had never heard from the mouth of a female in
his life. Then she said, "Who are you going after this
time?"

"A rogue gang led by a man called Gregor."

"Those assholes?" She shook her head.

"What do you know about them?" Reaper asked.

Roxy shrugged. "Only what I've heard. They're
skilled, they're mean, and they outnumber you."

"You know where they are?" Reaper asked.

"No. But when you leave to find them, I'm going
along."

"Absolutely not."

She met his eyes and smiled, a slow, sexy smile that
seemed to speak volumes. "You're telling me no? Since
when has that ever worked?"

Reaper closed his eyes and let his head fall back onto
the seat of the car.

"Who *are* you?" Seth asked her at last.

She smiled. "I'm Roxy. I'm the oldest living human
with the Belladonna antigen. At least, as far as I know."

Seth lifted his brows. "But I thought we—they all
got weak and sick and died young."

"All but me."

"How old are you?" he asked.

She fluttered her lashes. "How old do you want me
to be?"

Seth's throat went dry, and Roxy released a bark
of laughter and slapped her own thigh. "Don't worry,

pup. I wouldn't want to hurt you." She gave him a wink, then bobbed her head toward the windshield. "Here we are."

Roxy's place was a tiny cottage that looked like something out of a child's fairy tale, all cobblestones and little green shutters, flower boxes overflowing with fragrant herbs, gardens flowing like colorful streams around the place and between the flat stones that formed a meandering path to the front door.

She parked her car and glanced nervously at the sky. "Best get him inside, son, before dawn."

"I can manage on my own," Reaper said. But his voice sounded so weak and pain-racked that Seth thought he might as well have said, "I can't lift my little finger without help right now."

"Fortunately," Roxy said, "you don't *have to* manage on your own. You've got Seth now." She smiled at Seth, and there was so much affection in the look that he wasn't sure if she was hitting on him or just being friendly. The woman was a puzzle. He had no idea how to take her.

He didn't ask, though. Just got out, opened the back door and got a grip on Reaper's shoulders, so he could help him inside.

"Right through here," Roxy instructed. From the waist down she was wearing a long, flowing skirt in bright splashy colors. From the waist up, she wore what looked like a leotard. Skintight, revealing a figure that was close to perfect, short-sleeved, with a V-neck all plumped full of cleavage. A moonstone glittered from a long chain, resting between her breasts. She jingled when she moved, and he realized it was due to the ankle bracelet she wore, along with flat, woven sandals that looked to be made of straw or something.

Seth looked at her face again, baffled by his inability to guess her age.

She just smiled more warmly and tipped her head, so her hair fell over one cheek. "This way. Put him in the guest room. It's actually a walk-in closet, but I keep a bed made up in there for my undead friends." She opened a door and stood aside to let Seth pass, with Reaper's arm drawn around his shoulders. Reaper was silent, except for little grunts of pain every time he put weight on his leg. Seth figured it was taking all the guy had just to stay conscious at this point.

He helped Reaper ease his way onto the twin bed that sat at the back of the large-closet-slash-minuscule-bedroom. Roxy hurried away, then came back a second later with a porcelain basin full of water and a basket full of other items. She sat down on the edge of the bed, put the stuff on the nightstand, then went to work with a pair of scissors, snipping the leg off Reaper's pants, so she could better get to the wound.

"Duct tape," she said, eyeing the patch-up job Seth had done. "Hell, I don't know if I can even improve on this. It's not bleeding."

"And it'll heal as soon as the sun comes up, right?" Seth asked.

Roxy nodded, dipped her washcloth in the basin and began washing the drying blood off Reaper's thigh.

"You should drink, Raphael. You're as weak as a kitten from the blood loss."

Reaper met her eyes, then shifted his gaze to her neck, where it lingered and became suddenly intense. Seth felt hot under the collar and thought maybe he should leave the room.

Roxy said, "In your dreams, Raphael. I have bags in the fridge. I can heat it first, if you're craving a little warmth, though." She glanced at Seth. "Come with me, and I'll get you some, too. And then you'd best get to the basement. There's another bedroom down there. You'll be safe and comfortable."

Seth nodded, still not clear on what the relationship was between Reaper and Roxy. They seemed close. Almost intimate. He wanted to ask but sensed he wouldn't get an answer. And it was none of his business, anyway.

He followed Roxy into the kitchen. She stopped at the fridge, turned and faced him. "He's not going to want you to stay with him."

"I know."

"You have to stay anyway. He's going to need you, Seth."

Seth frowned, searching her face. She had eyes as deep and dark blue as sapphires glittering up from the depths of the sea. They were fringed by the longest black velvet lashes he'd ever seen on a woman, and all that hair, all that long, curly red hair, seemed too soft to be real.

"Are you listening, Seth? This is important."

He focused on her eyes again. "I'm listening. He's going to need me. But how can you know that?"

"Look around, Seth."

He did. The place was cozy and completely cluttered. There were bundles of herbs hanging upside down from every possible location in the kitchen and beyond it, in the little dining room and the sitting room, which were really one very large room with two parts. He saw a crystal ball on a glass pedestal all by itself. Incense was burning, sending spirals of fragrant smoke throughout the place. Chimes and sun-catchers and plants hung near every window. The dining-room table was covered with tarot cards, spread out in a mystical and complicated pattern, their images graphic and somehow disturbing.

Seth took it all in, and then returned his attention to her.

"I know," she said. "The same way I knew to be where I was when you had that accident that wasn't quite an accident. I know *him.* I've known him since he was a little boy at the hematology clinic where we were both patients. I already knew I had the Belladonna antigen. And I knew what it meant, though the doctors didn't. I was a student of the occult and the paranormal even then, you see. An expert already. Raphael didn't know anything. He was just a child with hemophilia and a rare blood type. I've been watching over him ever since."

"Kind of the opposite of the way it's supposed to work, huh?" Seth asked. "I mean, don't vamps ordinarily watch over the Chosen?"

"There's nothing ordinary about me, young man. And you'll never meet one of the Chosen who's anything like me."

"I totally believe you."

That comment brought a quick smile to her lips. Full lips. Moist. Nice white teeth behind them, too. Little laugh lines appeared at the corners of her eyes when she smiled, and when her expression turned serious again, he could still see the tiniest traces of them.

"I'm going with you on this mission, Seth," she said. "Raphael is a loner, and he's going to fight us. But he has two partners now, and we aren't going to take no for an answer, are we?"

"I owe him my life. And this mission is leading me someplace I need to be. So, yeah, I'm in." He thrust out a hand. "Shake on it."

Roxy smiled slowly, and closed her hand around his. She squeezed, and said, "Mmm. Strong. I like that." She released his hand, handed him a glass and said, "Come on, Seth. I'll take you to bed now."

He thought his feet would be glued to the floor, but they moved to follow her as she pushed open a door and descended a set of stairs down into the dark basement. He watched the sway of her hips, the play of her long thick hair over her shoulders, and he wasn't sure whether he was hoping for or fearing whatever might happen at the bottom. Sure, she wasn't his dream woman. But she sure as hell was something.

It didn't matter, though. She simply pushed open another door, flipped on a light and stood aside to let him pass. He walked into the room that was to be his. She said, "Good rest, Seth. And don't worry about Raphael. I'll see to it he's safe until sundown."

"Good night," he said, out of long habit. He was going

to have to stop doing that, he thought. A vampire should say good day or good rest or something, not good-night, not when he was forever going to sleep in the morning.

Roxy stepped out of the room and closed the door. Seth thought she had to be old enough to be his mother. He also thought he could develop a serious case of lust for her, if he let himself.

He got undressed and slid into the bed. But as the day sleep came in like a dark wave to claim him, it wasn't Roxy's face he was seeing in his mind's eye.

It was that other face, that frightened, innocent face with the exotic eyes pleading for his help.

5

━━ ◆ ━━

Reaper was lying in the bed, as instructed, surrounded by the freshly laundered scents of the white sheets and leopard-print comforter, when Roxy returned with his sustenance. She handed him the glass, and he drank and prayed she didn't want to stay and talk until the sun came up.

She sat down on the bed, though, so he figured he was doomed. Still, it wouldn't be more than a few minutes before dawn came and saved him from her knowing, probing mind.

"You're fuming," she said.

"I don't like being attacked by my own kind."

"Bullshit. You relish a good battle. You're fuming because you needed help tonight."

He slid her a look. "Don't go there. I didn't need help."

"No? You know you would have died in that car, Raphael. You were bleeding out, unconscious and about to go up in flames. Your stubborn fledgling hunk refused to leave, even though he could have been toast."

He nodded. "You don't have to sing his praises to me, Roxy. I know he has the soul of a hero."

"Really?" She seemed surprised to hear him say something nice about Seth.

"You think I would make a vampire out of an ordinary human? Even one with the antigen? No, he's special."

"I agree. You, um, might wanna think about telling him that."

"And let it go straight to his head? Please."

"You're a mean bastard, you know that?"

"*I'm* mean? Could you have teased the poor kid any harder, do you think?"

She shrugged. "I was only being myself."

"Right. It's not your fault young men want you."

"*All* men want me, hon. Young, old, humans, vampires. There are *dead* men who want me. Is it any surprise your young Seth wants me, too?"

"Don't—"

She shot him a look, a dangerous one. And he knew better than to presume to tell Roxy, the most independent female on the planet, not to sleep with his pain-in-the-ass charge. She slept with whomever she wanted. And God help anyone who presumed to judge her for it.

He licked his lips and started over. "Don't break his heart, okay?"

"I'm not planning to jump him, Raphael. He's got important work to do, and a night of my incredible body would only distract and confuse him."

"Important work, huh?"

"Hell, yeah. He's on a mission, that one. I don't know what it is—don't think he does, either—but it's practically sparking from his aura. Something big is in store for him."

"So he keeps telling me."

"Believe him." She got up from the bed. "Sleep, now. At sundown, the van will be packed and ready to go."

"Roxy—"

"You don't have wheels of your own anymore," she reminded him. "You can't go on foot, after all."

"I can get a car."

She shrugged. "Fine, get one. I'll follow you." She reached out a hand, as if about to lay it over his, but then she hesitated, because she knew he disliked touching unnecessarily. Drawing her hand away, she went on. "I know you hate accepting help, Raphael, but you'd damn well better believe me when I tell you that just this once, you need it. I feel it all the way to my gut. You'll die if you don't let Seth and me go with you."

"And you and Seth could die if I do."

"We won't—"

He reached out and grabbed her hand, maybe just to show her how damn serious he was about this. "You know what I'm capable of, Roxy. You're the *only* one who knows. Anyone who's near me for any amount of time is at risk."

"All the more reason to take me along. I won't let you hurt him. Or me. Believe me, I can handle you."

"No, you can't." He released her hand. The sleep was coming on strong and fast, but he had more to say. "I'd planned to come to see you while I was here. I'd planned to ask you to keep Seth, teach him until he's ready to be on his own."

"Yeah, I already figured that out. But it's not going to work. We're going with you. If you're so worried that you might hurt us, then I'll see to it we're both armed."

"You wouldn't be willing to shoot me. I know you—" His eyes fell closed. He opened them again. "You'd be too afraid of killing me." Again his eyes closed.

"You let me worry about that. As if I'd hesitate to kick your oversized ass to the grave and back if I thought you were gonna hurt me. Hell, Raphael, don't kid yourself. Now, get some sleep."

He tried to reply, but the sleep was on him before he could make a sound.

Vixen waited in the cell, wondering what was taking so long. She still wasn't sure she could do what they asked of her, but she couldn't stand any more torture. Why these people delighted in causing pain, she could not fathom.

Their footsteps came, just minutes before dawn. Briar was not alone this time. The one called Jack was with her. Longish brown hair, shot through with streaks of blond, parted on one side, so that it tended to fall over his eyes. An unshaven look that was always just that. Never more, never less. As if he meant it to be that way. Light blue eyes, almost shockingly pale.

Jack looked at her, smiled slyly, shook his head slowly. "Damn, she is a pretty thing, isn't she?" He stuck his arm between the bars of her cage and made smacking sounds with his lips, like calling a pet. "Come here, hon. Let me feel that silky hair, hmm?"

She backed up to the far wall, her eyes wide and darting from Jack to Briar. Of the two, it was the female she most feared.

"Fine," Jack said. "Your loss, babe." Then he turned to Briar. "So what is it you wanted to show me?"

"She's not human."

"No, not anymore. Not since Gregor changed her."

Briar shook her head. "Not even before. She's a shape-shifter. Spent half her time as an animal."

Jack grinned. "Right. Briar, have you been feeding on crack addicts tonight or what?"

"Gregor knows. That's why he wanted her. He had me stake out the places where she tends to show up when she's in human form and tell him her habits, so he could follow her. He set a trap, caught her in it when she was an animal, then waited for her to shift back and transformed her."

Slowly Jack's smile died. "He didn't make you do it for him? You know, he didn't have you suck her blood and then make her drink yours…?"

"No," she said with a disgusted look.

Jack pushed a hand through his long hair and shook his head. "Damn, that would've been hot."

"She's a shape-shifter. Are you even *getting* this?"

He shrugged, then looked at Vixen. Then, frowning, he *really* looked at her. His brows drew together. "Vixen. And that hair. And those eyes." He glanced at Briar again. "You saying she's some kind of a fox?"

"Pull your hair back, Vixen. Show him."

Vixen lowered her head, but not in shame, for she knew no such thing as shame. But she hated defeat. She hated obeying the girl with the blackest heart in all the world. Still, she pulled her hair back, and Jack looked, and then his brows shot up.

"Are her ears slightly…pointed?"

"Mmm-hmm. And now she's going to try to shift back into her animal form. If she can still do it, she can be of invaluable help to Gregor. I mean, can you imagine the places she could get into where we couldn't fit? Hell, we could set her loose inside a bank, then have her shift back and let us in after closing."

"Gregor's got more money than God already."

"You can never be too rich," Briar said. "You ready, Vixen?"

"I think so."

"Then do it."

Vixen nodded and sank down onto the floor. She lay down on her side and pulled her long, copper hair around her face. She closed her eyes and pretended to will her form to change. But in fact, she wasn't willing it at all. She didn't know if she *could* change, but she wasn't going to do it just for them. Especially not for Briar. She had to wait, because she wasn't sure she could fit between the bars. So she had to wait.

She lay there for several minutes.

"Dammit, Vixen, do it," Briar snapped.

"I'm trying…."

"This is bullshit. She ain't a damn fox."

"She is, I'm telling you. Do it, Vixen!"

Vixen said nothing, just lay there, trembling, because she could feel Briar's anger, and when that one got angry, it didn't go well.

"You are gonna be so fucking sorry," Briar whispered.

Vixen heard the keys in her cell door. Yes. Finally. Vixen focused. She honed her energy and saw herself in her mind's eye as a fox, running free, and then she felt her body shrinking, growing smaller, vanishing into her long protective hair, until the hair was her tail, curled around her body like a warm coat and covering her face.

She'd changed. Just as Briar swung the cell door open and came charging inside, probably to hurt and punish her, she sprang onto her toes, her clothes falling away behind her, and darted right out of the cell, racing between Briar's feet, dashing past Jack, who jumped and dodged her as if in fear for his life.

"Well, I'll be damned," she heard him say as she raced past.

"Don't just stand there laughing, get the damn thing!"

She didn't know which way to go and sought wildly for some means of escape. There! The door, and that gap in the bottom. Please, let her fit! She ran up to it.

Then the door swung open, and the master himself stepped in. She darted fast, intending to race between his feet and outside before the door swung closed, but Gregor was faster. He grabbed her by the tail as she rushed past and lifted her high.

"Well! So she can still do it after all!"

Vixen twisted her little body around, and sank her claws into his arm and her teeth into his hand. She sucked blood from him as he howled, and a hunger reared up inside her such as she had never known. They'd been starving her to keep her weak.

She drank all she could before he flung her away so hard that her body slammed into the stone wall and sank to the floor. Energy spent, she felt herself changing again, becoming a woman. A vampiress. She lay there, naked, her head aching, her tailbone throbbing, the taste of Gregor's blood on her lips.

"Jack, toss her back into the cell. Briar, you have some explaining to do."

"I didn't mean to let her get out," she began.

"Not about that. I understand you sent one of the drones on an assignment last night, without clearing it with me first."

Jack scooped Vixen up into his arms, and she remained limp, not because she was acting, but because she was exhausted, half starved and in pain. He seemed to try to be gentle with her, as he carried her into her cell and lowered her down onto the cot that was the only piece of furniture.

"You said this person, this hit-man vampire, was coming after you," Briar said. "I caught wind of where he was, and I didn't see any reason to delay and risk losing track of him again. So, yeah, I sent a drone to take him out."

"Well, the drone failed. Any task that takes thought isn't exactly their forte. But that's irrelevant. Next time, Briar, do not even *think* about giving orders. I'm in charge here, not you. You have no authority."

"But...but—"

Vixen heard pain in the dark one's voice. She was hurt and confused. The black-hearted bitch deserved it—and more.

"The thing is, Briar, I *want* him to come after me. I need him. Alive."

Briar blinked slowly. "Well, you could have just told me that."

"Easy, Briar," Jack said. "Haven't you figured him out by now? He operates on a need-to-know basis. And you didn't need to know. Just like I didn't need to know about our guest here and her special abilities." He looked at Gregor. "Even though I'm his right-hand man. Right, Gregor?"

Gregor shrugged, but the look in his eyes was chilling. "You complaining, Jack?"

"Not me. Not a chance. You're driving this rig, and I'm content to sit in the passenger seat and ride along. Always have been."

Gregor grunted but said nothing more. Instead, he looked down at his hand, which was dripping blood. "Briar, come with me and patch this thing up before I bleed out. Damn. Good thing it's almost dawn. Jack, you see to the vixen here. Make sure she's staying put for the day. We can use her." He took Briar by the arm, and left the horrible underworld where Vixen was forced to exist on stale air and darkness.

Jack closed the cage door, double-checked the locks, and then she heard his footsteps moving away. She expected that to be the end of her torment, but no. Only moments later, she heard his return, caught his scent.

Her cage opened once more. If she'd had the energy, she would have shifted again and tried to escape. But she was so tired.

She opened her eyes, saw Jack come closer. He was

hesitant, as if he were approaching an animal that might bite, which was probably wise of him, because that was what she was. His gaze kept lowering, sliding down her nude body, but he seemed to be trying to keep it from doing so. She didn't feel any shame about her form, or any shyness. It was just a body, after all.

He had a blanket and pillow under one arm, and a glass of red liquid in his free hand. He held the glass out.

She took it, noting how quickly he jerked his hand back. Sniffing, she wrinkled her nose, but drank, too hungry to be fussy. Then she handed the glass back to him, and he gave her the pillow and blanket. She tucked the pillow under her head, spread the blanket over her and curled onto her side.

"You're welcome," he said, an odd tone in his voice.

She frowned and lifted her head to look at him.

"When someone does something nice for you, Foxy, it's customary to say thank-you. And then they say, 'you're welcome.'"

"Oh. And you consider bringing me this blanket and pillow and that blood, to be *nice?*"

"Well, yeah."

"I'm being kept prisoner in a cage against my will. If you want to be nice, let me go."

He lowered his head. "Man, I can't do that. Gregor would have my hide."

"Then don't expect my thanks."

He shrugged, turned slowly and started to walk out of her cage, but then he stopped. "If you'd escaped to-night, you would have died, you know."

She frowned and looked up at him.

"You're a vampire now. It's almost daylight. If you go outside in the sun, it'll burn you alive. We can't tolerate it, Foxy."

She blinked three times, weighing his words. "Are you saying this so that I'll be too afraid to try to run away again?"

"Why would you be? You'd just try it by night."

"Are you forgetting that I'm in this place where I can't tell day from night?"

"Sure you can. When day comes, you fall asleep. It's irresistible. You feel that coming on, you know it's almost morning. When you wake again, it's just past sundown. Understand?"

Tilting her head to one side, she said, "Why are you helping me?"

One corner of his mouth pulled into a half smile. "I have a weakness for pretty women. And you are a— Well, hell, you're a fox."

She frowned at him, unsure why he was stating the obvious, but he just touched his forehead as if it were a way of saying goodbye and turned to leave her alone. He locked her cage again on his way out, though, the bastard.

6

"This thing is going to get us noticed—and probably killed—before we get within a dozen miles of Gregor's band," Reaper said, eyeing the vehicle Roxy had pulled out of her garage—where it had been, understandably, hidden—and parked in front of her house. He wore a look of distaste mingled with utter horror.

The customized conversion van was something to behold, and while Seth believed Reaper was a miserable curmudgeon about a lot of matters, he totally agreed with him on this one.

"No," Reaper said. "Absolutely not."

Roxy glanced at Seth, as if seeking a second opinion.

"Well, it's not exactly…inconspicuous." He wondered for just a second if he would be just as tactful if she wasn't such a hotty, then wondered why it mattered. She certainly didn't seem to care.

Shirley—and that was the van's name, as its custom license plates attested—was yellow. *Canary* yellow. Its—her?—sides sported murals depicting fields full of sunflowers, and the rear window was decorated with a translucent sunset.

"She's just what we need," Roxy said. "Look, we can rent a car or something for short trips once we get where we're going. But for getting there, and for emergencies, she's freakin' damn near perfect. Just look here." She pulled open the side door. There were four rows of seats, all sporting black seat covers with giant sunflowers in the center of each one. They matched the floor mats.

Of course they did.

Seth managed not to groan aloud as he poked his head in, then stepped up. The van was tall. Most people would be able to stand up in it, though for Seth and Reaper it required significant stooping.

"There are only three of us," Seth said. "Why do we need all this room?"

"Never mind *that,*" Roxy said quickly. "Take a look at *this.*" She went around to the back, opened the two rear doors, climbed in and pushed a button. The rearmost seats folded forward and down, then lower, tucking themselves neatly into the floor. Then Roxy lifted a piece of floor mat, tugged a handle hidden beneath it and the floor folded up, revealing a nearly full-sized bed underneath.

She met Seth's eyes and grinned. "Built-in coffins. This baby can sleep three vampires under the floor, well hidden. And we could close the floor over them, and put three more on top, because the windows tint all the way to black at the touch of a button."

Seth glanced at Reaper and saw that the man was impressed in spite of himself. There was a slight edge of approval nudging its way into his grimace.

"There's a minifridge," Roxy said with a nod, "so we can take a supply of that Kool-Aid you guys love so much. Her sides are reinforced steel. Bullet-proof. She's got a Hemi under the hood, and all-wheel drive so we don't get stuck. Big ground clearance for a van. She gets terrible gas mileage, but let me tell you, Shirley will fly. And to top it all off…" She moved to the center of the van, gripped a handle mounted to the inside of the sliding side door and lifted.

The inner panel of the door slid upward, revealing a cache of weapons stored behind it. Shotguns, rifles, handguns and several odd-looking little weapons that looked like dart guns. Boxes of ammo lined a number of small built-in shelves, and holsters and clips hung every which way.

"What are those little ones?" Seth asked.

"I call 'em Noisy Crickets," she told him.

Seth laughed out loud, shaking his head, and muttering, "Good one, Roxy," between chuckles. He was just getting it under control when he noticed that Reaper hadn't so much as cracked a smile. "That was a reference to *Men in Black,*" he told the sour-faced vamp. "The movie? You know, Will Smith, Tommy Lee Jones?" No reaction. "Hell, don't you see movies at all?"

"No."

Roxy handed one of the tiny weapons to Seth and took a second one off the wall for herself. "These shoot tranquilizer darts. I have a supply in the fridge, measured, loaded and ready to go. Seth, the only way Reaper will agree to let us come with him is if I can convince him that you and I will be perfectly safe. And the only way I can think of to do that is to give him our word that we will each carry one of these with us at all times. It needs to be loaded, and we need to carry spare ammo on hand."

Seth took the tiny weapon and turned it this way and that, looking it over. It seemed pretty simple and straightforward. "Why do we need tranquilizer darts? You guys expecting to run into a herd of angry elephants or something?"

"Those darts aren't for animals, Seth," Roxy explained. "They're for vamps. They're doped with the only tranquilizer that will work on you guys. The only one *I* know of, at least."

Seth frowned, then nodded. "I guess we could use it against the rogue vampires if we had to. Yeah. Not a bad idea." He looked at Reaper again. The man was oddly silent. "Don't you want to carry one, Reap?"

"The tranquilizer isn't to protect you from the rogues, Seth. It's to protect you from me."

Seth started to laugh, thinking the miserable fuck had actually made a joke. But there was a grimness in his tone, a darkness in his eyes, that had the laugh dying in Seth's throat before it was even born. His smile faded, and he searched Reaper's face. "What the hell are you talking about?"

Reaper lowered his gaze. "I'm not going to go into detail or bare my soul or my history or my flaws to you, Seth. This is not up for discussion. It's my personal business, and it's off-limits. I will only say that if I should ever turn on you in an apparently mindless burst of violent rage, you will need to act and act fast, or die. If it happens—if it even looks like it's happening—use the tranquilizer. Don't hesitate."

Seth opened his mouth, then closed it again as question after question tried to get out. Why would Reaper turn on him? What the hell was he talking about? Did he have some kind of split personality-Jekyll-and-Hyde thing going on, or a brain tumor or what? But Reaper wasn't going to tell him any more. He'd made that clear. So Seth settled on one question, the only one he thought might elicit an answer.

"Can the tranq do you any lasting harm?"

Reaper looked at Roxy for the answer.

"No," she said, and she said it firmly, with a shake of her head that had all that long hair swinging. "It'll knock him cold, and he'll wake up with a hell of a hangover. That's all."

Seth nodded and faced Reaper again. The guy looked really miserable. As if even broaching this subject was ripping into his guts, and Seth hated that. He needed to lighten things up. "Okay, then. I got it. I just need you to make me one promise."

"And what would that be?" Reaper asked.

"If I misread you and shoot you by mistake when you weren't *actually* intending to eat me for lunch, you can't be mad at me when you wake up."

Reaper scowled at him.

"Dude, I'm serious here. If I have to worry about being wrong and pissing you off, I'll hesitate, and you'll have time to rip me a new one before I pull the trigger. So you have to promise."

Eyes narrowed, Reaper nodded. "All right. I promise."

Seth grinned. "Man, this is great. You so much as look at me funny, I get to pop you with the Noisy Cricket. And you can't even get mad about it. You are *so* gonna regret this."

"*Seth.*" It was a warning, Reaper's tone dangerous.

"Whoa, that sounded menacing. Did it sound menacing to you, Roxy?" Seth glanced at the gun in his hand. "Maybe I should shoot him now."

Reaper glared at him.

Seth lowered the weapon and wiped the grin off his face. As usual, his attempts at humor were hitting a brick wall. "Hey, come on. I was kidding. I'm not gonna pop you with this thing. Come on, man, don't look like that."

Sighing, not saying a single word to Seth, Reaper climbed into the van and took a seat all the way in the rear. "Let's get going, Roxy. We need to see this Topaz woman before we can go any farther."

Roxy handed Seth a holster. She was already wearing one of her own, with a tranq gun tucked into it. Then she closed the weapon door and climbed up into the driver's seat. Seth took the one beside her.

As she backed the van out of the driveway, Seth glanced at her and whispered, "I was kidding."

"Hey, I thought it was funny as hell."

He smiled, relieved. "Does he *ever* lighten up, Roxy?"

"Not that I've ever seen. But I'll tell you one thing."

"What's that?"

"You're good for him. Real good."

"Hell, he can barely stand me."

"Trust me, I know these things."

Reaper sat up straighter in his far backseat and said, "People, I *am* a vampire. I *have* preternatural hearing. I could listen to your entire conversation from a half mile away. From here, it's as if you're on a loudspeaker."

Roxy looked over her shoulder at him and said, "Fuck you, Raphael." Then she grinned and sent Seth a wink. "Yep, you're gonna be good for him."

Topaz had packed several bags and dressed to kill. She wore a short skintight black dress, with a chain-link belt draped around her hips, black thigh-high stockings with seams up the back and lace on the top, and open-toed spike heels with straps that criss-crossed once, encircled her leg just above the ankle and buckled there. They had twenty-four-karat gold heart charms dangling from their straps. Her hair was sleek and smooth, and her makeup perfect.

She looked so good that Jack would probably weep when he saw her.

Bastard.

She was stacking her bags near the mansion's front door when she felt the presence of another vampire—no, two of them—nearby.

And one of the Chosen, as well.

Instinctively, she ducked to one side of the door, to get out of plain sight, and peered out the window. Yes, three people, two men and a woman, were standing near the end of her curving white gravel drive, just waiting there.

She squinted, and spoke with her mind. *Come any closer and you'll regret it.*

The reply came immediately, from a man she didn't know. *We only want to talk to you. It won't take long, and we're no threat.*

And I'm supposed to take your word for that? Any vampire who trusted unmet, undead strangers was asking for trouble, Topaz thought. And she was not stupid. *I wasn't transformed yesterday, you know.*

We need to ask a few questions, that's all. It's about a man who calls himself Jack of Hearts.

Her reaction was so instinctive that she couldn't hide it. A surge of emotions—passion, pain, desire, anger—all twisted up into one ball of feeling, just welled up and burst from her, and she wasn't quick enough or disciplined enough to hide it in time. She knew they'd felt it. Damn. She tried to pretend it hadn't happened, tried to move quickly past it, but she knew she wasn't fooling them.

Why do you want to know about him?

Because I'm looking for the leader of the rogue gang he's rumored to be running with. They're dangerous, Topaz. Deadly, to humans and vampires alike. They're even hostile toward the Chosen, or at least that's what the rumors claim. I need to know all I can about them before I get too close.

She swallowed the sudden dryness in her throat and looked at her bags. She'd been just about to go storming into the midst of a rogue gang? A murderous rogue

gang who killed their own kind? *Jack* was running with
a rogue gang?

That was *so* not Jack. And damn, from what she
knew about rogue vampires, she was pretty sure she
could have gotten herself killed tonight.

Sighing, she opened the front doors and stood between them, staring down the driveway at the three who
waited there. "Come in, then," she called. "Since you
may have just saved my life, I suppose I owe you a
favor."

Seth saw the woman standing in between the open
doors. She was backlit, and the total effect was as if
some kind of goddess had just flung open the doors to
heaven and invited them in. Her shape was willowy,
slender, graceful. Long arms and legs, long neck, long
hair. Gorgeous. And yet his first reaction to seeing her
there was one of almost crippling disappointment.

She wasn't the woman he'd been searching for.

He could have wept, but instead, he lifted his chin,
determined to press on. The sense that he was closer to
her than ever, and still on the right path, was the most
comfort he was going to get right now. So he clung to
that and got on with the business at hand.

They trooped up the driveway, and he was finally
able to see more than just her silhouette. She was of me-
dium height, with the youthful face of a prom queen.
Her hair was long, perfectly straight, satiny smooth
and the color of melted milk chocolate—the same color
as her eyes. She had Cupid's bow lips, high cheekbones and a dimple in her chin.

She was beautiful, in the most classic definition of the word.

"My name is Reaper," the boss said, but when she reached out to shake his hand, he just stuck his into his pocket, ignoring her offer.

Seth thought he was a moron. Not liking physical contact was one thing—he'd already picked up on that quirk of Reaper's in the short time he'd spent with him. But to avoid the touch of a woman who looked like this one…well, hell, that wasn't quirky, that was just plain crazy.

"I'm Topaz," she said. "We can sit, if you like." She waved a hand toward a small sitting room, just off the foyer. They went in, each taking a comfortable spot.

Seth picked a love seat, in hopes she would sit beside him. She didn't. Reaper took a rocking chair near the gas fireplace, which Topaz turned on with the touch of a button. Roxy plunked down right on the stone hearth, probably cold. She should have said something when they were standing outside, Seth thought vaguely.

Topaz remained standing while Reaper spoke. "I don't want to keep you, so I'll come straight to the point. I've been hired by some of the elders of our kind to deal with a man called Gregor, who is leading the most notorious rogue gang we've ever come across. Jack of Hearts is reputed to be Gregor's right-hand man."

She lifted her perfectly arched brows and studied his face. "And you're telling me this why?"

"You know him, this Jack of Hearts, correct?"

She shrugged. "I might."

"It's rumored you were recently robbed of a great deal of money by your former lover. Since that seems to be this Jack's modus operandi, I thought it a pretty safe bet he was the one." He shrugged. "How many vampire con men are there, after all?"

"They're all con men, in one way or another," she muttered.

Reaper frowned.

"Okay. You're right. I admit it was Jack. And, yes, he was my lover. But how do you know I'll help you? What makes you think I won't rush off to warn him?"

Reaper smiled slowly. It wasn't a happy smile; it was a scary one. "I felt your reaction to hearing Jack's name. You don't want me to kill him in the process of taking out his boss. I figure I can bargain with you for his safety."

She lifted her brows. "You're right," she said. "I don't want you to kill him, but only because I want to do it myself."

Seth had felt the rush of energy blasting from her at the mention of Jack's name, too. And while he wasn't as adept at reading other vamps as Reaper was, he'd always had a knack for reading people. He thought she was lying. It hadn't felt like a rush of murderous rage to him. It had felt like a rush of pain of the heartache variety, and an all-out effort to hold back a flood of tears.

She changed the subject. "So who are these two?" she asked.

"These are my..." Reaper hesitated, as if he couldn't quite think of the right word.

"Friends," Seth filled in, sending Reaper a disgusted look and getting to his feet to offer his hand. "I'm Seth. I'm new to all this undead stuff."

Topaz shook his hand and said, "You're kidding," in the most sarcastic tone he could imagine. Hell, was it that obvious he was a newborn?

Then she turned to Roxy. "And you are…one of the Chosen, but…there's something different about you."

"Roxy." She didn't offer a hand, and didn't get up from her spot near the fire. "And everything about me is different."

"What an odd little band," Topaz said. Then she shrugged, as if that was all the consideration she was going to give to that subject.

"You were about to go somewhere," Reaper said, with a glance at the luggage stacked near the front door.

"Yes. I was going to hunt Jack Heart down—and that's his name, by the way. Jack Heart. This Jack of Hearts nonsense is nothing but vanity. At any rate, I was going to hunt him down, get back the money he stole from me and then kill him. But I had no idea he was running with a pack of rogues."

"So you know where he is, then?" Reaper asked.

She studied him, and took her time about answering. "I might." She shrugged. "I must admit, I'm glad you came along when you did. I was walking into a dangerous situation without a clue it even existed. I could have been killed if I'd tried to get to him alone."

She looked at Reaper, then at Seth and Roxy, and back at Reaper again. Seth could almost see the wheels turning in her mind. And then they seemed to click into place.

The slightly irritated, out-for-vengeance woman scorned melted away like the outer wax of a candle. Topaz smiled all of a sudden, and it was a huge, bright, entirely false smile that was enchanting all the same. Her eyes took on the sparkle and innocence one would expect to see in the eyes of the prom queen he had already mentally compared her to. The aura of being a dangerous predator might have never existed.

"But now I don't have to go alone."

"Oh, no—" Reaper began, but she cut in immediately.

"I have to tell you, Reaper, this doesn't sound at all like Jack. He's no rogue. A total bastard, yes, but there's not a violent bone in his body. He's a con man. A lover, not a fighter." She sent him a sheepish, almost shy look as she said it.

"That's good to know—possibly more than I need to know, in fact, but thank you all the same. However, you must understand this, Topaz. All I want from you is Jack's location. If you could just tell me where—"

She wasn't paying attention by this point, but was, instead, leaning past him to look out through the door and down the drive to the end, where they'd parked. And then she was speaking again, her tone so innocent that surely not even the most gullible man on earth would have bought into it. "Oh, look at that van! God, that is so *cute!* And there must be plenty of room. Sam, why don't you—"

"Seth," he said. She blinked at him as if not understanding, so he clarified. "My name. It's Seth, not Sam."

"Whatever. Be a doll and carry my bags out for me.

Isn't the timing perfect? You don't even have to wait for me to get ready." She clapped her hands together and turned her full-high-beam smile on Reaper again. "Here I am, all packed and ready to go, and you guys show up like a limo service or something. This is great."

She played the spoiled, rich airhead well. But Seth saw right through it. She'd revealed her truer nature when they'd first arrived—when she'd threatened to kill them if they came any closer. This friendly, bubbly ditz routine was for the birds.

"We are *not* taking you with us," Reaper said, using his darkest, most bone-chilling tone.

Thank God, Seth thought. Reaper wasn't falling for it, either.

Topaz's false smile died. Her brows lowered. Her eyes grew dark and dangerous, and in that instant the transformation was so complete that Seth half expected a ghostly wind to start blowing through her hair as lightning flashed behind her. "Oh, yes, you are," she said. And her tone was every bit as chilling as Reaper's had been, and every bit as sincere. "Because I am *not* going to tell you where he is. I'll give you directions as we go. If you want to find Jack and this gang he alleg-edly runs with, you're stuck with me."

Seth grinned then. He couldn't help it. The prom queen had Reaper over a barrel, and she wasn't one bit afraid of him. He had to like that. And he wondered how long it had been since Reaper had come across so damn many people he couldn't bully with his nasty-ass tem-per and big bad routine.

Reaper glanced his way, and he wiped the grin off

his face in a hurry, but not before it had been seen. Seth
sent a quick glance Roxy's way, just to see if he could
tell what she thought about all this. She was studying
Topaz as if trying to figure her out. Seth couldn't tell if
she admired the woman's moxy or hated her guts.

Roxy met his eyes, read his questions and shrugged
almost imperceptibly before returning her attention
to Reaper. "We're wasting time," she said. "Raphael, I
don't see that we have a choice. And standing here arguing isn't going to do any good. You can see she's not
going to change her mind."

"Absolutely not," Reaper said.

Seth tugged his Noisy Cricket out of his pocket.
"Here," he said, handing it to Topaz. "You're gonna
need this."

Topaz took it from him, a tiny gun just the right size
for her small hand. "What for?"

"We'll explain later." Seth scooped up half her bags
and started trudging toward the van.

Topaz picked up the smallest of the bags, a tiny pink
suitcase about one foot square, and carried that. Roxy
followed, carrying nothing. She would be damned,
Seth thought, before she would wait on a woman who
was capable of waiting on herself. A few minutes later,
the three of them were in the van and looking back toward the house.

Reaper was still standing in the open doors, blinking at them in disbelief.

"Grab those last two bags, would you, hon?" Topaz
called. "And lock up on your way out." She looked at
Seth, who had retaken his seat up front after stashing

her bags. "Do you mind terribly, Steve? I get carsick in the back, so I'm going to have to insist on riding shotgun."

She was turning up those eyes again. "It's Seth," he said. "And you can quit the sweet-shallow-princess bit, Topaz. It won't work on me." But he got out and climbed into the next set of seats, as Roxy sent him a look that said, "Gee, thanks."

"That's funny," Topaz said as she stepped through the center aisle into the front to take his former spot. "It *seems* to be working just fine." She blew him a kiss, lips smiling, eyes warning, then glanced through the windshield.

He looked, too. Reaper was still standing by the house.

"Give him ten minutes," Seth said. "If he hasn't surrendered by then, we can just shoot his ass for practice."

Roxy slapped her thigh and laughed out loud, then blew the horn, which made a loud *Ooo-gaaa* sound that almost shocked Seth right out of his seat. "Come on, Raphael!" she shouted through her open window. "Get that tight ass into gear. We don't have all night."

7

"Now, once you've consciously closed your mind to entry by anyone," Reaper said, "you can, very carefully, direct a message to one particular person at a time. It takes practice. But you just put their face in your mind, think of them, and then think the words you want to say to them."

Reaper was in the fourth row, all the way in the back. Seth was sitting in the second row, with his eyes closed. Learning to block his thoughts from those he didn't want in on them was, at least, a way to pass the time. They were still heading in the right direction; he sensed that. But his patience was wearing thin. He hadn't dreamed about the redhead or felt that connection with her in far too long now, and it worried him.

"Try it, Seth," Reaper encouraged. "You've got the blocking down. I haven't been able to read your thoughts for at least ten miles now, and that's important. Now try sending a message to Topaz, but not to me."

Seth licked his lips, kept his eyes closed, brought Topaz's face into his mind's eye and thought about how hot she was, and tried to come up with a message to send to her.

"Got it," Topaz said.

Seth's eyes popped open. "But I didn't think anything yet."

"Uh, yeah, you did. And can I just say, in your dreams, Sol."

He frowned. "It's Seth. And I didn't—"

Reaper glanced at him and nodded once. "I got it, too, kid."

"Damn. I swear to God, I didn't think anything. Not on purpose, anyway."

"Right," Topaz said. "Roxy, we need to get off at the next exit."

Roxy followed the instructions, just as she'd been doing all along. She took the exit, made it to the stop sign at the end of the ramp, and sat there waiting.

"Well, this is it," Topaz said.

Roxy was still waiting. She turned in her seat, looked sideways at Topaz with a look of ever-thinning patience, and said, "What do you mean, this is it? *This* is an off ramp."

"*This* is all I know."

Roxy made a circular motion with one hand. "More, please."

Sighing, Topaz looked behind her, to Seth and then Reaper. "All I know is that Jack has been seen around Savannah several times lately."

"That's it?" Seth asked. "Savannah's a big place, hon."

"Don't call me *hon*. And I know it's a big place. I'm not stupid."

"Well, jeez, Tope, what do you suggest we do, start a door-to-door search?"

"Did you just call me *Tope?*"

"Don't take it personally," Reaper said from the far back. "He has, on occasion, referred to me as *Reap.*"

"Excuse the hell out of me while I make a list of the things I'm not allowed to call you two!" Seth folded his arms and slammed back against the seat.

They all fell silent and turned to stare back at Reaper, who shrugged, his face just as stoic as ever. "Roxy, take a right here, and start looking for a safe haven for the daylight hours. Shelter is the foremost concern at the moment. There's not much darkness left to us."

Roxy flipped on the signal.

"No, left," Topaz said. And when all eyes were on her again, she went on. "Well, you don't think I was on my way down here without having made arrangements for my comfort, do you? I rented a little place. A friend's winter home."

Roxy flipped the other signal light on, glanced both ways and pulled out just as the driver behind them grew impatient enough to blow the horn at her. Seth grinned as he wondered whether they would have been so quick to honk if they knew they were behind a van full of blood drinkers.

"How long did you arrange to use this little place of yours, Topaz?" Reaper asked.

"Indefinitely," she said. "I mean, they don't come down here until after Christmas, and it's only September, so…"

She said no more, and Roxy drove. Topaz pulled a slip of paper from a pocket and began reading from it, a frown between her brows, as Roxy followed her directions. About twenty minutes later they were pulling into a paved circular driveway that led to a ranch worthy of the world's biggest country star. The house was a huge Georgian, white and flat-roofed, with tall pillars holding up the front, and wide steps and giant windows. There was a garage with at least a half-dozen bays, and beyond it, white wooden fences, meadows, barns, stables—not an animal in sight, but plenty of room for them.

"This is a little place?" Seth asked, gaping at the back of Topaz's head. "Your friend's winter home?"

"Mmm-hmm. Cute, isn't it?"

"*Cute* isn't quite the term I would use," Seth said. "Who the hell is your friend? Donald Trump?"

"God, no." She rolled her eyes as if he were an idiot. "Sissy Spacek."

Seth thought he would be damned if he could tell whether she was kidding or dead-on-balls serious. It was impossible with her.

Roxy pulled up to the front, passed the house and followed the strip of pavement to the endlessly long garage. "This is great. We can keep Shirley out of sight."

"A blessing all its own," Reaper muttered. When Roxy shot him a sharp look, he went on. "Let's find an empty spot and park this thing. No point in drawing any more notice than we have to."

"All right." Roxy looked up to the row of overhead doors on the six-vehicle garage and shrugged. "So, Monty, should I take door number one, do you think?"

"What?" Reaper looked confused.

Topaz said, "The doors are automatic. All the bays are empty, too—or all but one. She said something about leaving a car here for the season. There should be a remote…" She looked through the van's side window, and then pointed to a plant hanging from an ornate wrought iron bracket between doors four and five. "There, in that ivy. Do you mind, Seth?"

"Hell, at least you got my name right this time." Seth slid open the side door and got out, then took his first breath of Georgia air. It was potent. He could smell about a million flowers and then some. Sweet, sweet air. He went to the ivy, a ceramic pot overflowing with the stuff, and reached in, feeling around the moist soil until he found the small remote control. He picked it up and pointed it at the door closest to where Roxy and her van had come to a stop, then hit a button.

The door opened, and the interior lights came on. "Nice," Seth muttered. Shirley rolled inside as Seth stayed outside, pushing buttons, opening other doors, curious to see what was behind them. And then he was standing there, feeling a rush of something very close to lust, and staring at his dream come true—well, his second best dream, at least—and muttering, "*Damn* nice."

The others came out to join him, gathering around, gradually picking up on his state of arousal and following his hungry gaze to where she sat, teasing him with the sultry expression in her headlights.

"Holy moley," Roxy said. "Is that a…?"

"Mustang," Seth whispered. "Shelby GT." He walked into the garage, moving slowly around the car, holding a hand out as if to touch it, but stopping short, not quite wanting to mar its gleam with a smudge. "Mint condition. Nineteen sixty-eight. I've never been this close to heaven in my life."

"Oh," Topaz said, "that's the one my friend left here. She said I could use it if I want. Keys are in the house." She wrinkled her nose. "It looks kind of old."

Seth swung his head toward her, gaping.

"And that color. It's like blood. Don't we get enough of that?" Topaz shrugged. "Whatever. I suppose it'll do."

"It'll *do?*" Seth repeated. "That car is a freaking work of art. Do you have any idea—"

"Not much legroom. We'll be cramped in there if we all squeeze in together." Topaz tilted her head. "At least it won't draw as much notice as the van."

"People will fall on their knees in the streets and worship it as we pass!"

Topaz looked at Seth, and broke into a full-blown smile. "You're kind of cute, for an irritating rookie, you know that?"

He rolled his eyes and headed to the van to fetch her bags, much as he hated doing it. She was still the woman who'd led him closer than ever to his redhead, and although she was dumb as hell about cars, he was pretty sure she'd just paid him a compliment.

Roxy eyed the surroundings as they trooped toward the front door, nodding in approval. "This place is defendable. That fence— Okay, it'd be easily scaled, but you couldn't drive up to the house. We'd see anyone coming for quite a ways, too. Good visibility. Up on a slight rise. Yeah—" she nodded "—I like it."

"I'm hoping it won't need to be defended," Reaper said. "But it's good that it can be, just in case."

The van was put away, and Seth had discovered the joys of projection TV. TV? Hell, this place practically had its own theater. He was flipping channels, and the others were running around making their own discoveries. If he had to guess, he would say Reaper was probably looking for the safest place to bed down for the day sleep, while Roxy was likely checking out the security system. As for Topaz…hell, Topaz was probably soaking in a Jacuzzi, sipping A Positive from a margarita glass with a little umbrella in it.

Eventually, though, they all came to him, as if he were their center somehow, and sank into comfortable chairs to stare at the images flickering across the screen at the far end of the room as he flipped channels. There had to be three hundred to choose from. Maybe he should just choose a DVD from the thousand or so in the custom-made case that took up most of the wall to his left.

"It's time to retire," Reaper said.

Seth glanced at him. "I don't feel the lethargy coming on yet."

"Best to be secure before you do, don't you think, Seth?"

With a grin, Seth said, "Aw, c'mon, Dad. Five more minutes?"

Reaper didn't smile, but he did roll his eyes. *Finally,* Seth thought, *a joke the guy actually gets.* Seth kept flipping channels, so the flashing images and the par-

tially uttered phrases of a hundred actors had to be irritating to everyone else, but he liked the noise. He kept
pausing for a second or two on the interesting-looking
programs, before moving on to see what else he could
find. But then he heard something that made him stop.

It sounded like a groan—like a tortured, pain-racked
groan from the depths of hell itself.

He turned slowly to see that Reaper, who was still in
the center of the room, was bent over now, holding his head
in his hands, and it looked as if he was starting to shake.

"Hey. Reap, what's up, pal? What's wrong?"

Reaper lifted his head from his hands. His face was
contorted into a grimace of utter hatred, utter vicious
rage. And his eyes were glowing.

Seth felt his own eyes widen, and he rose from the
sofa, dropping the remote. "What the hell?" He glanced
past Reaper at Roxy, who had gripped Topaz by the
wrist, and was watching Reaper and looking downright
terrified. Seth didn't know much about Roxy but he
didn't think she scared easily.

"Get out of here," Roxy said.

Topaz didn't hesitate. She turned and ran from the
room. Seth couldn't, because Reaper stood between
him and the doorway.

Hell.

And then Reaper lunged. Seth tried to dodge, but he
wasn't any match for the other man. Not in age, not in
power, not in experience. Hell, he thought belatedly—
just about the time Reaper's big, meaty and oddly hot
hands closed around his throat—he really shouldn't
have given that Noisy Cricket to Topaz.

And then he was feeling his windpipe being crushed in a merciless grip as Reaper stared at him with unseeing, bulging eyes full of nothing but murder.

And then it was done. There was a slight hissing sound, followed by a pop, and all of a sudden, Reaper's grip relaxed. His eyes bugged wider for just a second, and then he was dropping, first to his knees, his hands falling away at last, and then—as Seth pressed his own hands to his neck and sucked in breath after breath— forward onto his face.

Seth looked across the room at Roxy. She was standing there with the Noisy Cricket in her hands. He noted the dart sticking out of Reaper's ass. "Hell," he muttered.

"Yeah. I guess he was right to insist we carry these babies."

Seth knelt beside the man he had begun to think of as more than a mentor—as a friend—and touched his shoulder. "What the hell is this, Roxy?"

She didn't answer.

"Hey, it's my neck he tried to wring just now. Don't you think I ought to know?"

She pressed her lips tight, then nodded once. "All right," she said. "He'll be mad as hell that I told you, but the man needs to start sharing something with someone sooner or later." She lowered her eyes. "Seth, Raphael used to work for the CIA."

"He already told me that," Seth said. "Well, more or less."

"Did he tell you what he did for them?"

Seth nodded. "He was…an assassin."

8

"An...*assassin?*"

Roxy and Seth both turned to see Topaz standing in the doorway, staring at them, and then at Reaper, in blatant disbelief. "That doesn't make sense, Seth. That's not him." She shook her head. "Okay, okay, maybe I've only known him for a day—but we spent hours and hours in that van. He may have a mean streak, but he would never go after you like that."

"I know," Seth agreed. "That... I don't know what the hell that was, but it wasn't him."

Roxy thinned her lips. "It was never him. But he was recruited young, trained and systematically programmed."

"Programmed," Seth repeated idiotically.

"As in brainwashed," Topaz said. "Am I right, Roxy?"

Roxy nodded, her eyes sad. "That rage you just witnessed—we're pretty sure there's a word, or maybe a phrase, that triggers it. And if there is, then there's another one that stops it. But we don't know what those trigger words are."

Seth frowned down at his unconscious friend, then

hunkered low and scooped Reaper's oversized carcass up off the carpet. "So this has happened before, then?" he asked, moving toward the sofa, where he deposited the man.

"Yes. I've seen it happen three times now."

"And you don't remember any particular thing being said about the time he freaked out on you?" Topaz asked, her tone bordering on disbelief.

Roxy lifted her brows, annoyed at what had sounded like an accusation. "Do *you* remember any particular thing that was said just before it happened this time?"

Topaz frowned, searching her memory. "I…no. There were hundreds of things. We were all talking, and Seth was flipping channels on the damned TV."

"Exactly. That's the way it always is." Roxy sighed, and took a blanket from the back of a nearby chair, carried it to the sofa and laid it over Reaper. "It must not be a common word or phrase. This really is a rare thing. It's been a decade since he left the agency and was changed over."

"And in all those years, it's only happened three times?" Seth asked.

"I said I'd only *seen* it happen three times."

Which wasn't, Seth realized, an answer. "He ever hurt anybody?"

Roxy met his eyes, nodded once, said nothing.

"He ever…*kill* anybody?"

"It was his job to kill people," Roxy said.

"I meant after he left the job. During one of these… episodes."

Roxy straightened the blanket over Reaper, though

it was already straight enough. Stalling, or maybe deciding whether or not to reply.

The silence got longer, tenser, and it was Topaz who broke it, with a whisper. "Why do you think he always works alone?"

Seth shook his head. "Could be a hundred reasons. You don't know it's—"

"I think that's enough with the speculation. Neither of you knows shit, and guessing is a waste of time. I told you what I did for your own protection. You want to know more, you're just gonna have to ask Raphael when he wakes up."

Seth bit his lip to keep from asking still more questions about Reaper's past and condition. Instead, he said, "When do you think that will be?" he asked.

"Couple of hours. And it's nearly dawn now, so he's out for the day. By sundown he'll be fine." She looked around the room. "He can sleep right where he is," she said. "I can draw those heavy shades. They must have them in place for optimal viewing of their fancy-schmancy projection TV. Lucky for us. You two may as well go find yourselves a place to rest."

"You're staying in today, right, Roxy?" Seth asked.

"Well, I might make a run for some supplies, take a look around town. I'll be safe, it being daytime and all." She sent Seth a wink. "Besides, I have to admit I like the idea of taking that Shelby for a spin."

"Don't scratch her."

"I'd sooner scratch the Mona Lisa, Seth."

"God, the way you people go on," Topaz muttered. "It's a car. And it's not even a Mercedes or a Porsche or a Ferrari." She took Seth by the arm. "Come on, I'll help you pick a room."

He looked at her, utterly baffled.

She made a face, rolled her eyes. "Well, you haven't been at this very long. I don't want the scent of toasted fledgling all over the house when I wake up."

"Who do you think you're kidding?" he asked. "You like me."

"Dream on. I just don't want to deal with Reaper waking up hungover *and* pissed off at me for letting his rookie recruit charbroil himself."

"You like me, Tope."

"Screw you. And stop calling me 'Tope.'"

"By the way," he said, "I'm gonna need my Noisy Cricket back. You can ask Roxy for another."

Sundown.

Vixen rose and stretched, after sleeping all day long, which was what she did every day since they'd changed her over. But the nights were worse. At least when she was asleep she was unaware of time passing. It went quickly, painlessly. Oh, but at night… All she could do was pace the cell in which they kept her. Pace, back and forth, this way and that way. Eight steps from one side of her cage to the other. Only six from front to rear.

It was maddening. She needed room. She needed to run, to jump and play. She needed sunlight and meadows and field mice to chase. She needed *freedom*. It had been days since they'd taken her outside.

"Good, you're up."

Vixen wasn't surprised by the female voice. She'd

sensed Briar's approach long before the young female had flung open the noisy basement door and stepped inside. She was wary, though, never allowing herself to forget how much Briar liked to inflict pain. Vixen thought maybe it made her more at ease with her own inner wounds.

"Yes, I'm up."

"Gregor says I have to take you out for some exercise. But I'm telling you right now, if you try to get away from me, I'll make you hurt in ways you can't even imagine. Understand?"

"Yes. And I believe you." But Vixen knew she would try anyway. It wasn't in her not to try. Her freedom was too precious a thing to give away so easily.

"Great. Here, come up close to the bars."

Vixen eyed what Briar held in her hands. A leather collar with a metal loop through it, and a chain attached. It was the sort of thing she'd seen dogs wear, while being led about by their human owners. She blinked, and moved no closer. "I'm not a dog."

"No shit. But you can wear the collar and leash like one, or you can sit on your ass in your cage for the whole night again. Your choice."

She wanted to rage at Briar, to lash out with claws and teeth, to draw blood, but it would do no good. Instead, she subdued the urge and moved closer to the bars.

"Turn around, press your back right up tight—that's it." Briar reached inside, and with rapid, heartless movements, she buckled the collar around Vixen's neck, yanking it tight. Too tight.

Vixen tugged on it with her fingers, but it didn't help. "Please, loosen it," she asked.

"No." Briar opened the cage door. "You can breathe, that's all that matters. The tighter it fits, the quicker you'll come to heel when I jerk on your leash. Oh, and this baby has added benefits, too. See this?"

Briar held up a tiny device, black, plastic, with a button on it. As she did, she smiled slowly. "Wanna see what it does?"

Vixen shook her head slowly from left to right.

"Oh, come on. I'm dying to. Aren't you even curious?"

"No. I'll be good, I promise."

Briar sighed and dropped the device back into her pocket. "I hope you try to get away at least once. I really want to see how the shock collar works on you." She shrugged. "Then again, I suppose I don't have to wait for you to try to get away, do I? I can jolt you any time I want. As often as I want. Can't I, Vixen?"

Vixen lowered her head. "You could. But then what would be my incentive not to try to get away? If you're going to hurt me either way…?"

"Hmm. You're intelligent, for an animal. Just be aware, it has sensors. If you try to take it off or shift without permission, it'll jolt you hard enough to kill you. Come on." Briar swung open the cage door, snapped the chain to the collar and led the way across the basement. They went up two stairs, to the large, loud door. It was steel, and it creaked and groaned as it opened, banged and clanged when it closed. Vixen had come to hate that door. But once through it, they went up another set of stairs, then through a door at the top that opened to the night.

Vixen stood there for a moment, just breathing in the fresh, clean air. She smelled a thousand scents, far more even than she would have as a fox. And she could hear everything, as well, every bird, every insect, every animal skittering through the fields and forests that surrounded this place. She could identify all of them by their sounds and their scents.

"We'll walk out across that field and back. All right?"

Vixen turned to Briar, and she knew her eyes were wide and pleading, but she didn't care. "Can we run?"

Briar narrowed her eyes at Vixen, then looked out across the field. "You see that gnarled tree at the far end?"

"The apple tree? Yes."

"If you go one step beyond that tree, I'll use this remote to shock you. It sends a bolt of electricity out of that collar and straight into your neck. Do you understand that?"

"It would hurt," Vixen said.

"It would put you down on the ground, it would hurt so much."

"I won't go past the apple tree," Vixen said. Then she looked to the right of the tree and said, "Or any farther east than…"

"The boulder, sitting there. See it?"

"The boulder," Vixen said with a nod.

"Okay. Go ahead. Run till you drop for all I care." Briar unsnapped the leash and took a seat on a fallen log and nodded. "Go on, would you?"

It occurred to Vixen that she could shift forms, slip the collar and escape. But, no. The change would take too long. Briar would see her, then shock her.

Vixen was afraid Briar would use the device in her pocket just to amuse herself, but maybe not. At least she could run. She took off then, racing into the field, shocked at how fast she could move now. The cool lush grass felt good on her bare feet, and the air rushing past her face had never smelled as sweet. She neared the apple tree and came to a halt, then turned three cartwheels, before racing off to the east, all the way to the boulder.

When Briar didn't send any bolts of pain shooting into her, she began to relax a little more, and even caught herself smiling as she played in the meadow underneath the stars.

Once, she looked back, and thought she saw her captor smiling as she watched. But Briar quickly turned her head away.

Vixen frowned, sniffing the air, puzzled by the lack of evil she had felt just then. Usually it was the only thing she could sense coming from the black-hearted female. But just now she'd caught the faintest trace of what felt like…a tear.

Seth heard female laughter and wondered just what the hell Topaz thought was so damn funny. But when he shot her a look, she was straight-faced. Not even smiling.

"Look, all I have to do is pretend I'm in trouble," Roxy insisted. "I'm a good actress. I can project fear enough to have any vamp in the vicinity pick up on it. I know I can. Then they'll come to help me out, and I'll pick their brains about the rogue band—subtly, of course—and—"

"And if they *are* a part of the rogue band?" Reaper asked.

"You guys can follow them after they leave me."

"Right," Seth said. "Right after they rip out your throat." Laughter again.

He glared at Topaz. "Something funny over there you'd like to share with the rest of us?"

"Nothing funny about it. Vampires can't hurt the Chosen, Seth. Everyone knows that. It's just gossip that this gang does that. I don't believe it's possible. Vamps *never* hurt the Chosen."

"Yeah? And the Chosen never live beyond their thirties. Everyone knows that, too," he said, with a nod toward Roxy.

"Are you implying that I look as if I'm beyond my thirties?" Roxy stared at him with wide eyes full of mock indignation.

"I'm just saying—" He broke off. That laugh again. Sweet, soft, childlike. He looked around the room and saw that it wasn't coming from Topaz. Or from Roxy, either.

"Seth is right," Reaper said. "Roxy, we cannot let you risk your life to locate them."

"Does anyone else hear that?" Seth asked.

"Hear what?" Roxy frowned at him, then seemed to listen. Everyone else followed suit.

"It sounds like someone laughing. A woman," Seth said.

Now the others were looking at each other, speculation in their eyes.

"I've been hearing her for ten minutes now. It's like—Hell," he muttered as realization dawned, "I think it's *her*."

"Her, who?" Roxy asked.

He looked at her, then at Reaper. "She's one of us—or maybe one of the Chosen, I'm damned if I can tell which. I think she's in trouble." Or he *had* thought so, the last time he'd felt her presence in his mind. The laughter he was hearing indicated something altogether different.

"If there were one of the Chosen in trouble nearby, Seth, we would all feel her need," Reaper explained.

"I think I may be a little more…connected to her than the rest of you are."

Reaper lifted his brows. Topaz lowered her chin, fixed her eyes on Seth and blinked rapidly, affecting an attitude of "I don't fucking believe this," without saying a word.

Roxy moved closer to Seth and put a hand on his shoulder. "Whatever this is, it's getting to you, isn't it?" She turned to face the others. "Reaper, why not take a drive with Seth? He can steer you toward this chick, whoever she is. Maybe you'll pick up on something."

"We need to be tracking the rogues, not chasing down every distraction we come to along the way," Reaper said, and he sounded frustrated as hell.

"She's close. And I'm going after her," Seth said. "Either way."

"Where there's a Chosen one in trouble, Raphael," Roxy said, speaking slowly and with apparently endless patience, "there are damn sure going to be vampires, as well. And if it's a vamp in trouble, well, hell, maybe she'll be grateful enough for the assist to tell us what she knows about the local rogue population. This little distraction is as likely to get you information as anything else I can think of."

Reaper nodded, conceding the point, and Seth felt himself sigh in relief.

"Topaz and I will do some exploring in the opposite direction, see if we can find a few clues ourselves," Roxy said.

"Be careful," Reaper said. "Block yourselves well. You don't want them picking up on you."

"We will, but be aware they're probably doing the same thing." Roxy glanced at Topaz. "They know we're coming. Tried to annihilate our boys here with a semi the day before we met you."

"You didn't tell me that," Topaz accused Reaper, shock in her eyes.

He shrugged. "You didn't ask."

Topaz propped her hands on her hips. "So is there anything else you've been keeping to yourself that I maybe ought to know about?"

"Nothing I can think of at the moment." Reaper turned to Roxy. "Seth and I will go on foot. You can take the Shelby. I want you to keep that van of yours out of sight. Understood?"

"Right," Roxy said with a wink, "like you're telling me what to do now?"

Reaper rolled his eyes and turned to Seth. "Can you home in on a direction?"

"I think so." Seth led the way, every cell in his body tingling with anticipation. Reaper followed close on his heels.

Vixen felt him before she saw him. She was chasing a field mouse through the deep grass, trying to close her hands around him as he scurried this way and that, always just barely eluding her, when a feeling of eyes on her, a sense of another soul touching her, was so real and so intense that it made her come to a halt. She stopped dead and stood in the field, looking around.

And then she spotted him. He was crouching in the trees, watching her intently. When she saw him, something inside her clenched and tightened. There was another with him. Vampires, both, but the first was young, and still so very human, while the other was older, harder—and dangerous.

"Vixen, what is it?" Briar called.

Vixen quickly looked away, knowing better than to reveal the intruders' presence to that cold, cruel female. She would delight in tossing them both into a cage and torturing them.

"Nothing. Just a mouse."

Vixen slid her eyes toward them again, willing them to go away, even making a little shooing motion with her hands. Who were they? What did they want?

One—the younger one—touched her in some intensely potent way. She felt as if she knew him. And then she realized that she did. She'd felt him—he was the one! She'd felt him just that one time, but she'd dreamed of him only this morning. Not a complicated dream, just an image. Just his face. And he looked exactly the way he had looked in her mind's eye.

He was coming to help her. He was…he was here solely for *her.*

She didn't know why. And she had no idea what caused the heavy flood of warmth through her core, or the tightening of her throat or the knotting of her stomach.

But he was important. She was sure of it, even though she didn't understand it. And yet she felt on the verge of tears—and Vixen *never* wept.

"Come on," Briar called. "You've had enough exercise for one night. Gregor will be wondering where we are, and I need to feed. Babysitting duty is over."

"All right." Vixen didn't dare argue, not when Briar held that device in her pocket.

"You're awfully agreeable all of a sudden," Briar said as Vixen made her way back through the deep grasses, inhaling deeply to smell the night air as much as possible while she still could.

When she reached Briar, the dark woman snapped the leash back onto the ring on her collar and led her back to the door in the base of the mansion. She'd had her first good look at the place from outside, but could tell very little. Her door and this field were in the rear of the house, and there were trees and vines all around it. It was built of redbrick, and it was massive. Beyond that, there was little to see.

As they went inside, Vixen glanced behind her just once and was troubled when she sensed that the men were following. Fools. They were going to end up as badly off as she was herself. And they would be no help to her then.

If they even intended to help her at all. But while she couldn't be sure that was why they had come, she felt it, on a gut level. The knowledge didn't seem to be coming to her from the older vampire, but from the younger one, it practically poured out to her. A promise, unspoken, only thought, but thought with so much passion and so much will it was unmistakable.

I've come for you. I'll help you. I promise.

I know, she thought back at him, just before the door closed. *I've been waiting for you. Just please don't make me wait too much longer.*

9

————

"Did you see her?"

Reaper nodded, trying to school his heart to a more steady rhythm. He'd seen her. The wild child, dark hair like a thundercloud around her head, eyes like black velvet, and a coldness, a hardness, an edge of cruelty, to her that surrounded her like an aura.

"I saw her."

"The way she was running, and spinning in the field—like a little girl in love with every part of life. And did you *ever* see hair like that? My God, there's so much of it, long and thick and as shiny as copper."

"Copper?" Reaper glanced at his charge again, then shook himself. Naturally, Seth was referring to the childlike creature who'd been dancing her way through the wildflowers, not the cruel dominatrix who'd held the girl's leash. Naturally. Only *he* would find the latter so much more captivating.

"Did you see the way the other one—the mean-looking one—snapped that leash onto her?" Seth asked, looking toward the mansion in the distance. "Red must be some kind of prisoner there."

"Yes, it looks that way. And the dark one mentioned Gregor by name. I believe, Seth, that your instincts and your…connection to that young woman…have led us precisely where we need to be."

Seth smiled. Beamed, actually.

"You needn't look so inordinately pleased with yourself, fledgling. It's the kind of thing vampires do."

Seth nodded. "I'm just glad I'm getting better at it. Although, it really was *her,* Reap. Not me or my instincts. *She* drew me here. Somehow. Is she—"

"Vampire," Reaper said, knowing Seth's question before he asked it. "You could sense that for yourself, couldn't you?"

"Well, yeah. But…" Seth hesitated.

Reaper pushed. "Go on, tell me. What else?"

Pursing his lips in thought, Seth nodded, his decision made, and went on. "I could tell she wasn't one of the Chosen—not anymore. She's a vampire. A really young one, too."

"And?"

"And there's something else. Something…off. Different. But I can't tell what it is." He looked at Reaper, as if awaiting the answer.

Reaper nodded. "That's what I sensed, too. But like you, Seth, I don't know what it is. There's something more to her than vampire. That much I know."

"Way more," Seth said. His voice had softened, and Reaper saw the look in his eyes as he stared toward the mansion and the last spot the redhead had been. Reaper had seen the look before, and he pitied the kid. But he didn't suppose all the sage advice in the world would change it.

"What do we do now?" Seth asked. "We have to get inside."

"Let's wait just a bit longer, and watch," Reaper said. "The dark one mentioned wanting to feed. So I believe they'll go out soon, unless they keep a supply of victims in the mansion itself. And I can't sense any." Then he frowned. "It's odd, I can't sense anything at all coming from inside those walls. They must be extremely adept at blocking."

Seth swallowed hard. "They kill when they feed, don't they?"

"That's why they're called rogues, Seth."

"We have to stop them."

Even as he said it, a group of vampires emerged from the front of the building. They couldn't be seen from where Seth and Reaper were, but they could be felt. Reaper closed his eyes and focused. There were several. The dark one was among them. The redhead was not.

"Did you feel that, Seth?"

"Yeah. You were right, a bunch of them are leaving. But she's not with them. And I know you want to go after the gang, Reap, but I can't leave her here."

Reaper studied him for a long moment. "Seth, it's important that you not confuse the power of the bond you feel with this woman for something else. Something more. It's difficult to separate the two, especially for a vampire as young as you are. But there *is* a difference."

"I'm gonna keep that in mind, Reap."

Reaper sighed, nodded—resigned, he supposed.

Seth was a man, and a heroic one, at that. He had to do what he felt compelled to do, and Reaper had no business trying to talk him out of it. And the cocky fledgling would be inside that mansion before this night was out, no matter what Reaper might say or do to try to prevent it. So there was no point in trying.

"All right, then," he said at length. "We'll split up. You stay here, try to scan this place, and if you feel you can get inside to speak to the girl, do it. But, Seth, please, don't go in there if you're at risk of being caught. You wouldn't be risking just your own life, but my entire mission. Do you understand?"

Seth nodded, but his gaze was riveted to the back door, through which the redhead had vanished.

"I'll follow the others," Reaper went on. "See if I can keep tonight's body count to a minimum."

"All right."

"Be careful, Seth."

Seth nodded, and then Reaper was gone.

Seth decided he didn't really need to follow Reaper's instructions to the letter. Hell, he didn't need to follow them at all, he thought. He did try to scan the place, to get a feel for how many might be inside and the nature of those who were, but he sensed nothing. It was as if no one was alive beyond those walls.

So he waited, just until he was sure Reaper was long gone, and then he slipped out of his hiding place, and went to the door he'd seen the girl go through. He tried the knob, but it was locked, just as he'd expected it to be. And yet, it wasn't *that* strong a lock. Not for a vampire.

He still got a hell of a charge out of how powerful he was now. The way he could close his hand around the doorknob, twist it until the lock popped and snapped and broke. Then he put his shoulder to the door and pushed, not even very hard, and the other locks holding it gave way. The door swung open, and Seth stepped inside, looking around—remembering to *feel* around, too—in search of enemies lurking in the shadows. And he felt them. Lots of them, countless energies, all of them seeming off, but in a far different way from the girl. The vibes he felt were dull, heavy and slow. And none of them were in the immediate vicinity.

She was, though. Her essence called out to him, drew him, and he moved toward it almost blindly, knowing Reaper would kick his ass for being as careless as he was right now if he knew. And yet he couldn't resist the odd pull of her.

He walked down two steps, through a corridor of stone, and then he saw her. She was in a cell, a barred cell, like a cage, at the end of the passage. She was standing there, her hands on the bars, her beautiful, almost elfin face peering out between them at him, as if she had known he was coming.

And she probably had.

She was a vampire. But her energy was different from that of any of the admittedly few vampires Seth had met. Even Reaper had acknowledged that. It was wilder, brighter, more vivid and chaotic. And God, her eyes…

"I'm Vixen," she said. "You've come here to help me, haven't you?"

"Yeah." He could barely form the single word, much less explain the entire reason why they had come here.

"I knew you would. I've been waiting for you. I...I've felt you." She stared straight into his eyes, not at all shy about her declaration. "I've longed for you. But why do I feel you so strongly? And why do you want to help me?" she asked.

He frowned, searching inwardly for an answer. "I don't know. But I've felt *you,* too." He touched her hand, sliding his over one of hers where it gripped a bar. "Does it really matter?"

She stared at his hand on hers, and he thought she shivered. He knew he did. Then she bent her head, paintbrush lashes lowering over the most exotic, expressive brown almond eyes he'd ever seen. But she didn't answer.

"Why are they keeping you locked up like this?" he asked.

"I don't know." She lifted her head, met his gaze. "They hurt me sometimes."

Seth's muscles knotted up in pure need—the need to pound on someone. They *hurt her* sometimes? Fuck that. He looked around the place, hoping to see a key, maybe hanging like a steel cliché from a peg in the wall. Nothing. "Who has the key?"

"I don't know. Whoever comes down to torment me usually has it. Briar or Gregor or Jack, or one of those other ones. The big mean ones."

Big mean ones, huh? He looked at her—pixie-sized at best—and wondered what kind of big mean vamps got off on hurting a woman like her. He would like to meet them. But first things first. He didn't need any keys. *Screw* keys. He spotted an ax. It would be noisy, but…

He grabbed it and started swinging at the door to her cage.

He hit it again and again, and the lock was just starting to come free when he felt their approach. Other vampires were stampeding from above, racing down to where he was standing with nothing to defend himself but an ax.

He swung again. "When the door opens, I want you to run for it," he said. "I'll hold them off as long as I can. Look for the man I was with. Reaper. He'll help you."

"But…you can't stay here."

He hit the door again.

"They'll *hurt* you!" she cried.

And again. The cell door sprang open. "Go! Run!"

She lunged past him, grabbing his arm and tugging him with her. "They'll kill you. And I don't even know your name."

They made it to a wooden door, but the others were in the cellar now, a couple dozen, at the very least—big, oversized, graceless, with dull, dead eyes, and a dense, thick energy about them. They were closing in. Vixen reached the door, yanked it open, turned back for him.

She would never make it if he went with her. Neither of them would. He had to hold these oafs off, give her a shot. He met her eyes as the vampires surged toward him from behind. "Seth," he said. "My name's

Seth." Then he shoved her outside, closed the door and turned, raising his ax and preparing to fight.

The rogue gang split up once they hit the streets of Savannah. Reaper had seen Gregor, and he'd seen Jack. There were others, whose names escaped him as soon as he heard them, mainly because he didn't give a damn. He'd seen Briar and that seemed, to him, to be the most pressing matter. As little sense as that made. Gregor was his target, after all.

And yet, when they split, though he knew he ought to follow Gregor, he opted to follow *her,* instead. There was something about her that compelled him to see her, speak to her, to learn what it was that drove her. Why was she with this gang of murderers?

More importantly, why did he care?

Maybe he recognized, in her eyes, a soul very much akin to his own.

Or maybe he only wanted to.

So he followed her. Briar. The name fit her prickly, dangerous energy. She walked the streets as if she knew them, and not an ounce of fear emanated from her, no matter where she wandered. She was looking for something. Someone.

A victim.

She found one soon enough. A man—midthirties, blond, utterly ordinary—came stumbling from a bar, and turned first to the left, then to the right, his expression blank. Glimpsing something in the distance, he nodded in a self-satisfied way and groped in a pocket, hand emerging with a set of keys. He staggered along the sidewalk then, toward the car that was apparently his; a small, expensive-looking sports car. Reaper allowed himself a small smile when it occurred to him that his young protégé would probably know its make, model, year of production and engine size. Seth loved cars.

He was worried about that young man, and quickly opened his mind to listen for any signs of distress from him. But there was only dead silence.

Odd. He didn't think Seth was *that* good at blocking yet. He should have picked up *something*.

The hungry vampiress got ahead of the drunken man without his even noticing her, and when he reached the car, she was leaning on the passenger door, waiting. Reaper clung to the shadows, keeping his mind and his energy blocked, so she wouldn't sense him there. He was curious, compelled to watch her, part of him hoping that she wouldn't reveal herself to be a killer like the others in her gang.

"I don't suppose you'd consider giving me a ride, would you?" she asked. The drunk man stopped, standing on the sidewalk and blinking at her as if he wasn't quite sure she was real.

"I, uh, probably shouldn't. My wife—"

"Will never know. I promise." She let her gaze trail down his body, stopping when it was fixed on his zipper. "And I'll make it *so* worth your while."

The man licked his lips, and looked her up and down. Reaper didn't think the guy had it in him to turn her down, which didn't say much for his marriage. Then again, she was something. Tiny but curvy. Dark and exotic. She exuded sex like a perfume. It wafted from her. Sex…and violence. Reaper didn't want to feel it, but he did. Couldn't the drunken idiot sense that part of her?

"Wh-where do you need to go?"

"Five blocks that way." She pointed. "But maybe I should drive, hmm? You look like you've had a few too many."

"No way, honey. Nobody drives this baby but me."

"You'll wreck her," she said.

"I've made it home a lot worse off than this." He aimed the key ring at the car and pushed a button to unlock the doors, then nodded when the car's lights flashed him a welcome. "What's your name, anyway?"

"Briar," she said.

"I'm Jim."

"I don't really care."

He frowned at her for a second, then shrugged. "Get in."

She opened the door, slid into the car, slow and sexy. He watched, then went to his side and got behind the wheel. There was little traffic, no one to see what might happen next. Reaper could have stepped in then, but he was curious, and more than a little bit aroused. He wasn't going to let her kill the man, though. He vowed he wouldn't. He would stop things before they got that far, though he prayed he wouldn't have to. She wouldn't go through with it. She wouldn't kill the guy.

Reaper had a perfect view of the entire episode. And he could hear them, even with the vehicle's doors and windows closed. He was, after all, a vampire. The man—Jim—put the keys into the ignition. Briar put her hand over his. "One kiss first," she whispered.

Jim stared at her as she leaned closer. Her lips touched his, and his hand went slack, letting the keys fall to the floor with a sharp jangle. He twisted toward her, eager arms sliding around her, yanking her tight, and Reaper felt a flash of anger blaze up in her, felt her deliberately grab it and hold it back.

She slid her mouth from his, around to his jaw and closer to his neck, then closer still, and Reaper could sense that she thought she had to hurry, because she couldn't take much more of his clumsy pawing and groping. She reached his neck. She grasped the back of his head, tipping it sideways none too gently, and then she clamped her mouth onto him, sank her fangs deep and drank.

"Hey!" He started to pull away, but he was no match for her strength. She had him in a death grip, and in a second or two, he didn't care. He was falling into her thrall, drowning in the ecstasy of being devoured, of flowing into another being, of mindless, fathomless pleasure almost beyond endurance.

Reaper knew the feeling. He knew it well.

The victim's heartbeat started to slow, and yet she kept on feeding, kept on drinking. She was going to take all of him.

Reaper shook off the bloodlust that watching her feed had brought on and lunged, moving at preternatural speed. Yanking open the door, he gripped her by the back of her tiny black leather jacket and dragged her right out of the vehicle.

Jim slumped in his seat, the two punctures in his neck trickling scarlet.

Briar whirled on Reaper, lashing out with a clawed hand and raking his face. "How *dare* you?"

"Oh, I dare, Briar." He nodded toward the man in the car. "You've taken enough. Any more and he'll be dead."

"That was the plan."

"You'd take his life? The life of an innocent?"

"And his car, too." She slammed the door and stood facing him. "Who the hell are you, and where do you get off interrupting my meal?"

He stared at her for a long moment.

"Well? Don't you want to tell me who you are before I kill you?"

That made him smile, just slightly, and very bitterly. "You couldn't kill me, Briar. Don't even try. I don't want to hurt you. And because I don't want to hurt you, I'll warn you that you're in grave danger."

She looked around. "From who? You?"

"From that gang you're running with. From its leader."

Her eyes narrowed.

"You go around murdering innocents. You take no precautions. You don't care if you're seen. You leave the bodies to be found by other mortals. You're exposing the entire undead race to discovery, and you're making us the objects of hatred and fear—even more so than we already are. Surely you don't think the vampires of the world are going to let that kind of behavior go unhindered."

She studied him more closely, her eyes probing his.

"You're the one, aren't you? You're the one they've sent to kill Gregor."

He nodded slowly. "I am. I'm aware that he already knows I'm coming, so it costs me nothing to tell you."

"Oh, it's gonna cost you plenty."

Even as he tried to guess her meaning, she lashed out. Both fists, clasped together as one, came around like a sledgehammer, and when they connected with his jaw, he flew bodily into the air. His back hit a brick wall, and he barely kept from sliding to the sidewalk.

He gave his head a shake, and straightened, and then she was there, striking again, with a solid, powerful kick to the solar plexus that had him bending over and gasping in pain.

Fists again. She brought them down on the back of his head, put him on his knees. He pushed up with his hands, stunned at the ferocity of the attack.

"I'm going to kill you," she said. "Nobody is going to hurt Gregor."

"You in love with him?" he asked, though the words came in a raspy, pain-racked voice.

"I owe him."

He heard the sharp hiss of a blade sliding out of a sheath and realized he couldn't continue this passive routine. Swinging one arm outward, he yanked her feet right out from beneath her, and when she went down hard, he sprang, landing atop her, pinning her tight. He held her wrists to the sidewalk at either side of her head and straddled her thighs, his hips pressing hers down tight.

He lifted his gaze to her hands, one of which was still clinging to the dagger. "Drop the knife," he said.

"Kill me if you want. I'm not going to drop it."

"I'm not going to kill you."

"Then why the hell would I drop the knife?"

He lifted his head, fixed his eyes on hers, and then let them slide to her neck. "Because I'm going to drink from you if you don't."

She didn't move, just lay there, panting, frozen. So he lowered his head, let his lips touch the skin of her neck, parted them a little and sucked.

The knife clattered to the sidewalk.

But God, he didn't think he could stop now. He sucked a little harder, pressed just the tiniest bit with his teeth.

"I dropped the knife," she said. "Get your filthy mouth off me and let me up."

He didn't. He kept nibbling, suckling. He felt her heartbeat speed up to match his own. He was going to do it. He was going to take her—just a sip, just a taste.

And then he heard something that made him stop. A woman, a vampiress, speaking to him mentally, a sense of panic coming through with her words.

Reaper, if you're out there, Seth is in trouble. He needs your help or he'll be killed. Please hurry.

10

Seth swung the ax hard, lopping off the head of the first oversized vampire who attacked him. Blood spurted as the body collapsed like a sack of bricks, and the head went rolling away, its face contorted in a horrible grimace.

But there were three more of Gregor's henchmen right behind the first one. They didn't talk; they just surged, growling, and swinging beefy arms at him. One caught him upside the head, and he stumbled, then caught himself, pushing up, swinging the ax and lopping off one foot at the ankle.

The creature howled, falling down and rolling on the floor as the blood flowed. He would bleed out, and fast, right? Seth thought. That was the way Reaper had explained it— Hell, no time to think. There were more. God, where were they all coming from? He swung the ax again, hitting something, an arm or maybe a waist, and reached behind him to open the door. Surely Vixen had fled far enough by now to be safe.

He opened the door, but they kept coming. One grabbed him by the shirt and jerked him back inside. Another one pegged him with a meaty fist, right in the face, knocking him to the floor, and a third stomped on his arm, then yanked the ax from his hand. The thug raised Seth's ax up over his head, and Seth covered his face with his free arm, preparing to meet his doom.

And then he remembered the Noisy Cricket he'd reclaimed from Topaz. He rolled to dodge the falling ax, jerked the little weapon from the holster under his shirt, rolled and fired.

The guy with the ax fell, dropping the weapon to the floor. There were still two others in Seth's face, and more beyond them, but he pointed the gun at them. "Stop. Just back off. *Now*—or you're next."

The gun only held one dart at a time, but these gorillas didn't know that. They backed off, staring at the weapon, and then at their comrade on the floor.

"Pick him up," Seth said.

One of them did. Then Seth herded them to the cage where Vixen had been kept like an animal. He made them get inside, shut the door. He'd broken the lock, but he wedged the ax handle between the bars. It wouldn't hold long against preternatural strength, but it might buy him a minute or two.

Finally he turned and raced from the musty cellar, reloading his handy-dandy little weapon on the way. Up the stairs, grabbing a crowbar that was hanging from a nail on the wall as he went. Then he was outside, sucking in the blessedly fresh air. He closed the door behind him and stuffed the crowbar through the handle, to keep it from being easily opened.

Reaper said, "I *told* you not to go inside unless it was safe."

Seth turned from the door, gripped Reaper's arm and hurried up the drive. "Hey, you're way too slow for comfort, pal. Still, it's good to know you care enough to come when I call."

"I never heard your call, Seth. I was summoned to your aid by a strange female. Your redhead, I presume."

"She's all right, then? Do you know where she—" He broke off at the sound of an agonized scream somewhere in the distance. He glanced at Reaper, then broke into a dead run, pulling the tranquilizer gun even as he sped into the forest, following the sound. Seth had been hurting before, battered, bruised, even cut in places during his struggle with Gregor's apes. But now his entire body was alive with pain, and he knew it was Vixen's hurt he felt.

Someone was hurting her horribly.

"I'm gonna kill whatever son of a—"

And then he saw Vixen, on the ground, hugging herself, shaking and whimpering. He knelt beside her, touched her shoulder. "Vixen, what—"

"Get away from her!" a woman snapped.

Seth looked up to see the other one, the one who'd held Vixen's leash before. She was gripping a small black box in one hand like a weapon. "What did you do to her?" Seth demanded.

"Back off, or I'll do it again."

Reaper was behind her. Surely he would make a move at any second. Take the dark bitch out. Save Seth's redhead.

"But—" Seth said.

Big mistake. The dark woman thumbed a button on

the box, and Vixen shrieked and went rigid. Seth aimed the weapon and fired, but the bitch saw it coming and ducked. And then Reaper grabbed her hard, taking her completely by surprise—she'd been too focused on Seth to sense the other presence. Reap wrestled the box from her hand, holding her captive at the same time.

She clawed his face like a rabid cat, and when he recoiled in pain, she jerked free of him, then, as Seth fired a second shot at her, she whirled and ran for all she was worth. "You'll be sorry for this, Reaper!" she shouted.

Seth pocketed the gun and bent again, gathering Vixen, who had been reduced to a quivering mass, up in his arms. He held her as she trembled. "It's gonna be okay," he said. "We've got you now. We'll take care of you."

She managed to open her eyes and stare into his, looking for all the world like a small, wounded animal with no idea what was happening to it. Lifting a hand, she clawed at the collar around her neck.

"Shock collar," Reaper muttered.

Everything in Seth's body seemed to go cold at those words. He'd never felt hate the way he felt it right then. "If I see that bitch again, I'm gonna rip out her heart," he promised.

But then he focused again on Vixen, weak, small, trembling in his arms. He thought she was in trouble. "I think she needs help, Reap. She needs Roxy."

"You look like you could use a little patching up yourself," Reaper said.

But Seth couldn't take his eyes off the woman he held.

"Seth, you're injured and tired. Let me carry her."

Seth only shook his head. "No. I found her. I saved her. I'll carry her."

"I could probably take a turn driving," Topaz said, "you know, if you're getting tired or anything."

Roxy glanced at her, and Topaz pasted a mask of disinterest on her face and tried not to feel the engine's overly noisy growl reverberating deep in the center of her chest, the way she'd been doing for the past couple of hours as they drove around the known vampire haunts of Savannah.

Not that it had done them any good. Topaz had sensed only one vampire, at a nightclub at the edge of town, but whoever she was, she must have been decidedly shy of meeting others. The second Topaz tried to home in on her essence, she vanished beneath a shroud of protection, like a thick fog, blocking intrusion from any others. Topaz hadn't had the chance to discover the vampire's identity, much less whether she was one of the bad guys.

It had been a decidedly disappointing night.

"You know, I *am* getting a little tired," Roxy said. "You sure you can drive a stick?"

"Pssh."

Roxy grinned. "I take it that's a yes." She flipped on her turn signal and pulled onto the shoulder. They had just about given up and were headed back to home base. But there was still some distance yet to drive. Roxy brought the car to a stop and opened the heavy door.

Topaz didn't bother with such formalities. Instead, she climbed over the stick shift to slide behind the wheel, then worried that she might have made herself look a tad too eager. Hell, she *was* eager.

Roxy got in, closed her door and was just pulling her seat belt around her when Topaz slid the shift into first gear, eased off the clutch, pressed gently on the accelerator and felt the satisfying rumble of power underneath her as the car came to life. She tried to stifle a smile as she gave it more gas, then eased off to shift into second, then third. The power was all below and in front of her, and the sensation was like being in a chariot pulled by a thousand stallions. They'd named the car aptly, she thought. She shifted again, picking up speed with ease, and finally hit fifth gear and really cut loose.

"Hot *damn,*" she muttered. Then she bit her lip and shot a sideways glance at Roxy.

The woman was grinning. "Yeah, I had the same reaction. I won't tell Seth if you won't."

"Deal." Topaz took a corner without slowing down and came damn close to giggling. But she didn't. She did *not* giggle. But when she came to a steep hill and the Mustang ate the road without flinching, she almost broke that rule. Instead, she settled for putting her window down and letting the wind blow through her hair. She hadn't had this much fun since the first time she'd driven her Mercedes, and she thought this just might be better.

And then she felt him.

Jack.

She hit the brake hard, and when the car started to

lug and nearly stalled, she remembered the clutch, hit that, too, and pulled over.

"What is it? What's wrong?"

Topaz turned to Roxy, blinking. "I felt him. Just now. Close."

"Jack of Hearts?" Roxy asked, searching her face.

Topaz wished Roxy wouldn't look so closely, because along with the sense of Jack had come a tightening of her throat, a heaviness in her chest and a burning behind her eyes. Damn him. She hated that the very thought of him still hurt so much. And she would be hanged before she admitted that to anyone.

"Yes," Topaz said, swallowing to ease the hoarseness in her voice. "The bastard's here. Somewhere."

"Do you still sense him?"

Topaz closed her eyes, focused, the car rumbling, impatient to be on its way. She eased the shift out of gear, so she could let off the clutch. "It's…very slight now."

"You could try calling out to him. Tell him you're in town and want to see him," Roxy suggested.

Topaz opened her eyes wide. "Why the *hell* would I want to do *that?*"

"Because he might respond, might tell you where he is."

"Please."

"Well, why wouldn't he? Look at you. He'd be insane not to be tempted."

Topaz warmed to the compliment. "Thanks for saying that."

"It's only the truth. And I know you're furious with

him for what he did to you, but if you could fake it, maybe we could get a clue to where this rogue gang calls home."

"It wouldn't work. He wouldn't be tempted, because he never wanted me to begin with. Just my money."

"I seriously doubt that."

"Well, it's the truth. And besides, even if he wanted to see me, he wouldn't dare. He got to know me pretty well while he was playing the part of my devoted lover. He knows I'd rip his heart out if I saw him again."

Roxy blinked. "But you *are* going to see him again. I mean, that's why you're here, right?"

Topaz nodded.

"So why wait?"

"I'm just…not ready."

"Hmm." Roxy was quiet for a second. Then, "When you *do* see him, are you really going to do it?"

"Do what?"

"Rip out his heart?" Roxy asked.

Topaz sighed. "I don't know what I'll do. I just know I'm not ready. Not yet. And I don't want to tip him off that I'm here. I mean, suppose word is out that I'm with you guys, that we're after Gregor? It would give the entire gang an unnecessary warning, give them a chance to get away or, worse yet, get ready for us. Maybe even attack us first."

"Mmm, a preemptive strike. We're not prepared to handle that."

"No, we're not. So you can see why my calling out to Jack right now would be a mistake."

"Not really. But I can see why we need to get ready. Let's head back to the mansion. We have work to do."

Topaz frowned at her, but put the car back into gear and drove. She tried to lose herself in the power of the motor, the feeling of might that came with controlling such an incredible vehicle. But her heart wasn't in it anymore. She couldn't stop seeing Jack's face, hearing his voice, feeling his touch, shivering all over with the memories.

She ought to kill him. She really should.

Gregor paced the great room, while Jack and Briar, the two closest to him, the two he most trusted, Jack thought, stood before the fireplace. There were other vampires in the gang, mostly young and easily influenced. Easily controlled. Not as easily controlled as those damn drones, of course, and Jack would have given his right arm to know how the hell Gregor had created them. But Gregor would never tell.

As to the other vampires in the mansion, Gregor only used them for bringing wealth back to his coffers. He barely spoke to them, rarely interacted with them, and clearly didn't trust them.

Not that he trusted Jack or Briar either, at least not entirely. Gregor didn't trust *anyone* entirely. He couldn't afford to trust easily, or often. But he considered them both lieutenants in his rogue army.

Briar, devoted little idiot that she was, seemed truly remorseful and devastated by Gregor's anger at her. He himself, on the other hand, was laughing at the entire mess, keeping his head bowed to hide his expression rather than to show regret. He suspected Gregor was well aware of it, too.

There was more going on here than met the eye, Jack thought, and he wasn't naive enough not to have noticed that. Gregor wasn't just a rogue vamp bent on mindless destruction, self-gratification and amassing untold wealth. No way. He was too smart, too cunning, for that. He had a goal. Jack just wasn't sure what it was.

Gregor had been animated, almost excited, since word had come that a vampire hit man by the name of Reaper had been sent to kill him, more excited than Jack had ever seen him. He suspected Reaper's appearance was somehow related to Gregor's ultimate goal, and he was curious, but not for any other reason than that it would give him an edge. Jack was always on the winning team. Or at least, he pretended to be. In truth, he was never on anyone's side other than his own. He would always do what was best for him. Loyalty was bullshit, except when it came to being loyal to yourself. Look out for number one, because no one else is going to do it for you. Those were his mottoes, his rules.

He didn't trust anyone, didn't need anyone, didn't go out of his way for anyone. Never had, never would.

"I'm sorry, Gregor," Briar muttered for what had to be the twentieth time. "I tried. I did. I told you, they had some kind of weapon. A dart, with some sort of…drug."

"Yes. I'm familiar with it." As he spoke, Gregor lifted the tiny dart Jack had plucked out of Briar's belly when he'd found her lying unconscious in the woods. Gregor hadn't even been worried when she'd failed to return from the evening hunt.

Not that Jack had. He'd simply felt like taking a walk around the grounds, mainly to get away from Gregor's ranting over the missing prisoner and dead drones in the cellar he liked to refer to as the dungeon. The guy had a flair for drama.

"What do you mean, you're familiar with it?" Briar asked. Her voice was soft now. It sickened Jack a little, not that he gave a damn, to see such a feisty, spirited woman subjugate herself to Gregor, who was far from worthy. And granted, Briar was the most heartless, cruel bitch he'd ever had the misfortune to come across. But she was also hot and strong and damn capable. In her approach to Gregor, however, she was as submissive and obedient as a mistreated lap dog.

Sickening. Not that it was any skin off Jack's nose either way.

"It's a tranquilizer, the only one known to be effective on our kind," Gregor explained. "It was developed years ago by scientists in the employ of the now-defunct DPI."

"DPI?" she asked.

"It's not important," Gregor said, brushing off her curiosity. "What matters is that our enemies have it. It's good that we know in advance."

"I don't know why you didn't just let me have this Reaper killed before he found us, Gregor," Briar said.

"Because I need him alive. If anyone *does* kill him, even by accident, I'll have their head on a pike before dawn. Is that understood?"

She flinched at the volume of his edict, because he had all but shouted it. If anyone else shouted at Briar like that, Jack thought, she would probably drop-kick them into next week.

"Yes, Gregor," she said meekly.

"Oh, for the love of—" Jack bit his lip, but it was too late. He'd let it out. He was slipping. His role as Gregor's lackey wasn't going to survive if he didn't get a handle on himself. "Sorry," he said. "I just, uh—why is it you need him alive, if I may be so bold as to ask?"

"That's my concern."

Jack frowned.

"Getting the prisoner back is yours. It's too late now. Dawn is only a few hours away. But come sundown, I want that to be your top priority. The two of you."

"It won't be a problem," Jack said. Though he was secretly glad the little fox had gotten away. Even a hardhearted prick like him had hated seeing her caged—especially with a zookeeper like Briar, who so enjoyed seeing her suffer. So really, he didn't intend to try overly hard to recapture her. But he would make a show of it, just to stay in Gregor's good graces. And maybe he would manage to get a look at the other side, while he was at it. Whoever they were, they were already proving to be good. Maybe a little too good.

Seth was hurting pretty badly as he and Reaper walked up the long curving driveway to the plantation house he was already beginning to think of as home. He was carrying Vixen, and she was in far worse shape than he was. For a vampire, pain was magnified, and apparently so was the effect of electrocution. She was semiconscious, quivering in his arms, and he wondered if she would ever be all right again.

And he wondered, too, why it felt so good to hold her, to touch her. It was different than touching any other woman had ever been. *She* was different.

He couldn't get his own pain totally out of his mind, either, and even though The Reap-man had wrapped a few strips of cloth around his more serious wounds, they kept oozing blood at regular intervals.

The gash on his thigh was bleeding now. He could feel it trickling and dampening his jeans. It worried him.

"Hey, Reap, I'm not gonna bleed out, am I?"

Reaper glanced at him, then at the wound in Seth's thigh. His jeans were torn there, thanks to whatever weapon those fucked up vamp-guards had used on him. He'd been too busy trying to stay alive to notice what it was. Reaper had tied the rag right over his jeans, so it wasn't like he could see much of the wound.

"I don't think it's bleeding that heavily," Reaper said. "And Roxy will see to you as soon as we get inside."

"No way. Vixen first."

Reaper just crooked an eyebrow and kept walking.

The front door swung open as soon as they got close, Roxy and Topaz both standing there, looking alarmed and speaking at once.

"What the hell happened?"

"Who's the comatose chick?"

Seth climbed the steps, and they parted to let him pass. "Let's just get her inside. She's hurt bad. I'll explain as we go along," he said.

"Right in here." Roxy led the way up the stairs, flinging open a bedroom door for him.

Seth carried Vixen inside and lowered her to the bed, but her arms remained locked around his neck, and when he tried to stand up, she clung tighter.

As bad as the situation was, her holding on so tight made him smile just a little. "It's okay, it's okay," he said, trying for a soothing tone. "I'm not going anywhere."

"What happened to her?" Roxy asked, hurrying to the other side of the bed and bending over the beautiful redhead.

"She was being held captive—kept locked in a cage like a freaking animal—by Gregor's gang."

"You found them?" Topaz asked.

Seth nodded. "They had a shock collar on her, a fucking shock collar. There was this dark bitch of a vampires—heartless whore. She had the control, zapped her—I don't even know how many times. She was down by the time we got to her. She's been like this ever since."

Topaz looked from Seth to Reaper. "Did you see any sign of Jack there?"

"No. But I'm sure he's with them."

Roxy was leaning over Vixen, tucking a heavy blanket around her to warm her. Seth had pried Vixen's arms from around his neck, but he had to sit on the edge of the bed and hold her hands, instead, to keep the look of panic from coming back into her nut-brown eyes every time they opened to seek him out.

"She needs to feed," Roxy said. "Living blood. The

electricity hit her hard. She's way beyond weak—her entire system is out of whack. She's shocky. I think she'll probably rejuvenate with the day sleep, but the way she is right now, she's not very damn likely to live that long."

"I've got it," Seth said. He rolled back his sleeve to reveal a cut on his forearm, tore away the rag that Reaper had tied around it, and pressed it to Vixen's lips. Her eyes had been closed, but they fluttered open as her lips trembled against his skin. She met his eyes, her own full of questions and fear.

"It's all right," he said softly. "It's okay. Drink. It'll make you better."

Her gaze never straying from his, she closed her lips around the small cut and suckled him. The blood began to flow, and Seth was totally unprepared for the feeling that rose like a wave from the pit of his soul, bigger and more powerful with every movement of her lips, every touch of her hungry little tongue, until it engulfed him utterly. He was reeling, mouth agape, eyes wide, his entire body alive with unbearable sensation, incredible pleasure and intense desire. Vixen seemed to feel it, too, because her small hands closed around his arm, holding it hard to her as she fed more eagerly, almost desperately.

"Roxy, Seth's been wounded, too," Reaper warned. Seth heard him as if from a distance. "Don't let her take too much."

Even as Reaper spoke, Seth grew dizzy, and a peculiar weakness came over him. He swayed a little. And then Roxy's hand encircled his wrist. "Enough, Seth," she whispered, and tugged his arm away.

"I'll get bandages. God, Seth, look at you." Topaz hurried from the room, then returned only seconds later with supplies Seth didn't even know they'd had.

He sat there, stunned by the power of what he felt, unable to move or speak or take his eyes away from Vixen's as she lowered her head onto the pillows, still holding his gaze. Her eyes were wide, searching, glassy—maybe, he thought, glassy with the effects of the same powerful things he was feeling.

Roxy taped the wound in his forearm, then bandaged it. She did the same with the gash on his thigh.

"You should lie down," she said.

He didn't. He sat there, staring at Vixen, drowning in her.

"So are you going to tell us what happened, or what?" Topaz asked.

He nodded. Vixen's big brown eyes fell closed, and he was finally able to tear his gaze away from her. "I felt her…before," he said. "She's the one I sensed, calling out for help, the night you brought me over, Reaper. And several times since. And again tonight."

"It's true," Reaper said to the others. "That's how we found Gregor's band. Seth followed his sense of her, and I followed Seth. When we got there, we saw two women."

"One woman and one tyrant, you mean," Seth corrected. "Vixen was running, jumping, dancing in the tall grass, all while wearing a collar. The other one—dark as a demon and twice as mean—was watching her, holding that damn remote in one hand and a freaking leash in the other. When she took Vixen back inside and caged her up, she and some of the others left to go feed. Reaper decided to follow them, and I stuck with her."

"Yes, promising not to go inside unless you were sure it was safe," Reaper said.

Seth shrugged. "That's another thing. I tried to scan that place, and I couldn't get anything. Nothing. It was like a dead zone."

Reaper frowned. "That would explain why I never knew you were in trouble until she told me."

Seth nodded and continued his tale. "I couldn't just leave her there."

"We could have gone back later, Seth. We could have returned with more backup, with a plan of action, with a rudimentary map of the place and an idea of how many guards there were, of their strengths and weaknesses and habits. You were reckless. Walking into a den of rogue vampires like that could have been suicide."

Topaz widened her eyes in what Seth took to be sheer disbelief. "A den of them? How many were there?"

Seth grinned, more pleased with himself than was probably either wise or called for. Still, he lifted his chin a little as he spoke. "I think I took out seven or eight."

"Five," Reaper corrected. "I felt five deaths inside as you were closing the door."

"You barely had a second to sense anything, Reap. I know there were at least six," Seth went on. "Probably more. I took them out with nothing but an ax and one dart from the Noisy Cricket. You should have seen it. I was awesome."

"You're insane!"

Seth frowned, puzzled, because Topaz sounded angry with him, rather than impressed. "What, no praise for my skills? I know you didn't think I had it in me, Tope, but I do, and I just proved it. Would it kill you to give me a little credit here?"

"You don't need credit, you need your head examined. You could have been killed, you idiot."

The lightbulb flicked on over his head all at once. He found himself surprised, but also kind of smugly pleased, at what he saw when it did. "You really do care. Who'd have figured?"

"In your dreams, Seth."

Seth shrugged. "Hey, I don't need you to admit it. I *know*. Thanks, Tope."

"I should bite you."

He grinned at her, then glanced at Reaper. Fun as it was playing with the princess, there were important things he mustn't forget about. "There was something off about those vamps who were left behind to guard the place," he said. "Something…not quite on the bubble, you know?"

"How so?"

"I don't know. They just seemed…kind of zombified."

Reaper blinked. "Is that a word?"

"You know, like they weren't all there. Kind of dull-minded."

"Like drones," Reaper interpreted.

"Yeah, like that. Any idea what that could mean?"

"Perhaps Gregor has found a way to create them

that way. Maybe he's keeping them weak and complacent by feeding them very little, or by some other means. It would explain how you managed to take out five of them single-handedly."

That stung. "Six. And they weren't *physically* weak, pal. Just mentally a little slow. Can't I get props from anybody for this?" He glimpsed, just barely, a little spark in Reaper's eye that might have been humor, and almost gaped. The miserable bastard was teasing him! Seth didn't know he had it in him.

"The only *prop* you'll get from me is my sincere relief that you didn't get yourself killed. I suppose you *do* deserve credit for staying alive."

"And rescuing the prisoner," Seth said.

"Yes, because we *so* needed one more stray," Reaper muttered.

Seth pretended not to hear him. "What happened on your end, anyway? You never told me."

"The group I followed split up," Reaper said. "I stuck with Briar."

"Who?"

"That's her name. The, uh…the dark one."

"The evil bitch from hell? I figured her name was Lucifer."

Reaper averted his eyes. "She took a victim. A drunk man, as he left a local bar. Got him into his car and took him right there, on a public street where anyone could have seen."

"Brass ovaries on that one," Roxy said. "She kill him?"

"I pulled her off before it went that far."

"But I'll bet she intended to," Seth said, and he didn't make it a question.

"Yes," Reaper admitted. He drew a breath and went on. "She knows I've come for Gregor. I got the impression he knows, too, and that he's waiting. And now she knows I'm not alone, that I have Seth working with me, and that the two of us stole their captive."

"Well, we already knew they were on to you, Raphael, when they sent that semi to try to crush your ass in your car. But at least they didn't know you weren't alone," Roxy said, glancing at Topaz.

Topaz shrugged. "They still don't know that you and I are also on the team, Roxy."

"No, they don't. Which means you could still contact Jack without alerting him."

Topaz lowered her eyes. Reaper asked, "What's this about?"

"She sensed him nearby tonight, while we were running errands and searching for signs of the rogues," Roxy said. "I suggested she call out to him, tell him she's in town and wants to see him. Then see if she can get any information from him."

"Yeah, like where they're holed up." Topaz flipped her hair behind her shoulder. "But we know that now, thanks to Seth's bond with the damsel in distress, so it's totally unnecessary."

"You might learn other things, though," Reaper said. "How many of them there are, what their schedule is like, when they feed, what they were doing with this captive."

"You want to know that stuff, ask them yourself."

Topaz looked at the girl in the bed, deliberately changing the subject, Seth thought. "So what's her story?"

Seth studied Vixen for a moment. She seemed oblivious to their conversation, and he thought she might be sleeping. "I don't know. I mean, I think she and I are connected. You know that bond they say is stronger between one of us and one of the Chosen than it is with any other? I think she was that one for me before she was transformed. Or maybe I was for her, before I was changed. Either way, it's still there." He sighed. "Dammit."

"Seth?" Topaz stared at him and then at Vixen, then back again.

He tried to paste a look of practical, no-nonsense seriousness on his face.

She rolled her eyes, then shot a look at Reaper. "You knew this? And you let him feed her from his own body? Are you insane?"

Reaper sighed and waved a hand.

Seth frowned at them both. "Wait. Am I missing something here?"

"Sharing blood makes any bond stronger, Seth. Incredibly stronger. Good grief, no wonder you look like you've been smacked upside the head with a freakin' love-club. Rookies." Topaz shook her head, sent Reaper one more scowl for good measure, then said, "Go on, Seth, what else do you know about her?"

"I don't know anything about her, except her name. Vixen."

"No idea why they held her?"

"No."

"You didn't ask her?" Topaz asked.

"Of course I did. She didn't know, either."

Topaz studied Seth's prize where she lay in the bed. "I think she seems…strange. Different." She looked at Reaper. "Are you getting that, too? The sense of her, her scent, her energy? It's vampire, but…something else, too."

"Yeah, I'm getting it, too. Did from the beginning." Reaper sighed. "We should turn in, it'll be daylight soon." Then he looked at the windows, and Seth followed his gaze.

The windows were completely covered in black felt, taped firmly in place.

Roxy nodded when they both looked at her. "Yeah, Topaz and I did that tonight, while you guys were out picking up strays and battling drones. Shopped for supplies, and then did some decorating. All the bedrooms are safe for you to use now. And they all lock from the inside."

"I like sleeping in a real bedroom," Topaz said. "And there's no reason for us to be cramped up in some dank basement or all sharing that theater room, when there are a dozen perfectly good bedrooms in this house."

"For once, princess, I agree with you," Seth said.

She smiled. "Don't even *think* about the corner room at the end of the hall. I've claimed that one already. It's got a Jacuzzi."

"Actually, I thought I'd bunk in here tonight."

Everyone gaped at him, brows rising, eyes widening, speculation careening through the air like a bat on crack.

"If she wakes alone, she might not know where she

is. She might freak out. But she'll remember me. You saw the way she was clinging to me. I just want to make sure she's okay. That's all."

"Makes sense to me," Roxy said. "I've gotta go get a bite to eat, folks. My belly button's touching my backbone. And by the way, *I've* called dibs on the suite at the opposite end of the hall from Topaz's. It's got a sauna."

She left the room, Topaz right behind her. Reaper remained a moment longer. "I'll take one of the rooms next to this one, in case you need me," he said.

"Yeah." Seth sighed. "Just one question before you head out."

"Yes?"

Seth met his eyes and smiled a little. "Can I keep her?"

"We have too many people underfoot as it is."

"Yeah, but if she leaves us, they'll get her again. You saw her before, Reap. You and Tope are right, there *is* something different about her. Something innocent and naive and vulnerable. She's…she's like a child. They'll get her back if we turn her away, leave her on her own."

"Seth, we're here on a mission. Not to take care of homeless vampires."

"If they get her, they'll cage her again. Torture her some more. Maybe shock her, or even kill her, to punish her for running away."

Reaper's gaze moved from Seth to the woman in the bed. His expression softened. Seth saw it, surprised there was a soft bone in the man's entire body, and knew he'd won.

"If she wants to stay with us, she may. As long as she doesn't get in the way. But, Seth, you cannot afford to be distracted while this situation lasts, no matter how much you feel for her. You drop your guard, you could end up dead. Understand?"

"Absolutely," Seth said. But he was so busy studying the way the colors in her hair were lighter in some places and darker in others that Reaper could tell he wasn't really paying attention.

11

‒‒◄‒‒

She'd picked up their names and their faces as they'd gathered around her to tend to her wounds. Reaper, Topaz, Roxy. And Seth, of course. Seth. Her Seth.

Vixen woke to a soft mattress, thick blankets, fluffy pillows and clean, sweet-smelling sheets. It was warm and wonderful. This part of being human—the creature comforts in which they indulged themselves—was one of the few things she'd always enjoyed, and she let herself luxuriate for a moment. But then there was a disturbance, a mental shout delivered on a wave of energy that reverberated in her head and made her eyes squeeze tight.

Pay attention, you bastards! You'll pay—and pay dearly—if you don't listen to me now!

The threat frightened her so badly that she leapt from bed. "Gregor!"

She looked around, frantic, certain he must be very close, then raced from the bedroom through the hallway and down the stairs, instinctively following her senses to where the others had gathered—in the kitchen.

Vixen thought, from the way they looked—each of them still and attentive, focused on nothing, in a posture of listening—that Gregor's shout must have reached them all: Reaper, Seth, Topaz and any other vampire within range of Gregor's anger.

Even Roxy had stopped what she was doing, a large ceramic mug in one hand, freshly brewed pot of coffee in the other, and cocked her head. "Is something…?"

Reaper held up a hand, and Roxy went silent.

I want my captive back, Reaper! Before midnight, or I promise you, I'll take one of your little helpers in her place.

Seth spotted Vixen across the room, went to her and clamped an arm tightly around her shoulders. Too tightly. He shouted, and the anger in his voice made her flinch and try to pull away from him, but he held her all the same.

"Yeah, come on and try it, you bastard!" he shouted. "Send some of those brain-dead monkeys you had guarding her, why don't you? See how far they get."

"Seth." Reaper put a hand on his shoulder. "Enough. You'll give away our location."

"And why the hell are you yelling, anyway?" Topaz demanded.

"Not to mention crushing the poor little thing in the process," Roxy added.

Seth looked at her, captured in the circle of his powerful arm, and eased his grip. But he didn't let go, not entirely. He seemed to bank his anger only with an effort. "I haven't got the hang of shouting mentally yet. I still have to do it physically to make it work."

The impatience left Topaz's face for just a second, and she stared at him as if he were something cute enough to cuddle. If she said "Awww," he was out of here, he thought.

"I heard that," she said. "See, you can do it. You just have to stop over-thinking it."

Vixen eased herself free of Seth's arm and took a few steps away from him. "It was Gregor," she said softly. "Did you all hear him?"

Reaper and Topaz nodded.

"I didn't," Roxy said. She filled her mug. The aroma coming from the steam was one that Vixen loved. She moved closer, closed her eyes and inhaled the scent of fresh coffee.

"He said," Vixen told Roxy without opening her eyes, "that if he doesn't get me back by midnight, he will come and take one of you instead."

"Ha!" Roxy's bark of laughter made Vixen jump, and her eyes popped open wide as she searched Roxy's face. "I'd like to see him try," the mortal woman declared. "Don't you worry, hon, he's not getting you back, and he's not going to take any of us anywhere, either."

"He'll try," Vixen told her, and she knew it was the truth.

"He'll fail," Seth said, moving to stand beside her again. He didn't touch her this time.

She turned and met his eyes, and she felt something ripple through her. A pulling sensation that tried to make her sway closer to him, touch him. A tingle of pleasure and a rush of sensory memory—the way it had felt to suckle him last night. The power of it. And the way she'd felt since the first time his essence had drifted through her mind.

He was her mate. He was the one.

She liked his touch. But not when it seemed to convey ownership. She was no one's captive. Would never be again.

Still, this man's blood had made her strong, made her well when she'd been weak and in pain. And it had been spilled for her in battle. She fixed her eyes on his. "Thank you for helping me."

He smiled, drawing her gaze to his mouth, and she found she couldn't take her eyes away from his lips. Fascinating, so soft and touchable.

"You're very welcome, Vixen. And I want you to know, no one wants you to leave. You're staying with us for as long as we're here."

"Wait just a minute," Topaz said, verbally shouldering her way into the conversation. "You're presuming a lot, Seth. No one's asked me what I think about that. And the fact is, we don't need any more help here."

"We're not going to abandon her, either. Gregor's gang would get her back before the first night ended," he shot back.

"And that's our problem why?"

"Because I say it is, that's why. She's staying."

As they argued, Vixen backed away from the noise, her attention bouncing from Topaz to Seth and back again, and when she couldn't stand any more she pressed her hands to her ears and closed her eyes tight. "Stop!"

They fell silent, and when she dared open her eyes

again, it was to find them all staring at her. She took her time, tried to find the right words to convey her frustration without seeming ungrateful.

"You…helped me," she said. "Seth, you took me from that cage, and you risked your life doing it. But…I didn't ask you to. I didn't ask you to bring me here. I didn't ask you to feed me from your veins to make me well. I didn't ask for that bed, or for Roxy's ministrations. I'm grateful for all of it, but I didn't ask."

"I know that." Seth seemed confused.

"You don't own me just because you helped me."

His jaw went lax for a second, and his eyes seemed uncertain. "I don't…I don't want to own you, Vixen."

"Then why are the two of you arguing over whether or not I'm staying here, when the decision isn't yours to make?"

"I don't understand—"

"I have to run. I have to be free. I don't want to stay here. I'm sorry Gregor is angry with you, but that's not my fault. I'm free. I want to see you again, Seth. But I'm no one's captive. And I'm going my own way now." She smiled at them all, very brightly, and added, "Thank you, all of you, for your help. Goodbye." Then she turned and left the kitchen, wandering through the house in search of an exit.

Seth lunged so fast that he nearly tripped over his feet getting ahead of her, and then he stopped, blocking her path. "Wait!"

She was startled, and a little afraid. Maybe he *did* think he could keep her against her will just because he'd saved her. Maybe he was going to try, and maybe he was truly no better than Gregor and his band had been. And she had so hoped to mate with him. Disappointment came in waves. She had never felt so attracted to a male before.

"Why, Seth?" she asked softly. "Do you have a collar you want to put on my neck? A cage you want to push me into?"

"No. *Hell,* no. That's not it at all. Vixen, if you go out there on your own, Gregor's bullies are going to capture you again. If you stay here with us, we can keep you safe."

"I don't want to be *kept.* Safe or any other way."

"Could I inject a word here?" Reaper asked from behind her. She turned slowly, to see that he and the others had followed from the kitchen.

Vixen met the older man's eyes and nodded, wary. The one called Reaper had a darkness about him. A quality of danger. He held it tightly in check, but she sensed it was a constant battle, and one he did not always win. "Speak," she told him.

"Vixen, Gregor is our enemy. He's an evil man who does great harm."

She nodded. "He is a killer."

"And those with him are just as dangerous," Reaper went on.

"Not all of them," she said.

Reaper lifted his brows in surprise, but quickly set that aside and moved on. "I've been sent here to stop him, to stop them all. But I'm at a disadvantage. I know nothing about him or his band, who they are, what they're capable of. You've been with them. Even as a captive, you would have learned things about them that I need to know. You could help me, Vixen. Not because you have to, and not because you owe us anything for helping you. But just because you want to. *If* you want to."

She tipped her head to one side, considering his words.

"If you stay, you stay only for as long as you like. You stay as a guest—"

"No," Topaz bit out.

Every head turned in her direction, where she and Roxy stood just behind Reaper. Vixen sensed that Seth was about to shout her down, but she sent him a look that asked him not to. "Let her speak."

Topaz nodded and went on. "You can't stay as a guest. Or as a prisoner, though where you got the idea any of us would stoop to that is beyond me, and frankly, I find it pretty damn insulting. But I suppose you don't know us, and you've been treated pretty horribly, so…" She shook her head, as if shaking that thought aside. "If you stay, you stay as part of the team. You work, like we all work, to put this rogue band out of commission. You help us. We help each other. No one owns anyone, no one holds anyone here. We're all here because we want to be, and that's the only way you can stay. That's the deal."

Vixen bent her brows. The one who most disliked her was the only one treating her as an equal. How very strange.

"And if I wish to leave tomorrow or a week from now or…?"

"Then you leave," Reaper said.

Vixen slid her eyes to Seth, who seemed to be

searching his mind for a way to disagree without ensuring that she would bolt right then. But there wasn't one, so she was glad when he didn't try. Finally he nodded his agreement with what Reaper had decreed.

Vixen turned and looked out the nearest window at the fields, the woods, the starry night sky. How they beckoned her. But she supposed Gregor and his band would be a constant threat to her for as long as they existed. If she could help this group stop them, then maybe she could *really* be free. Free of captivity. *And* free of fear.

She drew a breath of fresh night air, then turned to face the others. "All right. I'll stay. For now."

"Good," Reaper said. "Now, before we make another move, Vixen, can we sit together and talk? I'd like you to tell me everything you know about Gregor and his gang."

She looked at the people around her and nodded. "Yes, if we can do our sitting and our talking outside, under the stars, and—" she looked up at Seth, right into his eyes "—if you will sit beside me."

She saw his Adam's apple swell and then shrink as he swallowed hard, and then he nodded. "Sure I will."

"Oh, brother," Topaz whispered.

"Hey, wait a second," Roxy said. "Come back this way. Let's go out the back door instead. There's a patio, gardens, furniture. It's a regular paradise out there."

Vixen smiled, turning and nodding at once. "Yes, that sounds better." She closed her hand around Seth's, and when he glanced at her with a surprised expression in his eyes, she only smiled. "I very much enjoy touching you when you're not trying to control me."

He just stared, as if he couldn't quite believe what he was hearing. "I, uh—I enjoy it, too."

"Good. Then we'll do more of it." She tugged his hand, and quickly followed Roxy through the massive house to the patios and gardens in the back.

"Tonight we plan," Reaper said. "We're going to go over this until we're sure we know the best course of action and the best way to execute it. Agreed?"

The vamps nodded, but Roxy said, "They'll be looking for us tonight. I'm not sure it's wise to wait."

"I think it's a bigger risk to rush into battle unprepared," Reaper said. He kept glancing up—distracted, Seth thought, by Vixen. She was the only one not sitting still. Rather, she was wandering, though staying within human earshot, likely for Roxy's sake. But she was moving about, curious, exploring. She sniffed every plant, paused to watch every bird or rodent that moved in the distance. She stood beneath a set of tinkling wind chimes for ten solid minutes with her eyes closed and a soft smile on her face.

Seth didn't blame Reap for being distracted. He was distracted, too, big-time. Not to mention confused. One minute she was pulling away from him, the next, holding his hand. Did she like him or didn't she?

"You're all adept at shielding by now, what with our practicing on the road," Reaper said.

"I wouldn't presume too much about the newbie," Topaz said, glancing Vixen's way.

Vixen responded right away, which Seth found a little surprising, since she seemed so absorbed in her explorations that he'd begun to think she wasn't listening. "I know how to camouflage my presence. I've been doing it all my life."

"But you've only been a vampire for—how long, Vixen?"

"Mmm, it was springtime. Apple trees were in blossom."

"Maybe a few months, at the most," Roxy muttered.

"How is it you've been shielding all your life, if you've only been a vampire for two months?" Seth asked.

She shrugged, walking in that bouncy way she had, up on her toes so she always seemed to be dancing everywhere she went, to inspect the contents of a hanging basket full of ivy. "Had to. Survival and all that."

Topaz frowned at Seth, who just shrugged, while Reaper went on. "Okay, so we're all actively shielding."

"I can help with that," Roxy said. "I can put up wards around the place, cast a reflective circle, draw some runes at the four directions, that sort of thing."

"I wonder if that's the sort of thing Gregor has done at his headquarters," Reaper said softly. "It's like there's no one there at all, no energy whatsoever emanating from that place."

"I think it would take more than magical charms to be that completely effective," Roxy told him.

Reaper sighed, but shrugged it off and moved on. "Okay, let's begin with what we know. Gregor is the leader, and probably the most dangerous of them all. Jack is likely the second biggest threat. Then we've got—"

"Jack is no threat at all," Vixen said. "He has... there's a goodness in him."

"You are a *terrible* judge of character," Topaz said. "Jack is evil, through and through."

"He's self-centered. But not evil. I don't think even he knows who he really is. But I do," Vixen insisted.

"How?" Topaz demanded, and she was searching Vixen's face with a dangerous look in her eyes.

Vixen turned away from the hanging flowerpot and flashed her a smile. "He brought me a blanket."

"Oh, well, there you have it, then. Proof positive. A blanket."

"See? I told you," Vixen said, totally missing the sarcasm in Topaz's tone. "And Gregor is dangerous, yes, and evil, but he's not the biggest threat."

"Who is?" Reaper asked.

Vixen's smile died, and her face lost its sparkling animation. It just went still, expressionless, and her gaze seemed to turn inward. "Her name is Briar. And she is the darkest, cruelest creature I've ever seen in my life. She's pure evil."

Reaper averted his eyes, looking genuinely troubled. Seth noticed it, and so, he saw, did Roxy.

"What makes her more evil than Gregor?" Topaz asked. Then she grinned. "I mean, this oughtta be good."

"Gregor kills for personal gain. He has no remorse, takes what he wants, grows richer and stronger. But Briar...she kills because she enjoys inflicting pain and suffering on others. She likes hurting them. She liked hurting *me*. I could feel it. It fed something in her, some darkness that has devoured her soul and still demands sustenance. Her own suffering can't feed it anymore. There's nothing left. She can't feel pain any longer, I think. She's numb to it. So she feeds that beast inside her with the pain of others."

She looked at Reaper, and he met her eyes, his own seemingly reluctant. "I've never been more afraid of any creature in my life. And I fear very little, Reaper. Briar is the biggest threat. Believe me."

He nodded, but said nothing. Seth felt some kind of turmoil going on in him, but he couldn't figure out what it was. Did he know Briar or something? "Having seen her, I agree with Vixen," Seth said. "She's mean."

"How many others are there?" Topaz asked.

"I don't know. I was kept in the dungeon. But I know there are other vampires. Younger ones, not close to Gregor. Mostly I only saw Gregor, Briar and Jack and my guards." She slid her eyes to Seth's. "I thought there were only two or three guards, Seth. I was shocked when so many came after you."

"We've got to get a handle on how many we're facing," Reaper said.

"I don't know why," Seth said. "The solution is obvious, if you ask me. We burn the place to the ground while they sleep. Wipe 'em out, all at once. Nice and clean. Anyone escapes, they're toast."

"That's the most ridiculous thing I've ever heard," Topaz snapped. Everyone looked at her, and she seemed to calm herself. "I mean, suppose there are other captives locked up in there somewhere?"

"She's right," Reaper said. "Besides, how can we attack by day? We'll be as asleep and helpless as they are."

"We locate shelter near the house." Seth was thinking it through as he went along. "We set everything up the night before, while they're out hunting. We rig a remote-control device, so we can set it off just as the day sleep kicks in."

"Or I could set it off for you," Roxy added.

Vixen stood there, staring at them. Her eyes were wide, black velvet lashes fluttering like butterfly wings. Seth thought she looked close to tears as her confused gaze moved from one of them to the next.

"Vixen, what is it?" he asked. "What's wrong?"

"You…you're just like they are." She shook her head, backing away a few steps. "You're going to *burn* them? Burn them alive? All of them? How can you… how…?" Shaking her head harder, she turned and ran.

Seth started to go after her, but Reaper clapped a hand on his shoulder. "Leave her alone. We gave her our word that she would be free to go. You chase her down now, she'll never believe us again."

"But—"

"He's right, Seth," Roxy said. "She'll want to come back—to demand an explanation, if nothing more. And once she sees we didn't try to stop her from leaving, she won't be afraid to come back, because she'll know we won't try to hold her. You see?"

"She really does bristle easily, doesn't she?" Topaz asked. "I wonder what her story is."

"I just hope she gets back before dawn," Seth muttered. And though it killed him not to go after her, he believed Reaper and Roxy were right. So he waited, and he waited.

But she didn't return. And when the day sleep was calling him, and he could no longer resist its pull, Seth told himself he should have followed her. Because now she was on her own, and anything could happen.

"I'm going after her tonight," he said, as he headed to his room. He would have gone then, if it wouldn't have meant certain death at the hands of the blazing sun. "Don't anyone even think about trying to stop me."

12

———

Vixen ran through fields and woods, played tag with field mice, and just enjoyed the sheer rapture of being alive; of being a fox.

She didn't have to stay and deal with her disappointment in the people she had been beginning to trust. She didn't have to deal with anything. She felt no angst when she was in vulpine form. There were none of the unfamiliar and silly human emotions she'd always managed to avoid, welling up so big that they choked her. No tears. There was just *life,* and God, how she loved it.

What she felt for Seth…it was powerful. There were moments when it was exciting and delicious, and other moments when it was frightening and hurtful. She didn't know what to do with the power of those emotions, having so little experience with them. But she wanted to be near him, that much was certain. She wanted to be touching him all the time. That was odd, wasn't it? She'd never felt the need to be in physical contact with anyone else that way. And when she thought of his face or the look in his eyes, of the feel of his hand on hers or his arms around her when he'd carried her—when she thought of him at all, her heartbeat quickened, and her tummy tightened and her breaths grew short and eager.

Such drama—she guessed emotions were as heightened as every other sensation seemed to be once one became a vampire.

God, she longed for him as if he were air and she were drowning.

Her respite from the drama of being a human was short-lived. She couldn't maintain her fox form for long. Not anymore, apparently. She was exhausted after only a few hours, her body straining to return to its human lines. No, not human. That part of her was gone forever. It was the vampiric form pulling her back, powerfully, irresistibly. It felt as if the part of her that embodied the spirit of the fox was dying, too. It had always been as real to her, as important to her, as her human side, and now…

She had been a shape-shifter, mostly human, but partly fox, just like her mother and grandmother before her. But now she was a vampire, and that seemed to be overtaking everything she had been before.

She *hated* it.

She began trotting on her toes, tail straight out behind her like a rudder, toward the plantation house and all its drama. She supposed she had no choice. The sun would come up soon. And she was determined to watch it rise, one more time, just in case it turned out to be the last.

She could bear the sun's touch in fox form for a

very brief time—this she knew on some instinctive, gut-deep level. But since she couldn't maintain that form much longer, she thought it best she get close to the house, find shelter and watch the sun rise from there.

Her plans, however, were cut off as surely as her dainty paw nearly was when there came a loud snap, and a set of iron jaws closed hard and fast on her foreleg. She yipped and jerked backward, but that only resulted in the cruel trap's teeth digging deeper. Oh, it *hurt!* She eased closer, to relieve the pressure, but the pain screamed on, and she could do nothing, only lie there, pawing at the metallic mouth with her free paw, pushing at it with her nose, licking at the bleeding wounds on her leg.

Then she felt warmth, and turned to look toward the east. It was the sun, climbing slowly from its place of slumber, rising bit by bit. The first streamers of golden light spilled across the sky, and then more, and soon the topmost yellow curve of the fiery sphere was peering at her from the horizon.

The sun. She loved it. And yet, right now, she feared it. Because the pain and the bleeding were making her even weaker than she had been before. And within minutes she would be too tired to keep from shifting back to her human form. Or rather, her vampire form.

And when she did, she was going to die. Jack had told her as much, back at the mansion when she'd been imprisoned there. She almost wished he hadn't. Death would be more merciful if she didn't know it was coming.

She pushed more desperately with her paw, whining and crying out as she tugged, because each movement sent bolts of pain through her.

And then, all at once, she stopped and went still. Her head tipped to one side, ears perking up high. She'd heard something.

"Vixen? Vixen, where are you?"

The voice was female, and familiar. Vixen sniffed the air to pick up the scent and recognized Roxy. Her first instinct was to return to human form as quickly as she could manage—it wouldn't take long. All she had to do was stop resisting it. Her body was fighting hard to shift. But if she allowed that now, with the sun climbing higher every second, she would die. And so she remained as she was, and she howled, a high-pitched, broken wail that she prayed would draw the woman closer.

And it did. She heard Roxy's steps in the brush, coming nearer, and she cried on and on, urgently. So weak, so very weak, and bleeding so much now…

"Oh, for the love of—all right, little one. All right, take it easy now." Roxy knelt on the ground, quickly yanking a shawl from around her shoulders and dropping it over Vixen's head. "Forgive me for that, sweetie. I can't have you biting the hand that saves you, though."

Then Roxy was prying at the trap. And it hurt. God, how it hurt, when she got the jaws to open, because sensation rushed into the area anew, and with it came crippling pain. Vixen moaned and whined, though even her cries were weak now.

"There now. My goodness, it's bleeding like hell. Hold on."

A moment later Vixen's pain was magnified as Roxy twisted something around her wounded leg and pulled it tight. The agony was unbearable, and Vixen screamed with it.

"I know. I know, I'm sorry," Roxy said. Then she was gathering Vixen up, bundling her in the shawl the way humans bundled their infants, and carrying her rapidly back to the house.

Within moments they were inside. Roxy laid her on a fainting couch in the darkened theater room. "Wait here now, little one. I'm going to get some bandages to patch you up properly."

Vixen stared into her eyes as she spoke, and Roxy paused before turning away, then turning again and staring back at her.

"It's almost like you're listening, like you understand every word I'm saying."

Vixen gave a yip to tell her to hurry, then lowered her head onto her good paw, careful not to touch the injured one, quivering and trembling with pain, dizzy now from the blood loss.

As she walked away, Roxy glanced toward the curtained windows and shook her head. "I just hope Vixen found shelter before now."

And then she was gone, and Vixen's weakness overcame her. She felt her body changing, her spine and limbs lengthening, her features shifting. And she was helpless to prevent it, and glad Roxy hadn't laid her down in a sunny room instead of this darkened one.

She couldn't move, could only lie there, her forearm throbbing just above the wrist, bleeding despite the wrappings, which were even tighter now. She was naked, except for Roxy's cloak, which was still draped around her, and she was rapidly giving way to the day sleep.

She heard Roxy's footsteps approach, then stop all at once.

"Well, I'll be dipped," the woman whispered. "It's *you.* Vixen. *Vixen.* Of course."

Vixen met her eyes and whispered, "Please don't tell." And then her eyes fell closed as the day sleep took her into its sunny embrace.

"What in the name of hell happened to you, Vixen?"

Seth whispered the question even as she stirred awake. Vixen found herself still on the sofa. Seth was sitting on its edge, close to her, and her gaze followed his, to where her wrist was swathed in thick wads of gauze, much of it stained with blood. Blood stained the couch beneath her, as well, and spots formed a trail across the carpet, still visible, though they had been cleaned.

Roxy was sleeping in a chair, still wearing the same clothes she'd had on before. She opened her eyes, and they met Vixen's.

Vixen held her breath, certain Roxy would reveal her secret—a secret she wasn't ready to share. Partly because she feared what they would think of her, particularly what Seth would think of her.

She hated this state of being, of caring so much. A fox *never* cared what anyone thought of her!

"Roxy, what happened?" Seth asked. "Where did all this blood come from?"

"No big deal," Roxy drawled with a casual wave of dismissal. "She had a run-in with a barbed-wire fence on her way back here, right after you all turned in. It was barely a scratch."

"Barely a scratch?" He looked again at the blood-soaked gauze, and the sofa and the floor.

"Well, you know how much your kind bleed. Honestly, I intended to have that all cleaned up by the time you woke. Guess I fell asleep." Roxy got up and moved closer. "It will be totally healed by now. We can get rid of the nasty wrappings." As she spoke, she reached for Vixen's arm, and Vixen held it up, too shocked by Roxy's behavior to do otherwise. The woman was going to keep her secret after all.

"I'll do that," Seth snapped.

Vixen looked at him sharply. He softened his expression, and his tone along with it. "If it's okay with you, I mean."

Vixen nodded, still wary, and Roxy quietly withdrew from the room, leaving them alone. Gently, Seth moved Vixen's forearm until it rested across his thighs. Then he began unwrapping the bandages. He slid his fingers over hers, twining them to lift her hand, so he could untwist the white gauze from beneath her arm. Over and over, around and around, he unwrapped her, until all the gauze lay in a tangle on the carpet and only the thick cushy pads remained on her skin.

Then he noticed a basin of water and a clean cloth nearby. He took the cloth, wet it and laid it on the pads, soaking them so that they would come away without pulling, stuck on as they were with dried blood.

Finally he peeled them away, washed the blood from her skin, patted it dry, and then looked very closely at the place where the wound had been.

Vixen looked, too, uncertain what she would see. But then she became distracted by the way his fingertips touched her skin, the way they trailed over it gently, his touch so soft.

She trembled, and wondered why the mating urge came alive so fiercely and so urgently at such a minute touch.

And yet, as he kept stroking her skin that way, the urge only grew stronger. Especially when he lifted his head to look into her eyes.

She stared back.

"Did it hurt terribly?" he asked.

She nodded. "It was horrible, worse than the collar. I've never felt pain like that before."

"It's because you're a vampire. All our senses are heightened far beyond what they were before, the sense of touch included. So we feel pain far more keenly. Pleasure, too, or so I'm told."

"Oh."

He looked away briefly. "Does it hurt now?"

"No. It's as if it never happened."

"Good," he said. "I'm glad." He drew a breath, seemingly thinking about his next words before he spoke them. "I want to talk about what happened. About why you ran away."

She lowered her head. "I'm free to come and go as I choose. You all said so."

"Yeah, I know. And you are. I promise. It's just that you were upset, and I don't like that we—that I—did something to upset you."

She blinked slowly, considering that. "You. It was definitely you."

His brows rose in apparent surprise. "Because I'm the one who suggested burning the killers while they sleep?"

"Yes. And because you're the only one who intends to do it."

"I am?"

She nodded.

"I don't follow. I mean, Tope argued, but no one flat-out refused."

"No, but I can sense things that others can't."

"We can all read thoughts, Vixen."

"It's not so much that. I *sense* things—anger, fear, reluctance. A person's scent changes, their stance changes, their eyes and faces and voices—everything. You can look at them and tell what they're thinking, even if they're guarding their thoughts. You don't have to read their minds. You can read their bodies, their scents."

"You mean, *you* can," he said.

She shrugged. "Yes, I can. So I know that Topaz has no intention of doing what you suggested. Nor does Reaper. They both had things on their minds, plans of their own unfolding even while you were talking about yours."

He lowered his head, and she thought he felt insulted. "If they had plans of their own, they would have shared them. We're a team."

"You think so? They were both keeping their own secrets for their own reasons, Seth. If you don't believe me, just ask them."

"I will."

He surged to his feet, his hand finally breaking contact with her arm, and for one mindless moment, all she wanted to do was grab it and pull it back to her. She *loved* him touching her.

Seth started toward the doorway, but Roxy came in before he ever got that far. "Where are Reaper and Topaz?" she asked.

Seth blinked, as if stunned, and sent a searching look back at Vixen, as if she might hold the answer.

"I don't know, Seth," Vixen said.

He turned back to Roxy. "I don't know, either. You checked their rooms?"

Roxy nodded. "Checked the whole damn house. They're both gone. Didn't leave a note or say so much as a freaking word."

"But…we're a *team*," Seth muttered.

Topaz very nearly borrowed the Mustang for her mission but decided against it. The car was loud, as if it liked to boast of its power to anyone within earshot every time you stepped on its accelerator. And it was noticeable.

It was an eye-catcher, and she supposed she should

admit, at least to herself, that she was enamored with it. She might just buy one for herself as soon as she got her money back from Jack.

Which was, of course, the *only* goal on her mind tonight. She didn't give a damn if Reaper and Seth burned the rogues' headquarters to the ground with Jack inside. She didn't care if he lived or died. But she wasn't going to watch her money go up in smoke along with him, so there was really no choice but to save him.

She mulled her plan over in her mind as she made her way through the night, cutting through woodlands, racing across fields, her pace faster than a human could possibly detect or perceive as more than a brief blur of motion; there and then gone.

She had to see to it that Jack wouldn't be there when the place was torched, so that he would be alive to return her half million dollars to her.

Period.

She was glad she'd decided to travel on foot, because a small, slender vampiress was much more silent and easily concealed than a bloodred muscle car any night of the week. She knew the location of the rogues' hideaway from what Reaper and Seth and even freaky little Vixen had said. She also knew that the vampires went out hunting within a few hours of sunset every night and returned well before dawn most of the time. So she would simply crouch outside the mansion and wait for them to come back from their nightly hunt, then try to catch Jack's attention mentally, while blocking her presence from the others. She would get him to come to her alone, and then she would figure out the rest.

She paused in her fast-paced journey at the shore of a glistening lake surrounded by woods, as if it were some closely guarded secret shared only by the trees and the wildlife. It was too beautiful not to admire, if only for a moment, while she pondered.

She couldn't really warn Jack of what was about to happen. He would warn the others, and then the entire mission would be ruined. But she had to make sure he wasn't in that mansion when it burned just after sunrise tomorrow.

The only method that came to mind was to take him somewhere and have sex with him until it was too close to dawn for him to make it back there. He would have no choice but to wrap his arms around her and hold her while they both slept through the day. And to be there, still holding her, when she blinked her eyes open at sundown.

The shore of this lake would be a perfect spot for making love to Jack Heart. At least until dawn drew close. But there must be shelter nearby. She looked around and spotted an upturned tree with a platter of roots and soil as big as a small house. They could huddle in the natural cave it created and pull brush in behind them to cover the opening. They could lie there all day long, their bodies entwined.

A shiver whispered up her body and emerged as a shaky sigh. She closed her eyes and tried to shake away the rush of desire. "I don't want him," she told herself. "This is about money. Nothing more."

But even as she said it, she knew it was a lie.

She turned in the direction of the mansion and, in a burst of motion, completed her journey. Then she took up a position in the woods across from the front drive and main entrance, crouching there and trying to sense Jack's presence anywhere nearby.

There was nothing. Vampires near, yes. But not him, and nothing from inside. The energies she picked up were odd—weak, or dulled somehow. Must be the dronelike vampire guards Seth had described, left behind to watch the place while the others went out to hunt. She suspected that she'd arrived too late to see them leave. But she would be here waiting when they returned.

13

— ◆ —

"I suggest you two find something to do to keep yourselves busy, instead of wasting your concern on Raphael," Roxy said.

Seth tried to read her. Was she seriously uncon-
cerned, or just trying to get him to stop worrying so
much? "But what if he's gone over there? To the rogues'
den? Alone?"

"He's not alone," Roxy said. "Topaz is gone, too.
Obviously the two of them are together. Maybe he felt
there was more groundwork that needed to be done.
Maybe they've just gone off to run an errand. Or maybe
they're having a wild roll in the hay someplace. Who
knows? It's not our business."

Seth didn't even consider Roxy's ludicrous sugges-
tion that Tope and Reap were having sex. Reaper was
the epitome of the lone wolf. He wouldn't be interested.
And if he were, Seth thought with an inner grin, Topaz
would tell him where to get off in a hurry. Not only was
she uninterested in a miserable loner like Reap, but
Seth was pretty sure she was still hung up on her con
man ex-lover, Jack.

Funny. He'd never thought of her as an idiot, but he guessed some women were where men were concerned.

He dragged his attention back to the subject at hand. "If they were leaving, they should have told us." He knew he sounded like a petulant child feeling left out by a beloved parent, and he told himself to get over it. "I just feel like we need to be really clear with each other if this mission is going to be a success, that's all."

"Mmm-hmm. Just remember whose mission it is, Seth. Raphael has been completing successful jobs like this one for a long time now, all by himself. He's not used to answering to anyone. And old habits are hard to break."

"I guess."

Roxy nodded, as if that was the end of the discussion, and glanced at Seth's companion. "Vixen, didn't you tell me earlier that you thought there was some trapping going on around this place?"

Seth glanced at Vixen, who met Roxy's eyes blankly for a moment; then suddenly her expression cleared, and she nodded. "Yes. There are traps in the woods all around us. Cruel things."

"Why don't you and Seth use this time to try to find them, then? Perform a service for the local wildlife? Spring the damn things, or, better yet, demolish them. It'll give you something productive to do while we wait for Raphael and Topaz to get back."

Vixen turned to Seth, which put her right up against his side, because she never seemed to move very far from him. His arm and shoulder, her breasts and belly…full contact. He loved it, and yet, he wasn't sure she meant it the way he hoped she did.

"Let's do it," she said, beaming her huge brown eyes up at him. "Let's destroy the traps so no more animals have to suffer."

"No *more* animals? You think some have already been caught?"

She averted her eyes a little too quickly, and said, "I wouldn't know. But if any have, we can free them, and maybe help mend their wounds."

"And maybe lose a hand," Seth muttered.

Her head snapped up again, but she wasn't beaming this time, she was frowning.

"Okay," he said. "That's what we'll do. Come on." He nodded to Roxy. "Be sure to let us know if the others show up."

"I will. Watch yourselves out there. Don't forget to keep your guard up."

Seth nodded, closed a hand around one of Vixen's, and led her through the house and out the front door.

Reaper had left the house before anyone else had even risen, so far as he knew, and all without being detected by the sharp-as-a-tack Roxy, who tended to be a real pain in the ass when she thought he was doing something he shouldn't be.

But he didn't have a choice here.

Seth had been dead right about the best course of action to take. Burning the rogues' base while they slept would be the quickest, cleanest, smartest way to be rid of them once and for all. He was proud of the kid, almost in spite of himself.

The problem was, Reaper couldn't do it. He couldn't

burn Briar alive, despite knowing that she was a cold-blooded killer. Despite having seen her delight in tormenting poor Vixen with his own eyes. Despite fully believing that odd little female's sense that Briar was the most dangerous one in the entire rogue gang. And despite that every instinct in him was telling him that he was making a huge mistake, maybe the biggest one of his existence—maybe even a fatal one.

He had no choice.

Looking into her eyes, it was as if he knew her. Yes, she was entombed by darkness, but it was darkness built upon pain. He'd seen it. And he'd felt something, some pull, some perverse attraction, that compelled him to save her. Or at least to try.

She might already be too far gone, but there was simply no alternative. He had to try, even though he knew she didn't want to be saved. And that she wouldn't come with him willingly.

He waited near the end of the lane that led to the rogues' mansion until they went out for their nightly hunt, his presence concealed by brush and, more than that, by his longtime skill at blocking discovery, his senses honed only to hers. And when the vampires passed, Reaper followed. When they split up, he trailed her, and then he watched and he waited, skulking in the shadows while she stalked her prey.

It was another man. She seemed to prefer feeding on men. He was in his twenties, a bit younger than the last one, walking down the street with a half dozen others of the same age. College friends, Reaper thought. The scent of marijuana was thick on their clothing, on their breath.

They were feeling very good, Reaper knew from reading their thoughts, heading to a party where they were sure to find willing females for a night of uninhibited sex.

"Excuse me," Briar said, stepping out of the shadows.

The young men stopped in their tracks, every set of eyes tracing her shape, up and down, every eager young member getting hard at the sight of her. Yeah, that part he understood. They wouldn't have his ability to feel the danger wafting from her like a strong perfume. They would only see her full breasts, the plump, enticing cleavage exposed by the scooped neck of the skintight black blouse she wore. They would see only the perfect curve of her backside encased in snug-fitting stonewashed denim, and the stiletto heels with their open toes, suggesting all kinds of things to their horny young minds. They would see those intense, burning eyes with the hungry look in them that could easily be mistaken for sexual lust.

Oh, it was lust, all right. Bloodlust.

"Can we, uh…help you with something?" one said.

"'Cause, damn, baby, I'd *love* to help you with something," said another.

"Maybe I have something *you* can help *me* with," said a third.

Her target, though, was silent, just staring at her. She met his eyes, ignoring the others, pointed a finger with a bloodred, dagger-sharp nail at its tip, and said, "You. I want you."

The young man swallowed hard, a tiny ripple of fear tiptoeing through him. But he wouldn't show that in front of his friends. Instead, he glanced at them, tried for a smug smile. "You guys go on ahead without me."

They muttered as they walked on. "Some guys have all the luck."

Briar watched them go, thinking she would get to them all, one by one. Of course, by the time she made her way through the entire group, they would know she was a predator. They would know that they were disappearing one by one. Each of them would begin to wonder if he were next. Their fear would be delicious.

Reaper closed his eyes as he read those thoughts. She was evil. God, she really *was* purely evil.

"Come here," she said to the young man, and as he moved closer, she opened her blouse, exposing her breasts to him, to the night. He stared as if mesmerized. "Suck them," she told him.

Blinking, he jerked his eyes up to hers, then looked up and down the sidewalk. People walked, traffic passed. "Right here?"

"Do it."

He licked his lips, and then he was on her, bending her backward, suckling her breasts, first one and then the other, as she closed her eyes and relished the pleasure he gave her, even while anticipating the kill.

After several moments, he lifted his head, and she straightened upright, slid her arms around his neck and said, "My turn."

"All right."

She kissed his neck. He closed his eyes and thought he was the luckiest man alive, until she sank her fangs into his throat and began to drink.

Reaper had intended to let her take enough to sustain herself, to fulfill her hunger, and then to step in and stop her before she killed the victim. What he hadn't expected was the sudden thought that rushed from her mind to his.

You're not fast enough, Reaper. Not this time.

And the instant that he realized what that meant—that she knew he was there, had known all along—even as he lunged from the shadows to stop her, she bit down harder and then tore the man's throat open wide. Blood gushed into her, and she took all she could swallow before Reaper yanked her away.

The young man slumped to the ground, blood pumping from his jugular, the flow slowing already. It was too late to do anything for him. He was gone. Reaper turned to stare at her in disbelief.

She only smiled at him, her lips coated in her victim's blood. "The more you try to stop me, the more of them I'm going to take."

He shook his head slowly. "No, Briar. You're not going to take *any* more of them."

She shrugged. "Maybe not tonight…"

"Not any night. Not ever again, Briar," he told her.

She frowned at him, not understanding his intent, and then he gripped her by one arm, flung her up and over his shoulder and lurched into motion with all the vampiric speed he possessed. "Because you're coming with me."

Briar shrieked. She screamed and swore and pounded the hell out of him. He did nothing about it, just took the pain, though it was significant. She was a vampiress, after all. He didn't do anything at all besides hold her and run, until he felt her shouting out mentally to Gregor.

And that was when he had to act. He stopped moving, flipped her onto the ground, and fell on top of her to hold her still even as she tried to roll and escape. He tugged the syringe from his pocket as she twisted and writhed beneath him. Her breasts were still uncovered, and they rubbed against his chest. His pelvis pressed hard to hers to hold her down, while he flipped off the needle's cap and resisted the fire she was causing to rage in his loins. Finally he jabbed her in the ass, right through her jeans, and depressed the plunger, sending the tranquilizer into her.

She went still instantly. Her eyes widened, then grew blank before they fell closed again.

His breath rushed out of him as he sat there, straddling her hips. She was out now. Helpless. He eyed her breasts, recalled the pleasure that unfortunate mortal had taken in tasting them, and how hot it had made him to stand in the shadows, watching. He licked his lips, knowing now that she had been putting on a show for his benefit. She'd known he was there.

He bent closer, wanting, craving, and when he was very, very close, he watched her nipple harden in anticipation, sensing him there, even though she was out cold. He used his tongue, one long, slow lap, then a teasing flick or two. Fire raged in him, but he didn't close his lips around her, didn't suck. The temptation to do more would have become irresistible if he had, and he knew his own limits.

Drawing away, he got off her, stood up, then bent to

pick her up and flip her over his shoulder, then began carrying her back toward the plantation, wondering how the others were going to react to his choice to abduct her, rather than burn her alive with the rest of her ruthless cohorts.

Seth walked through the woods, picking his way with care, watching for traps. Vixen more or less *skipped,* always on her toes, her face constantly to the wind, turning this way and that, almost as if she were scenting the air.

"Vix, slow down, would you? You're liable to step right into one of those traps you say are out here."

"No chance of that," she replied, her voice a happy lilt. "I know what they smell like now." She stopped skipping and opened her arms, then spun in circles, her hair blowing behind her, until she got so dizzy she fell to the ground, her laughter like tinkling bells to his slightly besotted ears.

He went to her, bent and reached down to help her up. She lifted her hand to his, then gripped him and tugged, so he fell forward. He landed on hands and knees—knees on either side of her hips, hands above either shoulder. She kept right on smiling. He wasn't able to take this quite so lightly.

"I really like you, Vixen," he said.

"I like you, too."

"You make me feel…" He searched his mind for words, the kinds of flowery, romantic words that would sweep a woman off her feet, take her breath away. "You make me feel—"

"Like mating?"

He almost choked, but clamped his mouth shut so he wouldn't end up spitting down into her face. He swallowed, cleared his throat and croaked, "What?"

"That's how you make *me* feel. Like mating," she said. "The urge has never been this strong in me before." She tipped her head to one side, studying his face. "Do you want to?"

"Don't you think we should try something a little lighter first?"

"Like what?"

"Kissing, maybe?"

She frowned at him. "I guess that is the usual method. All right."

"All right." He was a nervous wreck, never sure if she was teasing him, or whether her little red caboose had skipped the tracks. Or could she just simply be this innocent, this naive?

Seth licked his lips, hoped his breath was still minty fresh, and lowered his head until his lips met hers. And, God, those lips were so incredibly soft under his mouth. He pressed, nudged them apart, kissed her over and over, and she kissed back, first curious, then eager. He tried using his tongue, and she jerked her head back in surprise, eyes flashing wide.

"I'm sorry," he said.

She shook her head, a smile coming out of nowhere. "No, I *like* it." And she wrapped one arm around his waist, the other hand cupping the back of his head, and yanked him down to her, full body to body. He was on top of her, and she was kissing him, and it only took him about half a second to get over his surprise and start kissing her back. She opened her mouth to his tongue this time, even using her own.

Her hips arched against him, and her breath came in short, desperate little gasps. She was so incredibly responsive.

"Seth? Vixen?"

He went still, though she kept right on clinging and grinding and kissing. "Wait, wait, babe, I hear someone."

"I don't care."

"I think it's Roxy."

"Seth, where are you?" the voice called again.

This time he was certain it was Roxy. He looked back down at Vixen, her wet lips, parted and still so hungry for his, her eyes filled with sexual need, pure and unrestrained lust. He loved that. Who would have expected it in a woman who seemed so damned innocent?

"I'm sorry. It sounds like she needs us."

And then he rolled off Vixen and bounced to his feet, gripping her hand and pulling her up on the way.

"We're over here," he called.

Within a few seconds, he heard Roxy coming, and then she appeared on the path, amid the pines. "Best get back to the house. We need you."

"Trouble?" he asked, gripping Vixen's hand in his and moving fast.

"Yeah. Raphael brought it home with him. Just to keep things interesting, I guess. Stupid, stubborn, son of a—"

"Whoa, whoa, just what kind of trouble is this?"

"The worst kind." Roxy slid a sideways glance at Vixen when she said that, and the look was almost one of pity. "I've never seen Raphael act like a typical male before, but I have now."

"In what way is he acting male?" Vixen asked, sending Roxy a curious look.

"Thinking with his dick, honey."

Vixen frowned and looked at Seth. "What does she mean?"

"Uh, I think she means Reaper's mind is more on, uh…" What was the word she'd used? Oh, yeah. "More on *mating* than on common sense."

"You got that right," Roxy said. She wasn't walking through the woods so much as *stomping* through them. And her hands were clenched at her sides, swinging more than they normally did when she walked. "Never thought I'd see the day," she muttered. "All these years, and it isn't that I haven't been trying to get that man laid all along, because I have. Sex is *good* for a man. But damn, of all the females in all the preternatural world, why the hell did it have to be her?"

"Who?" Seth and Vixen said in unison.

"No wonder he never went for any of the women I picked out for him. They were freaking *sane!*"

"Who is it, Roxy?" Seth asked again.

The house was in sight now, and with their vampiric hearing, he and Vixen could pick up the sounds of struggle coming from within. Growls and shrieks, and the crash of things breaking. It sounded as if Reaper were battling a badger in there.

"Tell you what I *ought* to do. I *ought* to march right in there and kick that idiot square in the *cojones*. Maybe that would knock some sense into him."

They opened the front door and hurried inside, following the sounds of battle to Reaper's bedroom, where he had a furious, wild-eyed female pinned to the bed. She struggled and twisted, spat and growled. Her hair was all over, her face red. Reaper was bruised and scratched, and his clothing was torn.

"No," Vixen whispered. "She cannot be here!"

Seth was looking around, though, a new concern etching itself into his mind. "Hey, where the hell is Topaz?"

"No one knows," Roxy said. "She wasn't with Raphael. We have no idea where she went."

"But we'll damn well find her," Reaper said through gritted teeth. He was clearly in pain. "Just as soon as someone finds me some restraints strong enough to keep our captive still."

"Why didn't you tranquilize her?" Seth demanded.

"Did, but I didn't use enough the first time and I'm not sure how much more she can handle. Find me something, dammit."

"I'm on it, Reap," Seth said, and he turned and picked his way back across the bedroom, avoiding the broken lamps and upended furnishings that littered the place from one end to the other. He made it to the closet down the hall, where Roxy had put her supplies, and started rummaging, hoping she'd thought this far ahead.

"I have something that will keep her in line," he heard Vixen say from the bedroom. And then she left, heading down the same hallway he had, moving past him and on to her room. When she emerged, she was holding the shock collar that had so recently been buckled around her own slender neck.

She held it up, to show him.

"That's the best idea I've heard all month," he said, reaching for it.

Vixen tugged it away before he could grab it, and he searched her eyes, only to see them lower, and she quickly shook her head. "No. No, it's a bad idea. It's... it's too cruel. Even for Briar."

14

—▶◀—

Topaz had waited far from the rogues' mansion, until she was certain they had, indeed, all left for their nightly feeding frenzy. If anything, she gave them extra time, but she had to be careful.

Okay, so maybe it was pathetic of her. To be used, to be taken, to be robbed by a man like Jack, was bad enough. What was worse was that she'd enjoyed every minute of it. Every second. *Intensely.* Right up until the big revelation at the end, at least, where he'd done a vanishing act with her money. But the rest—the rest had been blissful. To add insult to injury, she missed him. And she still got hot every time she thought of his kiss, his touch, his hands on her body. God, the man was a master at lovemaking.

And yeah, she hated the idea of Jack burning alive, even though that was exactly what he deserved. She'd tried telling herself and everyone else that she wanted to keep him alive only because she needed her money back, and if he died, she would never be able to get it. And she would *keep on* telling everyone *else* that. But deep down, she knew better. It wasn't as easy to lie to herself.

So she waited, and then she moved closer to the mansion and waited some more. It was a long wait, and she figured the others in Reaper's band of misfits would be wondering where she was. Maybe even worrying about her, though she supposed that was doubtful. She wasn't the kind of person people actually liked. Never had been. Which was why she was so stupid to have let herself believe Jack had ever really cared about her. No one had ever *really* cared. It didn't matter. She had to do this.

It was, she figured, a couple of hours past midnight when the rogues began returning to their lair. Sometimes just one solitary vampire, sometimes a group of two or three. She opened her senses while trying to keep her own presence concealed—a difficult task. It was easier to block your own essence while closing yourself off entirely. To be open, searching, reaching out for someone while blocking others, that was trickier. She thought she could handle it, though.

Finally she felt him. He was with a small group making their way to the front of the mansion, talking about the night's kills the way mortal hunters would discuss every detail after taking a deer.

"You should have seen her," a male vampire Topaz had never seen before was saying. "She never realized anything was wrong until I sank my fangs into her pretty neck. It was fantastic." He was tall, painfully thin, recently made, with silver gray hair and a gaunt face that spoke of endless hunger.

Jack laughed with the strange vamp, but Topaz could feel him squirming a little. "Sixteen, you say?"

"Or thereabouts."

"So, you, uh, killed her, then?"

"Drained her dry." The vampire slapped him on the back. "Young blood is so much sweeter, don't you think?"

"Always," Jack said. "I was just saying the other night how—" He stopped there, breaking off in midsentence and tipping his head in just such a way that Topaz knew he'd sensed her presence, just as she'd intended.

Jack quickly glanced at his companion. "You know, Merlin, I completely forgot what I was going to say just now." He gave his head a shake. "I think the victim I took tonight was on something that's not agreeing with me."

"You all right?" the other one asked.

"Fine. I think I'm going to stay outside for a bit, though. Take in the night. It'll refresh me far more than being inside that stuffy mansion would."

"I can stay, if you—"

"Please." Jack rolled his eyes, and the other vampire grinned, nodded and went inside. Then Jack looked around, listened, *felt* for her.

She knew he was scanning for others in the area, not only of his own band, but of hers. He probably suspected a trap.

She stepped out of the shadows, and said, "I'm alone. I need to talk to you."

He saw her, and his eyes registered surprise, but only briefly. For just a moment there was a flash of something that looked almost glad to see her, and then his gaze moved up and down her body, blatantly appreciative. She tried not to remind herself how stupid she'd felt dressing up tonight in a slinky black number with a slit up to her hip and a plunging neckline. Putting on makeup, brushing her hair until it gleamed. God, she was pathetic. And yet, he noticed, and it felt good to be looked at that way. By him, only by him.

He came closer, and she stood there, waiting, letting the wind move her hair and knowing it turned him on. She could feel that it did. Good. Let him suffer. When he was a foot from her, he stopped. "You look amazing, Topaz. It's been too long."

"It hasn't been nearly long enough," she said, hoping he felt only her anger and resentment, and none of the hurt and ridiculous longing welling up inside her. "Never wouldn't be long enough. But I couldn't very well demand my money back without seeing you."

"Ah. So you're here for your money."

"What else?"

He shrugged, but his gaze was on her cleavage, then her neck and her lips, and his fingertips were suddenly running down her arms from shoulder to elbow and back again, and she shivered involuntarily.

"Stop it, Jack." She could have taken a step back, but didn't. It had been too damn long since he'd touched her. And he didn't obey. Just kept on stroking, so lightly. "I just want my money." God, her voice was shaking.

"I earned that money, love. Fair and square. I gave you enough orgasms to pay for twice what I took from you."

"I didn't know I was being charged for them. And

as I recall, I gave as good as I got. You had plenty of pleasure, too."

"I'd like some more."

Before she could react—not that she was even sure she would have—he jerked her to him and took her mouth with his. And, oh, God, it was everything she'd been dreaming about since he'd left her. Everything she remembered and hungered for. The way he had of moving his lips against hers as his tongue teased—didn't plunge, that would come later, but just teased—dipping, tempting, tasting. He had the softest lips of any man she had ever kissed, and everything in her wanted him in that moment. She couldn't help it when she twisted her arms around his neck, tipped her head to get a better angle.

He slid his magic hands down her back, cupped her ass and pulled her slowly, powerfully, against him as he arched into her. Hard. She felt him. At least he wanted her, too. But then again, that had never been the issue.

"God, you're a hot little thing," he whispered against her mouth. "I'm so glad you came back for more. Did you bring your checkbook?"

Just like a slap in the face, his words snapped her out of the haze of desire that had held her. She jerked herself out of his arms and blinked up at him, stunned, hurt and angry. "You bastard."

"Sorry. Just checking." He shrugged. "I suppose I could toss you a freebie, if you—"

She hit him, and it wasn't a girlie face-slap, either, but a full-blown, clenched fist to the jaw that snapped his head around and spun his body in a half circle.

He wobbled, caught himself, put a hand on his jaw and lifted his head slowly to face her. "You *are* pissed."

"Half a million dollars will do that to a woman."

"I think that was more feeling than fortune, love."

"In your dreams, Jack. Give me back my money, and I might just tell you something that will save your sorry ass from annihilation."

That caught his interest. Finally the smug look left his face. His brows rose, and he searched her eyes. Good, at last an honest expression—something beyond his act. She'd seen it before, or thought she had. But it was rare that he let the slick veneer slip away.

"My ass is in danger of being annihilated?"

"Soon, too."

"Well, now. That *is* interesting." He took her arm. "Why don't we find a cozy, private place to discuss it further?"

Her heart beat faster, even while her mind told her to send him packing, or, better yet, deck him again. But before she could do either, she sensed others coming from the castle.

It hit her fast that she'd let her guard down—he'd kissed her, and she'd forgotten everything except feeling, sensation, passion. God, he was good.

He seemed to become aware of their discovery at the same time she did, because he shoved her away from him and whispered, *"Run."*

She ran, and the other vampires came charging toward them, but Jack stepped out, held up a hand, and they stopped. After that, she couldn't see or hear them anymore. She was entirely focused on making her way, silently and with all the speed she could muster, through an unfamiliar forest, in hopes of eluding the rogues.

Jack had spent the entire encounter, minus its final minute or so, feeling extremely pleased with himself. She still wanted him. That much was clear. That he still wanted her just as much didn't really enter into it. He was male, she was hot and quite possibly the best sex he'd ever had. Naturally he still wanted her. It didn't mean anything.

For her, however, it did. It must. She was female. They were emotional things by nature. He'd stolen from her, used her, hurt her, abandoned and betrayed her, and she still had it bad for him.

Damn, he must be better than even *he* had realized.

Of course, the kiss had hit him a little harder than he'd anticipated, and not wanting to reveal that, he'd had to cover by insulting her. It was second nature. Keep them close enough, just not too close.

At any rate, all those thoughts had dissipated when she'd made her cryptic comment about his impending doom, and then they'd vanished entirely when he'd realized that her presence on the grounds had been discovered.

He stood there now, grinning like an idiot at the two members of what he had dubbed Gregor's Goon-Squad—the GGS for short. God, they were all so alike—Gregor chose them that way. Weak-minded and bulky, they looked enough alike to have been blood kin in life. Beetling foreheads, eyes a tad too close together, thick necks. Big heads full of dark hair, and bearded.

All of them. Why Gregor insisted on that, Jack couldn't be certain. His best guess—to make it easy to tell them apart from the full-blooded vampires.

Though he wasn't quite sure what made them less than full-blooded. And he had to admit to a burning curiosity, though he wouldn't break his neck trying to find out. It was no skin off his nose either way.

The drones lumbered up to him and stopped.

"I sensed a presence, too," he lied. "Came out to check, but there's no one. Maybe around back—"

Before he could finish, he heard and sensed something that made his stomach turn, and he turned to see two more of the oversized, under-witted vampire drones dragging Topaz between them. Dammit to hell, where had they come from?

Her face was bruising already, silken hair hanging in her eyes, sexy dress—the one he was sure she'd put on just for him—torn. The slit that had reached to just below her hip now gaped to the curve of her waist, revealing the slender band of the thong panties she wore underneath it. One vampire clutched each of her arms, and he knew they were holding her far harder than was necessary.

She lifted her head, met his eyes.

Jack averted his, because he couldn't stand seeing her in pain. He *liked* women. This one in particular. He didn't approve of, much less have the stomach for, harming them—at least not physically. Financially, emotionally, those were entirely different things.

"Nice work, men," he said, forcing a smile of approval. "How about I take her from here, then?"

"How about I do?"

The voice was Gregor's, and it came from behind him. He turned to meet the boss's eyes and found them furious. Frowning, Jack said, "Gregor, what's happened? The anger's coming off you in waves."

"Briar is missing. I believe *they've* taken her."

"*Who* have taken her?" Jack asked, though he was sorely afraid he already knew.

"Reaper, the one sent to destroy me, and his gang. The same bastards who took Vixen from us." He looked past Jack at Topaz. "Fortunately, we have one of theirs now. Don't we?"

She lowered her eyes, refusing to answer.

"Yes, of course we do. Who else would be sneaking around here in the dead of night?"

"Gregor, I don't think—"

"Shut up, Jack. You two, take her inside, down below. She can have Vixen's old cell."

They nodded and dragged her onward. Topaz didn't struggle, didn't fight, just kept looking at Jack, her eyes asking why the hell he wasn't doing something to help her. But dammit, he couldn't.

As they dragged her past Gregor, he stopped them, then gripped her chin and lifted it so that he could stare directly into her eyes. "I'm going to enjoy punishing you for the crimes of your comrades, pretty one. I'm going to enjoy it very much."

She spat in his face, and Jack closed his eyes and turned his head away so he couldn't see the back of Gregor's hand when it slammed into her already bruised cheekbone. But he heard it, and dammit, he felt it. He felt her pain like his own.

"Downstairs into the cell—*now.*"

The goons towed her off. Her feet were no longer moving, just dragging behind her, and Jack was pretty sure Gregor's blow had left her unconscious. Dammit, now what the hell was he supposed to do?

Briar passed out on the bed when Roxy managed to inject her for a second time with the tranquilizer, as Seth helped Reaper hold her down. Roxy'd had a hard time convincing Reaper that the hell-cat could handle another dose, but in the end, they'd had no choice. She was tearing up the place, and her anguish was bound to give away their position, given time.

And that wasn't the only problem with her being there. Vixen was petrified, absolutely traumatized by Briar's presence, and Seth was madder than hell about it.

"We can't just keep injecting her," Reaper muttered. He looked at Roxy as he said it. "We don't know how much of this stuff a vampire can handle all at once."

"Good call, Einstein," she snapped. "Maybe you should've thought of that before you brought her here." She turned away and muttered under her breath, "Dumb-ass."

Reaper looked at her quickly.

"She's right," Seth put in. "Not only that, but you didn't even bother to consult us."

"*Consult* you?"

"Yes, consult us. We're a team, aren't we?"

"No," Reaper said. "I wouldn't call us a team. Look, you've joined me one by one, against my will, not to mention my better judgment. But this is *my* mission. It's *my* job. It's what *I* do, and I don't intend to *consult* any of you about how I choose to do it."

Seth felt the sting. "Fine. Don't consult. Care to explain, then?"

"No."

"Well, what the hell are we supposed to do with her, Reap?"

"I'll let you know when I've decided."

Seth rolled his eyes, pushed his hands through his hair and wound up facing Vixen, who was standing on the far side of the room, near the open door, staring at Briar and, he thought, trembling a little.

He swung his head around to look at Reaper again. "Do you see what this is doing to her? She's on your side, man. Yet you traumatize her by bringing home the woman who tortured her, without even a word of warning or so much as an explanation. Dammit, Reaper, what are you thinking?"

"For the last time, I'm not going to explain myself to you!" Reaper seemed to grab hold of himself before he lost it entirely. He glanced at the wild thing on the bed, sleeping now, and then turned to face Vixen. "I'm sorry this upsets you, Vixen. Believe me when I tell you, I will keep her from hurting you in any way. I promise you that. And she'll have a hell of a time trying to contact Gregor mentally until the drugs metabolize out of her system. At this dosage, they should keep her from giving him our location even when she comes around."

She held his gaze and whispered, "I believe you

mean what you say. I just don't think it's a promise you can keep. She's strong."

"I'm stronger."

"I'm not so sure about that," Vixen whispered. She lowered her head, hurt showing in her eyes, and turned to leave the room.

But then she stopped—they all stopped—when they heard Gregor's mental shout ringing loudly, almost deafeningly, in their heads. Only Roxy couldn't hear it, but she went still, watching them.

You have taken two of mine. But now I have one of yours. And believe me, her stay here will not be pleasant.

"Topaz," Vixen whispered. Her voice was choked with fear, and Seth went to her automatically, put his arms around her and drew her close to his side.

Return Briar and Vixen, or this one will die.

Don't hurt her! Reaper replied, speaking without making a sound.

Oh, it's too late for that. I've already hurt her, and I will continue to do so. It's killing her that I'll hold off on. But not for long, Reaper. Not for long. I want you to bring my women back to me personally. And alone. Or she dies. You have until one hour past sunset tomorrow. I'll let you know when and where.

Reaper closed his eyes.

Vixen drew herself out of Seth's embrace. "I'll go back. I'll go right now. And I'll take Briar with me."

"No." Seth gripped her shoulders, turning her to face him and staring hard into her eyes. "No way in hell."

"Yes, Seth. It has to be done, and it has to be done now. He's hurting her. You don't know what it's like—"

"We have time to make a better plan," Reaper said.

"He's hurt her already! He's hurting her now!" Vixen cried.

"It's nearly dawn. He can't hurt her while he rests," Reaper promised. "Topaz is tougher than she looks. Have a little faith. We'll get her back, safe and sound. I promise."

Vixen seemed to want to accept that, although she clearly had her doubts. As for Seth, he didn't see any possible solution, and he was sick at the thought of Topaz being tortured. He wished to God he could sense her, send her a message of encouragement or let her know they would get her out of there somehow. But he couldn't feel anything from her. Once inside that mausoleum, it was like a vampire had fallen into a black hole. There was no way to know what was happening to her, and his imagination was supplying dreadful possibilities.

Thank God it was almost dawn, because he couldn't bear to think about it for much longer.

Topaz hit the far wall face-first, scraping her palms, elbows and, she was pretty sure, her chin, when the burly thugs shoved her into the cell. The door closed, a jarring clang of iron on iron, and locks turned, squealing in rusty protest, but clicking into place all the same.

She pushed her face away from the damp stone wall, refused to press a hand to her chin, because that would be admitting they'd hurt her. She didn't like admitting to pain. She didn't like anyone to have that kind of power over her—the power to hurt her—much less admit it on those rare occasions when someone did.

Instead, she turned her head slowly, and sent a look

over her shoulder that should have had the goons shaking in their jackboots.

But, of course, they'd already turned and lumbered away by then.

Cussing under her breath, Topaz touched two fingertips to her chin, sucked air through her teeth and jerked them away again. Okay, the skin was intact. But she bet she would have a hell of a bruise marring her complexion before daylight. Thank God for the day sleep's regenerative powers, she thought. She examined her elbows, and saw that they were skinned and speckled with droplets of blood. "Bastards are gonna pay for that." Turning her palms toward her, she saw that they, too, were skinned up, mostly on the heels of her hands. She was glad her reflexes were practically instantaneous, or her face would have taken a considerably more serious beating.

She crossed the cell, gripped the bars and peered between them to get a look at her surroundings. It was a lightless tomb of a place, but she could see better by darkness than any mortal could in full light. It was a cellar, maybe had been a wine cellar once. The gut-level perception of it as a dungeon was ridiculous; there were no dungeons in the old South when this place had been built. Slave quarters, yeah, whipping posts, more than likely. Or maybe not. They wouldn't have needed to resort to a shock collar for Vixen if they'd thought to whip her raw and bloody.

Then again, they might just be lazy.

For a moment the thought of Vixen in this place for God knew how long, being tortured by these assholes, made her feel sick to her stomach. She could handle anything they could dish out. But Vixen—she was such a little thing, so odd and fragile-seeming. Yeah, okay, she was freaking weird, but that didn't negate the disgust Topaz felt at the thought of those burly animals hurting her.

The cellar was built of hand-hewn stone blocks, its floor packed earth. And beyond the cell, she couldn't see much of use. A bench on one wall, some pipes running up the sides here and there, and criss-crossing the ceiling—recent additions, relatively speaking. A pail and washboard dangled from a nail where they'd probably been hanging for a century. Cobwebs were plentiful. Ahead and to the left there were two stone steps that led upward and a tall door, beyond which she knew were more steps and the outside world.

There must be another door somewhere, with stairs that led up into the main part of the mansion, but it was out of sight. The thugs hadn't gone out the way they'd brought her in. She craned her neck to see around the corner to the left of her cell, where the goons had gone, but it was useless. Even vampires couldn't see around corners or through walls. None that she knew of, at least.

She gave the cell door an experimental shake, but she knew damn well it wasn't going to give. They wouldn't have put her in here if they thought she could get out. And she doubted a faulty cell would have held Vixen for very long. The little thing might be strange, but she wasn't stupid. She struck Topaz as kind of cunning, in a naive sort of way.

The lock looked new. As if it had been recently replaced.

Sighing, she turned to examine the inside of her cell, but it only made her angrier. Stone walls, concrete floor—probably so prisoners couldn't tunnel out with their bare hands. *As if,* she thought with a look at her nails. Screw that. She would use one of their fat heads to bash the hinges off the door instead. It beat messing up a ninety-dollar manicure.

There was a cot—a slab of wood, really—bolted to the wall, further supported by chains at the head and foot. A small blanket was wadded up on the cot, and she remembered Vixen saying Jack had brought her a blanket. Was that the one?

Hell.

"I know it's not what you're used to."

She spun around and hated the way her heart skipped at the sight of that bastard Jack coming across the cellar toward her. He stopped at the cell door, not close enough to reach. He didn't trust her.

He was smart.

"It's a shit hole."

"I'm sorry, Topaz. Believe me—"

"If you were sorry, you would have stopped them."

"If I'd tried, they would have killed me without batting an eye. I was outnumbered, in case you failed to notice."

She narrowed her eyes to mere slits, glaring at him. "What?"

"Seth was outnumbered, too."

"Seth who?"

"Seth, the young fledgling barely out of braces, who

charged in here and took on six or eight of those Nean-
derthals you have lumbering around just to get that odd
little Vixen out."

"Oh." He pursed his lips. "I, uh…oh."

"Don't worry. I know you could have done the same.
I'm not questioning your manhood here, Jack. Just
pointing out that you're a self-centered snake."

"How so?"

"You let them throw me in this cell because doing otherwise would have ruined your position here. And if I
know you, you're hoping to cash in, in some manner or
other, before you check out. Correct me if I'm wrong."

"I wouldn't risk your life for money."

"Why not? You don't give a damn about me."

He shrugged. "True, but I don't like hurting women."

She released an involuntary snort that spoke volumes.

"Physically," he clarified.

"Right."

He shrugged. "Believe what you want. I think I can
get you out of this without the need for violence."

"You going to con me right out from behind iron
bars, Jack? Come on, even you're not that good."

He sighed, lowered his head, shaking it, then raising it again and stabbing her eyes with his. "Why did
you come here tonight?"

"To get my money back."

"Come on, Topaz, what's the point in lying now?"

She averted her eyes. "I want my money, Jack."

"Fine. I'll get it for you. Not that a quarter mil is
going to do you much good in that cell, now, is it?"

"Half a million," she corrected.

"Uh, well, yes, but I had to hand half over to Gregor, love. I can't return what I don't have."

"What?" She looked up swiftly, eyes wide with disbelief. "Why the hell would you give half to that maniac?"

He shrugged. "Secure my position here, win his trust, that sort of thing. It's confidence-man stuff. You wouldn't understand."

"Fuck you, Jack."

"All in good time, babe." He shrugged. "Do you want me to get you out of here or not?"

"You think you can?"

"Somebody has to. Gregor's angry as hell."

"I know. He mentioned that he thinks someone has taken…Briar?"

"Yes, Briar. Meanest bitch ever to drink blood. Your pal Reaper took her tonight. We heard her cry out for help, but it was so brief no one could locate her."

"The man's a freaking idiot."

"You don't know the half. If I were Gregor, I'd let him keep her. It would be the most damaging thing we could do to your side, if you ask me."

She thinned her lips at his words, though his expression told her he was being anything but sarcastic.

"You have any idea what The Grim One wants with our hellion?"

"I can't even imagine." She shook her head. "Poor Vixen. She's terrified of Briar."

"You should be the one terrified right now, Topaz. You're the one being threatened here." He glanced toward the door, the one she couldn't see. "He probably won't bother you tonight. Dawn's too close, but come sundown—"

"I need to feed," she said, cutting him off.

He blinked, then frowned. "You haven't fed tonight?"

"No. I wasted all night waiting to warn you—" She bit her lip, but too late. She'd said too much.

"Warn me?" His brows rose skeptically, and Jack searched her eyes while she avoided his. "So Reaper was planning some kind of move against us, was he? And you couldn't bear to let it happen with me sitting here, a perfect target."

"I want my money. I won't get it if you're dead."

"Nor if you are. Yet you risked your life to warn me. Admit it."

"You are *so* full of yourself."

"Doesn't matter. I don't suppose your friend will do anything too destructive while we have you here, anyway." He moved closer to the cage. "Now, don't try anything vicious. All I have to do is shout to bring a dozen of the goons down on you. All right?"

He reached through the bars, gripping her shoulders, one in each hand, and drew her closer. She stiffened, and he met her eyes. "Come here, Topaz. You said you were hungry. I can't bring you sustenance, since Gregor's taken to keeping careful track of the supplies. My blood will have to do."

Her eyes shot to his in spite of herself, and she felt heat spike inside her and knew it showed, though she would deny it to the death.

"Come here," he whispered. So much the way he used to say those very words to her in bed, when he was changing positions, moving her, turning and pulling her close again.

She moved close to the bars, drawn to him like a magnet to steel.

"There now," he said. One arm encircled her shoulders, his hand resting at her nape, while the other rose, palm up, wrist near her chin. "There's a good vein there. Go ahead, drink."

Her breath came faster; her eyes fell closed. "I'd rather go hungry."

"You're a terrible liar. We both know you want it. If you were paying attention to anything besides trying to conceal your own desires, Topaz, you might know I want it, too."

Her eyes flew open.

"We were good together. You can't deny that."

"It wasn't real. You used me."

"I did. But it was still good." He lifted his wrist higher, closer to her mouth. "Take me the way you want to."

"Can't," she whispered, closing her hands around his forearm. "The damn bars are in the way." Then she bent and sank her fangs into his flesh. She tasted him, and everything she had ever felt came screaming back to life inside her. She suckled and swallowed. She drank him. And she burned for him so badly that her entire being seemed swathed in a thick, red-hot haze of blood-lust.

All too soon, he was tugging his wrist away, pushing her head away gently, or perhaps weakly. Her eyes parted just a little, and she knew they were glowing with need—and with hunger—as they met his. She was shocked to see that his were bright with craving, as well.

"As good as ever," he said, his voice throaty, almost a growl. "I wish Gregor hadn't taken the damn keys. If I could get in there with you right now, I'd—"

"Don't." She closed her eyes and turned away, tried to douse the fire raging in every cell of her body. God, it was too much. She was *shaking* with it.

He took a deep breath, blew it out. "Tonight, when Gregor comes to question you, you need to tell him that you came here for me. Convince him that you're in love with me, that you couldn't forget me, and that you came here to try to win me back."

Her head came up, her eyes opening wider as his gall did what her own will hadn't been able to do—douse the fires he'd lit inside her. "Not even in your wildest dreams," she promised.

"Convince him that you came to join up with his gang, just to be close to me. Make it believable, Topaz."

"You're out of your mind if you think I'm going to do that."

He sighed heavily, the glow fading from his eyes. "Tell me, do you think Reaper will bring Vixen and Briar back to him right away?"

"I don't think he'll bring them back at all."

"Well, the torture—*your* torture, Topaz—begins at sundown, unless you can convince Gregor you're on our side. And you'll have to give him something to prove your sincerity; some information about the other side to show him you're on the level. Do you understand?"

She shook her head. "I won't betray the others."

"I'm not asking you to. Make something up, but make it something he can't verify. Better yet, tell him something true, something that isn't going to do any harm to your friends."

She shook her head again. "You're asking me to sell out."

"If you don't, you'll be tortured and probably killed. And there won't be a thing I can do to save you, Topaz."

"You mean, there won't be a thing you're *willing* to do to save me, don't you?"

He turned away from the cell. "Sleep, Topaz. When you wake up, take my advice and do exactly what I've told you. But only if you want to live."

And then he was gone.

Topaz sank onto her cot, furious with herself for wanting him so much, for risking so much to come here to warn him, to *save* him, when he clearly wasn't willing to risk a hair on his head for her.

When had she become so pathetic?

15

Sunset, and as she rose, Vixen battled a feeling of dread and an urge to run that was like nothing she had ever felt before. Reaper had brought Briar into the house where she had begun to feel safe—safer than she'd ever felt around others, mortal or vampire. Safer than she'd ever felt since she'd become what she now was. Seth was a big part of that. She craved him, relished his touch, felt eager, excited and yet tranquil all at once when he was near. But there was more than just Seth and his odd effect on her. There were the others. She'd begun to grow fond of them, to trust them, even. She'd begun to think of this place as a haven, but it wasn't the place, really. It was them, the people—Seth and Reaper and Topaz and Roxy—they were her haven.

But her haven had been ruined, and it felt like a violation.

It occurred to her that she didn't really know these vampires she'd been so close to trusting. Especially Reaper. She never would have imagined him bringing Briar here. Of course, he might be very close to deciding to turn her over to Gregor again—to returning both of them to captivity.

She should run. Every instinct told her that.

And yet she couldn't, because Topaz might pay with her life if she did.

So she rose, and she took her time showering, dressing, fixing her hair, giving the others plenty of opportunity to discuss her fate without her. And then she joined them just in time to hear Seth saying, "We need to know for sure."

"Gregor doesn't strike me as the kind of man to make idle threats," Reaper said.

"Then why don't we sense anything from Topaz?" Seth countered. "If she were in pain, being hurt, we'd feel it."

Reaper pushed a hand through his hair and paced the room.

Stepping into his path, Vixen said, "You can't judge anything from the fact that you don't sense her. You can't read anything from inside that place, I think."

Reaper met her eyes, his own narrowing. "I got that feeling when I was there, but I didn't think such a thing was possible. How can Gregor accomplish it?"

"I don't know. I don't even know for sure that it's true. But I could only sense Seth, feel him, when I was outside. Never when I was within those walls. And yet when I was out, I sensed him constantly, with every fiber of my being."

Seth met her eyes and told her without a word that he felt just as powerfully connected to her.

She held his gaze for a long moment, then tore it

away to face Reaper again. "I can find out what's happening to Topaz."

Reaper looked into her eyes, his gaze probing. "You can't risk going back there."

"They won't know. They won't even see me."

"You couldn't even get inside, Vixen."

"Yes, I could."

Reaper studied her, frowning. Seth came to stand beside her, and he was searching her face, too. "How?" he asked.

She swallowed and pursed her lips. "I can't tell you that. Or rather, I *won't* tell you that. Not now. Maybe not ever. It's my secret to keep. But I can do it."

"Yes," Roxy said. "She can." She smiled at Vixen. "Don't worry, little one. It's not my secret to tell, and I'll take it to my grave, if that's what you want."

Somehow, Vixen believed her.

"Let me go," she said, turning her attention to Reaper again. "I can be back in an hour. I can tell you everything that's going on with her."

Reaper looked at Seth, as if waiting for his approval. Seth shook his head and started to say no, absolutely not; she felt the words spring to his lips before he even spoke, so she spoke first. "I don't know why I'm asking. It's not your decision. I'm going. I'll be back in two hours, at most. I hope you won't do anything until then."

She turned to run toward the door. Seth raced after her, gripped her arm and spun her around. "Vixen, please don't. If they catch you again—"

"They won't."

"But if they do—"

"If they do, you'll come for me." She stared into his eyes, wanting to see in them some confirmation that what she had just said was absolutely true, and unsure *why* she wanted it. Not just to make her feel safe. In fact, her own safety had very little to do with the unfamiliar longing suffusing her core. "Won't you?"

"You're damn right I will."

She blinked in reaction to his words, spoken with passion, with conviction, without a hint that they might be false. She believed them. She believed he meant it, and meant it just as powerfully as he'd spoken it. Why?

"If you'll let me come with you, I can make sure it won't be necessary, though."

"You can't come with me."

"Vix—"

She stretched and pressed her mouth to his, telling herself it was only to make him stop arguing, but knowing as soon as his arms closed around her that she had other reasons. He kissed her in a way he never had before, almost desperately, and she clung and kissed him back with everything in her, and wondered why she'd never understood the appeal of kissing before. It had seemed a waste of time. Now it seemed like heaven.

Finally she pulled free, turned and ran to the door.

She didn't stop running, either. Not until she was nearly at the enemy mansion, crouching in the woods near its boundaries and sending out her senses to determine whether she'd been followed.

It didn't feel as if she had. So she found a quiet

spot, and there she focused her energy, relaxed her body and let it begin to change.

Gregor showed up just slightly after Topaz awoke in her cell. She was unimpressed with the man so far. For a bad-ass leader of a gang of rogues, he didn't look like much. Fit, yeah, but in a stubby way, and his close-cropped red hair showed signs that it had been thinning when he'd been brought over. His cheeks were pock-marked, his eyes pale blue, brows so blond they were almost invisible. He looked like a joke.

And yet she knew he was dangerous.

She'd been giving a lot of thought to Jack's sugges-tion, and no matter how she tried, she couldn't come up with a better idea.

"It's about time," she said when he used the key to unlock her cell. "If you'd waited any longer, it might have been too late."

"Too late for what?"

She pursed her lips. "No, no way, you've treated me like shit. Fuck you and your entire gang. I've changed my mind."

Gregor shrugged. "Don't play games with me—Topaz, is it?"

She scowled at him. "Who said I'm playing? You think I came here to play? You think I risked my freak-ing *life* because I was playing with you?"

"I don't know. I *do* know that I'm about to find out." He swung the door open wide and motioned her to come out.

She did, but slowly, warily. "I came here with an offering for you, you idiot. A gift, but you don't know the difference between a friend and an enemy."

He lifted his pale, pale brows but kept walking, gripping her arm to tug her along at his side. They rounded a corner, into a larger basement room. On the far side, she saw the stairs that led up to the main house, the ones she couldn't see from her cell. But more importantly, she saw the chair in the middle of the room, with a goon from hell standing on either side of it. There was a coal bucket full of glowing embers on the floor, with an iron poker thrust into it.

"Friends don't usually run away when spotted."

"I ran because I was being chased by some kind of oversized, demi-vamp or something. What *are* those things, anyway?" He didn't answer, just kept watching her. She sighed and went on. "I came here looking for you, Gregor. How was I supposed to know they worked for you?"

He pushed her into the chair. She sat, and tried not to tremble in fear, tried to keep to her plan. She'd deliberated all night long, but in the end, she'd realized she had no choice but to do as Jack had suggested.

Where the hell was he, anyway? You'd think he would at least show up.

"So why were you looking for me?" Gregor asked, even as he nodded to the goons. One of them moved behind her, grabbed her hands, pulled them back and began tying them way too tightly.

She could tear through that rope. What were they thinking? Then she glimpsed the hot coals and knew. The pain would leave her too weak to break free, probably after the first few minutes. And if she tried before-hand, well, they outnumbered her, so…

"That's a lie, actually," she told him. "I wasn't look-ing for *you,* I was looking for Jack."

"Again, I ask you. Why?"

She lowered her eyes. "To warn him. About Reaper."

"And why would you want to do that?"

"That's personal," she said. "Suffice it to say that I don't want to see him hurt. And if he stays with you, he will be."

"By Reaper?"

She nodded. A thug was tying her ankle to the chair leg now. Then he moved to the other one. "Reaper is going to do his best to kill you and everyone else in this gang," she said.

"So far, Topaz, you've told me nothing that I didn't already know." He moved slowly toward the bucket of coals, gripped the handle of the poker.

"You touch me with that thing and, I swear, I will never tell you *anything* that could help you. I swear to God, one burn—"

"That's up to you, isn't it?" He pulled the poker from the coals. Its tip was glowing cherry red. "When does he plan to attack?"

"It was supposed to have been tonight," she said. "But he won't if he knows I'm here. At least, I think he won't."

He was still moving closer, still studying the tip of the poker. "And how was he planning to attack?"

She blinked rapidly, tried to look away from the poker, but couldn't. "I—I don't know."

He lowered his head as if he were sad, shook it

slowly, and moved the poker toward her face, closer and closer, until she could feel the heat searing her skin, even from an inch away.

"All right," she said quickly. The poker's progress stopped, but still it hovered near, too hot. "He hadn't decided yet, but he was leaning toward burning the place while you all rested."

"And how would he manage that? He has to sleep by day, too."

She would be damned before she would mention Roxy. The mortal was the most vulnerable member of the entire group. "He mentioned using some kind of timing device."

He nodded slowly and drew the poker away, but only a little. "Why did you want to warn Jack?"

"I—I c-can't—"

"Why?" He moved the poker closer again. "He stole from you, betrayed you."

"I know. But I—" Her head fell, eyes on her lap. "I still love him," she whispered.

"That's quite an admission."

"That's quite a hot poker," she shot back.

"One more thing, just one more, and then we'll see. And this, my little one, this will tell me all I need to know about your motives. Where are Reaper and your other friends staying?"

She couldn't betray them, not like this. Not when it might mean their lives. If this man knew where they were, he would annihilate them. He would destroy them. As irritating as they were—and as much as she hated to admit it—she cared about them. All of them.

"Hold her head still," Gregor ordered.

And before she could react, huge, meaty hands clapped to either side of her head, smashing her ears, squeezing to the point of pain. Her face tipped up at the whim of those hands, and the poker touched her cheek.

She screamed in pain, even though the red-hot iron only grazed her skin. She could have burst into flames, but didn't. Instead she felt her flesh searing, smelled it, heard the snakelike hiss as glowing metal brushed across her cheek for the space of an instant. It didn't matter. Nothing hurt like a burn, and no one felt pain more acutely than a vampire.

Her agonized scream died away as the drone released his grip on her, and her head sagged forward.

"Where are they staying?" Gregor asked again.

"Nowhere." The word emerged on a whimper of pain. God, it hurt. "Please, please, put something cold on my face."

"Where are they staying?"

"I told you, nowhere. We've just been finding shelter wherever we can at dawn. Sometimes it's in the woods, sometimes an abandoned barn." She gritted her teeth as waves of hurt crashed against her nerve endings, causing her to shiver all over.

"Again," Gregor commanded.

The vamp behind her clamped her head again, and Gregor lifted the poker. But suddenly, the door at the top of the stairs burst open, and Jack leapt from the top of the staircase to the floor, nailing Gregor with two fists clamped together. Gregor stumbled, almost went over sideways but managed to catch himself, and just

then a small missile made of copper fur with a white
tip seemed to fly from nowhere. When she could focus,
Topaz realized it was an animal, a fox, and it had its little jaws clamped around Gregor's wrist. The poker he'd
been holding clattered to the floor, and he dropped to
his knees, howling in pain.

Topaz gazed up at Jack, unable to take her eyes off
him. Her relief, her joy at him actually showing up to
help her, was so overblown that it even overwhelmed
the excruciating pain.

He wasn't looking at her, though; he was looking at
the fox, and Topaz realized he was speaking to it, mentally. She could tell by the intent look in his eyes, by his
focus. But he was blocking so no one else would hear.
She shot a look at the fox, which seemed for all the
world to be listening intently, because it stared at him,
ears perked forward, then spun, flicked its tail and shot
out of the room like a bolt of lightning. Topaz glimpsed
a crack in the stone wall, through which the animal vanished.

And even before she could begin to make sense of
any of it, Gregor was on his feet, and two of the goons
had Jack by the arms.

He didn't fight them, just smiled and shook his head.
"You can let go, or I can rip you apart. Your call." Then
he glanced at Gregor, who was brushing the dust from
his pants and scowling. "You're already short a few
goons, Gregor. You really want to lose two more?"

"I can make others," Gregor said, but he nodded at
the drones. They released Jack, who straightened his
shirtsleeves.

"Care to explain yourself before I kill you?" Gregor asked.

"What's to explain?"

Gregor grunted, but said nothing.

"She came here to warn us. And you respond by torturing her?"

"I never claimed to be a nice guy," Gregor said.

"No, but at least a loyal one. I've been your right hand. Is this how you repay me? By marking up my woman?"

"*Your* woman?"

"*My* woman. She risked everything to warn me. That tells me she can be trusted, and if you were less than an idiot, it would tell you the same."

"All she needs to do to prove herself to me is tell me where Reaper and his band are staying. If she's really on our side, she'll tell us. If not, she's an enemy and will be dealt with as such."

Jack glanced at Topaz. She saw his gaze move to the mark on her cheek, saw him flinch and quickly hide it, and then his eyes met hers, and he spoke to her alone. *Tell him.*

Never!

Vixen will warn them. She's on her way to do just that, even now, I promise you, they'll be out before he can get to them.

Vixen? Topaz blinked at him, then quickly looked away, because Gregor was looking at them and maybe noticing the exchange. If he wasn't now, he would soon.

"I'm out of patience. Jack, if you can't stand to watch, you'll just have to leave."

"Tell him, Topaz. For God's sake, tell him."

She lowered her head, closed her eyes, wondered

when the hell Jack had been able to converse with Vixen, and what the hell had been up with that little fox, and—

And then she paused, her eyes going wide. Fox. Vixen. What the hell?

"Bring me an ax," Gregor commanded.

Topaz brought her head up sharply.

I swear to you, they'll be warned, Jack's voice whispered in her mind.

She sent him a look, then slid her gaze toward Gregor's. "There's an antebellum manor house on a former plantation known as Mariposa—five miles due east of here."

He lifted his brows. "I know it." Then he smiled. "Oh, I know what you're thinking, pretty one. You're thinking you could warn them, mentally, from here just as soon as I leave you alone long enough. But you can't. We've taken precautions. This place is a dead zone. You can't send thoughts through its walls."

"How…how is that possible?"

He sent her a look that said she was an idiot if she thought he would tell her that. Then he nodded to the drones. "Toss her back into the cell."

"Gregor," Jack snapped. "It's enough. I told you she's mine. She's coming upstairs with me. Or I can take her and leave. Your choice."

"We still don't know if we can trust her."

"I'll take responsibility for that," Jack said. "I'll keep her in line. Watch her."

Gregor narrowed his eyes. "She's our only leverage to get Vixen and Briar back."

"Within forty-eight hours, Reaper will be begging you to take Briar back. And Vixen's no great loss."

"Bull. You saw what she did just now. With her abilities, she could be an asset like nothing else."

"Could be, but won't be. She hates you, Gregor, and she'd rather die in captivity than help you. Take my advice. Settle for Briar. Let the little shape-shifter go."

Shape-shifter, Topaz thought. Holy God.

Gregor stood silent for a long moment; then he finally sighed and nodded. "Untie her. Take her where you want, just don't leave the premises with her and don't let her out of your sight. She's your responsibility, Jack. You fuck up, you die. Right after she does."

"The depth of your caring for me is overwhelming," Jack said. "I swear, I'm going to cry if you keep on with the sentimental bullshit."

"Don't even *think* of betraying me, Jack. I'm not one of your marks. You can't con me."

"Wouldn't even think of trying," Jack said. Then he knelt in front of Topaz, putting his back to Gregor. He bent to untie her ankle and ran his hands over her calf in the process, and though she knew it was probably all for show, for Gregor's sake, damn, it made her shiver all over, just the same.

"I've missed you," he told her. "I hate to admit it, but I have."

"I've…missed you, too," she whispered. It hurt to say it, because it was true. And she knew that in his case it was only a line, spoken by an actor. He was the best actor she'd ever seen.

She had to remember that. He was running a con.

Maybe not on her, this time, but she was definitely a part of it. No, this time it was Gregor he was conning, though she wasn't entirely certain why, what he stood to gain from it. There had to be something though. Jack never did anything unless there was something in it for him.

Gregor left, stomping up the stairs to the main part of the house. The drones faded away, as well, and the minute they did, those fingers tenderly caressing her flesh went all business. Jack quickly untied the other leg, then moved behind her to release her hands.

"How bad is the pain?"

"Excruciating," she said, and she wasn't referring entirely to the physical pain of the burn on her face. It was the pain of having to sit there and bear his pretending while hating him, while wishing it was real, while loving him, while wishing he was dead.

Her hands were free. He came around in front of her again, scooped her up and carried her to the stairs.

"You don't have to—"

"It's nothing."

"There's no one here watching you, Jack," she reminded him.

"You can never be too sure about that. Besides, there will be witnesses upstairs. Always are."

She relaxed into his arms, let her head fall against his chest. She was too weak from pain to stand on pride. "What will Gregor do now?"

Jack glanced down at her face, and his eyes seemed to get stuck there for a moment as he strode up the cellar stairs. "My guess is he'll go check out your friends' headquarters, see if you were telling the truth. Don't worry, though, they'll be gone by then. Vixen's probably warning them even as we speak."

"That was Vixen, that little fox?" she asked. "God, Jack, how can that be?"

"It's a great story. I'll tell you in bed, all right?"

She shot her gaze to his again and kept it there as he carried her through the mansion. She probably should have paid attention to the layout of the place, to where the exits were, to what other people they passed on the way. But her observation was limited to noting the ceiling above his head, the glittering crystal chandeliers, the lamps mounted on the walls that resembled old-fashioned gaslights, but which were, in fact, electric.

She noticed that his steps were muffled in some places and guessed the floors were carpeted. She heard the click of his shoes in other rooms and presumed marble or tile or granite.

But mostly, she noticed his eyes. His hair. His face, so beloved to her. And she remembered vividly staring up at it, while he lay on top of her, or down into it when she lay on top of him, making love, time after time.

And she hoped to God he wasn't just teasing about taking her to bed. Because she wanted him. She always had.

16

───▶ ─◀───

Vixen raced all the way back to the secluded spot she'd chosen earlier, and then shifted back into her normal form. She was exhausted, but slightly less than she might have been, thanks to the substantial sips she'd had of Gregor's blood.

It was evil blood, but powerful enough to help her through the struggle of shifting. The process had always drained her—much more so since she'd become a vampire. But it was less exhausting tonight. And maybe, she thought, Gregor's blood was only part of the reason. Part of it was surely her own all-too-human emotions. She was angry, furious at Gregor for inflicting pain on Topaz. She was frightened for Topaz's safety. She was desperate to get back to the mansion to warn Seth—to warn everyone that Topaz would have to reveal their whereabouts. Maybe she already had. Maybe Gregor and his band of evil vampires were on their way to raze the place, even now. Maybe she would be too late.

All of these things drove her, so that she shifted far more quickly than she normally would have, and then threw her clothes on in a rush and raced through the for-

est back to the mansion, praying all the while that she
would make it in time, and fearing what she might find
awaiting her if she didn't.

The image of Seth, dead or dying, lifeless eyes staring up at her, haunted her mind and propelled her ever
faster through the night. Until, finally, she arrived at the
plantation house and sensed that beyond the doors, behind the walls, all was well. Relief washed over her,
nearly leaving her limp. So much so that she paused
there in the gravel-lined drive and lowered her head into
her hands with the sheer magnitude of the feeling.

Then hands closed on her shoulders, gently, comfort-
ingly. "What happened? Are you all right?"

She lifted her head and stared into Seth's worried
eyes as they probed hers. It was genuine fear she felt
wafting from him, fear…for her.

"Did they hurt you again, Vixen? I swear to Christ,
if they hurt you I'll—"

"No. No, no one hurt me." She had hurt *them*,
though. With a secretive smile, she recalled sinking her
teeth into Gregor's arm and hoped she'd reached the
bone. And then she reminded herself of the urgency
with which she'd fled that place. "We have to leave
here."

"What? What happened?"

She looked past him for the others, but no one was
in sight. It was only Seth, then, who'd waited for her
all the way at the end of the drive. Waited and worried.
For some reason the knowledge made her feel warm
inside.

"Let's go inside. We have to tell the others."

He nodded, not pressing her further, and walked with her up the gravel driveway toward the towering front doors. As they walked, he closed his hand around hers, interlocking fingers, squeezing tight. She glanced down at their joined hands and felt that they symbolized something beyond just physical contact. It was a possessive gesture, but an intimate, caring and protective one all at the same time.

She liked it, she decided.

They entered the house, and the others crowded around her before she even got through the entry hall. Roxy was barking questions about whether Topaz was all right. Reaper wanted to know what she'd seen and when she'd seen it. Briar was howling from the room above, but Vixen paid no attention to what that one was saying. She held up her hands for silence, then kept her voice low, her thoughts guarded, as she spoke.

"First, none of this must be revealed to *that* one," she said, with a look toward the ceiling to indicate that she meant the wild thing on the second floor.

"Of course not," Seth said, shooting a look at the other two. They both nodded in confirmation.

Vixen nodded, too, then swallowed and tried to think where to begin. "We have to leave this place."

Reaper lifted his brows. "Topaz told them where we were staying?"

"She hadn't when I left, but I imagine she has by now."

He looked disgusted. "I can't believe she would—"

"Gregor held a hot poker to her face, Reaper. He burned her."

Roxy turned her head away as one hand flew to her mouth. Seth swore under his breath and clenched his fists. Reaper lifted his gaze slowly, and there was, Vixen swore, murder in his eyes.

"Then Jack attacked Gregor, knocked him to the floor and kicked the poker away."

"Jack Heart? Gregor's right-hand man?"

"I've never believed Jack to be anyone's man, besides his own. He tried to convince Gregor that Topaz had come there to join them and to give information, and that torturing her wasn't necessary. But Gregor insisted she had to prove herself by telling him where we're staying."

"And she *did?*" Seth asked.

"No, and that's when he burned her."

Reaper swore under his breath.

"Jack spoke to me mentally. Told me to get back here and warn you, that Topaz *had* to betray us or face a slow and cruel death, and that he was going to convince her to cooperate, for her own sake."

Reaper nodded slowly, and Vixen couldn't read his thoughts on the matter. They were guarded.

"We have to go," she insisted. "Gregor won't waste any time giving us a chance to elude him. He's coming, Reaper."

"All right. Grab what we'll need, and anything that might give them information we don't want them to have. Roxy, take the van. Seth will ride with you. Vixen, you ride with me in the Mustang."

Seth started to object, but Reaper shot him a look full of meaning. Vixen didn't understand it, and she shiv-

ered a little at the thought of riding with Reaper. He was
a powerful man, dark and tormented, and, she'd sensed
from the start, a dangerous one.

They made quick work of gathering their belongings
and trooping out to the garage. Reaper tranquilized
Briar again, though he was reluctant to do so, and bound
her, then carried her out to the garage. He moved toward the Mustang, where Vixen stood waiting.

"Will you get the door for me?" Reaper asked.

Arms crossing over her chest, she shook her head.

Reaper frowned.

"If you insist on me riding with you, that's fine," she
told him. "But I will *not* ride in the same vehicle with
her, drugged or not."

He looked down at the woman he carried, then
sighed and nodded. Then he turned and carried her to
the van. Seth opened the door for him, and Reaper laid
Briar, unconscious, onto the rear seat.

Vixen reached for the passenger door of the Mustang, but before she got it open, Seth came to her and
put his hands on her shoulders.

"He only wants to speak with you alone, Vixen.
There's nothing to be scared of."

"Then why am I afraid?" she asked in a whisper.

"A lot of people are afraid of things when they
shouldn't be."

She shook her head slowly. "Not me. I'm not the
kind who feels fear without cause, Seth. It's instinctive,
a survival mechanism. And it's never let me down
before."

"Look, as soon as he seems to be finished with whatever it is he wants to discuss, just tell him you want to ride with me. Ask him to pull over so we can put Briar in with him, all right?"

She nodded. "All right."

"You sure?"

She tipped her head to one side. "Why are you so protective of me, Seth?"

He smiled a little, but it died when he saw in her face that it was a serious question, not a teasing one. "Because I care about you, Vixen."

"Care," she repeated, turning over the word's meaning in her mind. "But you care about all of us, don't you?"

"Of course I do. But it's…it's different with you."

"How is it different?" She searched his eyes, really wanting to know the answer.

He seemed to hunt for words, but before he found them, Reaper was clapping Vixen on the shoulder. "Time to go. Don't worry, I'll have you back with Seth in no time. I just want a private word, okay?"

She turned, nodded, and felt that her instincts were pointing toward risk, rather than impending doom.

Seth touched her chin, turning her face to his again, and then he leaned close and pressed his lips to hers for just a moment.

"See you soon," he promised.

"Yes. Soon."

Then he left her and got into the van, while Reaper reached past her to open the passenger door of the Mustang. She got in. He went around and climbed behind the wheel, and moments later the engine roared to life and they were leaving the plantation far behind them.

"Torch it."

Immediately a dozen of Gregor's drones surged forward with their tools in hand: cans of gasoline, matches and lighters, fuel-soaked rags and too few brains to realize they could go up in flames just as easily as the stately plantation house could. Or maybe they realized it and had too few brains to care.

Jack watched them, saying nothing, though he thought it was a crying shame to burn such a valuable piece of real estate. There was no reason whatsoever, besides Gregor's temper. Not a single member of Reaper's gang was inside.

Then again, he figured the drones had probably trashed the place anyway, when they'd been sent in to search. Gregor hadn't sensed his enemies within, but he'd already learned how adept Reaper was at blocking his essence.

Jack had never seen Gregor quite as furious as he'd been when the drones returned to report the place empty. Abandoned.

"How do you suppose they knew?" Gregor turned to face Jack as he asked the question. The look in his eyes made it feel more like an accusation, though.

Jack squared his shoulders and looked Gregor squarely in the eye as he answered. "You know the answer to that as well as I do. You saw the fox—up close and personal, as I remember it."

"Yes, but I've since decided it was just a fox. It wasn't Vixen."

Jack was struck mute for a second. Was the boss truly that dense? "What other fox would be lurking around the place, attacking when you tried to torture one of Vixen's rescuers? You think that was random?"

"There was no essence. No sign of vampiric presence, and I would have felt it."

"She could have been blocking," Jack countered.

"She didn't even know she couldn't go out in sunlight until you told her, Jack. We transformed her, we didn't teach her anything."

"Perhaps Reaper has."

"She was right on top of me. There's no way she could have learned to block *that* well in so short a time."

Jack shrugged. "Maybe, when she's a fox, she's not exactly a vampire."

"Don't be stupid."

Jack didn't think he was the one being stupid, but he hesitated to say so just then. Gregor was in a murderous mood, and Jack needed to stay on his good side until he got a better feeling for which way the wind was blowing. He didn't owe any particular loyalty to Gregor. His only loyalty was to himself. He could play any role in any situation, convince anyone of anything he chose. His intent, always, was to be on the winning side, the side most profitable to him—and, he supposed, the side most likely to ensure his continued survival.

He hadn't decided just yet which side that would be.

"It wasn't Vixen," Gregor said again. "Though I

suppose she could have sent some animal to act on her behalf."

Jack blinked, but bit back his comment. That Gregor thought it impossible she could fail to emit the essence of the undead in fox form, but entirely rational to think she could command other wildlife— Damn, the man was deluded.

Or maybe he was fishing. Looking for a reason to lay this at Jack's feet, or, worse, at Topaz's.

No, wait, that wouldn't be worse, that would be better. Slightly better. Because he only looked out for number one. Odd how he'd forgotten that for a moment.

Flames were lighting the night now. Every few yards, near the base of the mansion, flames leapt to life. And there were several more on top of the wide staircase near the front door. The drones who had set them were already heading back toward Jack and Gregor, while the ones who'd gone inside to set the fires there were taking a bit longer. Jack didn't suppose it had occurred to the idiots outside to let the ones inside get clear before lighting up the outer walls.

Gregor was still watching him, awaiting some kind of response. He decided not to dance around it but to meet the accusation head-on. "It certainly wasn't me. And it wasn't Topaz, I guarantee you that."

"And just how can you be so sure?"

"Come on, Gregor, do you need the details? I've *been* with the woman. I've shared blood with her. You know what that does to the psychic connection between vampires."

"Not to mention the bond."

Jack shrugged that off as if it were of little consequence. "I can read her. Even when she's blocking, I can read her. I would have known if she'd been trying to warn Reaper and the others."

"Perhaps," Gregor said. "But would you have told me?"

Jack tipped his head back slightly. "Ah, now I see your point. I suppose, in your position, I'd wonder the same thing. So I won't swear my loyalty or beg for your trust based on our past camaraderie. If you're doubting me, none of that would convince you, anyway."

"True."

"But let's not forget your own precautions, Gregor. You've made our headquarters into the vampiric version of a soundproof room. Psychic messages can't seem to get in or out. And I have to admit, I'm dying to know the secret."

Gregor looked at him sharply. "Then you'll die not knowing. I don't give away anything that might prove to be an advantage."

"The strategy of a true warrior," Jack said, kissing up just a little. "But even the greatest general shares secrets with his captains during times of battle, my friend."

"Not this one. You never know when the two of us might be on opposing sides of the battlefield."

"Right. Like that's going to happen."

"It's not impossible."

"Don't worry, Gregor. I know on which side my proverbial bread is buttered."

"Good. Then tell me again that your girlfriend had nothing to do with warning her people."

"I guarantee you, she didn't. And they are not her people. Not anymore. We are. She's loyal, Gregor."

"To me? After I burned her pretty cheek? I seriously doubt that—which is why I left her locked in your room under heavy guard while we tended to this little errand. I have a feeling she'd stake me in my sleep if she could."

"True, she's madder than hell at you. But she's loyal to me. She risked her neck to warn me about Reaper. That tells me all I need to know."

"She's loyal to you. On that we agree. But the question remains, just how loyal are *you* to *me?*"

"I gave you a quarter of a million dollars, even though I was beginning to have…sentiments toward the woman I conned out of it. I walked away and brought you the take. In my estimation, that should buy me some trust." He watched Gregor's face, saw a bit of the doubt beginning to leave his eyes. "Besides, if your theory is correct and Vixen can somehow communicate with animals, wouldn't it make sense to think they can communicate back? Perhaps her furry friend told her that Topaz was being tortured. Anyone with half a brain would take precautions and move themselves, rather than trusting in her ability to withhold information under those conditions. Wouldn't they?"

"Yes. I suppose they would."

Now that Jack had offered an explanation that fit with Gregor's warped theories, the boss man seemed more able to believe him. That was Gregor. He was smart, but he also liked his people to tell him what he wanted to hear, to validate his own theories rather than shooting holes in them by pointing out their flaws. And that was his greatest weakness. His biggest point of vulnerability. The one thing that could probably be used against him successfully.

"We'll figure out where they've gone and strike again," Gregor said. He clapped Jack on the shoulder by way of apology and turned, at last, to survey the progress his drones were making on the mansion.

The ones who'd set the outside walls burning stood in a huddle a few yards away. The walls were engulfed, and just now the idiots who'd gone to torch the place from within began trying to find their way out. It wasn't pretty.

One flaming hulk fell, screaming, from a second-story window, while another burst through the front doors and ran toward them like a walking torch. He was cinder before he made it halfway.

Gregor sighed, shaking his head, then glanced at the group who were safe, and Jack heard him counting mentally. Then he rolled his eyes. "Down six more. I wish I could find a way to make them smarter while still keeping them perfectly obedient."

Jack shrugged. "If I knew how you made them at all, I might have a suggestion or two."

Gregor sent him a look. "You know better."

"Of course I do. So keep them stupid but obedient, then. That's better than smarter but rebellious. You don't want a bunch of independent thinkers on your hands. It's a trade-off, I suppose."

"I suppose you're right." Gregor turned and shouted to the drones, "Back to the mansion. Now."

They trooped back, obeying without question, as they always did.

Jack smiled to himself at the thought of getting back to Topaz. Then he wiped the smile off his face. *Don't start believing in your own con, Jack,* he told himself. *That's the kiss of death.*

17

—◄ ►—

Vixen was afraid Reaper would stop at the first suitable place he found, but she was relieved to find she'd been wrong. He passed by several abandoned houses and barns without even giving them a second glance. She sensed Seth's frustration coming from the van that followed behind them, but she knew Reaper was making the wise decision. You didn't elude a predator by hiding in the first place he would search. You had to put distance between yourself and him. Distance meant safety.

"I wanted you to ride with me, Vixen, so that we could talk a bit in private."

"I know."

Reaper looked at her, and his eyes were narrow, observant and wise from experience. "Will you tell me the secret you're keeping?"

She only blinked at him.

"You've made it quite clear—not just to me, but to everyone now—that you're hiding something from us. Something major, something about yourself and your… nature, I think. For you to be so certain you could get back into Gregor's lair without being detected or caught—and then to actually do it—while refusing to tell us how—"

"It's my secret to keep."

"Yes, I know that. I agree with you, it's just that… you're a part of this team now."

"It's not a team. I heard you tell the others so."

He lowered his chin slightly, not taking his eyes off the road. "This nature of yours could be an asset to us."

"It *is*. It was tonight. It was an asset to you without you needing to know how or why. If it can be again, I promise you, it will."

He licked his lips. "Your logic is tough to argue with."

"Then don't argue with it." She faced him and smiled at the frustration on his face.

To her surprise, he smiled back. "That's the first time you've seemed at ease in my presence."

She nodded. "That's true enough. I'm nervous around you."

"Why is that, Vixen?"

She felt her expression turn serious. "You know why. You're dangerous. You're capable of causing harm and even death to those around you, whether they deserve it or not. I don't understand how or why that's your nature—just as you don't understand the details of mine. But I do sense it, and I always trust my instincts."

He was silent for a moment, driving and, apparently, thinking, his brow furrowed. "If I reveal my secret to the others, will you reveal yours?"

"No. But you should."

"That's hardly a fair trade."

"Isn't it? You could harm them, maybe more so if they don't know your secret. I could help them, whether they know *my* secret or not. Which seems to you to be more important to reveal?"

He lowered his gaze, and in the tension of his jaw and in his aura, she sensed a hint of anger. "I've told them I could be dangerous to them. They all carry a tranquilizer weapon that will render me harmless should I turn into a threat."

"It's beyond your control, then? Your nature?"

"Yes. I'm afraid so."

She thought about that for a moment, then nodded slowly. "I'm better off, I suppose. At least I only change when I want to."

"Change?"

She met his eyes, then shook her head slowly from side to side. "Can we switch vehicles now? I'm eager to be with Seth."

"Just one more thing, and then we'll pull over. I'm not entirely comfortable with Roxy and Seth trying to handle Briar, anyway."

"All right. One more thing, then."

He nodded. "It's Seth. He's…falling in love with you, I think."

She frowned, and searched his face. "I know about love, of course, but I can't say that I understand it. Is it bad? For him to feel that way toward me?"

"Well, that depends on whether you feel the same way toward him."

"I don't understand."

He sighed, and drummed his fingers on the steering

wheel. "I'm not good at this, being male. But…if you love someone and they love you back, it's the best feeling in the world. The best, most satisfying thing you could imagine. But if you love someone and they *don't* love you— Well, I don't think there are too many situations more painful—emotionally painful, that is, not physically. Do you understand?"

"Emotionally painful. Like being sad, you mean."

"Yes, being so terribly sad it feels as if your heart is broken."

"That *is* very sad."

He smiled a little, and she wasn't sure why. "When you *do* love someone, you tell them things. Things you don't tell anyone else."

Tipping her head to one side, she said, "Are you saying this to convince me to tell Seth my secret, so that he can tell you?"

"If he loves you, he will never repeat your secret to anyone."

She opened her mouth, closed it again, searched the ether with her eyes and finally gave up. "There are too many rules in this love thing."

"They're not rules. They're human nature. Instinctive."

"Not to me. My instinct is to mate and leave it at that." He seemed to have something caught in his throat for a moment, and while he coughed and tried to clear it, she added, "Besides, we're *not* human."

"Doesn't matter, it all applies. If anything, vampires feel love and sadness and every other emotion even *more* keenly than humans do. Just the way we feel physical sensations more keenly."

She pursed her lips, nodded. "What if knowing my secret makes him stop loving me?"

"I don't think that could happen, Vixen. I really don't. He's not a shallow person. He's actually pretty damn deep."

"Shallow, deep. It doesn't matter. He would change his mind. I know he would."

"I guess you have to trust your gut on that, then. But for the record, I disagree."

She sighed, thought some more. "How does a person know if what they feel for someone is love? Are there rules for that, too?"

"I think it's probably different for different people. And with you and Seth, there are added complications that make it even harder."

She looked at him, frowning.

Reaper shrugged. "Well, there was already a bond between you. A natural connection that's probably embedded in your DNA. But beyond that, you've, uh, well, you've shared blood. That makes the bond even stronger."

"Oh," she said, nodding. "I see."

"But some things about being in love seem to be pretty universal," he went on. "You'd rather spend time with that person than anyone else. You care more for them than anyone else. You want to see them happy, to *make* them happy, and it becomes as important to you as your own happiness, even intertwined with your own. You know?"

She tilted her head, thinking she felt all those things for Seth, but hesitant to admit to any of them. "I'll give the idea some thought. A lot of thought," she told him.

Then she turned to him and smiled. "Thank you. You can be...very kind."

"Yeah, well...don't spread it around."

"So can we stop now?"

He nodded. "Yes. I'm pulling over right now."

He angled the car toward the side of the road and slowed down. Within a few seconds they were coming to a gradual stop, and Vixen turned to look behind them, then watched as the van came to a halt, as well.

She opened her door and got out, and Reaper got out his side. They met in the back and walked side by side toward the van. She glanced up at him. "It was wise of you to pass by all those places where we might have holed up. You're right to put distance between us and our enemies."

"I'm glad you approve."

She paused. "If you think I can help you with your... problem—you know, the one you won't explain—I hope you'll tell me. I...I'd like to help you, if I could."

"I'm afraid it's beyond even your powers, Vixen. But thank you for the sentiment."

She lowered her head, then lifted it again, and quickly snapped her arms around his neck and hugged him hard. "I'm glad we talked. I like you better now that I know you don't *mean* to be evil."

He seemed too stunned to react, and even before he could have, she pulled away and ran to the van.

When Reaper opened the door and reached for her, Briar hissed like a cat about to lash out. It was enough to make him stop with his hand a few inches from her shoulder. Then he shot a look toward the middle row of seats, where Seth sat. "Why isn't she still unconscious?"

"Because I figured if you wanted to kill her, she'd have been dead by now," Seth said. "You said yourself, no one knows how much of that shit a vampire can handle. So when she started to come around this time, I let it be." He shrugged. "She's been drifting in and out. Mostly quiet, so far."

"Only because...I don't have the strength to...to take on all of you at once," Briar said. Her voice was soft and deep, and it had a raspy quality to it like silk on velvet. It was the first time she'd spoken since they'd taken her, other than to scream, swear, threaten and demand. "Yet."

"Can you walk?" Reaper asked.

She looked at him from the corners of her half-lidded eyes. "I can if you're...taking me back to Gregor."

"I'm only taking you over there." He helped her into a sitting position and pointed. She turned to face front and looked through the windshield at the Mustang, with its running lights glowing in the night. "You're riding with me."

"Afraid I'll kill your...misfits?"

"Afraid you'll force them to drug you again. And as Seth pointed out, we have no idea how much more of that your body can handle." He closed the distance between his hand and her arm. She jerked away from his touch. "Come with me, Briar. I don't have time to play games with you. You're getting into that Mustang one way or the other, and we both know it. I won't hesitate to drug you again if you force the issue. I don't have half the ethical issues my friend Seth has."

"I don't want your hands on me."

He tipped his head a little in acknowledgement and sent her a single thought. *Liar.* Her eyes widened slightly, and he knew she'd heard him. Aloud, he only said, "Then they won't be. Let's go."

"Bastard," she muttered, gripping the sides of the van to pull herself out and down to the pavement. He moved aside to let her, then followed, fully expecting her to break into a run at any moment.

She didn't. He saw her looking for markers, though, probably so that she could broadcast her thoughts to Gregor, telling him where they were.

"I chose a spot without a road sign in sight, Briar. You're not going to be able to tell him where we are that way. Besides, you probably can't get through to Gregor anyway."

"Of course I can."

"No. He's put some kind of a field around the mansion. From what I've observed, it blocks psychic communication, both incoming and outgoing."

She frowned. "He doesn't know how to do anything like that. If the mansion is a dead zone, it's always been that way. Some natural phenomenon or other."

"How can you be so sure?"

"Because if Gregor knew how to do that sort of thing, he would have told me."

"Really." The skepticism in his voice was obvious. They reached the car, and he opened the passenger door for her. She glared at him, but got in. Leaning in over her, he flipped open the glove compartment and pulled out a blindfold—one of those Roxy had brought along. It was black on one side, leopard print on the other, and bore a tag with the brand name Slap & Tickle and its logo, a whip crossed with a feather. He didn't even want to think about what Roxy had been doing in that particular shop, or whether this blindfold had seen a lot of use.

Briar drew back. "I'll just take it off."

"Then I'll inject you. Your call." And without waiting, he slid the elastic band over her face, print side in, because he didn't want to have to look at it. His fingers brushed through her hair, and he tried to ignore its silken texture as he settled the blindfold in place, then closed her door. He went around to the driver's side, got in and drove.

Roxy pulled out onto the road behind him.

"So Gregor tells you everything, then?" Reaper asked, picking up the thread of their earlier conversation.

"Important things, yes."

"Then you know how he created that army of drones?"

She pursed her lips. He didn't like not being able to see her eyes, trying to read them, but it was necessary. "I wouldn't tell you if I did."

"I didn't ask you to tell me. I asked you if you knew."

She didn't answer.

"So there's another important thing he neglected to tell you." He drew a breath, certain from her pursed lips that she wasn't going to say a word. "I've heard of vampires who make slaves for themselves. They drain their victims, then give them only a small amount of their own blood, rather than doing a full exchange. The result is a vampire very much like Gregor's drones, mentally. Physically, though, they're as weak as kittens. Gregor's drones are powerful."

"He chooses powerful victims with less-than-average intelligence levels."

"That alone wouldn't be enough to account for it, though," Reaper told her. She was young, he knew that. She probably didn't know a hell of a lot about her own nature. Possibly only what Gregor wanted her to know.

He spotted a sprawling warehouse in the distance, far off to the left, and sent out his senses to investigate. The place gave off no indication of human presence. Of course, it was the dead of night. Still, it was worth checking out. He picked out the winding shape of a side road that led to it, but couldn't see where that road connected with this one. So he kept driving until he found a road that went to the left, took it, and then another, until eventually, he located the place.

He pulled the Mustang to a stop and shut it off, looking around without yet getting out. There were rusty piles of scrap metal, old barrels, uneven stacks of wooden pallets. Some of the windows in the giant teal-colored steel building were broken. Others were boarded up. No Trespassing signs hung crookedly in two places along the front, their colors faded. A third sign lay on the ground, where weeds were growing in the doorway.

No one had been using the place for quite some time.

"Why have we stopped?" Briar asked, her tone impatient.

"Because we've found our place."

"Good. I can start trying to contact Gregor, then. He'll home in on my position and destroy you all."

He knew she would do just that, and that it was only a matter of time before Gregor stepped outside the walls of that radio-silenced mansion and heard her signal. "Gregor has offered to trade Topaz back to us in exchange for you and Vixen. And I'm considering it. But if he attacks before that, I'll never give you back to him, even if I have to kill you to ensure it. I promise you that."

"If he attacks you, you won't survive."

He reached to her, ignored the way she flinched away when his hands touched her head, but only until she realized he was taking off the blindfold. He removed it, and she blinked, rubbed her eyes and stared at the area around them.

"Do you have any idea who I am, Briar? Have you even heard of me? Has your beloved Gregor told you anything about me?"

She turned toward him, meeting his gaze.

"I'm an executioner. I am a professional killer. It's what I did in life, for the CIA. It's what I do now, for the undead."

She narrowed her eyes on him. "You murder your own kind. And you're proud of that?"

"Only those who need killing, Briar, for the good of the rest of us."

"Oh, and who gets to decide who needs killing? You?"

He frowned, searching her face, wondering just how little she could possibly know about her own kind. "Rogues need killing. There's no choice in that." The confusion in her eyes told him that she didn't even understand what the term meant.

"Briar, vampires do not just go around killing mortals at will and leaving bodies to be found. It's forbidden among us. We feed from blood banks, mostly. Some prefer living blood, but there are ways to do that without committing murder."

"Right. Take just a little and leave them to tell the tale. How is that preferable to leaving a body lying in the street to be found? At least the body can't talk."

"You leave them with the memory of an erotic dream. Nothing more. They never know."

"How?"

"With the power of your mind, Briar. You focus, you command them, and they obey. If you tell them to remember it as a dream, they do."

She lowered her eyes. "And the marks in their throats?" Her question was a mere whisper.

"Vanish the moment they are touched by the sun. Gregor didn't teach you these things?"

She didn't confirm or deny it. "So other vampires… never kill?"

"Oh, some do. They take serial killers, rapists or child abusers. They're performing a service, really. But even they take care to dispose of the bodies where they will never be found."

"Because if they're dead, then the marks in their throats don't heal?"

"Exactly. And because a body drained of its blood causes a lot of questions. We do not wish for the world of man to know about our existence. Some do already, and it's caused nothing but problems—they tend to want to hunt us down and exterminate us."

"Humans are stupid."

"Why would that be stupid? If they think we're all like Gregor and his band, it would be stupid of them *not* to try to eliminate our kind before we eliminate theirs."

She turned, reached for her car door and opened it.

He got out his side, noticing at last that the others were already walking around the place, trying doors, checking things out. He joined Briar in front of the car, then walked beside her toward the abandoned warehouse.

"When a vampire kills at will, kills innocents, leaves evidence behind," he told her, "he is known among our kind as a rogue, and for the good of all of us, he is hunted down and destroyed. It's how we survive."

"And Gregor is a rogue," she said softly.

"Gregor is the most dangerous, deadly rogue in the history of our kind, so far as I know it."

She looked him squarely in the eye. "You're a very good liar, Reaper. But I'm not an idiot."

"You don't believe me?"

She held his gaze steady, shaking her head side to side, very slowly. "We are predators. They are our prey. It's the natural order. And if you think I will believe that an entire race of predators, aside from a few so-called rogues, has made an agreement not to take the prey nature has provided out of some idiotic sense of morality, then you are wrong. But it was a lovely story, all the same. You should write fiction."

And with that, she turned, lifted a foot and kicked in the white door of the warehouse. "You're vampires!" she shouted at the others. "If you want to go in, then stop messing around trying locks and just go in."

18

— ⬤ —

Jack was heading down the vaulted second-floor corridor, on his way back to his own room and the woman who waited for him there. He'd accompanied his boss most of the night, in search of the enemy, but without luck. Fortunately, there was still enough darkness left to make the most of this opportunity to…renew his acquaintance with Topaz.

Her face flashed in his mind's eye, and he tripped over his feet, then had to stop to get his balance again.

Damn. There hadn't been sex like the sex with her since he'd left her. Or before. Or…ever. If nothing more, he had to admit that much. She was the best. So if she was willing… Who the hell was he kidding? Of course she would be willing. He was Jack Heart, for God's sake. King of cons. Talking people into doing things he wanted them to do was his stock in trade.

He smiled to himself and noted the spring in his step as he moved again along the hallway. But then he stopped short, because of what he heard.

"Yes, sir. I know that, but Rivera isn't alone. He has a band, of sorts, helping him. And he's moved them all to a new location, along with two of my own recruits, taken against their will."

Jack frowned, because he had never heard Gregor address anyone as *sir.* The boss's tone was uncharacteristically respectful, too. Almost apologetic. And who the hell was *Rivera?*

"I *will* find him. I plan to arrange a prisoner exchange. By the time I finish with Reaper, the entire vampire community will believe *he's* the one in need of annihilation. The mortal world, as well. He'll be hated, and he'll be hunted. He'll have nowhere to turn, and his little gang will be history—dead, all of them. At his hands. And *then* he'll be at my mercy."

Jack frowned. Just how the hell did Gregor plan to fulfill such huge promises? And what made him think he could convince Reaper to kill his own crew? He was one of those moral vampires, from what Jack had seen. One of those ethical saps who did what was right. So Reaper's real name was Rivera, huh? Interesting.

"Yes, sir, of course I intend to bring him to you once I have him. That goes without saying. I do need a couple of things from your end, however." There was a pause. "Nothing major. But we've suffered some losses here. I need you to send me more drones."

So Gregor wasn't making the drones himself, then? Hell, this had just gotten pretty interesting. If Gregor wasn't making them, then who was? And how?

"A dozen should do. And there's one other thing. You told me you'd give it to me when I needed it, and that time has come, sir. I need you to give me his triggers."

Triggers? What the hell…

"Yes, sir. I won't use them unless absolutely necessary. Good. No, let me grab a pen." Jack heard the sounds of drawers opening as he stood just outside the slightly open door to Gregor's suite. "I'm ready. What's the word that activates him?"

Jack heard the pen scratching across the surface of a pad.

"And to deactivate?"

Again with the scratching.

"Yes, sir. Yes, I understand. I'll report in just as soon as it's over. Thank you, sir." The telephone hit its cradle.

Jack straightened away from the door, even as he felt Gregor's attention turning his way. Too late to walk away. Gregor knew he was there. Nothing left but to try to act as if he had only just arrived. He lifted a hand, knocked on the door and tried for all the world to act as if he hadn't heard a damned thing.

Gregor yanked the door wider and stood staring at him, his eyes so full of suspicion that Jack felt an icy finger slide over his spine. He suppressed a shiver and pasted a big grin on his face. A grin he felt fading as he saw Gregor's displeasure and heard his gruff excuse for a greeting.

"What the hell do you want?"

"Nothing. Just wanted to see you before heading to bed. Is anything wrong?" He glanced past Gregor. The desk stood there, with the notepad on it, pen beside it, top page already ripped off. What Jack wouldn't have given for a look at whatever words Gregor had scribbled there. Beside the desk was a birdcage, hanging from its floor stand, and a poor imprisoned rat, Gregor's pet, on its hind legs inside. It stared out at Jack with hate in its beady eyes.

"What, you mean, *besides* the fact that Reaper and his band of do-gooders eluded us yet again? *Besides* the fact that they still have Briar and Vixen, and *besides* the fact that we lost a dozen drones in that fire tonight?"

"Yeah," Jack said with a wink. "Besides all that."

Gregor scowled.

"Sorry. I know it's not funny. So what's our plan, boss? What do we do next?"

Gregor lifted his brows and looked at Jack. He seemed to give his words some thought before he spoke. "I'm going to arrange a prisoner exchange. Briar and Vixen for Topaz. They have no way of knowing she's changed sides, after all."

His heart sank a little. "When?" he asked.

"Two hours past sundown."

"Oh." Then he wouldn't have her for very long at all, would he? Damn. And meanwhile, he knew Gregor had a whole hell of a lot going on that he hadn't revealed to his own right-hand man.

A hell of a lot. Which confirmed what he'd begun to suspect. Gregor no longer trusted him. And the journey from not trusting him to staking him out to await the sunrise, or hosing him with a flame thrower, was a very short one.

It was probably getting close to time for Jack to either cut his losses or hedge his bets. He was going to have to change sides and get the hell out of here, or else win back Gregor's trust. Either plan would take a grand gesture of some sort.

"Well, I'm off to bed, then," Jack said. "Good sleep, Gregor."

Gregor grunted a reply and slammed the door.

Jack went about five yards down the hall, then waited, knowing Gregor would emerge. He never went to his rest without first walking the entire house—a touch of OCD, or maybe just a control issue. He liked to make sure everything was in order before he closed his eyes.

As soon as Gregor was gone, Jack slipped into his rooms. He crept past the desk and the caged rat. The damn rodent watched his every move as if planning to report back to Gregor at the first opportunity. Stupid. And impossible, thank the gods. He moved through the sitting room and into the bedroom. Then he crossed to the painting—it was titled "The Offering," and depicted a nude woman bound and lying on a slab of granite, clearly terrified and awaiting God only knew what. Jack pulled on the frame, and it swung out, on hinges.

He paused there, sensing something, someone, another presence in the room.

His gaze was drawn to a large, sheet-draped square in the corner of the room. "Oh, hell," he muttered. Too much. There was too much to do right now, and very little time. He focused, punched in the combination he'd acquired and memorized long ago, and opened the door.

Then he took the stacks of bills that waited inside. There were far more of them there than just the ones he'd contributed. Nonetheless, he took only what he'd given. Half of the five hundred grand he'd taken from

Topaz. Five neatly banded, fat, fragrant stacks of fifty thousand dollars each. He looked around the room and didn't find what he was looking for, then hurried into the adjoining bathroom to grab a towel. He dropped the bills into the towel, knotted it into a bundle, picked it up, closed the safe and righted the painting.

And then he turned to go.

A sound from behind the sheet brought his head around. "I absolutely promise I'll find a way to help you. Hell, I can't do otherwise, now, can I? But it can't be tonight. Soon, though. Very, very soon."

Then he left, closing the door behind him and praying Gregor would never know. Everything in him rebelled against leaving her there. And yet, he couldn't risk giving himself away too soon. He needed to figure out which way the wind was blowing, come up with a story to get himself and Topaz clear of Gregor's wrath, and then come back for her. Doing otherwise would only ensure that they would all end up as munchies for those damned drones.

They sat around Roxy's gas lantern as if they were sitting around a bonfire at summer camp, and Briar hated them. It wasn't a new emotion. She hated most everyone. Always had.

But she wasn't going to rip out their throats or devour their still-beating hearts or even try to escape them tonight. Not tonight. Gregor, the one person she *didn't* hate, had finally stepped outside the mansion's walls long enough to contact her mentally. And even as she'd damn near blown a gasket trying to let him feel where she was being held, he'd interrupted her to tell her to stay put. He'd said he would be meeting Reaper soon, setting up an exchange. He needed her to stay with his enemies for just one more day. There were things he needed her to do. She listened, memorized, tried not to let the inner conversation she was having show on her face, tried to feign interest in the nonsense going on around the lantern's white-gold glow.

"The story goes that Gilgamesh, the greatest king in the history of the land known as Sumer—or, as some call it, Sumeria—was the first vampire," Reaper said.

Vixen, like a child begging for a ghost story before retiring to her girl-scout pup tent, had asked him about the beginning, and he was obliging her.

"What part of the world is that?" Vixen asked.

"Northern Iraq," Seth answered, even though she hadn't addressed the question to him.

"When Gilgamesh's best friend died, the king decided to seek out the only immortal he knew of, the old man of legend who had been the sole survivor of the great flood."

"Noah," Roxy said.

"Exactly, only this was a far earlier version of the story. His Sumerian name was Ziusudra, or, to the Semites, Utnapishtim. So Gilgamesh sought him out, and the old man gave the king the secret to immortality. This was something the gods had forbidden him to do, so, as punishment, he lost the gift himself. The legends say the king lost it, too, that he dropped it into a river, where it was swallowed by a snake. But that's highly symbolic. The truth of the story is that Gilgamesh became the first vampire. But unlike Utnapishtim, who had lived as any ordinary mortal so far as anyone knows, the king had to feed on blood to survive, and he couldn't go out in sunlight. Moreover, becoming a vampire did not give him the ability to bring his friend Enkidu back from the dead."

"But he lived on, yes?" Vixen asked.

"Oh, yes. He's still alive today. He goes by the name of Damien Namtar now. Utnapishtim made one other vampire—a rogue, who came to his cottage on the trail of the king, whom he intended to murder. He forced the old man to give him the gift, as well, and then he killed him and took his young nephew as a slave. He was the first rogue."

"Wow," Vixen said softly. "They were like brothers. The first. Like Cain and Abel."

Briar rolled her eyes, unimpressed and slightly disgusted by the naive one's enthusiasm, but the gesture was lost on the little fox, who tilted her head to one side questioningly. "What about you, Reaper? How did you come to be a vampire?"

"I was working for the CIA. I was on a mission, in Syria, and I was ambushed, shot and left to die. Then this woman showed up."

"Who was she?" Vixen asked. Her face was pale as porcelain in the lamplight, her eyes wide and her attention utterly riveted. Briar tried very hard to remain detached, but even she found herself vaguely interested in the story.

"Her name was Rhiannon. She was originally called Rianikki, and she was the daughter of an actual Egyptian pharaoh. And she never lets anyone forget that fact." Reaper smiled just slightly, and Briar felt something dark rake over the surface of her temper. "I remember opening my eyes and seeing her, like some kind of demonic angel, leaning over me, this endlessly long raven hair touching my face, and she was looking at me with eyes so intense that it felt as if she could see right through me. She asked me if I wanted to live or die. And then she changed me."

"So you were made by a powerful vampiress."

"More powerful than you know. She was made by one even more powerful. You see, that slave boy, the one taken by the first rogue, later came to be known by a name you'll recognize. Dracula. He made Rhiannon. And Rhiannon made me."

"And you made me," Seth muttered, his tone one of awe.

"Oh, for Pete's sake, what difference does it make?" Briar snapped. "Who cares about lineage? It's not like it means anything."

"It means everything, Briar," Reaper said softly, and he turned to her when he spoke, looked deeply into her eyes. "A vampire's strength and powers are based on those of the one who made him, and the one who made them, and so on, back to the beginning." He paused, as if to give her time to think about that. "You were made by Gregor, yes?"

"Yes." She didn't offer any more.

"Why don't you tell us your story, Briar?" Vixen asked. She spoke softly, her voice trembling a little, as if she were still afraid of her.

As well she should be.

"I ran away from my stepfather because he wouldn't stay out of my bed. Lived on the streets, fucked for money so I could buy cocaine and get something to eat now and then, got weak and thin and sick, and probably would have wound up dead sooner or later. But Gregor found me, and changed me and took me in. End of story."

They all nodded, except Vixen. She looked away—unable to stand looking at her, Briar thought. Probably thought she was too good.

"So what's your lineage, Briar?" Reaper asked. "Gregor made you, but who made Gregor?"

"I don't fucking know or care." Briar pushed herself up off the floor. "It'll be light soon. I'm going to find a place to crash."

No one said good-night, or good day, or whatever the fuck they were in the habit of saying, as she walked away. She stopped and turned. "I almost forgot. Gregor sent me a message for you while you were all playing Bible camp."

Reaper shot to his feet, and she smiled, knowing she had his full attention. "Is he on his way, then?"

She shook her head. "Not necessary. He wants a prisoner exchange. You and me, Reaper—alone. To-morrow night, nine o'clock. He picked a public place—probably for your peace of mind. It's a goth bar called The Crypt, in downtown Savannah. I've memorized the address."

Then she turned and walked away to find a dark corner where she could rest away from them. Their goodness made her want to puke.

19

"I don't trust him," Vixen said. She was walking through the warehouse at Seth's insistence. He had hold of her hand, guiding her to where they were going to sleep for the day, though he hadn't told her yet where that was.

"Gregor or Reaper?"

"Gregor." She tilted her head. "Reaper…is dangerous. But he wouldn't betray us. Not deliberately, at least."

"I'm not even sure what that means."

She shrugged. "It could be dangerous tonight. The exchange."

"It's in a public place. That will help."

"No, Seth." She stopped walking and turned to look straight into his eyes. "It makes no difference whatsoever to Gregor. He doesn't care if innocents die, or if his bloodlust is witnessed by mortals. He never has. But Reaper does. Don't you see that doing this in public puts Reaper more at risk, not less? He'll be at a disadvantage from the start, because he'll care about protecting the innocents."

Seth shook his head. "I hadn't thought of that."

"Something is wrong—I feel danger right to the core of me."

"All right. We'll talk to Reaper."

She nodded, started to pull her hand free.

He held tighter. "At sundown, when we rise. There will be time enough then." And he started walking again, tugging her along at his side.

"Where are we going?"

"There," he said. He pointed to the van, which had been parked inside, to keep it from view. It was in a small section of the warehouse, separated from the area where the others had taken up residence. The car was parked beside it. "Roxy said we could sleep in the van, if we wanted."

"Oh."

"You're disappointed?"

One shoulder rose, a half shrug that came automatically. "I used to curl up beside a fallen tree, or beneath a pine, snuggled and warm with the stars overhead. But now I can only sleep by day, and it has to be indoors." Her eyes closed slowly. "I miss…my old life."

"I'm sorry."

"It can never be the same. But I can get some of it back. As soon as this is over, and Gregor is stopped and Topaz is safe, and I know that you'll be safe, too, then…" She let her words trail off as she searched her mind.

"Then…" he asked.

Vixen smiled. "I don't know, exactly. I only know I'll be free again. To do what I want, run wild, and play and explore. I won't be able to sleep in the sunlight, but maybe I can get some of my old life back again. Somehow."

He looked sad then. She tipped her head to one side,

then the other, studying his face. "Why does that make you feel badly?"

"I guess because…you didn't mention me as being a part of those plans of yours."

"Don't be silly, Seth. I can't make your plans for you. Only my own, for me."

They'd reached the back of the van, and she opened the doors. Then she paused to look. Seth had folded up the rear seats, leaving plenty of room for a bed on the floor. There were blankets and pillows spread out, ready and welcoming. She climbed inside and stretched out among the softness. "This is almost as good as being under the stars."

"Is it?"

His earlier mood had been upbeat, even excited. Now he seemed brooding. It wasn't like him.

Laughing, she reached for him, and pulled him so hard that he fell into the nest of blankets with her, landing on top of her. His groin was nestled between her thighs, and his face was close to hers. She felt him growing hard against her, and smiled even more. "Oh, I see how it is. That's what you have in mind, is it?"

"What?" he asked, feigning innocence.

"Sex. Mating."

"Not exactly."

She frowned, disappointment dousing her excited anticipation away. "No? What, then?"

"Lovemaking," he said.

Her smile returned. "But isn't that the same thing?"

"Not by a long shot, Vixen. Tonight I'm going to teach you the difference."

She lifted her eyebrows, and her smile widened. "You mean, we get to do both?"

The look of sadness fled from his face. He smiled, slowly but deeply; it reached his eyes and, she thought, his soul. "Yeah," he said, "we'll do both." Then he slid his hands around the nape of her neck and kissed her. But it was a light, teasing kiss. His lips danced over hers, first upper, then lower, and they almost tickled, their touch was so featherlight.

She parted her own lips, longing for the heat and passion of his earlier kisses. Mouths open, tongues questing, suckling and biting as their bodies strained to press closer, even when they were touching at every possible juncture.

But he didn't give her that. Instead, he kissed slowly, tenderly. His fingers drifted back and forth over her nape, the touch exquisitely gentle and yet incredibly arousing. God, he was killing her.

His kisses moved to her jaw and down to her neck, where he nibbled and sucked, but softly. So softly.

She felt an arousal the likes of which she had never felt before. The bloodlust rose inside her, creating a red haze over her vision. His mouth near her throat was an image, a sensation, that drove her wild. She wanted him to bite down, to drink from her. She wanted to push him down and spring on him and drain him. She wanted him inside her. She wanted all of him.

And yet he held himself above her, not even letting his body's weight rest on her, just gently nibbling, his entire demeanor one of infinite control. Except, perhaps, for the hardness between his legs. He arched his hips against hers in a slow, primal rhythm that spoke of mating.

She was trembling now. She was panting.

"We have more than an hour," he whispered.

"If you make me wait that long, I swear on the undead, Seth, I will rip out your heart."

His eyes, lazily half-lidded before, widened a little at that declaration.

"Please?" she whimpered. "Seth, could we do the mating first, fast and urgently, the way it's meant to be, and save this slow lovemaking for after? If I don't achieve release soon, I think I'll surely die of need."

He smiled then, his features relaxing. "I'm a little eager myself, to be honest."

"Then take me, Seth. Take me now. Make it hard and fast and deep. Please."

The smile died, and his eyes became darker. Passion-glazed, she thought. He looked different. Intense and deep. He reached down to peel his shirt up and over his head as she watched.

His chest was magnificent. She'd noticed as much before, and she noticed it all over again now, with an even deeper appreciation this time, though it hadn't changed. Maybe *she* had, though. She'd become more and more fond of him, and that might make him appear even more physically attractive to her. Had his abs been that taut before? Had his chest been that smooth and firm? Had his biceps *really* been that hard? Had his shoulders…

Suddenly her hands were on him, running over every spot she had admired and every place in between.

Touching him, feeling his skin and muscle slipping beneath her palm, had suddenly become as necessary as breathing. She couldn't help herself.

He'd been undoing his jeans, but he stopped when she began caressing him. He went still, watching her, and then his eyes fell closed as she stroked and rubbed his shoulders and his chest, his arms and his belly.

"You're killing me, Vixen."

"As you were me, a few moments ago. It serves you right." But she stopped running her palms over him and instead peeled off her own blouse. Then she quickly shimmied out of her skirt and panties, and leaned back to observe him.

He was kneeling in front of her but had only managed to unsnap his jeans before he'd apparently lost the ability to do anything but stare at her. She blinked up at him. "What?"

"You."

"What about me?" She looked down at her body. "Is something wrong?"

"Nothing's wrong." He reached out, touched her arm, traced his hand down it. "You're beautiful, that's all. The most beautiful woman I've ever... God."

"That's very nice, Seth. But you're doing it wrong." She clasped his hand, removing it from her arm and placing it squarely on her left breast.

"Impatient little minx, aren't you?"

"I'm not a minx at all, though I've known a few, and you're right, they're terribly impatient."

He laughed, adjusting his hand, then using it to knead and squeeze her flesh. Then he brought his fingers together to press her nipple between them. She closed her eyes and breathed through smiling lips. "Yes, yes. That's better."

And then his lips were on hers again, but no longer with those useless, teasing kisses he'd been giving her before. Now he kissed her the way she'd been wanting him to: fully, deeply, almost desperately. It made her body heat, made the trembling he'd already elicited come on more strongly. Full-body shudders racked her now. And she loved it. She loved it all.

She twined her fingers into his hair and tugged his head away from her mouth, guiding it toward her breast, until he latched on and took her nipple with his lips, his tongue, even his teeth, which made her scream with pleasure.

She wrestled with his jeans, shoving them down his hips; then she lifted her legs and wrapped them around his waist, locked her ankles behind him and used them to pull him down, until his hard, erect member slid right inside her. Deeply inside her.

She closed her eyes, and her mouth formed a perfect O, which was also the sound that emerged. It was a cry of sheer sensation, of physical bliss.

He moved then, sliding back and forth, in and out, but not only that. Sometimes he moved his hips in circles, rocking so deeply into her that she went into an instant orgasm.

His hands slid beneath her, gripping her hips tight and holding her to him so he could penetrate even more deeply as she climaxed. She moaned and cried, then came again as her body tried to shake itself apart. And all the while he held her, pushing her more and more, making the pleasure go on and on.

Finally he eased back just a little, changing his movements to slower, gentler ones, just to give her time, she thought, to come back to earth again.

Panting, she managed to stammer one word. "Ah-ma-zing."

"We're just getting started. Come here."

He wrapped her in his arms, hooked a leg around and beneath hers, and rolled them both over, until she was lying on top of him.

She liked that *very* much. Her knees were down, her body upright, her thighs straddling him. She rode him that way, hard and deep, fast, and she enjoyed knowing that he was getting incredible pleasure from watching the way her breasts bounced as she worked him. She could tell. After a while he used his hands to torment her nipples, pinching and pulling while she drove herself into a frenzy on top of him.

It wasn't enough, so she began to lean back, just to see how far she could go, changing the angle of entry and slide, the contact points, just enough. New nerve endings came to screaming life, and with a few more strokes she was coming again, screaming his name, shivering all over, bouncing faster than before, and then losing herself in a torrent of spasms that rocked her right to the core.

She didn't realize at first that he had climaxed, as well. She only figured that out when he didn't start moving in and out again. He held her close, kissed her mouth, her neck, stared into her eyes in between.

And there was something… Something way beyond the intense sex they'd just had and the momentous orgasms he had given her—the likes of which she'd never known. There was something else, twisting in her gut. It was big, and not entirely pleasant. It felt like a stirring of panic, of utter, heart-rending fear. It felt like the fight-or-flight response she'd heard spoken of, taking hold. It was hard to breathe, because for some reason her throat was constricting painfully, and her eyes were burning, as if someone had dumped them full of acid.

"What did you do?" she asked.

"What do you mean?" He stroked her hair, unable to see her face, because she was resting it on his chest just then. "Are you all right, Vixen?"

"I feel… Something's wrong."

He sat up a little, lifting her from his chest and searching her face. "What is it?"

"Is it—is it possible for a vampire to have a heart attack?"

"I don't think so."

"Well, that's what it feels like. It hurts. Right here." She pressed a balled-up fist to her chest. "I think you made me climax so powerfully I damaged my heart."

He grinned, but when she didn't respond in kind, he wiped the look from his face and studied her seriously instead. "I promise, there's nothing wrong with your heart. Maybe it's just starting to feel something for the first time, hmm? Could that be it?"

"*Feel* something? Of course it felt something. That was *incredible.* Every single part of my body felt something. But it shouldn't *hurt.*"

"I meant emotional feelings, not physical ones," he said.

"Don't be stupid, Seth. Sex is physical. Not emotional." And yet his suggestion rang true, somehow. It wasn't just the sensations that had coursed through her. It was *him*. It was something very specifically about him.

He'd flinched when she spoke, almost as if he were the one with the inexplicable pain pulsing through his chest. She soothed him with a pat on the shoulder, then sat up straighter. "I need to be alone for a while, before the day sleep."

"Oh." He looked so incredibly sad when he said that. As if she were hurting him, somehow.

"I'll come back. I need… I can't explain what I need, but believe me, it will help. And I *will* come back. I'd like…I'd like to sleep in your arms, I think."

His brows rose, the sadness in his eyes replaced by a thin look of hope and a dense one of confusion. "Oh. Okay."

"Okay. I won't be long." She climbed, naked, out of the van.

"Your clothes," he began, but she only tossed a smile over her shoulder and called, "Don't need them," as she raced out of the empty warehouse and into the night.

Seth followed her. He couldn't help himself; he had to know, dammit. She'd been keeping a secret. He knew that much. And he had a feeling it was something that was having a huge impact on their relationship—on the way she felt things—or, more accurately, didn't feel them. Hell, how could she not feel something after the sex they'd just had?

How could she even claim to feel nothing, when she looked at him the way she did? When she touched him as if she adored every inch of him, as if she couldn't keep from running her hands over his skin even if she wanted to? When she took his body into hers the way she did? How the hell could she not realize that what had been happening between them went way beyond sex?

How?

He crept out of the warehouse just in time to see her running and leaping, stark naked, through the tall grasses and wildflowers and weeds of a vacant lot-turned-field, until she seemed to stumble, seemed to bend, seemed to fall down into the grass.

Almost as if she really *were* having some kind of heart attack. Hell, it wasn't possible. Was it?

He ran into the field, because he couldn't see her anymore. Her body was hidden by the deep grasses. He ran through the night, his preternatural vision probing, until he found her, about ten feet ahead of him, lying on the ground, writhing and flattening the grass all around her.

He lifted a hand, opened his mouth to call her name, to ask what was wrong, then froze when he realized what he was seeing.

She was changing. Vixen's very shape was changing. Her body curled in on itself, and she buried her face beneath the thick mass of red hair, and then she seemed to shrink, and shrink, and…change. Skin vanished beneath sleek shiny fur. The hair covering her face became a long, lush tail. And when it flicked away, the face of a fox—a vixen—peered up at him. Big brown eyes, exotically slanted, blinked once, and then she sprang onto all fours and darted away through the grass.

Seth just stood there, staring after her. "What the hell just happened?"

A hand closed on his shoulder. "So now you know," Roxy said.

He turned. "*That's* her secret? That she's not really a woman but an animal?"

"She's not an animal, Seth, she's a shape-shifter. Or was. Now she's a vampire, just like you."

"Not just like me."

"Of course she is."

"Bullshit." He shrugged her hand off his shoulder and stomped back toward the warehouse. A shiver worked up his spine. "Shit," he muttered. "I just fucked a goddamned animal."

20

— ◆ —

"This prisoner exchange," Topaz said softly, a little while after Jack had finally returned to his room, where she'd been pacing, waiting, nervous and eager and unsure, for most of the night. "Is it some kind of a trap?" She studied Jack's face, his eyes, as she awaited his answer.

Several drones had been left here to guard her. He'd sent them packing as soon as he'd come through the door, though she wasn't convinced they'd really gone. A few of them were probably still lurking in the shadows, keeping a safe distance, outside in the darkness beneath the windows, in the hallways of this place. Probably also posted at every possible exit.

No, not every exit, she thought. There wouldn't be enough of them. She was a vampire, after all. Any window, door or chimney could serve as an exit for her.

Not that she planned to leave tonight. She intended to stick around long enough to learn something valuable about this gang, something she could take back to Reaper, so that he could use it to his advantage. And maybe she could learn a little something about Jack, as well.

He'd prevented her from being killed, had put a halt to her torture. No question, he'd helped her, and probably at no small risk to himself.

The question was, why? Did he have some new con in mind? Was he running some new game on her? Or on someone else?

She wasn't stupid enough to think there could be any other reason. Like that he cared. No, she'd bought into that once already, and it had cost her a half million dollars. She wasn't falling into that trap again. Trusting Jack Heart was like trying to pet a king cobra on the head. Just as foolish, and just as deadly.

He'd returned with a bundled-up towel in one hand, dismissed the drones, and then told her that she would be going back to Reaper's gang tonight, just two hours past sunset.

Now he sank back on the bed, sighing. "I know as much about Gregor's plans as you do, Topaz. You know that."

"Bull. You're his right hand." She was pacing away from him, too nervous to stand still.

"And he no longer trusts me—largely thanks to you, I might add."

"Thanks to *me?* What did *I* do?" She turned to face him, made her eyes go round and filled them with innocence.

He didn't fall for it; she could tell by his expression. "Please," he said. "You show up here out of the blue and risk your pretty neck, forcing me to step in between you and disaster like some kind of storybook hero, and you want to know what you did?"

She blinked rapidly. "I showed up here to warn you that your life was in danger, risking my own life to do it. I'm the storybook hero here, Jack. You're the con man who used me, cheated me, left me and doesn't deserve my efforts. You're more like the storybook villain."

"I risked my standing with Gregor to protect you."

"A hero wouldn't be with Gregor in the first place. He's the bad guy, Jack. Or hadn't you noticed?"

He shrugged, but averted his eyes, which was as good as admitting guilt.

She slid her glance to the towel he still held in one hand. Something was inside, but she had no idea what and didn't want to ask, because she thought that was what he wanted her to do. "So what's going to happen at this prisoner exchange tomorrow night?" she asked instead.

"I don't know. I swear to you, Topaz, I honestly don't know. If I did, I would tell you."

"Hmmph. Only if it benefited you in some way."

He closed his eyes and sighed. When he opened them again, he was patting the spot beside him on the bed. "Come on. Get in."

She crossed her arms over her chest, pursed her lips and shook her head firmly. "I don't think so."

"Why not? You afraid of me? Or yourself?"

"Neither. I just know us both too well. Having sex with you right now—"

"Is exactly what you want, and you know it. You've had it on your mind since before you even got here." Again he patted the spot beside him on the bed.

She turned her back to him. "I have not," she said. But it was a lie.

"Yes, you have. Look at the way you dressed for the occasion. If those aren't the clothes of a woman bent on seduction, I don't know what could be. I know women, hon. And I know you."

She didn't face him. "You're so damn full of yourself, aren't you? So sure I'm dying to get back into your arms."

He was off the bed before she was sure he'd moved, coming up behind her, sliding those aforementioned arms around her, pulling her body back against his, nuzzling her neck.

"Aren't you?" he asked. "Tell the truth, Topaz. I'm not ashamed to admit I'm as eager as you are."

Her eyes fell closed as a shuddering sigh stammered from her lungs. "The truth is, you broke my heart, and I let you. I fell for you, even though I knew better. I let myself love you, even though you never said you loved me, too. Acted like it, played the role, but you never said the words. That should have told me all I needed to know, but I refused to listen. I'm not going to let you get to me like that again, Jack. Not now. Not ever."

"All right." He kissed her neck, her shoulder, pushing the neckline of her dress aside to get to them. She shivered. His fingers caressed her collarbones.

"And I want my money back, and I'm going to keep my head long enough to get it."

"It's on the bed, Topaz."

She stiffened as the words sank in. Then she stepped away from his embrace and turned to stare, first at him, then at the towel he'd left on the bed.

"Go on, take a look. See for yourself," he said.

She barely knew what to think. Swallowing hard, she opened the bundle and peered inside. Stacks of bills, neatly wrapped, were haphazardly piled inside.

"I'm sorry that I can only give you the half that I kept for myself. I honestly don't know what to do about the half I gave to Gregor," he told her.

The part of her that still loved him damn near whispered, *That's okay, baby. This is enough. More than enough.* But she bit her lip before that part could speak. Then she bitch-slapped it into a corner and called on the part of her he had burned instead.

"I want it all," she told him. "You stole it. What you did with it afterward doesn't negate the fact that you stole it. Therefore, you owe it to me. All of it. And I want it, Jack."

"I want *you*," he said. He moved closer, slid his arms around her waist and nuzzled her neck again.

She closed her eyes and tipped her head sideways to give him more neck to nibble. It felt so incredibly good. But dammit, if she let him make love to her, it would be all over. She knew it. She would fall for him again, even knowing he didn't feel the same and never would. It was a world of hurting just waiting to happen, and she wanted no part of it.

"I can't. I can't put myself through that kind of pain again, Jack. As much as I want you, I just can't."

He sighed, but he backed off. Kept his arms around her, but stopped the kissing and caressing, which left her wanting it back again. He turned her toward the bed, urged her closer. "I wasted so much time running around with the boss that tonight, there's probably no time anyway. It'll be dawn soon." He glanced at his watch. "Twenty minutes or so."

"Oh." She was relieved. Surely she could keep her willpower strong for twenty minutes.

"We have to stay here, together, just to make sure Gregor believes the bill of goods we're selling him. And there's only the one bed."

"Yes, I see that."

"I'll keep my hands to myself, I promise." He held up one hand, making a Scout's-honor gesture.

She pressed her lips together, but finally nodded. "All right." And without another word or look, she marched to the bed, peeled back the covers and crawled inside, still fully clothed. She tucked the bundle of money underneath her side of the bed.

"You're not getting undressed?" he asked.

She made a face at him.

He shrugged and pulled off his jeans, then his shirt, leaving him garbed only in boxers and socks. He looked good. As good as she had remembered, or maybe even better. So long and lean. She'd loved that about him right from the start. Everything about him was long and lean, even his fingers. Elegant fingers. The fingers of a musician, he had. And God, they were so talented when it came to playing her.

She closed her eyes and averted her face so he wouldn't see the blatant hunger in it as he approached the bed.

He climbed in beside her, stretched his arms over his head and yawned, then lay down on his back. She was lying on her side, facing away from him, longing with every cell in her body to roll over, wrap her arms around his waist and lay her head on his chest, the way she used to.

But that would lead to more. And more would lead to pain.

Although maybe avoiding all that wasn't going to do any good at all, because the pain was already there, gnawing a hole in her chest like a rat chewing through a wall. Hot tears welled in her eyes, and her throat constricted, until she had to force herself not to suck in a choking sob or two.

Dammit. Why did it hurt so much to be this close to him?

"Topaz?" he said.

"Hmm?" She didn't dare say more in answer. Any more and he would hear the tears in her voice, choking her.

"For whatever it might be worth, I'm sorry."

She blinked. "For what, exactly?"

She felt the bed move as he shrugged. "Everything. Leading you on, taking your money. Using you, conning you, tricking you. Leaving you."

She thinned her lips as she let the words make their way through her ears to her brain, trying to block them from entering her heart. "Why are you sorry? It's what you do, after all."

"It was different with you."

She was quiet for a long moment. Anger built. She wanted so badly to believe that, but she wasn't quite that stupid.

"I honestly think there was something real between us, Topaz," he went on. "Or could have been, if I'd—"

She sat up in the bed so suddenly that he went silent in surprise. Then, with a tug, she yanked the covers off him, leaving only a sheet, slid to the floor, grabbed two pillows under her other arm and strode across the bedroom. Blankets dragged behind her like a bridal train.

"Where are you going? What did I say?" He was sitting up now, but he didn't get out of the bed.

"If you have any respect for me at all, Jack—even a crumb of it—don't insult me by starting the con all over. You never felt a thing for me. Don't try to tell me you did."

"But—"

"I can forgive you. Maybe. In time, and only if you return the rest of the money. But I damn well can't forgive what you did if you keep right on trying to do it. I'm not going to fall for it again, Jack. So just…just don't bother, okay?"

He couldn't meet her eyes. "I wasn't. I really wasn't."

"Bullshit. I want my money. Period."

She slung the pillows into a pile in the corner of the floor, then spread the blankets over them. When she finished, she crawled in, lying on top of one blanket and beneath another, which she yanked up to her shoulders before turning on her side, facing away from him and closing her eyes.

"I'll try to get you the rest of your money."

"I'll believe it when I see it."

"I mean it. I *will* try. I just…don't know if it's possible. Gregor has a safe, and shit, I gave you half."

"Good for you. I want it all."

"Can I have a blanket?"

"No."

She heard him sigh, heard the mattress move with his weight as he lay back down, and congratulated herself on her resolve and her willpower.

Thank God she wouldn't have to be here long, though. She wasn't certain she could make it last.

That thought led to another, as she returned to her original concern: the prisoner exchange that was to take place tonight, and the question of whether it was legitimate or some kind of a trap.

She didn't like Gregor. What she knew of him, what she'd seen and sensed about him, told her all she needed to know. He was a bad apple. And he wasn't to be trusted.

Sadly, neither was Jack. She was frightened about what was going to happen tonight. She was frightened for Reaper, for Roxy, for Seth and Vixen. She was even frightened for Jack. And, a little bit, for herself.

She wished she knew what to expect.

When Vixen returned to the van to bed down for the day sleep, Seth wasn't there. She didn't know where he had gone, and there was very little time to search for him. Thinking he would come back before sunrise, which was only moments away, she burrowed into the covers, and got comfy and warm.

It had been a great run. She'd danced and jumped and chased her tail, hunted field mice and snatched a butterfly from midair, catching it between her paws. She'd relished her time in the wild, even though it had been brief. She couldn't sustain her fox form for very long anymore, and she wondered if someday she would be unable to shift at all. It seemed to be getting harder.

Her run hadn't helped her to better understand anything, though. Not her own odd feelings, not Seth's. But it helped her to know that none of it mattered. All that mattered was being alive and relishing that life. No matter what it was or what it brought.

And that was what she intended to do.

It got harder, though, as the sun rose, and her eyes grew heavy and the day sleep crept over her. Because she realized that Seth hadn't returned, and a feeling of darkness and hurt came into her heart.

The sun set, and Seth rose, stiff and uncomfortable from spending the entire day on the hard concrete floor of the warehouse. Not wanting to explain to his nosy comrades why he wasn't with Vixen after all the preparations they'd seen him making, he'd opted to duck into a hidey-hole he'd found for himself. It was a tiny, unfinished room off the rear of one of the large areas and had probably once been a place to store tools, if the shelves along the walls were anything to go by. It was dark, and it was cold and the floor and walls were hard. Perfect to suit his mood.

He probably needed to think this thing through a bit, but he was damned if he even knew where to begin. What the hell was he supposed to think, anyway? Why hadn't she *told* him? Didn't she think her being part animal was something he would have wanted to know?

He covered his head with his forearms and moaned.

"Seth?"

Lowering the arms, he lifted his head, almost groaning again at the interruption. He'd been getting ready for a full-blown self-pity party. "In here, Reaper."

Reaper ducked into the tiny room, its doorway, sans door, barely wide enough to admit him. "What the hell are you doing in here?"

"I was sleeping. Now I'm waking."

Reaper looked him up and down, and Seth could see the questions in his eyes. To Reap's benefit, though, he didn't ask. Instead, he extended a hand. Seth took it, and Reaper tugged him up onto his feet. "Things didn't go so well last night, I take it."

"I don't want to talk about it."

"I didn't ask you to. She's, uh, looking for you, though."

"She can keep looking. What time is it?"

"Almost seven-thirty."

"And we need to hit that club by nine. Let's focus on that, then. Where's Roxy?"

"She sneaked out for coffee, predawn. Now she's sitting on a tree stump outside, drinking it."

"I think I'll join her."

Reaper frowned at him, not understanding.

"Just do me a favor and tell Vixen to get ready for the night, and that we have very little time for... anything else."

"You want me to buy you some time before you have to talk to her."

"Bingo."

"You sure you don't want to talk about this, Seth?"

"With you? Yeah, I'm sure."

Reaper lifted his brows, looking wounded.

"Well, hell, pal, you're not exactly an expert on women, are you? Much less relationships. Or was that someone else who's been insisting he's a loner since the day I met him?"

Licking his lips, Reaper nodded. "I guess you have a point." Then he shrugged. "Roxy's probably a much better choice. Go out the front. You'll sense her right away."

Nodding, Seth clapped his friend—and yes, he realized, he did think of Reaper as a friend, though he doubted Reaper would call *him* one—on the shoulder, and moved past him and through the narrow doorway into the larger room, then crossed it and headed out the front door.

The early evening air hit him with a blast of freshness and floral scents that he hadn't noticed the night before. Of course, it had been nearly dawn then, and he'd been pursuing a half-vampiress, half-*fox* through the grasses.

It was dark enough that the stars were already starting to appear here and there in the sky. He moved a few paces away from the warehouse, then stopped and stood there, scenting the air, feeling for Roxy.

He didn't pick up on her until she cleared her throat to let him know where she was. Then he turned in that direction and spotted her, sitting on a fallen log, not a stump, holding a cup between her palms. He should have smelled that fragrant steam, even if he didn't sense her presence. Damn, he must be even more distracted than he'd thought.

"Don't kick yourself, hon," Roxy said. "I'm blocking."

"Doing a hell of a job of it," he said, walking toward her. "For a mortal."

She shrugged. "Been perfecting my skills for a long time. And I didn't want to give our position away to the bad guys. Not that they know me from Adam, but a Chosen in the area might be enough to make them curious."

"Good call." He reached her, but remained standing, rather than taking a seat beside her on the log.

She stared up at him for a long moment, then nodded sagely. "So you've had time to knock things around in your brain now. About Vixen's secret."

He pursed his lips, nodded twice.

"Pretty freakin' amazing, isn't it?"

"It's fucking horrifying, is what it is."

Roxy sipped her coffee, her placid expression never changing as she watched him. He pushed a hand through his hair, paced away from her, paced back again. She sipped and waited.

"I just…I don't know what the hell to make of this. I mean, did I…is she an animal or a human or…what the hell is she?"

Roxy grinned. "Worried you committed bestiality, huh?"

"Don't even joke about that!"

Her smile faded, but the twinkle remained in her eyes. It pissed him off no end that she was amused by his discomfort. "This is serious, Roxy."

"I know it is—to *you,* because you're making it into

a federal case. But it shouldn't be. You need to get the hell over yourself, Seth. So she's a shape-shifter, or was, before she was changed over. Now she's a vampire. Just like you."

"A vampire who can change into a fox!"

Roxy shrugged. "I've heard of a few who can change into bats, or ravens or wolves. Why not a fox?"

He shot her a look, his eyes wide. "Really? I thought that was just, you know, fiction. Like the crosses and the garlic."

"Shows just how much you know, Einstein." She shrugged. "You're just a fledgling. You don't know shit about anything yet. The truly ancient ones, one or two of them, at least, can change their forms."

He nodded, mulling on that for a moment. "Still," he said, "those are ordinary vampires. They got older and more powerful until they acquired the ability to change. She's brand-new, just changed over. I think she was shape-shifting before she was ever undead."

"Well, duh," Roxy said. "And that makes a difference why?"

"Because I don't know if she's a woman or a fox, that's why."

"I told you, she's a vampire. Maybe not an ordinary one, but I've never really thought there was any such thing as an ordinary vampire, myself."

He shook his head. "I don't know what to make of this."

"Maybe if I kick you in the balls—"

He shot her a look. She bit her lip and started over. "Talk to her, Seth. Talk to her, let her tell you who she is, who she was before and who she is now. She can tell you all you need to know if you'll get off your high horse and listen."

He clenched his jaw. "I don't know. She should have told me before this."

"Yeah, maybe. But she's still figuring out what's, well, polite and what's not. I get the feeling she's spent her life avoiding relationships—maybe avoiding other humans altogether. And she hasn't been a vampire all that long. Just yank the stick out of your ass and give her a chance."

He sighed, stared off into the distance for a long moment, then faced Roxy again. "We should be getting ready to head to the club, for the rendezvous."

"*We?*"

"Well, yeah."

"No, you're wrong, hon. Reaper's going alone, just as Gregor instructed. He's taking Briar along, of course, but no one else. He doesn't want any of us hurt, in case it's a trap."

Seth forgot his own issues and turned back toward the warehouse. "He can't do that."

"He already has. Probably left right after he sent you out here to me."

He ran back inside, flung open the door and shouted for Reaper, but there was no answer, and no sense of him anywhere near. "Dammit."

Vixen came out of nowhere, hurrying toward him, but stopped a few feet short, seeming uncertain. Her eyes searched his face, full of questions, but aloud she only said, "What's wrong?"

"Reaper went to the rendezvous alone."

"Oh." She took two steps closer. "I'm sure he'll be fine."

"Of course he'll be fine." Roxy had come inside behind Seth, silent as a cat, and now she sounded as if she were trying to convince herself, even more than them, of what she was saying. "He's been working alone for a long time now."

"He's got Briar with him," Seth pointed out, he thought unnecessarily. "Even if Gregor doesn't spring some kind of a death trap on him, that bitch is liable to get him killed." He turned in a slow circle, then stopped and said, "We have to go after him."

Roxy was silent. Vixen, though, nodded.

"We should take the van, so there will be room for all of us to get back here," he said, heading for the next room, where they'd parked the vehicles. Roxy and Vixen followed, but when he opened the door and saw the van sitting there with its back doors open, and the cozy nest of blankets and pillows inside, he remembered the night before, the night with Vixen, and went still.

Roxy moved past him, heading around to the driver's door. "Stow the blankets, close that up and get in."

Seth took a single step toward the rear of the van, but Vixen stopped him cold with nothing more than a hand on his forearm.

"Where did you sleep?"

He turned slowly, to look at her. "I…we don't have time for this right now, Vixen."

"Why didn't you wait for me?"

He drew a breath and decided to get it over with. "I followed you when you ran off. I was worried. I...I saw."

Her eyes widened, and she backed up a step, perhaps involuntarily. "You...*saw?*"

"Yeah. I saw you change, okay? I know what you are."

"What I am."

He nodded.

"And just what is it you think I am, Seth?"

He lowered his head, shook it rapidly from side to side. "I don't know, I just know it's not...natural."

"And being a vampire is?"

"Of course it is. We've existed almost forever."

"Shape-shifters have existed just as long. Maybe longer. We're just as natural. But I suppose you don't see it that way."

He didn't answer, couldn't just then. Her words were coming out coarsely, as if her throat was tight, and there was moisture pooling in her eyes.

"You're repulsed by me now, aren't you, Seth?"

Again he didn't answer.

The van's horn sounded, making them both jump.

Vixen turned and climbed into the back of the van, pulling the doors closed behind her. Seth caught them just before they closed all the way. "Look, we need to talk about this. Just not now."

"Just not ever. If I repulse you, obviously you no longer want me. And it was only sex, after all. If we don't have that, we don't have anything."

He glimpsed her tears spilling over just before she shoved his hand off the door and yanked it closed.

He felt bad, mean, even sorry. And hurt by her words. But he wasn't so naive that he didn't realize she might be lashing out, returning pain for pain. He'd clearly hurt her, after all.

The front passenger door swung open. Roxy called, "Get in, Romeo."

Sighing, he obeyed.

"Nice job," she said, with a nod toward the back, where Vixen was angrily folding blankets and stowing them in the compartments beneath the floor, tears streaming down her face.

He'd never seen her cry before. "Yeah," he said, "I know."

21

— ✦ —

Reaper had taken the Mustang to the meeting place. Briar was in the front seat beside him, and she was tense enough to tell him that she expected trouble.

"So you think it's a legitimate exchange, or a trap?" He asked the question just to see if she would answer honestly.

"What makes you think I would know?"

"Gregor's your man, isn't he? He tells you everything—except how to make drones, that is. Right?"

"He didn't tell me this." She faced him in the dimness of the dashboard lights. "How do I know *you* haven't got some kind of a trap planned for *him*?"

"You're with me. Do you *see* any signs of a trap?"

She shrugged. "You didn't bring your friends."

"I don't want to risk them getting killed."

"Or maybe they're setting up an ambush somewhere." She leaned back against the headrest, closed her eyes.

He was under no delusion that Briar might just be resting her eyes. He was certain she was speaking to

Gregor, telling him they were on the way, who was coming, who was not, asking for instructions to help get Reaper's ass killed.

After a few moments she stirred and opened her eyes. Huge, brown, beautiful eyes. Dangerous, dark, deceitful eyes.

"I hope you said hello for me," he said.

She smiled, and he thought anyone who didn't know her would think she had the face of an angel. "You can say hello yourself soon. We're nearly there." She pointed. "There's the club."

He saw it just ahead. It sat in the center of a city block, a two-story brick building with darkened windows and a solid red metal door, probably lead lined. The only noticeable thing about it was the neon lettering above the door that spelled out The Crypt.

He drove up the block, found a spot to park where he was unlikely to get blocked in, pulled over and stopped the car.

He reached for the door handle. She reached for it, too, sliding her arm over his waist, covering his hand with her own. "It's not nine yet."

He met her eyes, instantly suspicious. "So?"

"So he said to come at nine. *Precisely* at nine. He can be an asshole about details like that. And since he's agreed to make the exchange even though you haven't brought Vixen, you should do whatever you can to keep him happy."

"He asked you to stall me. Why, Briar?"

She shrugged. "I'm just trying to make sure this goes

off the way it's supposed to. I want to get back to my people. You want Topaz back with you. Let's do this right."

"I'm not buying it."

She drew a deep breath, sighed, then reached to the hemline of her blouse and tugged it up, over her head, and tossed it to the floor.

He was caught for a moment by the sight of her naked breasts, large for such a small woman, round and full, creamy and supple, with hard little nipples that aroused him beyond reason.

Then he forced himself to look away. "You *really* want to slow me down, don't you?"

"The exchange won't happen before nine, Reaper. Going in early won't change that. But it might be the last chance for…this." She trailed her hand over his jeans, over his erection.

He shivered. And he didn't pull away. His aversion to being touched didn't even begin to apply here. He tried to ignore his arousal and opened the car door.

"Kiss me just once," she said, sliding a palm to his cheek and turning his head toward her. "Just once, and then we'll go inside."

"Stop with the delaying tactics, Briar. They're not going to work."

"How can you be so sure that's what they are? Tactics? How do you know I haven't been dying to do this since the first night? You kissed me then. Remember?"

He tried not to.

"Remember how good it was? How I tasted?" Her fingertips brushed his lips, while her other hand stroked him through his jeans, up and down. "Taste me again,

Reaper." She rose up onto her knees on the seat and brushed her lips over his.

Dammit, he was only human. He snapped his arms around her, and he kissed her. His mouth wide, his tongue thrusting, he kissed her hard and deep. His hands twisted in her hair, holding her face to his as he fed from her mouth. And then he jerked her head back, none too gently, and went after those incredible breasts. He didn't take his time or work up to it. He sucked them hard, bit them harder.

And then her hands were fisting in his hair, and she panted and moaned and shivered.

"Stop," she whispered after a moment. She yanked on his hair, pulling his head away from her. "We have to stop."

"The hell we do." He growled the words, the blood-lust giving his vision a thin red haze, the arousal beyond tolerance. "Not now, Briar. No way in hell."

She tipped her head down, and he saw it in her eyes. The glow, the hunger. She wanted it as much as he did.

"Make it fast," she told him. She hiked up the short, short skirt she wore. There was nothing underneath it. "Fast and hard and fucking angry."

He reached for the fly of his jeans, undid them, freed himself. He was so hard he was throbbing. "Not a problem."

She straddled him, lowered herself, took him all the way in. He lifted his hips from the seat to go deeper, as she bounced up and down, working herself into a frenzy on him. He fed on her nipples again, biting harder than before.

She moved, faster and faster, nails raking his scalp, she whispered, "I'm gonna come."

"Me, too."

"Drink me, Reaper. Pierce me and drink me!"

He bit down harder, fangs sinking into her breast as he pumped into her. The blood welled, and he sucked harder, his entire being overtaken by physical pleasure, and the taste and rush of her blood in his mouth, on his tongue. He thought he would explode, it was so incredibly, unbearably good. And then he did, and his entire body climaxed as his brain lost its ability to do anything but feel.

And what he felt was her, shaking so hard it was like a seizure as the orgasm ripped through her. He felt her bending her head, sinking her teeth into his shoulder, drinking, suckling his life from his very flesh.

And he thought maybe she was crying.

"You should stay in the van," Seth told Vixen when they pulled to a stop directly in front of The Crypt. "Actually, you should drive around the block until we come out."

"What is that expression I've heard your kind use?" she asked. "Oh, yes. I remember. 'Fuck you.'"

"Play nice, kids," Roxy chirped. She shut off the engine. "Let's settle this like grown-ups. Vixen, Gregor wants you back. If he *has* set some kind of a trap, he's liable to take you, as well as Briar. That's not what we want here, is it." She didn't make it a question.

"No."

"So drive the van around until we come out."

"I don't know how to drive," she told Roxy.

Seth sighed. "Just wait here. Lock the damn doors."

She stared at him, hurt to the core and not liking it. No wonder she'd avoided emotions for so many years. They were absolutely awful.

She turned her gaze to Roxy's. "If you think I should."

"I do, hon. And Seth is only trying to keep you safe. Idiot that he is, his motives are pure here."

"I'm not an idiot."

Roxy rolled her eyes, then met Vixen's. "He's male. Same thing. Climb up here, hon, so I can show you how to unlock it and let us in. And hell, how to make the thing move, just in case you're forced."

"If forced, I'll get out and run," Vixen said, but she climbed over the seats until she was in the second row and watched as Roxy told her how to move the van— *just in case.*

"It's time," Briar whispered into Reaper's ear, as she climbed off him, righted her skirt and tucked her breasts back into captivity. "You ready?"

He tried to steady his pulse by the sheer force of his will, but it wasn't easy. Briar was acting all business, as if nothing had happened, and he was damned if he could see a hint of anything else in her face. Though he couldn't get her to meet his eyes.

She slid to her own side of the car and opened the door, then got out and started walking along the sidewalk toward the club. Reaper got out and hurried to catch up with her.

"Here we are," she said when they stopped outside

the door. A thrumming beat came from beyond it. She nodded at him. "Well?"

"Well."

Rolling her eyes, she reached past him, yanked the door open and strode inside. Reaper followed, his senses opening as he got his wits about him. He stepped into a rush of noise, a pounding beat, colored lights pulsing on and off in time with the music. The door slammed behind him, and he turned fast, startled.

Briar stood there, smiling. He saw her turn the lock, and that was when he smelled the blood.

"What the hell?"

He turned again, his eyes scanning the place, and he saw them, bodies, torn and bloodied, lying all over the place. Mortals. Humans. Young ones, barely more than kids, dressed to party. Their blood slickened on the floor.

"For the love of God," he whispered. "Why? What the hell is this?"

For just a moment he thought she looked as surprised by all the carnage as he was. But then she plastered the hard, cold expression on her face again. "Why do you think I would know?"

He heard movement, felt life, and looked toward the opposite end of the building. "Ah, that will be your friends, coming to join you," she said. She started to walk away from him, toward the sound, but he gripped her arm and jerked her back toward him.

"What the hell is going on, Briar?"

"I don't know." She shrugged, and looked him square in the eye. "But I do have a message for you, from Gregor. If your friends are inside, that is." She turned to look over her shoulder just as Seth and Roxy came around a corner and into sight. Then she looked him squarely in the eyes, and said, "Nightingale."

And everything went black.

Seth and Roxy went in the back door, which was unlocked, but no sooner had they opened it than a hand came from nowhere, shoving them through, yanking the door closed and locking it behind them. Seth heard the lock turn and smelled the death all around him.

"Oh, my God," Roxy whispered. She was staring, pointing. "Seth, my God."

He looked. She'd moved a few steps ahead of him, and he joined her, coming around a corner onto what must have been the dance floor and main room of the nightclub, only to see bodies littering the place like fallen leaves. Tables were smashed, broken glass everywhere. Music played, and colored strobes still flashed in time, but there was no other mortal left alive in this place. It had been a massacre.

Roxy turned away, lowering her head, and Seth automatically lifted his arms toward her, but he froze when he glimpsed Reaper across the room and saw Briar leaning close, her lips moving as she said something to him.

And then something changed in his face. It went blank. Lax. Eyes empty. Almost dead. Something made him grab Roxy and move her behind him, just before Reaper released a deep growl and lashed out.

He reached for Briar, one hand gripping her arm, and then hurled her. She shrieked and flew bodily through the air, landing amid the bodies on the floor, sliding in the blood of the innocent. And then she scrambled, trying to get up, but slipping in the slick scarlet mess, falling, whimpering.

Seth moved closer, calling out. "Reap, what the hell? What's going on?"

Reaper didn't answer. He looked toward Seth's voice, reacting as if on some kind of auto-mode. His head turned, his gaze locked on, but there was no recognition, no life, no nothing.

"Reaper?" Seth asked again, uncertainly.

Reaper came toward him, and Seth backed away, unsure what was happening. He heard Roxy shout a warning, but too late. Reaper swung a fist, and it caught Seth in the jaw, launching him until he collided with a wall and crashed to the floor.

He shook himself, and looked up to see Reaper moving toward Roxy as she struggled to get the tranq gun out of her holster and level it on him.

"No!" she cried, but Reaper hurled a chair at her all the same. She blocked it with an arm, and her weapon flew from her grip. "Dammit! Reaper, stop it! I'm your friend!"

He went after her, and Seth scrambled, dove onto Reaper's back.

"What the hell is the meaning of all this?" an unfamiliar voice shouted.

"He doesn't know what he's doing!" Roxy cried.

Seth was holding on for dear life while Reaper swung him in circles, then smashed him against the bar, trying to dislodge him.

"Seth!" That voice he recognized. It was Topaz's. She'd arrived with a vampire who had to be Jack Heart.

"Tranquilize him!" Seth shouted.

But now Reaper was heading for Topaz, despite the fact that Seth was on his back and pounding on his head, and despite the fact that Jack Heart stepped in front of her and brought a big chair down over Reaper's head.

Reaper swatted Jack away like an irritating mosquito, then reached for Topaz just as she lunged for the gun on the floor.

Her fingers touched the grip just as Reaper's foot connected with her rib cage, launching her into the air.

She grunted, then couldn't seem to breathe well enough to make another sound as she crashed into a wall and lay there, gasping.

Jack dove on the gun, rolled and threw it all at the same time, just barely avoiding Reaper's rampage on the way. As he tossed it toward Seth, Seth released his grip on his mentor's neck, dropped to the floor and reached to catch the weapon.

Reaper whirled, bringing a beefy fist around with him, but Seth leveled the gun and pulled the trigger fast.

The dart hit Reaper right in the neck, front and center, at the same moment that Reaper's fist hit Seth on the side of his head and made him see stars.

He also saw Reaper falling to the floor.

"Hell."

"He's out!" That was Roxy. She hurried to Reaper's side, where he lay in a heap on the floor.

"What the fuck just happened here?" Jack was asking as he scooped Topaz up. She was barely conscious. "Why would he…"

"He couldn't help it, and we don't have time to go into it now," Roxy said. "No doubt Gregor planned all this and will show up any minute. We need to get out before he does."

She was at Seth's side, helping him to his feet.

"Agreed," Seth said. He glanced at Briar. "What did you say to him?"

"Just…a word. Gregor told me to lock the door when he came in here, make sure you all were inside, as well, and then say that word."

Roxy nodded. "Gregor *knew,* Briar. He knew what that word would do to him. And yet he let you lock yourself in here with him. He fully expected everyone in this room to be killed. You included."

"That's not possible. Gregor wouldn't do that to me."

Seth lifted Reaper up, heaved him over his shoulder and strode toward the door. "There's another word that makes him stop," he said, addressing Briar without looking at her. "I don't suppose Gregor told you what it was, did he?"

"No."

"No. Well, you can wait here for him if you want. I could care less. Just be aware, he expected Reaper to kill you."

"He…he *wouldn't.*"

"He did," Jack said.

Seth glanced at him. "You can bring Topaz out to the van. Just so you know, she's going with us."

"So am I, if you'll let me. My boss tried to kill *me* tonight, too."

Seth narrowed his eyes, but without time to argue, he didn't see much point.

"There are liable to be drones outside, probably surrounding the damn place," Jack said.

"We've got a van waiting. We'll just have to run for it." Seth went to the door, opened it a mere crack and peered out, Reaper still over his shoulder. But he didn't see Vixen or the vehicle. He could sense others out there, though, watching, waiting to ambush them the minute they stepped out of the club.

"Where's the van?" he whispered. He turned toward Roxy and spoke louder. *"Where the hell's the van?"*

Vixen had waited until she'd noticed them, the drones, dozens of them, surrounding the nightclub. They didn't go in, just waited outside. And she was afraid of them. If they noticed the van and her inside it—she shuddered to think what they would do. So she moved the thing, as carefully as she could.

It wasn't as easy as Roxy had made it sound. They'd left the engine running, so all she had to do was put her foot on the brake, move the shift from Park to Drive and then press on the gas while using the steering wheel to control the direction.

However, pressing on the gas made the thing buck and shoot forward far faster than she had anticipated, and she could barely control its direction. She let off and the van stopped, and then she tried gripping the steering wheel with both hands and pressing on the gas far more lightly.

Despite the bucking and jerking of the van, the drones paid it no attention. They just stood there, staring at the nightclub as if they could only focus on one thing at a time. As if it didn't even seem odd to them that the van was spluttering and bounding through the parking lot.

She started to get a feel for the thing about the time she emerged onto the street, but there were other vehicles vying for space, and horns sounded and tires squealed as she pulled out into the flow of traffic.

Fighting to control the vehicle, she was distracted by her senses, by the feeling of death reaching her now from inside the club—and then the surge of violence and danger she sensed, coming from Seth's mind to hers.

He was in trouble! Worried that she was getting too far away, she turned right, and after another block or two, right again, her focus entirely on her friends. Their energy. Seth's energy.

Something was terribly wrong! When she sought Reaper's vibes, she felt only a dark black hole that swirled like a whirlpool, sucking reason into it. There was only fury. Rage.

"Reaper?"

And then she felt it, Seth's mind reaching out to hers. *Come back, fast, and be ready to take off again as soon as we're in the van. We need you, Vixen.*

I'm coming.

She drove the van as best she could, speeding right up

to the front door, where several of the drones were closing in. She hit them and sent them flying, falling, crushing some beneath the wheels. She grimaced as her
stomach turned, even as she stomped on the brake pedal.
The club's door flew open. Roxy surged out, with Seth
right behind her. Reaper was limp, hanging over Seth's
shoulder.

Drones closed in on them just as Roxy reached for
the sliding side door. Jack Heart, of all people, kicked
one of the drones away as he carried Topaz in his arms.
Briar—*Briar*—protected Roxy's other side. Roxy got
the door open and leapt inside, quickly hitting the button that opened the door of the weapons cache, even as
Seth hurled Reaper off his shoulder onto the floor.

"What happened?" Vixen shrieked.

A drone was trying to wrest Topaz from Jack's arms.
Another was wrestling with Briar.

Roxy threw Seth a gun. He caught it, spun around
and fired at the hulk who was after Topaz. The vampire
staggered backward, and Jack was able to climb into the
van with Topaz in his arms. He stepped over the prone
Reaper, managing to get Topaz into the back, then
whirled around fast, taking a weapon from the wall and
firing at one drone while Roxy fired at another, and Seth
gripped Briar and hurled her bodily into the van, where
she landed hard.

Seth was the only one still on the ground, and the
drones were closing in on him, despite Roxy's and
Jack's efforts. He gripped the side of the van to pull
himself inside, and the drones latched on to him, yanking him back into a sea of them.

"Go," Seth shouted. "Leave me and go!"

Vixen shoved open the driver's door and jumped from her seat out onto the sidewalk to his side, and was immediately surrounded. She heard Roxy swear, but she crouched protectively in front of Seth, and then she cried out, yipping, releasing a warbling sound that was half mewl and half howl.

For a moment the drones froze, stunned, even while Jack and Roxy, and now Briar, too, kept firing at them with conventional guns, as well as tranquilizer darts.

Several drones fell, and others shook free of their shock and resumed their attack. But even as they did, a peregrine falcon dove from high above, drilling one of them in the head. Dogs came like floodwaters, surging from down the block, snarling and growling, running full bore and launching themselves at the drones. Other animals flocked. Pigeons dive-bombed; cats flung themselves at the bastards; rats scurried from the alley, leaping on the thugs' legs, gnawing on their ankles.

The crowd of thugs fell away, busy trying to shake free of the animals attacking them, fighting for their lives.

Vixen had turned instinctively, putting Seth behind her, between herself and the van, leaving her between him and the drones. She was crouching, backing up slowly, when she felt herself gripped and lifted. It was Seth. He picked her up, spun around and set her firmly in the van. Then he leapt in behind her, slung the door closed and shouted, "Go, Roxy!"

"Going!" she replied, already behind the wheel. The van jerked into motion, rocking Vixen into her seat.

Seth didn't sit, but he did turn to Vixen. "Are you all right?" he asked.

The way his eyes searched her face, scanned her body, she almost felt as if he cared about her answer. She supposed she was as all right as any of them. Everyone was bruised, cut, bleeding, in pain. "Yes," she said.

He nodded; then he bent to drag Reaper from where he'd been dumped in the middle of the floor and into the back. He stretched his friend out on the floor in front of the rear seat, where Jack had laid Topaz. They were both still out cold. Jack was beside Topaz, looking concerned.

"She okay?" Seth asked.

"I think he broke her ribs when he kicked her. The pain was too much. I don't think she's bleeding, though, and she should heal with the day sleep." Jack glanced at him. "You?"

"I'll survive. You?"

"Yeah, I'm good. I'm Jack, by the way."

"I figured." Seth looked around the van as he took a seat beside Vixen in the middle row. Briar was sitting stock-still on the floor between the middle and front sets of seats. She looked shocky.

"Briar? Are you hurt?" Jack asked.

She looked at him. "I don't understand what happened." She looked around the van, her gaze lingering on each of them only momentarily before settling on Roxy. Then she climbed up into the front passenger seat and addressed the mortal woman. "Tell me. I know you know."

"Reaper used to work for the CIA, when he was human," Roxy said. "They brainwashed him, programmed him to kill. To destroy. There was a word that would trigger him to go into a murderous rage. You know now what that word is."

"Nigh—".

"No, Briar. Don't say it. He's unconscious, but I don't know what it might do."

"Briar," Seth said. "There's another word that will snap him out of it. Are you sure you don't know that one? Gregor didn't give you any clue at all?"

"No."

"Gregor tried to get you killed tonight," Seth said. "He tried to get all of us killed."

"That makes no sense," Briar said. "What would he have to gain? Reaper's the one who is his enemy, and he would have been the only one left alive."

"I think he *wants* Reaper alive," Jack said. "And maybe the only way he thinks he can get him alive is to get rid of all his helpers. And anyone else he's not certain he can trust. Like you and me, Briar."

She closed her eyes, turned her head away. "He wouldn't hurt me. Not Gregor."

"Briar, what, *exactly,* did he instruct you to do tonight?" Jack asked.

She pursed her lips, not talking.

Jack sighed. "Well, I'm willing to share. I heard something interesting last night, as I passed Gregor's office. He was on the phone with someone. Calling him *sir.*"

"Gregor wouldn't call anyone *sir,*" Briar argued.

"That's what I thought, but I heard it. He was asking about the *trigger.* I can only assume those key words are what he meant. And I know he was given two of them. I heard him writing them down, but I didn't get close enough to see." He paused in thought for a moment. "He told me to meet him here, and to bring Topaz. I arrived before you all did. I heard you and Reaper come in the front door, Briar. And then I heard the others come in through the back."

"As soon as we opened the door someone shoved us inside and locked it," Seth said. "Probably one of the drones."

"Same thing happen to you?" Jack asked Briar.

"I locked the door after Reaper and I came in."

"Why?" Roxy asked.

"Because it's what Gregor told me to do. He said to keep Reaper from arriving even a single minute early. He said to get him inside and lock the door, then to wait until I was sure you all were inside, too, and say the word." She paused. "He didn't tell me why, or what would happen next. He said he'd explain later."

"Yeah. But for you, Briar, later was never supposed to come."

She tightened her lips. "I don't believe that."

Roxy came to a red light and slowed, looking into the rearview mirror.

"I can't believe that. I have to see Gregor," Briar said.

"Briar, don't—" Jack began.

Too late. Briar yanked the door open and flung herself from the van, rolled to her feet and took off running full speed. She vanished like a blur of darkness in the night.

"Damn," Jack whispered.

"We're better off without her," Vixen said softly. "She's evil."

"And you're a fox," Jack said. "We all have our little imperfections."

22

---- ◆ ----

Reaper opened his eyes and tried to take stock. His head was pounding, and he wasn't sure where the hell he was. He seemed to be lying on the floor of a small place, and there were others there, too.

"He's awake," someone whispered.

Reaper turned his head slightly to the right. Two men were sitting in a seat ahead of him. A vehicle seat, its back between him and them. So they were in a vehicle. But it didn't seem to be moving. Both men were turned sideways, their eyes on him intently, expectantly.

His brain cleared a little. The one on the left was Seth. But he didn't know the other man. He closed his eyes tightly, because looking at them hurt. Thinking hurt even more.

"Reaper?" Seth asked. "Can you hear me?"

"Of course I can hear you." He brought his head up—too sharply—with his reply, and the kid jerked backward at the movement.

There was fear in his eyes. And it was a fear Reaper had seen before. He blinked and tried to remember, but found only a black hole. Then he looked past Seth and

the stranger to the next set of seats, where Roxy sat behind the wheel, staring at him, a sadness in her eyes that
went beyond anything he'd ever seen. Beside her, in the
passenger side, Vixen watched him with all the wari-
ness of a wild animal awaiting attack. She sat very still,
the way a rabbit did, as if thinking that made it invisible to a predator stalking slowly toward it. She might
even have been trembling a little. And her wide eyes
were riveted to him.

A sickness was beginning to uncoil in his stomach. It
was one he'd felt several times in his past. He recognized
that he was in the van, and that it was parked. He was
lying on the floor. He knew some members of his little
tribe were missing. Topaz. *Briar.* Slowly he turned his
head the other way, to the bench seat in the rear of the
van.

Topaz was lying there, still, unconscious, her face
bruised, her body in pain—he felt it, and opened his
mind to the signals and energy wafting from her. Her
ribs were broken.

He'd done that to her.

He sat up all at once, lurching onto his knees, toward
the van's side door, then hauled it open and all but fell
out. Dragging himself to his feet, he stumbled into a
nearby stand of weeds and gagged.

A hand pressed to his back, firm but comforting.
Seth's hand.

"Dude, it's all right. Tope's gonna be fine. It'll be
daylight soon, and she'll recover with the day sleep."

Gasping for breath, Reaper wiped his mouth with the
back of his hand, even though nothing had come up. His

eyes were watering until he could barely see, but he wasn't sure he could look his young protégé in the eyes anyway. "I did that to her."

"It wasn't your fault. Briar locked you in the club, and then she said whatever word it is that sets you off. Look, it wasn't you, Reap. I know that. We *all* know that."

"Briar?" He frowned and searched Seth's face. "She did that?"

Seth lowered his eyes and nodded.

"You're sure. It wasn't Gregor or—"

"She admitted it. Everyone heard her. I mean, she said she didn't know what would happen. She said she was just following orders, but I'm telling you, man, I'm not sure I believe her. That bitch is evil."

"She locked herself in with us, Seth." Roxy had come out of the van and was standing only a few feet away. "If she knew what that trigger word would do to Reaper, she would have said it, then ducked out and locked the door behind her. She would have been stupid not to."

"She *was* stupid," Seth argued. "Following that bastard Gregor's instructions without even knowing why or what the consequences would be. She could have gotten us all killed."

"I imagine that was the intent. She never claimed to be on our side," Roxy said. "And I agree, she's a bitch. But I don't think she's a suicidal one. And we can't assume she would have acted the same had she known the consequences."

"Bullshit."

Reaper held up a hand, and they both fell silent. "Where is she now? Did I—did I kill her?"

"No, of course you didn't kill her!" Roxy snapped. "Raphael, I've told you before, I do not believe you could murder an innocent, even when you're under the control of the brainwashing."

"Are you calling that lunatic an innocent?" Seth muttered.

Reaper ignored his comment, instead flinging out an arm and pointing toward the van. "Look what I did to Topaz. *Topaz,* for God's sake!" He lowered his arm, because it was shaking and he was ashamed. He needed to get away from these people—for their own good. If Gregor—and now Briar—had his trigger, he was a weapon, and he could be used to kill even those he…cared for. "I don't suppose you know what the trigger word was?"

"No," Roxy said. "Briar…left before I could get her out of earshot of you to tell us. And Gregor never gave her the second one, the deactivation word."

"She left," Reaper said. "Explain that, please."

Roxy nodded, coming closer, taking him by the arm and leading him back toward the van. "We stopped at a traffic light, and she jumped out. Not, however, before helping us get out of that club alive."

"She was helping herself," Seth snapped.

"That's your opinion," Roxy said calmly.

"She left with us because it was the best option for her. And I'll tell you something else, that Jack character did exactly the same thing. Those two cannot be trusted. I'm glad Briar left, and I'd just as soon drop her comrade off at the nearest cemetery and be done with the both of them."

They were at the van now, and none of them was under any illusion that their conversation had been private. Vampire hearing was, after all, acute, and they'd been speaking aloud.

Reaper gripped the sides of the van and pulled himself in. Vixen still sat tensely in the front passenger seat. Jack had moved all the way to the rear, sitting on the edge of the seat where Topaz lay, his eyes on her still form, but he turned when Reaper entered.

"Your fledgling friend is right, Reaper. I left that club with you because it was the option that gave me the best chance of survival. But you can believe any loyalty I felt toward Gregor is long gone. He tried to get me killed tonight. And her, too," he added, with a long look at Topaz.

"So your loyalty lies with us, now?"

"Don't you believe it," Seth said, climbing into the van behind Reaper. Roxy got into the driver's seat. "How do we know he's not a plant?"

"If he was a plant, Gregor would have taken steps to ensure he wouldn't get killed with the rest of you when I was triggered," Reaper said.

"How do you know he didn't?" Seth shot a hateful look back at Jack. "How do you know Gregor didn't give him the second word, the deactivation code? He could have had it all along, with instructions to use it only when his own neck was on the chopping block. Maybe Briar's, too."

"If I knew the deactivation word, don't you think I

would have used it when he was kicking the hell out of Topaz?"

"Right, Topaz, the chick you screwed out of a half million bucks. The chick you left with a broken heart. *That* Topaz, right?"

Jack lowered his head.

"This is getting us nowhere," Reaper said. "It's enough. And none of it matters, anyway, because it's clearly me Gregor wants, not any of you."

"He wants us, all right. He wants us *dead*." Seth sat down hard in the middle seat.

"Only to make it easier for him to get to Reaper," Vixen said. Her voice was very soft, barely more than a whisper, but she spoke with certainty. And when they all looked at her expectantly, she went on. "I know him. Jack does, too. Gregor is lazy, and basically, a coward. He gets others to fight his battles for him. Others take all the risks, do all the work. He reaps the benefits."

Then she hesitated, as if suddenly unsure of herself.

"Vixen, keep talking," Reaper said. "Tell us what you think. You clearly have an idea about all this."

She brought her head up again, her eyes meeting Reaper's. "He set you up. Locked us all in a room together and convinced Briar to trigger you into a rage. He expected everyone in that room to be killed. He expected all of us to die, except for you, and what would have happened after that?"

Reaper frowned, searching his mind. "I would have continued raging until I was spent, I guess. Until I passed out or the day sleep took me."

Seth picked up the story. "I can tell you what would

have happened next. Reaper would have been found right there, at that club, surrounded by dead bodies. Mortal authorities could never hold him, but they would try. Word would get out that he had become the most deadly rogue of them all. The vampire community would turn against him. He would be hunted, just as Gregor is." Seth looked Reaper in the eye. "You would have had no one left to come to your aid. And you would have gone after him for vengeance, but you would have gone alone."

Reaper turned in his seat to look back at Jack. "You agree with that assessment?"

"I do. I don't know why he wants you or what he has planned once he gets you. But this all fits with what I overheard on the phone. He said something about making you the most deadly, dangerous rogue in history, turning both mortals and vampires against you. It's pretty clear he wants you alive. And I personally think he's working for someone else, rather than himself. But, yeah, he wants you alone," Jack said.

"Then that's what he's going to get."

"You can't, Reap," Seth said. "He's still got you at a disadvantage. He's got the damned drones, a whole army of the bastards. He's got your triggers. He can control your freaking mind, pal. It's no good, not like that."

"We need to stick together," Vixen said. "If getting you alone is what Gregor wants, then that's the last thing we should give him. Why play right into his hands?"

"Because by staying with you, I'm putting you at

risk." Reaper looked around the van at each of them, his gaze lingering on Topaz, lying so still in the back. "I could have killed you. All of you. Gregor will trigger me again. If getting me alone is his goal, then getting rid of you is essential to his plan. Unless I get rid of you first."

"I won't leave you, Reap," Seth said. "No way. No way in hell. I'm with you in this. You saved my life, and I owe you."

Reaper sighed, knowing he wasn't going to be able to give Seth, or any of them, a choice in the matter. He needed to go after Gregor alone. He needed to see to it that his little gang was safe while he did so. And he needed to find Briar.

His last clear memory, before the moment when they'd walked into the club, was of having explosive sex with her in the front seat of the Mustang. It had been intense. It had been insane. And more than just a mating of bodies—they'd shared blood. That created a bond.

He could feel her, even now. She was thinking about him, too. She was alone, and she was angry. Furious. Cursing him as she searched the night for another man.

For Gregor.

You might as well forget him, Briar, Reaper thought, sending the message out to her on the wings of the night. *You belong to me now, and I promise you, I'm coming to claim you. Soon.*

He didn't expect a reply, so he was surprised when he heard one whispering through his mind, so full of turmoil that it felt like a million tiny electric shocks were zipping through his brain along with the message.

I belong to no one. It was just sex, Reaper. It was a delaying tactic. Get over it.

You lie.

You think so? Try to come for me again and you'll find out, I promise. I'll kill you if I can.

I'm not your enemy, Briar.

You beat the living hell out of me, and all your friends tonight. You took me from Gregor, gave him cause to distrust me. If you're not an enemy, then I've never had one.

I hurt you? The realization almost made him want to throw up again. *I'm sorry.*

Fuck you, Reaper.

She threw a block around her mind then, cutting herself off from him so thoroughly that there was no chance of him reaching her again. He sighed, glanced up to the front seat at Roxy. "Why are we just sitting here?" he asked.

"Well, I didn't dare take us back to the warehouse. Briar's liable as not to tell Gregor where we were. You didn't blindfold her on the way to the meeting."

"I didn't intend to let her leave with him."

"I know. Anyway, we need another place. And we'd probably better make it soon."

"There's a freight yard," Jack said.

Everyone turned to look at him. He shrugged. "Boxcars make good beds. No windows. I've used them before, in a pinch. Not exactly five-star accommodations, but—"

"Do *not* trust that man," Seth said.

Reaper narrowed his eyes on Jack, wondering if he was a good enough con to set them all up for another attack by Gregor. And that was when Topaz spoke, her lips moving slowly, her voice weak. "You can trust him," she said.

Jack looked more surprised than anyone else in the vehicle.

"Not with your hearts, but…yeah. With your lives, he's okay."

"I agree with her," Vixen said.

Jack's apparently stunned expression grew even more amazed.

Reaper nodded. "Jack, climb up front and give Roxy directions, if you would."

Jack made his way to the front, and once he'd gone by, Reaper moved to the back and sat where Jack had been, beside Topaz. He stared down at her, afraid to touch her, unsure how to begin.

She opened her swollen eyes. "I owe you a kick in the balls," she said. Her voice was strained. "Remind me when I'm feeling better, will you?"

"I'm sorry," he whispered. "I don't know what I can do to make this up to you, princess, but I promise, I will."

"Oh, you are *damn* right you will." She lifted a hand, closed it around his. It was ice-cold, her grip weak, and she was trembling. "I know it wasn't you," she whispered.

"That doesn't make it all right. I put you all at risk by letting you come along with me on this mission in the first place. I never should have done that. I knew better."

"We were forewarned. We made a choice."

"She's right," Seth said. He was in the center seat, leaning over, listening in. "You gave us all the information, even armed us so we could shoot your sorry ass if you got out of line. We can choose to leave if the reality is too scary for us."

Reaper lowered his head, certain that it wasn't a choice he would or could give them. It was his choice, his responsibility. If he killed one of them next time— hell, how would he live with that?

He realized with no small measure of surprise that he'd come to care about these misfits. In spite of himself.

"We're vampires," Seth went on. "Maybe not as old or as wise or as strong as you. Maybe not as experienced or as tough as you. But we're vampires, Reaper. Immortals. The undead. We have as much right to make our own decisions, take our own risks, as anyone else. As much right as Damien himself. As much right as the oldest, the first."

Reaper nodded as if he agreed. He didn't, but they would only argue if he tried to reason with them. Turning, he glanced through the windshield at the sky. "How long before we get to the freight yard?" he asked.

"Ten minutes," Jack said. "Give or take."

"Good. We have just under an hour until dawn." Then he closed his eyes. "I wonder where…"

"Gregor is?" Seth asked. Then he grinned. "I'd have damn well loved to see his face when he walked into that club, expecting to find us all dead and you out of your mind, exhausted or unconscious, just waiting for him to take you. And instead he found us all gone, and a few dozen bullet-hole-riddled drones littering the sidewalk."

"And a few more torn to shreds by Vixen's friends," Roxy added with a laugh. She met Reaper's puzzled eyes. "We can explain that later," she said.

Reaper hardly noticed what she said, because he hadn't been wondering where Gregor was at all. He'd been wondering about Briar. Had she made it back to that black-hearted bastard? Was she even now curling into his arms?

Having sex with him? Drinking from him? Letting him drink from her? Kissing him?

The thought damn near sent him into a brand-new frenzy. And that made him angry, because dammit, he didn't want to give a shit about her.

She was treacherous, and she was deadly.

And he wanted her more than he wanted to wake up at sundown.

The boxcars didn't offer much in the way of privacy. Not that Vixen thought it really mattered anymore. Seth, however, seemed to have other ideas.

As the others were claiming their space in the forty-foot-long-by-ten-foot-wide metal box, Vixen reached for the handle to pull herself up and in. Seth stopped her, a hand on the small of her back to get her attention.

She jumped and looked back at him, startled by the contact.

"Sorry. Didn't mean to scare you."

"I'm tense and jumpy after…after all that death back there. It was—"

"I know."

She nodded. "So many innocent lives, just snuffed out. And for no reason. Why didn't he just clear the place out? Why kill them all?"

"You heard Jack's theory. Gregor wants to convince the world—the undead world, at least—that Reaper is no better than he is. That he murders the innocent just as brutally, just as carelessly."

"But how would that benefit him?"

Seth shrugged. "Until we know what he's after, we can't even guess. But I don't want to talk to you about that."

"No, I don't suppose you want to talk to me at all." She lowered her eyes, nodded once and turned to reach for the handle again. It was high above her head. She didn't really need it; she could have jumped. She just didn't feel moved to expend a single ounce of energy. She felt dead inside. Like the mortals littering the floor of The Crypt.

"I do, actually. I think…I think we need to talk."

"I don't think I can."

He frowned. "I want to know about you, who you are. What you are, or were. What it means. You know?"

"No, you don't."

He frowned at her. "Yes, I do. You…you called in the help of the animals back there. You saved our asses by doing it. And you risked your neck for me."

She shrugged. "It was no risk. I could have shifted and run away before any of those clumsy drones could have touched me."

"Now *you're* lying."

She shot him a glare.

"I saw you change, remember? It took a few minutes. They would have killed you before you changed completely."

Sighing, she turned to face him fully. "Fine. I'll tell you what I am. Or what I was, anyway. I was a human who was possessed by the spirit of the fox, my totem, in a way far beyond what is normal, as were my mother before me and hers before her, and on and on. My great great great grandmother was full-blooded Iroquois. Daughter of the chief of her tribe, whose family totem was the red fox. My great great great grandfather was a Scot, blood and bone, of the clan McFarland. His family crest bore the face of a fox. And since the days when those two reproduced, the firstborn female of every generation has had the gift.

"And it *is* a gift, Seth, though it might seem a curse to you."

He lowered his head, seeming ashamed. "So you really *are* human."

"No," she said. "I'm a vampire. Now."

"But before…"

She closed her eyes. "Human, yes. But not by choice."

He closed a hand around her shoulder, turned her to face him. "Explain that to me. Come on, let's sit a while."

"We don't have much time."

"We have a little." He led her to a nearby handcar, took a seat.

Reluctantly, she perched beside him, but on the very edge, her toes touching the ground, knees bent, hands braced. She was ready to spring up and run.

He'd hurt her. She didn't like that kind of pain, emotional pain. She wasn't used to it, didn't understand it. She only knew for certain that she never wanted to feel it again.

The night was waning. Crickets and frogs chirped, and the cool breeze chilled her, though not in the usual way. She felt cold, but no discomfort.

"You said you were human, but not by choice," he prompted.

She nodded. "I've always preferred the company of animals to that of people. I've always loved my time as a fox far more than my time as a woman. Human emotions seemed foolish to me. All heat and anger, joy and sorrow. All pain and pleasure. No balance, no common sense. Just a roller coaster of dizzying highs and heartbreaking lows and sudden twists and turns you could never anticipate."

"And life as a fox?"

"Oh." She sighed, and she felt her shoulders relax a bit, and her lips curve into a smile. "So much better. It's logical, you know? It's about finding enough to eat, avoiding enemies, hunting, playing and being warm and comfortable. It's about using your senses, paying attention, listening and watching and scenting the air. It's about being wild and free. Free of so much, of worry, of stress. You don't worry when you're an animal. What happens, happens. It's nature."

He nodded slowly, and said, "I see," but she didn't think he possibly could.

"So I spent as much time as I could in that form. Several hours every day. I lived among the wild things, far more than anyone else in my family ever had. I learned to communicate with them. But I couldn't be one with them, because I didn't belong. I didn't feel I belonged with people, either. So when I was in human form, I kept to myself. I avoided others. Relationships. Complications. Worry. I tried to live the way my friends in the forest lived. Without worry or fear or highs and lows. Just surviving and taking as much comfort as possible in every day, every hour, every moment."

"And how has that changed?"

She shifted her gaze. It had ostensibly been directed at the sky, but in reality it had been turned inward. She hadn't been seeing anything other than the past as it unfolded behind her eyes. Now she looked at him. And she thought he was truly listening.

"The longer I spent in fox form, the stronger I became. The stronger I became, the longer I could maintain the form. The easier it was to shift. By the time Gregor found me, I was able to spend around six hours each day as a fox. Some days, I could even manage four hours in the morning and four more in the evening."

"How did he find you?"

She lifted her brows. "I got caught in a trap while chasing rabbits near his mansion. I didn't know I was one of the Chosen. He must have felt me near, known instinctively I was in trouble and come to my aid, as every vampire is compelled to do. But instead of a human, he found a wounded fox. And yet he felt it, that I was one of the Chosen. So he took me back to the mansion, held me in a cell, and watched and waited. And when I changed back, he saw, and then he knew."

Seth was nodding very slowly. "And then what happened?"

She averted her eyes, turning her head away, getting to her feet. "He changed me. That's all. The rest you know." She swallowed hard. "Since the change, I've been weaker. I can only manage to shift forms a few times a week. And I can only maintain my fox shape for an hour or so. I've found I can go out in daylight as a fox, without harm. But if I changed back while exposed to the sun, I'm certain I would go up in flames."

He got up, too. "I'm sorry, Vixen. I mean it. I'm sorry you lost something so precious to you, but more than that, I'm sorry I reacted the way I did to learning your secret. I…I'd like another chance."

"I wouldn't," she said without looking at him. And then she started walking back toward the railroad car.

He ran to catch up, caught her by the forearm, turned her to face him. "Wait a minute. What do you mean?"

"With you, Seth, I experienced those emotions I've avoided all my life," she told him. "And do you know what I ended up feeling most of all?" She watched his face, waited for him to answer. When he didn't, she went on. "More than desire, more than passion, more than love and longing and need, I felt pain. And it was far worse than the pain of the collar I wore for Gregor, when Briar's sadistic nature made her press the button and send shocks through my body. It was far worse than the pain of having my leg bitten almost in two by the teeth of a cruel trap. It was the most crippling, most horrible pain I have ever felt in my life. And you inflicted it on me. *You,* Seth. When you rejected me."

"I'm sorry. God, I'm so sorry."

She shrugged. "Being sorry doesn't take it away. It's a fresh wound, Seth, but one I'm certain will leave a vivid scar. It's not something I can ever forget. And it's definitely not something I ever want to feel again. For you to say 'give me another chance' is as if Gregor were saying to me, 'give the collar another chance, Vixen. It won't hurt this time. I promise.'" She held Seth's eyes, though his image became distorted through her tears.

"No, Seth," she whispered. "I'm afraid I can't give you another chance to hurt me that way again. You or…or anyone else, for that matter."

"I swear to God, I'll never hurt you like that again."

She smiled very gently, lifted a hand to touch his cheek and whispered, "I know you won't."

And then she lowered her hand and turned to walk to the boxcar, ignoring his calls to her to wait, to listen, to give him a shot. She climbed inside and strode straight to Reaper, who sat with his knees bent upward and his back against the wall. Her mind spoke to his, and his alone.

I know what you're planning, and I'm going with you.

I don't know what you're talking about.

You're going to go after Gregor alone. I know him. I know the mansion. I know Briar.

You could be hurt.

I'm a shape-shifter, Reaper. That's the secret I've been keeping. Everyone knows it now but you, so I suppose I might as well tell you. I can change into a fox and maintain that form for an hour at a time. I can go out in daylight in that form. I get into places where others cannot hope to go. I can go unnoticed. And I can speak to and command the aid of animals of any sort, in any form. I can help you, Reaper. And if you go without me, I'll know where you've gone, and I'll simply follow.*

Lowering his head, he thought to her, *Seth will never forgive me if anything happens to you.*

She lifted her brows. *Seth has no rights here, and no say in the matter.*

Reaper met her eyes and nodded once, firmly.

She nodded back, then turned and went to the opposite corner to lie down. But even as she curled up into herself, she glimpsed Jack staring at her.

"What are you up to?" he whispered.

She widened her eyes to their most innocent setting. "Nothing at all. Why do you ask?"

Topaz glanced at her curiously. She was sitting next to Jack, though not close enough to touch. Clearly, she was trying to keep him at arm's length, despite the obvious attraction between them.

Vixen supposed she understood that now.

Jack slid a look toward Reaper, his eyes full of meaning. "No reason."

Vixen lowered her head onto her folded arms, closed her eyes and, without opening them, whispered, "Jack?"

"Yeah?"

"You know that conversation you overheard in Gregor's office? The one where you said he was calling someone sir and asking for triggers?"

"Yeah."

"I don't suppose Gregor keeps any sorts of…pets in his office, does he?"

"Yeah," he said for the third time, "he has a rat."

She blinked her eyes slowly. "I hate rats."

"I know." He paused, then went on. "There's something else in his rooms that you'll want to set free. Check the bigger cage with the sheet over it."

She frowned, but asked no further questions. "Thanks, Jack."

Give him my best, will you? Jack thought.

Who? Vixen asked.

Jack sighed, folded his hands behind his head and lay his head back on them. *The rat.*

23

—▸ ◂—

Briar arrived at the mansion in the midst of a downpour. She was soaking wet, and her clothes were torn from her dramatic leap from the van, not to mention her struggles with the murderous drones.

They would be around. If she just walked up to the doors, they would probably kill her before she got any farther. So she hesitated at the far end of the drive, though she stood in plain sight, in the open.

Gregor.

She waited. He didn't reply. Of course he didn't. He couldn't hear her inside the mansion. The drones would sense her soon, though, and she had to get his attention before they did.

She cast her gaze around in search of a way to get Gregor's attention, coming up with no ideas, until the wind picked up and a small twig snapped from a nearby tree and landed at her feet. As her attention turned down to where it lay, she noticed the pebbles, slick and wet, on the ground around it. Bending, she picked one up and, taking careful aim, hurled it toward Gregor's bedroom window.

Then she waited, but this time only for a moment. The heavy curtains parted, and his face appeared in the window, staring outward, searching the night. She sensed his attention on her. Then the curtains fell closed again, and moments later the huge front doors opened, and Gregor stood silhouetted in the opening.

She stared at him, at the man she'd found irresistible from the moment she had first awakened in his arms, the taste of his blood on her lips, a new energy singing through her veins. He was tall and strong. Not handsome, but it didn't matter. He had saved her life. He had made her immortal. He had shared the very essence of himself—his own blood—with her. And for that, she would always be grateful.

She stood there, dripping wet, while he remained in the shelter of the house, staring at her just as she stared at him. She knew he was surveying the area, as well, trying to sense whether others had come with her.

"I escaped them," she said. She didn't raise her voice. He could hear her, even at this distance.

"And returned to me."

She nodded. "I'm alone, Gregor. I need...I need to speak to you."

He considered that for a moment, then, slowly, lifted his arms toward her and smiled gently.

A sob choked her, and she ran to him, relieved at his welcome, though her mind was still full of questions. When she reached him, she flung her arms around his neck, and he twined his around her waist and hugged her close for a moment. "I'm very glad you've come back, Briar. So very glad."

"I wasn't sure of my welcome," she whispered.

"Why would you be? You helped my enemies escape me, after all." His arms loosened from around her waist then, and he put his hands on her shoulders, held her away from him and studied her face. "You killed several of my drones, and helped Reaper and his minions get away. Why did you do that, Briar?"

She blinked twice, a new tension coiling in her belly. "To save my own life. Gregor, your drones were trying to kill *me* along with the others."

He said nothing. Just waited.

"Did you order them to kill me, Gregor?"

He narrowed his eyes on her. "Why would you ask such a thing? Has this Reaper brainwashed you?"

She shook her head. "No. But you didn't warn me what would happen when I said the word to him. You didn't tell me that he would explode into a rage and try his best to kill everyone within reach. He could have killed me."

"I had every confidence in your ability to protect yourself."

"But you didn't do a damn thing to make sure of it." She looked at the floor. "You could have told me what would happen, told me to say the word and then get out fast. You could have given me the second word, the one that would make him stop."

"I see. So that's why you've come back, then?"

"What?"

"To get the second word from me," he said. "So you can take it back to him."

"No." She frowned, and took a backward step away from him.

"No? Don't lie to me, Briar. I know you too well. And I saw you with him, in that car. I saw you mount him like an animal in heat. I saw—"

"I *had* to do that! You told me not to let him arrive at the club early, no matter what it took. You told me to do whatever I had to do to keep him out until the appointed time."

"Yes, I did. I rather thought you would apply some less dramatic tactics first, though, before resorting to fucking him senseless."

"Sex means nothing to me. You know that."

"Just a means to an end, right, Briar?"

"That's all it's ever been."

"But you liked it. Admit it. You enjoyed having sex with him."

"No."

"You came."

"No!"

"I was watching. You betrayed me, Briar. First by giving him what you've refused me all this time, despite the fact that I saved your worthless life, pulled you from the gutters and the streets, the drugs with which you were poisoning yourself, the men to whom you were whoring yourself. Despite knowing what you owed me, you gave yourself to him. And then you helped him get away."

"It wasn't like that." She backed up some more, realizing now that she was in danger here. She needed to get to the door, escape through it.

"And now you have the nerve to come here, pretending to be loyal to me, and ask me to give you the ability to disable the only weapon I have that can destroy him."

"Gregor," she said, and she spoke in a level, firm tone, slowly and clearly, as if that could somehow help him to hear and understand. "I *am* loyal to you. That's why I left them. And I didn't ask for the word. I don't give a damn about the word."

"You're a very poor liar, my dear."

She was nearly to the door and, she sensed, completely out of time. She turned in a whirl of speed, only to collide with the solid chest of a drone. Its beefy hands closed on her arms and hurled her backward. She landed on a table, breaking it in half before hitting the floor.

Pain surged as she pushed herself up, and then Gregor had her by the throat, raising her to her feet but not letting go.

"You are mine, Briar. Mine, and mine alone. You're going to learn that in short order."

"Gregor, please," she rasped.

He glanced at the drone. "Hold her."

The creature came around behind her, gripped her arms and pulled them painfully behind her back, holding her hard. She struggled, but it only served to tug her shoulders against their sockets.

Gregor released his death grip on her throat and took something from his pocket. She recognized it and went still, as ice water rushed into her veins. A collar like the one Vixen had worn. He came closer, moving it toward her neck.

"No, Gregor, no. You've got it all wrong. I was never on their side."

He smiled slowly as he slid the thing around her neck and buckled it tight, so tight it constricted her breathing. "I own you, Briar. And you're going to repay me for all I've done for you. You're going to repay me by helping me get Reaper. I'm going to lure him to me, and I'm going to drink him dry. I'm going to take all his power for myself. And once he's dead, I'm going to make you forget he ever lived."

"Gregor, I'm telling you, I didn't betray you," she whispered.

"Take her to the dungeon. Put her in the cage. I want her naked and in chains. No blood. No blanket. No comfort of any kind."

The drone tugged at her, and she jerked against him. And then suddenly she was jolted as electricity surged from the collar. Her entire body went rigid in pain, and when it stopped, she sank to the floor, her muscles twitching spasmodically.

Gregor knelt beside her. "I'm going to break you, Briar. By the time I finish with you, you'll be begging. Begging for sustenance, for relief—and for me. Do you understand?"

She lifted her head, her eyes on his. "I'll never beg anyone for anything," she whispered.

He smiled and hit the button again. She screamed this time, and when it stopped, she was too weak even to move. She thought of Vixen wearing the collar, of the way *she* had pressed that button. She closed her eyes and felt the first true regret she had ever known.

Then the drone was lifting her and carrying her away, to the basement, the dungeon, the cell.

She supposed that was where she would die. Because she would never give in. *Never.*

Sundown. Vixen woke to find the others all still sound asleep—except for Reaper. He was gone. *But he'd agreed to let her go with him, damn him.*

Startled, she leapt to her feet and went to the boxcar's sliding door, which stood slightly open. She peered out and saw him. He was at the van, gathering weapons.

Glancing back at the others, her gaze lingered on Seth's sleeping face. Just for a moment, she drank it in. She loved to look at him. He was beautiful to her, the shape of his jaw, his chin, his nose, the way his eyes lay closed so lightly. A lump came into her throat, and she closed her eyes, forcing herself to turn away. Quickly, she slipped through the open door, then turned to pull it closed, all the while straining not to make too much noise.

"Don't worry, they won't wake," Reaper said.

She turned sharply to face him. He'd returned from the van, coming up behind her unheard. He held weapons in his hands. "How can you be so sure?" she asked.

"Mind control is more difficult to exercise on vampires than on humans," he said. "But I'm older and stronger than they are."

"You commanded them to stay at rest?"

He nodded. "Don't worry. They'll wake within the

hour." He hefted a leather strap lined with tiny loops, each one of which held a bullet. A holster hung at the end, heavy with the handgun it cradled. He lowered it over her head. "Put one arm through." She did as he told her, and then he repeated the process with a second contraption, and bent to adjust the straps and buckles. When he finished, the straps crossed one another, and a handgun rested at each of her hips. "These are powerful—forty-caliber Glocks. They're what most police officers use. But they fire ordinary bullets. You still have your tranq gun?"

"Yes." She pulled it out to show him. "I need more darts, though."

He took a handful of them from his pocket, handed them to her. She loaded one into the tiny weapon, pocketed the rest and tucked the tiny gun into the back of her jeans.

"Are you afraid?"

She nodded.

"Good. It would be foolish not to be." He studied her face, then frowned. "What else?"

"What do you mean?"

"I mean, there's something else bothering you. You look...sad."

She shrugged and turned toward the van. "We should go, before they wake."

"You're not coming back with me, are you, Vixen?"

She licked her lips, lifted her chin and battled the tears that tried to gather in her eyes. "No. Once we rid the world of Gregor, I need to move on. Alone."

"Seth really blew it, didn't he?"

"I don't want to talk about that." She had reached the van, opened the door and climbed into the passenger seat.

Reaper went around to the driver's side and got behind the wheel. He started the engine and was driving before he spoke again. "Vixen, Seth is young. Whatever he did or said to hurt you, I know he didn't mean it. He's crazy about you."

"Not all of me," she said softly.

He frowned, and she knew he couldn't possibly understand what she was feeling.

"There's a part of me he cares for. Perhaps very deeply. But there's another part of me that repulses him. And it just can't work between us like that."

Reaper sighed. "I think you should give him another chance." He focused on the road as he spoke. "And I'm older and wiser than you, so you should really listen to my advice."

She glanced at him quickly, caught a teasing light in his eyes, and felt a sad smile tugging at her lips. She liked Reaper, she realized. "Do you have any sort of a plan?"

"Not much of one. I'm going to fall back on my childhood heroes and call him out."

"I don't understand what that means."

"No? You never watched any old cowboy movies?"

"No."

"Well, I don't blame you. I've never been much for television or films myself. But when I was very young, there were a few I couldn't get enough of. And those were westerns. You just watch and learn, little one. Watch and learn." He drove on.

Seth knew something was wrong the minute he woke. It was far later than it should have been, for one thing. He opened his eyes, sensed the hour and came fully awake fast, sitting up and scanning the dark interior of the boxcar. Roxy was curled up in one corner. Topaz lay not far from her side. Jack was stretched out against the far wall.

Reaper was nowhere in sight, nor was Vixen.

Surging to his feet, he raced to the door, yanked it open wide.

"Seth?" Roxy's sleepy voice came to him, and he heard her getting up. "What's up, kiddo? What's going on?"

He turned, saw Topaz and Jack coming awake, as well. "The van's gone. So are Reaper and Vixen."

"I expected as much," Jack said. He stretched his arms over his head, and before he lowered them again, Seth was in front of him, gripping his shirt.

"What do you mean, you expected it? Where are they?"

Jack lifted his brows and glanced down at the hands on his shirt. "You really don't want to do that."

"You don't have a clue what I want. What do you know, Heart?"

"Let go of him," Topaz said. She said it calmly, and in a low, steady tone. Didn't shout or raise her voice. But it was intense, and brooked no argument. Seth released Jack, for her sake and for the moment. He knew he'd been out of line, though he would never admit it.

Jack smoothed his shirt. "I don't *know* anything, pal. But I sensed the two of them having a private conversation before dawn. Had a feeling they were planning something of this sort."

"Something of what sort?" Seth demanded.

"Use your brain instead of your temper for a change, kid. What do you *think* they're doing?"

"They went after Gregor, didn't they?" Topaz asked.

"That would be my first guess," Jack said dryly.

Seth swore, turning in a slow circle and pushing a hand through his hair.

Roxy got to her feet, began folding her blanket. "I expected him to try to shake us off and go it alone," she said. "He believes he could have killed us all last night, after all. He wouldn't want to risk that happening again. And if Gregor has his triggers, he can send Raphael into a killing rage with no more than a word." She sighed deeply. "What I can't understand is why he would take Vixen with him."

"I doubt she gave him much of a choice," Seth muttered. "She can be stubborn as hell. Dammit, I'll never forgive Reaper if anything happens to her."

"Given her abilities, he was probably wise to take her along," Jack said. "I've never come across a vampire with such unique talents."

"She's one of a kind, all right," Roxy said.

"I hope she's okay," Topaz put in.

Everyone looked at her, and she shrugged. "I was getting used to having the little weirdo around."

"We have to go after them," Seth said.

"Be reasonable," Jack told him. Seth shot him a look

of disbelief, and the other man lifted his brows. "What? How do you suggest we go to the rescue? They took the van, and presumably all the weapons with it."

"Right," Roxy said. "And the Mustang was abandoned when we fled The Crypt. Though I suppose it might still be wherever Reaper parked it."

Jack nodded and went on. "Gregor's place will be surrounded by hulking drones who can snap us like toothpicks. And they'll likely be expecting us. Are we going to charge in there and let them murder us all?"

"We *have* to go after them," Seth repeated emphatically.

Roxy nodded. "I don't disagree with you, hon. But we have to do it wisely. It won't do them any damn good whatsoever otherwise."

24

— ◆ —

Vixen crouched in the sheltering trees outside Gregor's mansion. She was trembling with fear but determined to do this thing, to help her friends.

It was odd, having people she considered friends for the first time in her life. She actually cared about them and believed that they cared about her, too. Even Seth, in his way.

Reaper put a hand on her shoulder. "Gregor can trigger the rage in me at any second, Vixen. It's important that you put some distance between us. You're in twice the danger that I am here, because you have to fear my attack, as well as that of our enemies. So be careful. Don't be seen. Don't risk yourself, no matter what."

She met his eyes in the darkness and smiled gently. "I'll get the information we need. I promise."

"Listen for me. I'll block everyone but you and Gregor. He won't hear me until he's outside the mansion. Wait until he leaves, and even then—"

"I'll be careful." She nodded once, then turned and raced away from him, circling the mansion, to a secluded spot near the back. And there she waited, working to pull in her focus, her energy, preparing for the shift.

Moments ticked by, and finally she heard Reaper as he called out mentally.

Gregor.

The reply was immediate, and there was no sense of fear in Gregor's mind. Vixen heard his reply through Reaper's mind. *Hello, Reaper. I've been expecting you. Which is why I've been listening through the open window.*

Reaper looked up, guided by his sense of the man, and spotted him near an open window on the second floor. The bastard waved in his direction, even though Reaper was concealed by trees. Gregor knew he was there, must sense him there. Oh, he was good.

I hope you haven't come for Briar, though. If so, I'm afraid you'll be sorely disappointed. She's terribly glad to be back where she belongs.

I'm here for you, Gregor. And I'm alone. There's no one here you can make me hurt.

Smart move, I suppose. But I don't need to trigger your insanity to take you out. I can do that all by myself.

Now's your chance to prove it. Come out, meet me. And come alone, Gregor, or I won't be there when you arrive. I'm watching. I'll know if you deploy drones or set traps for me. This is you and me, one on one. If you're man enough.

When and where, Reaper?

Fifteen minutes. There's a vacant lot, where kids play baseball. Ten miles north of here, turn left and take the dirt road another three miles. It's on the right. No cover, nowhere either of us could hide reinforcements. Nothing.

I'll be there.

I'll be waiting.

Vixen closed her eyes, but only briefly. She had to watch the mansion. She had to watch until she saw Gregor leave, and make absolutely sure he left alone and no one followed. If anyone did, she would be able to alert Reaper instantly.

So she watched, and she waited. Ten minutes ticked past before she sensed Reaper leaving in a blur of speed. And a minute after that she saw Gregor leaving the mansion.

But he wasn't alone. He had Briar at his side.

No one else followed. No drones, no backup.

Vixen focused on Reaper's mind and worked hard to apply Roxy's lessons in blocking anyone else from hearing her thoughts. She envisioned a pure beam of light surging from her mind to Reaper's, but traveling through a pipeline of solid lead, a pipeline nothing could penetrate.

Reaper.

I'm here.

He's on his way. Briar is with him. No one else, at least not so far.

Good enough. Thank you, Vixen.

Be safe, Reaper.

Briar walked beside Gregor through the night to the waiting vehicle, his shiny black Porsche. Wherever they were going, she was glad they were driving. She wouldn't have been able to go very far on foot.

She'd been taken to the cell in the hours before dawn. She'd been stripped, her wrists shackled to the wall on either side of her, her ankles encased in a single iron band. And there she'd stayed, almost unable to move, in a pose reminiscent of the crucifixion.

Every little while, perhaps at fifteen-minute intervals, the collar at her neck came alive with cruel jolting energy. Her entire body went stiff, every muscle tensing until she thought they would tear apart. Her back arched, and her head slammed back against the stone wall. Her body jerked against its restraints, and she couldn't control that, so the iron cut into her wrists and ankles more deeply every time. And when it ended, she would hang there, trembling, weak, shivering, her entire body in pain.

She could only assume Gregor was above, comfortable at the fireplace, hitting the button maliciously whenever the mood struck him. The pain was intolerable. Maddening. And after the first few jolts, she began to feel terror as the minutes ticked past and she awaited the inevitable.

By the time the sun rose, she'd lost most of her ability for coherent thought. She only knew intense relief as she sank into the vampiric day sleep and waited for the healing power of a vampire's rest to restore her.

But when the sun sank that dusk, even as she began to wake, the jolting came again. And again. And again. Yes, the day sleep had restored her, but she was weak— in dire need of blood to complete the healing and replenish her energy. Instead, she received only torture and pain, weakening her body and mind even further.

And then Gregor was there, standing at her cell door. She hadn't even sensed his presence until she heard the key turning in the lock, metal on metal. She lifted her head weakly, squinted through eyes not quite focused.

Gregor swung the door open and stepped into the cell. He slung a handful of clothing onto the floor and came to her, unlocking her ankles and then her wrists. She sank to the floor.

"Get up and put the clothes on. And do it as quickly as your current state allows, Briar. We have an appointment to keep."

She pushed herself up onto her hands. "I…can't."

"Oh. Well, in that case, I might as well keep the electricity surging, I suppose." He reached to his chest, and she saw the blurry shape of the remote, his torture device, hanging from a chain around his neck.

"No, please."

"Then do as I say."

"I need…sustenance, Gregor. I'm not even sure I can stand."

"I anticipated your needs. Here." He took a flask from his pocket and removed its thimble-sized lid. He filled it with a sip of blood from the flask, and then he bent and held it to her lips.

She drank, but it was barely a swallow. Nowhere near enough.

"That's all you're getting. Ask for more and you'll get another taste of my power over you. Now, get dressed."

The blood caused a slight tingle, a dim echo of the power that would thrum through her veins if she could truly feed. She prayed it was enough to keep her alive, because truly, she felt nearer to death just then than she had ever felt before. And maybe it would be better if death took her. At least there would be no more of this agony.

She struggled to her feet, shuffled to the corner and began to pick up the clothing he'd thrown there. They were her own things. Black leather pants, skintight and difficult to put on. A leather jacket. No blouse, no undergarments. She struggled into them, then sank to the floor again to pull on the black boots, wondering how she would manage to walk in their spiked heels when she could barely stand.

As soon as the second boot was zipped, Gregor grabbed her by the arm and jerked her to her feet.

"You'll walk beside me. You'll hold your head up. You'll appear for all the world as if nothing is wrong, and you will also appear to adore me. Waver from these instructions in any way and I'll put you on your knees, Briar. Do you understand?"

"Yes."

"You'd better. Now, come along. We're going to meet your lover. And you're going to watch me kill him. I might even make you help." He smiled slowly and tugged her along beside him, through the basement and up the stairs to the main house, then through it and out the front door.

He led her to the sleek black Porsche, settled her into the passenger seat. And then he was behind the wheel and driving through the night. Briar couldn't stop looking at the remote control he wore around his neck, or thinking about the flask of blood in his pocket. If she could get those things from him, she might be able to stop him from murdering Reaper.

That thought gave her pause, and in her pain-fogged mind, she clarified her goal. If she could get those things from him, she might be able to survive. That was the goal—the *only* goal: her own survival.

It always had been.

Moments after Gregor and Briar sped away in the black car, Vixen trotted on furred toes toward the house. She went straight to the front door and launched herself bodily toward it, colliding hard enough to make a loud thump she knew would be heard. She landed on her feet, jarred but determined, and quickly darted behind a large potted plant on the landing to wait.

Soon the door opened, and one of the drones stepped through it and stood there, looking around.

She trotted past his feet unnoticed and into the house, shooting underneath a sofa and curling up there, waiting.

Soon enough the drone returned, closing the door. He tromped across the floor, returning almost mindlessly to whatever he'd been doing before. And when she was sure the room was once again empty, Vixen darted out from her hiding place, her tail flying behind her, and up the stairs to Gregor's suite.

Once there, she faced a closed door, and she knew it was likely locked. There was no way to open it, not in her current form. But shifting back would take so much energy—and she wouldn't be able to change again for hours. She might very well become trapped in Gregor's lair.

And yet she didn't see any other option. She looked up and down the hallway, and seeing no one nearby, she lay down on the floor, curled into her luxuriant tail and focused on shifting back.

Minutes ticked by as her body strained and morphed, lengthened and broadened. A haze of oblivion lay over her mind like a silk blanket, and as it cleared, she found herself curled on the floor, in plain sight. She'd left her clothes in the woods and so had nothing with which to cover herself. But first things first.

She rose to her feet, willing the strength to return to her body quickly, as she looked again up and down the hallway, and again saw nothing. No one. But she could hear the heavy footfalls of one of the drones in the great room below.

Turning to the door, she quickly twisted the knob. It opened—unlocked, by some miracle. Or maybe it wasn't a miracle at all. There was no one left here but the drones, so far as she knew. And they would never defy Gregor's orders, so he had no reason to lock his door.

She pushed the door open and ducked inside, just as the drone's footsteps began slamming on the stairs. Quickly, silently, she closed the door behind her, and unlike Gregor, she turned the lock.

She waited there, listening as the drone's steps came closer, then slowly moved past. Sighing in relief, she turned to examine Gregor's rooms. The first, the one

she'd entered, seemed to be a sitting room of sorts.
There was a desk, with the usual supplies littering it:
pens, telephone, blotter, laptop. Beside the desk, a birdcage dangled from its stand, a rough-looking rat sitting
silently inside, staring at her.

There was an open doorway leading into the bedroom, and something about the energy coming from there
drew her attention quickly and without warning. She realized she was not alone. And, just as suddenly, she felt
drawn to whoever was inside—irresistibly drawn.

Frowning she moved forward, as if compelled. There
was something square in one corner, covered with a
sheet. She moved toward it, and the energy now had a
familiar feel to it. Very like Roxy's energy, but altered
in some way.

Quickly she reached out and yanked the sheet away.
A woman was cowering in the corner of the metal cage
underneath the sheet. Her clothes were ragged and filthy.
She was far too thin, her collarbone and shoulder blades
protruding as she hugged herself. Closely cropped pale
blond hair contrasted madly with her dark, lush brows
and lashes, and her eyes were a stunning, vivid violet. She
was trembling and staring in wide-eyed terror at Vixen.

Vixen lifted a hand, put a finger to her lips.

The frightened woman didn't respond in any way.
Just stared, waiting, petrified. And no wonder. God
only knew what she'd suffered at Gregor's hands, but
the marks on her neck were a good indication. She was
snack food. And, Vixen realized as she stood there,
naked and unashamed, the woman was something
more. She was one of the Chosen.

It stunned her to realize that Gregor had tortured, harmed and used one of the Chosen. No vampire could do such a thing—or so the legends said.

Glancing left and then right, Vixen spied a satin robe hanging from a hook on the wall, and she went to it, then quickly pulled it around her. It was far too big—Gregor's, no doubt—but at least it covered her. Then she went to the cage. It was perhaps four feet square, its tiny door padlocked. Inside there was a bowl of some sort of meat made into a distasteful looking hash, and another one filled with water. No utensils.

Kneeling in front of the cage, Vixen whispered as softly as she could, "You must be very, very quiet. I promise I'll help you."

The woman remained unmoving in the corner, her eyes watchful and completely untrusting. Why hadn't the other vampires sensed her here? Vixen wondered. Why hadn't *she,* when she'd been held here? Or Topaz? And then she recalled that Gregor had somehow surrounded this place in a shield that prevented mental messages from getting out. Perhaps he'd surrounded his own rooms in the same manner, so this one's presence couldn't be detected by others in the house.

Turning away from the captive, Vixen went to the desk in the adjoining room, feeling the woman's desperation at being left behind. And yet she remained quiet.

Beside the desk, in his cage nearby, the rat looked at her, twitching his whiskers.

Vixen looked right back at him and initiated a conversation. But asking a rat to recall a conversation that had taken place in a language he did not know was no easy task. However, he did convey that Gregor had jotted things down on a notepad as he'd spoken on the phone.

She found the notepad. Its top sheet was completely blank. She took a pencil and used the old trick of shading in the top sheet to see what had been written on the sheet above it, but Gregor must have torn off several, or else never written anything at all, despite what Jack thought he'd heard, because nothing showed up. She checked the wastepaper basket, even as the rat showed her, with his mind's images, Gregor's habit of crumbling notes and tossing them into the fireplace when he finished with them.

She would find nothing of use in the wastebasket.

She had so hoped…

Quickly she went through everything on the desk, searching for any clues, but she found nothing of use. Turning, then, knowing it was time to attempt to escape, she showed the rat what she was going to do, to ensure his cooperation. Then she tipped the pole slowly over, lowering it to the floor, until the cage lay on its side. She freed the latch, let the door fall open, told the rat he was free to go.

He leapt out, raced across the floor and vanished from sight. He would be all right. He could make his own escape.

The woman in the dog-sized cage couldn't. And now Vixen had to get both herself and the strange, traumatized female out of the lion's den alive.

How she was going to manage it, she didn't know. She went to the window, parted the curtain carefully and peered outside. There were drones posted at every corner of the house, and some here and there in between.

No doubt the one who'd heard her "knocking" on the front door had deployed them to watch the grounds.

Hell. She was trapped.

Now what?

She lingered at the window for a moment longer, seeking an answer, when she saw something move at the edge of the drive. Frowning, straining her eyes, she looked again and thanked the fates for her vampiric night vision when she glimpsed a small group gathered there: Topaz, Seth, Roxy and Jack. She wanted to call out to them—even attempted it, but it was like shouting from within a lead chamber. She thought of opening the window, then wondered if there might be an alarm attached and thought better of it.

Seth convinced the others to scope out the place with him first, then come up with a plan. It was the best option he could come up with, because it would put him in close proximity to Vixen in the least amount of time. No one had any better ideas, so they went along.

They didn't get too close, only close enough to see the drones standing around the mansion at regular intervals, eyes scanning the darkness around them with a nervous apprehension that convinced him that they knew something was up.

Dammit. Where the hell was Vixen?

Vixen, he called silently to her mind alone. *Where are you?*

There was no answer. Nor would there be, if she were inside the house. "I wish to God I knew how he manages to keep messages from getting in or out of that godforsaken place," Seth whispered.

"It's something electronic. That much I know," Jack replied, crouching close beside Seth.

"How do you know that?"

"Power went out once. Big storm. And you could feel the shield, or whatever the hell it is, go down."

"Then we have to knock out the power." Seth glanced at Roxy and Topaz.

Roxy shook her head. "We don't even know for sure they're in there. What if they're not? Taking out the electricity would only tip them off."

"Well, just how the hell do you suggest we find out?" Seth snapped.

Topaz put a hand on his shoulder from behind. "Get a grip, Seth. We're just trying to be smart. Cover all the bases. We want to get them out of there as badly as you do."

"I know." He sighed, lowered his head. "I know— What the hell!" He jumped up suddenly as he spoke. "It's a freakin' *rat!*"

The others rose, too, backing off a little, except for Jack, who remained crouched, staring at the rodent that had, inexplicably, come scurrying right up to them. As they watched, the creature rose up on its hind legs, its nose twitching, forefeet moving as if it were shadow-boxing.

"What the hell is it *doing?*" Topaz backed away three full paces, rapidly, then shuddered and rubbed her arms.

"I think it's Lucifer," Jack said.

"You think the rat is the devil?" Roxy asked, sounding mildly amused. She'd backed away at first, but now she came closer again, bending a little to watch the animal's antics.

"Not *that* Lucifer. It's a pet, well, a captive, to be more accurate. Gregor keeps it in a cage in his rooms."

Seth narrowed his eyes on the rodent. It was down on all fours again, but turning back toward the house and twitching its snakelike tail.

"So then how did he get out?" Seth asked.

They all looked at him, each reaching the same conclusion. "Vixen would do something like that. Set a caged rat free," Topaz said slowly.

"Not only that, but she can talk to animals," Seth went on. "We all saw it outside The Crypt that night."

Roxy shook her head in disbelief, but her eyes remained riveted to the underfed black animal as it turned around to face them and rose up on its hind legs again. This time it emitted a squeak.

Topaz covered her ears and backed up again. "All right, all right. We hear you. Timmy's in the well. We're on it, okay? Now, get out of here, you gross little beast!"

The rat went motionless, still upright, blinking at her.

"Go!" she said in her loudest whisper yet, and she stomped her feet closer, as if she were about to trample it. The rat dropped to all fours and ran away.

"Dammit, Topaz, why did you do that?" Seth demanded.

"It was freaking me out!"

"We could have used it to communicate with Vixen."

"Oh, well, hell, Seth, you never mentioned that you could talk to vermin."

"Dammit, Tope, we could have strapped a note to it and sent it back inside or something."

"Uh-huh. And how were you going to tell the rat where to take the note?" She rolled her eyes.

Seth stared at the house, and his eyes were watering. "She must be in Gregor's rooms."

"Or was recently enough to set Lucifer free and send him to us," Jack agreed. "It's that window there." He pointed. "She must have seen us."

"That bastard. If he laid a hand on her—"

Jack shook his head firmly. "Gregor wouldn't touch her, Seth. Don't worry on that score. He was the kind of idiot who was disgusted by the very thought of it. Referred to her as a half dog."

"That is so wrong on so many levels, I don't even know where to begin," Topaz muttered. "But I suppose, in this case, it's a blessing. At least she's safe from that."

Roxy eyed Seth, and he squirmed inwardly. He hated like hell to think of himself as anything like Gregor, but he realized he'd had the same initial reaction. Okay, maybe not disgust. He'd been confused; he'd felt betrayed and lied to. He'd been hurt that she hadn't confided in him, and yeah, it had creeped him out a little. But only briefly.

"Where the hell do you suppose Reaper is? Why doesn't Vixen just shape-shift and dart out of that freaking place?" Seth asked.

"If she could, don't you think she would?" Topaz

sounded short on patience. "I don't like this waiting. We have to do something."

"I have an idea," Roxy said. "If she really is in Gregor's rooms, those rooms right there, she can escape through the window. It's an easy jump for a vampiress. All we need to do is get those drones out of the way, lure them around back or something, and give her time to get out."

Seth stared at her, stunned at the simplicity of the plan. He gripped her shoulders and kissed her full on the mouth. "I love you, Roxy."

"Yeah, yeah, most men your age do." She smiled and fluttered her lashes. "But there's one caveat to my plan."

"And what's that?"

"We don't get ourselves captured or killed in the process."

Everyone nodded in agreement, and they huddled close to finalize their strategy.

25

—▸—◂—

Reaper was standing in the field, out in the open, armed but feeling uncomfortably vulnerable, when the black Porsche pulled in. The headlights blinded him, but he quickly stepped aside, out of the glare. The door opened, and a man emerged.

"Hello, Rivera."

Reaper was surprised that the man knew his real name. He'd thought no one besides Roxy knew that. But there was something vaguely familiar about the voice, and as the man stepped closer, Reaper strained to see him clearly.

"Do we know each other?" It was impossible to see him with the blazing lights at his back.

"Turn off the lights," the man commanded someone in the car.

Briar—or so Reaper assumed—obeyed. The lights died, and he blinked and refocused on the man's features. And then recognition dawned. "Gregory Adams?"

"A sharp memory is a good quality in an operative. I see yours hasn't dulled with time."

He remembered the man. A CIA agent he'd worked with once or twice during his former life. And rapidly the pieces began clicking into place. "You're working for the Agency. Now. As a vampire."

Gregory shrugged. "They want you back. A vampire for an operative, one trained to kill, one they can control with a pair of trigger words—can you imagine how valuable you are to them?"

"They know about me."

"They know everything about you, including that you've reinvented yourself as an executioner of rogues like me. Hell, Rivera, you're one of their biggest operations. They made me into a vampire, set me up as a rogue, gave me your triggers. My mission was to lure you to me, capture you alive and return you to them."

"Was?"

Gregor smiled slowly. "I've found I like my new life a lot better than my old one. The power. I kill at will, I take what I want. I've amassed a small fortune already, and all I want is more. More money. More power."

"*My* power."

"*Now* you're getting it."

"You'd have to kill me to take my power, Gregor. And that's not going to be an easy thing to do."

"Easier than you think, my friend. Now, let me tell you how it's going to go." He turned slightly, though he never took his eyes off Reaper. "Briar, love. Get out of the car."

The passenger door opened as Reaper watched, and she stepped out. His eyes narrowed. She didn't look well. She looked haggard. She was trying to block but, in her condition, not succeeding. He could feel the pain, the weakness, rolling from her in waves. He shot a furious look at Gregor. "What the hell have you done to her?"

"Just this." Gregor moved his hand, and Briar screamed and dropped to her knees, hands flying to her neck.

And that was when Reaper saw the collar around her throat. He felt ill when he realized… "Stop. Damn you, stop it!" He took a single step toward Gregor.

Gregor held up the remote in his hand. "Uh-uh-uh," he said. "One more move and she gets another jolt."

Reaper went still as Briar fell face-first on the ground and lay there, trembling and moaning. Grimly, he shifted his gaze to Gregor. "All right. Just tell me what you want me to do."

Seth, Topaz and Jack each went to a corner of the house with an apple-sized rock and a haphazard plan. Peg the chosen drone with the rock, laugh uproariously and run like hell. They planned to lead the drones into the forest behind the house, hopefully with enough of a head start to get to the designated spot first, take up their positions and ambush the bastards when they arrived.

While they did so, Roxy would—with luck—be leading Vixen and Reaper to the van and driving them to safety.

Seth didn't even know if Reaper was still inside the house. He was certain Vixen was, though, and if he got himself dead, that was fine by him, so long as the result was that she got out in one piece.

He gave the others time to get into position, waited for Jack's whistle, which was the agreed-upon signal, and then he wound up like an all-star pitcher and let fly.

"His" drone stood at the front left corner of the house and was very close to Gregor's window, which was now Vixen's window. Roxy was crouching in the bushes, ready to rush to that very window and pitch pebbles at it to try to get Vixen's attention the minute the drone was gone.

The rock hit Mr. Big But Dumb right between the eyes, and he dropped like a sack of potatoes.

"Shit!" That wasn't what was supposed to happen.

Roxy parted the azalea bush and peered out at Seth with a look of "what the hell now?" on her face. Seth shrugged and made a slicing motion across his neck with a forefinger. Then he quickly located another rock, targeted the next closest drone and flung his missile.

This one reacted as predicted. He rubbed his shoulder where the stone had slammed into him, cussing a blue streak at the pain and scanning the night to see who the hell had thrown the rock.

Seth stepped out of his cover, sent the guy a smile and a wave, then turned and ran full bore into the woods. He could hear Topaz and Jack racing through the trees, as well, brush crashing, twigs snapping, footfalls pounding in a regular, rapid rhythm, then stopping suddenly when their owner leapt over some obstacle or other.

The plan should work, Seth thought, as he ran, weaving around tree trunks, ducking to avoid low limbs, and leaping over stumps, deadfall and roots. The drones were big, bulky, far from graceful. Powerful, yes, but not lithe or flexible. Meanwhile, he, Jack and Tope could run and leap like freakin' gazelles.

And that was what he did. When he hit the clearing, he could still hear the drones coming, and they didn't sound far away. But Jack and Topaz were there waiting, each standing directly beneath a large tree. Topaz had chosen a willow, Jack an oak. Seth moved quickly to his tree, a sugar maple, and at his nod, they each pushed off, jumping high, catching hold of a limb, pulling themselves into a secure position.

Seth settled into the crotch of the tree and took out his tranq gun. He didn't know how many drones would be coming—all of them, he imagined—but they'd taken every bit of ammo they could find. He hoped it would be enough.

He glanced across the clearing and spotted Topaz, seated far from the tree's trunk on a fat limb, looking as comfortable as if it were a park bench. Tendrils of willow hung before her face like a lace curtain. She was ready. Jack stood in his oak, feet braced on two separate limbs that forked outward from the center, while his back was pressed to the trunk. He was ready, too, his gun in his hands.

And then all hell broke loose as the drones came thundering into the clearing. Seth took aim, then fired. Then he loaded another dart, took aim again, fired again. Two drones fell. Two more, as Topaz and Jack did just as he had. And then another pair.

The tranq guns were silent, the sound of their darts hissing through the night barely noticeable, but by the time the second round of drones dropped, the others knew something was going on and began looking around.

There must have been twenty of them, besides those already out of commission, Seth thought. And within a second or two they were going to narrow down the source of those tranq darts, and probably yank him and his colleagues out of their trees like bears plucking juicy blueberries.

He loaded and fired again. And again. And then one of the drones was looking right at him, snarling, pointing, charging.

He shot the bastard, and the one behind him, but a third was leaping into the tree before Seth could load again.

A dart rocketed into the drone's shoulder, though, and he went stiff, fell backward out of the tree and hit the ground.

Topaz gave Seth a wave and went back to targeting drones. They were on to her location now, as well, surging toward her, but Jack and Seth managed to hit them before they did any damage. One got up high enough to grab her by the leg, and she bashed him in the head with her gun; then Jack managed to sink a dart into his backside, sending him tumbling to the ground.

Dammit, they just kept coming, and ammo was running low. Seth only had three darts left, and he could see at least seven or eight more drones. He shot one. A second went down, hit by one of his cohorts. A third came to his tree and started up it, as a fourth roared toward Jack's tree. Numbers five, six and seven were still on the ground. Two more darts, Seth thought, and fired at the drone climbing up his tree but missed.

The dart landed on the ground as the drone climbed higher. It took a swipe at Seth, hit him in the side and damn near knocked him right out of the tree. Pain screamed through him as he struggled to get his last dart into the gun. He glanced across the clearing for help, but both Topaz and Jack were busy with drones of their own.

Seth got the gun loaded as the drone hit him again, and this time he fired at close range and the dart sank deep into the drone's neck. He released Seth and fell to the ground, landing back-first. The three other drones on the ground looked straight up at Seth and then came at him, reaching for the tree. One jumped and landed on a limb right beside him. Seth had to react on gut instinct, and gut instinct said, "Get out of the tree where the two-ton drone vampire just landed," so he did. He jumped, clutching his now-useless gun.

He had no more ammo. The two other drones were under the tree, and they turned as they followed his progress through the air and onto the ground, and then they came at him, flanking him.

He could hear Topaz struggling with her drone, and the last time he'd looked, Jack had his hands full, as well. Seth was cornered, but then he glimpsed the misfired dart lying on the ground, and he moved fast. He dove for it, rolled as he grabbed it and leapt to his feet again in one smooth motion. Then he jammed it into the gun, aimed at one drone and fired.

The hulk went down, and Seth pointed the gun at

the second one. "Hold still now, unless you want what he just got."

The drone stood still, frightened by the unloaded weapon, at least momentarily. Seth glanced over his shoulder at Topaz just in time to see her gun falling to the ground as a drone leaned over her in the tree. Then she jammed a dart into her attacker's chest with her bare hands.

Seth shifted his gaze left and spotted Jack beating in a drone's skull with the butt of his weapon, until the bastard finally toppled from the tree.

Topaz shoved with all her might, pushing the now unconscious drone off her chest and letting his body thud to the ground. Then she jumped out of the tree, bent to pick up her tranq gun, walked calmly over to where Seth stood and shot the only remaining drone, the one standing before his unloaded gun.

The guy went down in a heap, and she nodded at Seth. "You're welcome."

"Uh, thanks."

Jack jumped down, as well, and came to join them. "You both okay?" he asked, but his eyes were only asking Topaz.

"I'm fine. You, Seth?" She looked him up and down.

"Yeah, I'm good," he said, noting that Topaz's eyes were on Jack almost before he'd answered.

"I'm okay, too," Jack said. "Let's get out of here, okay? Before more of these brain-dead lummoxes show up."

"Best idea you've had all night," Seth told him.

Vixen broke the lock on the little cage and opened the tiny door, reaching inside to help the woman crawl out, but the woman in the cage cringed away from her touch, so she backed off a little. "It's all right," she whispered. "I'll get you out of here somehow."

"You're one of them."

They were the first words the woman had spoken, and her voice was weak and raspy—and yet there was an underlying strength to it. A defiance that seemed out of place, given her situation. Vixen was surprised to hear it, and a little bit awed, as well.

"I'm a vampire, yes," she admitted. "But I'm nothing like the one who's been holding you. Although I guess, in your place, I'd be just as wary. He's the only one you've ever met, isn't he?"

The woman nodded shakily, pulling herself out of the cage, then standing straight with obvious difficulty and trying to hold her shredded dress together. "I didn't even know they were real before," she said.

Vixen went to a closet and took out a large white shirt, one of Gregor's. She handed it to the woman, who quickly grabbed it, then backed off and pulled it around her.

"What's your name?" Vixen asked as the woman slowly, clumsily, fastened the buttons with trembling hands.

"Ilyana."

"I'm Vixen."

"What will you do with me, if you *do* manage to get me out of here?" Ilyana asked.

"Nothing. I mean, help you if you need it, but other than that, what you do is entirely up to you. Though— before you take off, it would probably be good if you'd let me tell you a few things about yourself."

Ilyana stared at her. "What could you tell me? You don't even know me."

"I know about your rare blood antigen, your bleeding disorder, and the weakness and lethargy that have probably begun to show up."

The woman's eyes widened. But then she turned sharply, gasping, as something hit the window.

"Easy. Let me check." Vixen hurried to the window and peered out. Roxy was standing below, waving her arms. "Ilyana," Vixen said softly. "You've been in this room a while. Is there an alarm on this window?"

"No. He opened it tonight, only a little while ago. There was no alarm. I didn't see him do anything to shut one off or anything."

"Thanks." Opening the window and almost holding her breath while she did it, Vixen sighed in relief when no alarm sounded, then leaned out.

"The others lured the drones away," Roxy called as softly as she could and still be heard. "Now's your chance. But hurry."

Vixen nodded and pushed the window up all the way. "Come on, Ilyana. We have to go now."

The woman came to the window and looked out. "There's no way to climb down."

"That's why we're jumping."

Ilyana swung her head toward Vixen, staring. God, she had stunning cheekbones, Vixen found herself thinking. "That's impossible," the violet-eyed woman said.

"It's barely a hop for me. And you're going to have to trust me on this one. You won't be hurt. Just get on my back."

"I weigh more than you do. You can't possibly—"

"You're taller but thinner. Besides, I'm a vampire. I could take three of you out that window without a problem. Now, are you coming with me, or do you want me to leave you behind?"

Vixen turned, presenting her back to Ilyana, and waited.

"I must be out of my mind," Ilyana whispered, but she moved closer and wrapped her arms around Vixen's neck. "Then again, even if we land full force and break every bone in us both, it'll be better than staying here."

"We're not even going to break a nail," Vixen said. She dropped her hands to grip Ilyana's legs, then drew them around her own waist, hiking the woman up higher on her back as she did. "Hold on."

Roxy hadn't liked what she'd had to do, but that hadn't stopped her from doing it. As soon as Seth took off and every drone guarding the mansion had lunged into the woods in pursuit, she emerged from the azalea bush, slipped her blade from its sheath and knelt over the unconscious drone Seth had hit with his first stone.

Quietly and cleanly, she sliced his throat. Blood flowed, though not with the high-pressure-hose-type force she would have expected from a vampire. But then again, these drones *weren't* vampires—exactly— though she didn't know what they were. His blood flowed slowly, gently, but steadily. He was dead in a matter of moments.

Next Roxy turned and pitched pebbles at the window until Vixen opened it and looked down. Roxy waved at her, told her to come on, and Vixen nodded, vanished, and then a moment later returned to the window again.

Roxy had only an instant to glimpse a pale silvery blond head behind her, and then Vixen was sailing to the ground, her own red hair flying in the wind. She wasn't alone.

She hit the ground, bending deep to absorb the impact, then straightened slowly, lowering the other woman's legs to the ground at the same time.

The blonde got her footing and stared at Roxy, fear in her eyes. She wore a large white shirt, a man's shirt, buttoned and hanging to her thighs. Beneath that, the ragged remnants of a dress were visible. She had hair that reminded Roxy of David Bowie.

"Ilyana, meet Roxy. Roxy, Ilyana," Vixen said. "No time for more, we've got to go find Reaper and Gregor. Where's the van?"

"We're not taking on another—"

"She's one of the Chosen, Roxy. I found her in a four-by-four cage in Gregor's bedroom. We have no choice but to help her out. Now, where the hell's the van?"

Roxy met Ilyana's eyes and nodded once. "Sorry. I didn't know. Shirley's this way. Hurry, before more drones show up."

"What's that mean?" Ilyana asked. "'One of the Chosen.' What is that? And who's Shirley?"

"Shirley's my van. The rest—" Roxy gave her head a shake. "No time for the rest. We'll explain it all to you later, hon. Just come with us."

"We've got another friend in serious trouble," Vixen

said. "Ah, the van. Thank God." She'd spotted it in the distance and picked up the pace, running toward it, leaving Ilyana to accompany Roxy at a more mortal gait.

"Where are the others?" Vixen called from the passenger seat.

"Good question. They were supposed to lead the drones into an ambush in the woods, but they were limited on ammo and—"

Vixen?

Hearing Seth's summons in her mind, Vixen held up a hand. *I'm here. I'm safe. But we have to go to Reaper, Seth. He's in trouble.*

Before she could say any more, he was opening the van's side door and climbing in. He reached for her, but when she drew back, he settled for a hand on her cheek. "You really *are* okay."

"Yes."

Only then did he notice the blonde in the middle seat, right in front of him. "And you brought us another stray. Welcome to the gang, Blondie."

Ilyana frowned, clearly unsure what to make of Seth. He didn't fit the mold, Vixen thought. He probably didn't seem like a vampire at all to the woman.

"What's the deal with Reaper?" Seth asked.

Topaz and Jack climbed into the back and closed the doors, and Roxy started the van and began driving.

"Turn around, Roxy," Vixen said. "We need to go the other way. I remember the directions exactly. Reaper asked Gregor to meet him there alone, but he didn't go alone. He took Briar with him."

"Hell," Seth said.

"How far?" Roxy asked.

"Not far. Turn right—there," she said and pointed. "Three more miles on the right."

"Got it," Roxy said, and floored it.

26

— ◆ —

"I'll tell you how this is going to go," Gregor said softly.

Reaper wasn't looking at him but at Briar. She'd gone from kneeling to bending forward over folded knees, her face on her thighs, her arms wrapped around her head, her entire body trembling.

"Here," Gregor said.

His voice drew Reaper's head around, and he saw that Gregor was holding out a blade to him. It was golden and four inches in length, its handle carved of bone. Its edge appeared razor-sharp. "Take this," Gregor said.

Reaper took it from him.

"Now I want you to kneel."

"Gregor, this is—" Reaper began.

Gregor thumbed the button. Didn't threaten to, didn't suggest he might, just thumbed it. Briar howled in pain, and her body slammed flat to the ground, face-down, outstretched. Then, when he let off the button, she curled up into the fetal position in her side, hugging her knees to her chest, trembling.

"You didn't have to do that."

"Waste time speaking to me again and I'll do it until she dies. Now kneel. Don't speak, don't question, don't argue, just obey."

Reaper nodded, and then he knelt. Being on his knees before this worthless piece of preternatural refuse made him want to throw up, but he didn't see that he had any choice.

"Now, hold out your right arm, palm up."

Reaper lifted his arm, turning it so his wrist and palm faced upward. In the other hand, he clutched the blade, and he was even then wondering if he could bring it across the bastard's throat before Gregor would be able to press that damned button again.

"Slice your wrist, Reaper. Then drop the knife to the ground and kneel there, docile and silent, while I drink your power into me, until there's nothing left in you at all. I'm going to drain you. I'm going to take your blood and your power. I've got you here, at my mercy, for myself, not for the CIA, not for anyone. Slice your wrist, Rivera. Feed me your life."

Reaper opened his mouth to argue, but the bastard held up the remote again, his thumb hovering over the button. "You want me to hurt her? I'll reduce her to insanity, maybe even torture her to death, right now if you refuse me, Reaper. Say the word. I'd rather enjoy it."

Reaper closed his eyes. He lifted the blade, brought it to his other arm and laid its edge against his skin. Then, biting his lip and opening his eyes, he focused on Briar. She was lying there, hurting, and he knew he had to do this, had to spare her any more pain. But looking at her would make it easier.

He looked at that mass of dark hair, and he prepared to draw the blade across his flesh and end his own life. A vehicle was racing toward them, but he paid its glaring headlights no heed. It didn't matter. It was too late.

And then, as he watched her, Briar lifted her head weakly from the ground and, with her fingers making claws and digging into the very earth as if for strength, she met his eyes, opened her lips and whispered a single word.

"Nightingale."

Seth held on for dear life as Roxy swerved into the vacant lot so fast that the van rocked up onto two wheels. She braked to a skidding stop the second her headlights illuminated the nightmarish scene.

Reaper was kneeling before Gregor, holding a blade in one hand and looking for all the world as if he were about to slice his opposite wrist with it. There was a dark, low-slung car nearby. Briar lay on the ground near it, barely moving, and Seth wondered for a moment if she was dead.

As they piled out of the van, though, Briar lifted her head. Her eyes fixed on Reaper's, and she moved her lips.

The word emerged on a whisper.

"Nightingale."

"Noooo!" Roxy shrieked, racing forward, hands ahead of her as if she could somehow prevent disaster, but, of course, it was already too late. Seth knew that.

"Dammit, we need a tranquilizer dart," he said.

"We used them all on the drones," Topaz told him. "Just get him before he loses it!" They rushed forward, even as Reaper's eyes went blank, the blade in his hand frozen in midair.

"Bitch!" Gregor barked, thumbing the button on a small device that hung from his neck as he said it, sending Briar into screaming spasms on the ground. Seth realized it was the damned collar in the space of a heartbeat, but there was no time to give it more than a passing thought.

Gregor opened his mouth to say something more, but he never got the words out. Reaper grabbed him by the throat and picked him up off his feet, crushing his larynx as he kicked and twisted and gagged.

"Stop him!" Roxy cried, as the vampires ran forward, leaving her to catch up. "We have to stop him. We need to know the second word, the one that will bring Raphael back. If he kills Gregor—"

Seth didn't need to hear more. He poured on speed, surprised that Jack came along, right at his shoulder. Topaz and Vixen were right behind them, Roxy struggling to catch up.

Seth and Jack jumped at Reaper, prying at his hand to get it off Gregor's throat. Reaper used his free hand—the one holding the blade—to drive them away. He took a swing with it, his arm arcing, the blade flying toward Seth's face.

No time to duck, Seth thought, getting ready for the cut.

But something thudded to the ground just before Reaper's hand connected, and Seth realized in a brief flash before the pain exploded, that Reaper had dropped the blade.

And it couldn't have been an accident.

Seth landed hard on the ground, then pushed himself up in time to see Jack tumbling along the ground and coming to a stop beside him. Beyond Jack, he glimpsed the van and the blond woman standing in its open door, watching them with wide eyes. Then he shifted his focus to see that Reaper still had Gregor.

"His eyes are starting to bulge," Seth observed.

"Funny-looking, isn't he?" Jack asked.

He would have been content to sit right there and let the bastard suffer, but by then Topaz and Vixen were leaping on Reaper. Vixen wrapped her arms around his forearm, the one holding Gregor, and tried with all she had to pry his fingers loose.

Topaz jumped on his back, wrapping his neck in a choke hold, and talking rapidly and demandingly into his ear.

Roxy joined in, too, yanking Gregor as hard as she could, and adding her fingers to those already prying against Reaper's grip.

"Hell," Seth said. "We'd best go protect the women-folk."

"I hear that." Jack got up with him, and they both joined the fray, yanking and pulling and prying, until finally, Gregor's body dropped to the ground, free at last of Reaper's grip.

But it didn't much matter by then, because Reaper had turned on them now. His fists were flying, feet kicking, and his friends were taking the beating that had been aimed at Gregor only a moment earlier.

Gregor got to his feet and dragged himself toward

the car. On the way, he grabbed Briar by the hair and jerked her upward, toward the passenger door.

"Stop that bastard! We need the second word!" Seth shouted. Reaper decked him, and he hit the ground, then bounded back to his feet and tried again to subdue his friend, gripping Reaper's arms and pulling them behind his back. "Reaper, stop it. It's us!"

Vixen rose to her feet, turned, and ran toward Gregor and the car. Seth tried to keep one eye on her, even as he sought to reason with his mentor. "Reaper, you don't want to hurt us. You know you don't. Search your heart. We're your friends."

Gregor didn't see Vixen coming. She raced right up behind him, as he dragged Briar by the hair toward the Porsche, and she snatched the chain from around his neck, breaking it. The remote fell to the muddy ground.

Gregor released Briar and turned to face Vixen, who immediately punched him in the face. His head jerked with the blow, but then he backhanded her, knocking her flat to the ground beside Briar.

Then Seth couldn't watch anymore, because Reaper let out a growl of pure animal fury, tearing his arms free of Seth's grasp and reaching for Topaz, who'd gone to stand in front of him and was still trying to talk to him.

Seth leapt forward, even as Jack yanked Topaz behind him, and stood nose to nose with Reaper. "Afraid not, big guy. You're *not* going to hurt her."

Seth heard the car squealing and knew Gregor had gotten away. He dared to glance that way in a panic, but Vixen was all right and kneeling beside Briar, who was still lying on the ground. It was probably too late to hope for the second word.

Topaz and Jack were about to grab Reaper again, but Seth held up his hands. "No. Stop. Everyone else, just back off. Get out of the way. Vixen," he called, "get that collar off Briar before the bastard decides to torture her some more."

She held it up, already in one hand. Way ahead of him, as usual. The remote dangled from its chain in her other hand. He nodded and said, "I want you all to keep your distance. It's him and me."

"But, Seth, he'll kill you," Vixen cried. She bounded to her feet and ran closer, stopping only a couple of feet from where he stood, facing Reaper, crouching, ready. Reaper had adopted much the same pose.

"You know what? I don't think he will," Seth said. Then he licked his lips and glanced her way, but only briefly, because Reaper was ready to spring, circling him slowly now. "But just in case he does, baby, I gotta tell you—I was an idiot, and I know it. I'm in love with you. All of you—the woman, the fox, the vampire. And if I live through this, I hope to hell you'll give me another chance. Not another chance to hurt you—that's not gonna happen again. But another chance to make you happy, since I blew the first one. I need another chance to prove to you that what I feel is real. And total."

She blinked, shaking her head. "Seth, I—" Her words turned into a scream as Reaper lunged, and Seth couldn't do anything more than defend himself from then on.

Jack and Topaz gripped Vixen's arms, and tugged her toward where the car had been, where Briar lay unconscious on the ground. "We have to try to help her. It's a long time before daybreak."

That was all Seth heard. The blond woman, Ilyana, was still peering from the van's open door, watching everything with frightened eyes. Roxy stood nearby, but she didn't interfere.

Reaper attacked, and Seth defended, blocking blows, rolling out of the way of punches, ducking, weaving, but not hitting back. His plan was to let his friend exhaust himself.

But he was the one getting exhausted. He tripped Reaper, watched him fall, but then Reap sprang up again and landed a kick that sent Seth flying through the air. He hit the ground hard, and it knocked the wind out of him. He had to shake his head to clear his vision.

He glimpsed Topaz and Jack carrying Briar between them, heading back to the van. He saw Vixen coming closer, her hand closing around Roxy's as they watched wide-eyed. Reaper was coming toward him, and Seth would have been content to wait, to rest a minute, but then Reaper turned, catching sight of Roxy and Vixen, and started to move toward them instead.

Seth surged to his feet and ran to intervene, putting himself in Reaper's path. "Not so fast, pal. You're not finished with me, yet."

Reaper swung.

Vixen lifted her head, opened her mouth, and Seth read her thoughts and screamed, "Vixen, no!" The blow landed, and Seth went down again. Hard. He was dizzy and hurting. "Don't go summoning any wildlife," he managed. "They might hurt him."

She lowered her head. "*He's* hurting *you!* Stop it, Reaper. Stop it!" she cried, and she tore free of Roxy's restraining hand to jump onto Reaper's back even as he prepared to club Seth in the head yet again.

Seth scrambled backward. Vixen clung. Reaper reached behind him to fling her aside, but before he could, the blonde popped up out of nowhere, jabbed something into Reaper's arm and ran like hell.

She only went about five yards, then stopped and turned to watch.

Reaper blinked as if stunned, and staggered a little. Vixen clung to his back, her arms anchored around his neck, as she looked down. Seth looked, too, and saw the little dart sticking out of Reaper's shoulder.

Then the big man sank to his knees.

Vixen released her hold on him, lowering her feet to the ground. Reaper fell slowly forward, facedown in the dirt.

Vixen lifted her head, meeting Seth's eyes. He was on the ground, the prone Reaper between them. But then she leapt the fallen leader, and even as Seth rose, she flung herself into his arms.

Her face wet with tears, she clung to him, trembling, shaking all over. Seth kissed her face, her neck, held her so hard he had to consciously ease off, afraid he might hurt her. "It's okay now," he said, over and over. "I love you. I love you, Vixen. I love you. I've never loved anyone else. Never. Never will. It's you. Only you."

She was sobbing, and he wasn't sure if there were

words or just tears coming from her. He didn't know if she was happy, sad, heartbroken, traumatized, injured or all of the above. So he just held her, thanking his stars that she was okay.

The blonde stayed where she was. Roxy went up to her and said, "I think you may have just saved the day."

"I found the dart on the floor of the van. I heard Seth wishing for one, so I figured it might help."

"It was the only thing that could have."

Her eyes narrowed on Roxy. "You're not one of them."

"No. I'm one of *you,* actually."

The woman frowned, clearly confused, and Roxy slid an arm around her shoulders and started walking her back toward the van. "Come on. We have a long talk ahead of us, Ilyana. And when it's done, I'll give you a ride to wherever you want to go, okay?"

Ilyana nodded.

Jack and Topaz had left Briar in the van, and now they crouched on either side of the fallen Reaper. "He's really out," Jack said.

"Yes, and he'll wake with a hell of a headache and a nasty temper. But he'll be alive, at least," Topaz added.

Together they picked him up and dragged him toward the waiting van.

Vixen lifted her head and stared into Seth's eyes. "Gregor got away."

"We'll hunt him down sooner or later," Seth said. "He can't be allowed to run around with that kind of control over our friend."

She nodded. "I agree with you. And I'm…I'm staying with you."

"Why?" He searched her eyes, awaiting her answer. She blinked as if confused. "Vixen, what I'm asking is, are you staying with me because you want to stay with the gang and help us bring Gregor to justice, or repay Reaper for something? Or—"

"I'm staying for all those reasons, and for one more. I love you, Seth," she told him. "I thought love was the most foolish and useless of every human emotion. Until I felt it. And now, I think—now I think it's the most wonderful."

Seth smiled, pulled her closer, pressed his mouth to hers. "I love you, too, Vixen. And I know now that's what I was put on this planet to do. I always felt I was destined to do something big, something important. I think you're it. Saving you from Gregor's prison, bringing you into the gang, falling for you. Hell, loving you…I think that's my destiny."

She stared into his eyes and whispered, "Part of your destiny, perhaps. But there's more, I think. In fact," she whispered as she looked toward the van and all the others, "I'm sure of it. There's something more, and it's not just your destiny. It's ours. All of ours."

He held her close to his side, and they started walking toward the van. "He could have killed me seven times over just now, you know. But he didn't."

She nodded. "You're sure of that?"

He made a face, then shrugged. "No. But I want to be." He glanced down at her. "You kept Gregor from taking Briar."

She nodded. "I couldn't let— I had to."

He nodded. "She'll never hurt you again, you know."

"I know." She smiled and glanced up at him. "I kept the collar."

The stars looked down, and they climbed into the van. Seth pulled the door closed and said, "Let's go, Roxy."

"Where to?" the other woman asked.

"To our destiny," Vixen told her. "Where else?"

REQUEST YOUR
FREE BOOKS!

2 FREE NOVELS
FROM THE ROMANCE/SUSPENSE
COLLECTION PLUS 2 FREE GIFTS!

YES! Please send me 2 FREE novels from the Romance/Suspense Collection and my 2 FREE gifts. After receiving them, if I don't wish to receive any more books, I can return the shipping statement marked "cancel." If I don't cancel, I will receive 4 brand-new novels every month and be billed just $5.49 per book in the U.S., or $5.99 per book in Canada, plus 25¢ shipping and handling per book plus applicable taxes, if any*. That's a savings of at least 20% off the cover price! I understand that accepting the 2 free books and gifts places me under no obligation to buy anything. I can always return a shipment and cancel at any time. Even if I never buy another book from the Reader Service, the two free books and gifts are mine to keep forever.

185 MDN EF5Y 385 MDN EF6C

Name _____ (PLEASE PRINT) _____

Address _____ Apt. # _____

City _____ State/Prov. _____ Zip/Postal Code _____

Signature (if under 18, a parent or guardian must sign)

Mail to **The Reader Service:**
IN U.S.A.: P.O. Box 1867, Buffalo, NY 14240-1867
IN CANADA: P.O. Box 609, Fort Erie, Ontario L2A 5X3

Not valid to current subscribers to the Romance Collection,
the Suspense Collection or the Romance/Suspense Collection.

Want to try two free books from another line?
Call 1-800-873-8635 or visit www.morefreebooks.com.

* Terms and prices subject to change without notice. NY residents add applicable sales tax. Canadian residents will be charged applicable provincial taxes and GST. This offer is limited to one order per household. All orders subject to approval. Credit or debit balances in a customer's account(s) may be offset by any other outstanding balance owed by or to the customer. Please allow 4 to 6 weeks for delivery.

Your Privacy: Harlequin is committed to protecting your privacy. Our Privacy Policy is available online at www.eHarlequin.com or upon request from the Reader Service. From time to time we make our lists of customers available to reputable firms who may have a product or service of interest to you. If you would prefer we not share your name and address, please check here. ☐

BOB07

MAGGIE SHAYNE

32279 PRINCE OF TWILIGHT	___ $6.99 U.S.	___ $8.50 CAN.
21503 BLUE TWILIGHT	___ $6.99 U.S.	___ $8.50 CAN.
20944 COLDER THAN ICE	___ $6.99 U.S.	___ $8.50 CAN.
32229 DARKER THAN MIDNIGHT	___ $6.99 U.S.	___ $8.50 CAN.
66737 THICKER THAN WATER	___ $6.99 U.S.	___ $8.50 CAN.

(limited quantities available)

TOTAL AMOUNT	$ _____
POSTAGE & HANDLING	$ _____
($1.00 FOR 1 BOOK, 50¢ for each additional)	
APPLICABLE TAXES*	$ _____
TOTAL PAYABLE	$ _____

(check or money order—please do not send cash)

To order, complete this form and send it, along with a check or money order for the total above, payable to MIRA Books, to: **In the U.S.:** 3010 Walden Avenue, P.O. Box 9077, Buffalo, NY 14269-9077; **In Canada:** P.O. Box 636, Fort Erie, Ontario, L2A 5X3.

Name: _____

Address: _____ City: _____

State/Prov.: _____ Zip/Postal Code: _____

Account Number (if applicable): _____

075 CSAS

*New York residents remit applicable sales taxes.
*Canadian residents remit applicable GST and provincial taxes.

MIRA®

www.MIRABooks.com

MMS1207BL